MARGARET WAY

Outback Marriages

Containing

Master of Maramba
& Strategy for Marriage

All the characters in this book have no existence outside the imagination of the author, and have no relation whatsoever to anyone bearing the same name or names. They are not even distantly inspired by any individual known or unknown to the author, and all the incidents are pure invention.

*Harlequin Mills & Boon Limited, Eton House,
18-24 Paradise Road,
Richmond, Surrey TW9 1SR*

Master of Maramba and *Strategy for Marriage* were first published in Great Britain by Harlequin Mills & Boon Limited in separate, single volumes.

ISBN: 978 0 263 85839 6

010-0707

*Printed and bound in Spain
by Litografia Rosés S.A., Barcelona*

Master of Maramba

MARGARET WAY

Margaret Way takes great pleasure in her work and works hard at her pleasure. She enjoys tearing off to the beach with her family at weekends, loves haunting galleries and auctions and is completely given over to French champagne 'for every possible joyous occasion'. She was born and educated in the river city of Brisbane, Australia, and now lives within sight and sound of beautiful Moreton Bay.

Look out for Margaret Way's new novel *Promoted: Nanny to Wife* in Mills & Boon® Romance in September 2007.

CHAPTER ONE

SHE didn't see the car until it purred right up to her. A big opulent Jaguar. Platinum. This year's colour. Only seconds before she had scanned the jacaranda-lined street: traffic moving at a clip along the terrace, nothing in this narrow side street where she always tried to park when visiting her favourite uncle, in fact her only uncle. James Halliday of Halliday, Scholes & Associates, solicitors and tax advisers to the seriously rich. The busy professional area which included architects, engineers, town planners, and two very trendy but non-flashy interior designers, was fully parked except for the spot she'd had the great good fortune to drive into as another driver moved out. There was a space of sorts behind her suitable for a pokey little car like her own. She'd tried that in the past with the rear end showing the scars. No way could the driver of the magnificent Jag, she could see it was a man, squeeze into the spot. The thought gave her a certain perverse satisfaction.

Carrie locked her car, hoping the Jaguar would glide past, instead the occupant drove alongside, coming so close she could feel the familiar agitation start up inside her. She flattened her whole body against the side of her own car watching in sick fascination as the driver turned his coal-black head over his shoulder preparatory to putting the limousine into reverse.

The usual male derring-do. This one had more than his share.

No way could he miss hitting the trunk of the jacaranda tree unless he knew the exact dimensions of the Jag and the spot down to the last millimetre. She knew she was staring after him, her upper body now slumped sideways giving every appearance of a woman who had narrowly missed being run over. She didn't know whether to laugh or cry. She only knew she couldn't control her reactions. Ever since her accident she'd lost her emotional equanimity becoming almost a stranger to herself, fearful, wary, her nerves running on overdrive.

While she awaited the ker-uuun-ch the driver confounded her by manoeuvring that great big car into that teeny little space, startling her into unwilling admiration. But it happened sometimes. Especially with men. Even the total idiots among them seemed to know exactly how to reverse park. Had it been another woman she would have burst into applause but no such luck for his lordship.

Carrie looked away, pretending utter indifference. Her heartbeats had quietened now she was free to go about her business, realising at the last minute she'd forgotten her sunglasses and the spring sunshine was dazzling. Shafts of it flashed through the lacy canopy of the trees. Another month and they would be out in glorious lavender-blue flower, an event the whole subtropical city of Brisbane looked forward to. Except maybe the students. Jacaranda time. Exam time. She knew all about that. An honours graduate from the Conservatorium of Music. Winner of the Gold Medal for outstanding achievement. Winner of the National Young Performers' Award for her playing of the Rachmaninoff 2nd Piano Concerto. Accepted into the prestigious Julliard Academy in New York. A young woman with a very bright future.

Until the accident.

With an unhappy shrug, Carrie opened the door, reached in, and picked up the glasses, before giving the door a good healthy slam to work off excess energy, panic, irrational hostility, whatever. She'd have a lifetime to come to terms with her broken dreams. A whole world opened to her. Now shut.

She turned, watching the man get out of the car. He was looking straight at her, something questioning in his expression as though he saw things going on in her face. Or her *heart.* The thought shook her. She had instant impressions of her own. Dark-haired, dark-eyed, dark tanned skin but with a healthy glow. As tall as Mount Everest and just as impressive. Very likely a huge source of income. An aura like that only came with tons of money. But he wasn't deskbound. Too powerful. Hard muscles rippled beneath his beautiful, elegant city clothes. The walk was purposeful, athletic, the action as superlative as the powerful cylinders of the Jag. If a halo of light had surrounded him she wouldn't have been a bit surprised. The tan hadn't come from lying around on the beach, either. He put her more in mind of some godlike explorer gazing off into sun-scorched infinity. The Red Centre. The Dead Heart. She particularly liked that image. It seemed to suit him yet she stared back as though he were transparent. She had to find someone to hate today. He was it. Mr. Heartbreak, Mr. Trouble, Mr. Larger than Life. Men who irradiated their surroundings always were.

''Have a problem?''

Like the rest of him his voice riveted her attention. Overly authoritative from where she was coming from. Super-confident, super-resonant, dark in colour. A man of substance and it showed. She assumed he was the boss of a huge corporation. A guy who gave orders all day while other people jumped. Not her. She prided herself on kowtowing to no one, though her body carried the odd conviction something significant was happening to her. Why was he looking at her like that? She was feeling the impact right through her body.

Yet she answered coolly giving off her own aura. ''Not

in the least. I share your enthusiasm for parking in cramped spaces. Only I didn't think you could make it.''

''Why not? It wasn't difficult.''

He sounded amused. Carrie watched him approach her, billowing that male aura. He stopped just before it completely enveloped her. Above-average height for a woman he made her feel like a doll with a slight case of hysteria. It was way too humbling. And it stiffened her backbone.

His brilliant eyes—how could black eyes be filled with such light?—continued to sweep her, missing absolutely nothing including the tiny heart-shaped beauty spot above the swell of her right breast.

''I had the decided impression you thought you were about to be run over?''

''What, on the basis of a raised eyebrow?'' she parried.

''Actually you appeared to crumple. You couldn't really have been frightened. *Were* you?''

''Of course not.'' She tasted a faint bitterness at the back of her throat.

''I'm glad,'' he answered. ''You were in absolutely no danger. Perhaps you have a thing about male drivers.'' He answered mildly, she considered. For him. ''Pretty much all of us can park better than our womenfolk. Your left rear tyre is rammed into the gutter by the way.''

Carrie didn't give him the satisfaction of turning to look. ''I'm not one of the world's greatest parkers I admit.'' She made it sound as if one only needed to be if one drove an armoured truck.

''That's perfectly clear,'' the vibrant voice lightly mocked. ''Be assured I'm not sore at you.''

''I didn't imagine you were.''

''Then confess. Why so nervous? I'm almost positive you're nervous. *Why?* It's broad daylight. I don't normally make women uneasy.''

"Are you sure?" He couldn't fail to hear the astonished irony in her tone.

"It's obvious you don't know me." The jet-black eyes glinted over her as though no one *but no one* spoke to him this way. "Look there's no traffic," he pointed out in an unexpectedly gentle voice, glancing up and down the street. "Would you like me to escort you to the other side?"

And let him touch her? This dominating man. She didn't dare. She held up her two palms, then dropped them in one graceful gesture.

"Surely you jest?" She spoke sweetly when she could cheerfully have pushed him over. An enormous not to say impossible job.

"I jest not." His mouth was handsome, sensual in cut, but very firmly held. "You on the other hand seem to be kneading the hem of your skirt."

She glanced down. She was, too. Another nervous habit. "All right, if you must know I thought you came much too close to me."

"You should talk to somebody about it."

"About what?" Colour whipped into her cheeks, antagonism into her tone.

"I suppose the best word would be phobia." He looked squarely at her.

It was a big mistake to have spoken to him at all. "You're saying *I* have a phobia?" She gave him what she thought of as her dagger look. "That's a bit much for a complete stranger?"

He seemed mightily unimpressed, shrugging a nonchalant broad shoulder. "Seems very much like it to me."

That was the final straw. To be caught out. So easily. By a stranger. Carrie turned away so tempestuously her thick silky amber hair whipped around her like a pennant in a sea breeze. "Have a nice day," she clipped off.

"You, too." He sketched a brief salute, watching her stalk away, on her beautiful long legs. Sort of angry. And it showed. She was muttering something to herself as she went.

Then abruptly she turned, like a woman determined on having the last word. Point of honour. He almost laughed aloud.

"I hope you're not planning on parking there too long?" she threw at him with that rather tantalising hauteur. "An inspector might just wander by. It's not actually a parking space, you know. I should warn you. I might be forced to back into you in order to get out. You've virtually jammed me in."

"Not at all."

He moved with dark energy to double-check, giving her a sudden smile that did strange things to her. Formidable in height and demeanour—his employees probably addressed him staring at his feet—that smile was extraordinary, making nerves twitch all over her skin.

"Anyway I'm not worried," he pronounced casually. "Just leave your name and address under the wiper should anything go wrong."

"I'll try very hard to see it doesn't."

How could he be enjoying this? he thought. He almost never got into conversations with strange young women. And this one was not only hostile, but intriguingly familiar. A firehead to match her rare colouring. Hair like a good sherry with the light glinting through it. Beautiful clear skin with an apricot blush. Golden-brown eyes, almost a topaz. Her hadn't seen a woman with such clarity for years. And she was just a kid. She carried the beautiful scent of youth with her. Probably ten or more years his junior. He would be thirty-two his next birthday. A thirty-two-year-old divorcee with a child, Regina. He cared about her deeply. But the devastating fact was Regina wasn't his child. She was the result of one of Sharon's affairs. Funny the young woman who was stalking away from him had put all thought of Sharon out of his mind.

"Take care!" he called after her. "You city girls are so damned aggressive."

Carrie despite her avowed intention found herself stopping. Wasn't that strange. *City girls.* "So where do you hail from?" she challenged, wondering what imp of mischief had taken possession of her. He was Someone. She was sure of it.

"A long way from here," he drawled.

"And here was I thinking you're the sort of man who *always* knows what to expect."

"Careful," he said. "I might be still here when you get back."

Carrie waved a backward hand as though everything he said was of no real importance. She supposed she was being very rude but crossing swords with that man had helped to bring a little pleasure into her blighted young life. She'd never had an experience quite like that. But then as far as she knew, he hadn't, either. Maybe he would be there when she returned. The little flurry of excitement made her furious at herself.

James Halliday's secretary announced her arrival like an aide might announce a candidate for a court investiture, Carrie thought. She'd known Ms. Galbally since she was a little girl but the secretary had never once veered from the very formal. As a child and adolescent she'd always been Catrina, not Carrie. Once she turned eighteen she became Miss Russell. Ms. Galbally was a middle-aged saturine woman of handsome appearance and Carrie knew other people found her intimidating, but according to her uncle she was just about "perfect." So much for appearances, Carrie thought trying but not succeeding in looking honoured.

"Carrie, sweetheart!" Her uncle himself opened the door, handsome, genial, charming, fifty and looking nothing like it, four years older than her late mother but very much like her in appearance which was to say like herself, ushering her into an office as big as Central station but cosy as a den. It had a great view over the river; the walls were mahogany-panelled, lined with deep antique bookcases holding leather-bound legal tomes, a series of excellent quite valuable architectural drawings took up the rest of the wall space along with a few striking oil paintings, seascapes in gilt frames. James Halliday was a well-known yachtsman.

A magnificent Persian rug, all wonderful dark blues and rich rubies adorned the discreetly carpeted floor. Glass display cabinets set off a few choice pieces of James Halliday's collection of Ming dynasty Chinese porcelain, heralding the fact James Halliday was a collector, as well. An enormous partner's desk held centre court with a splendid high-backed chair ranged behind it. It was abundantly clear her uncle was doing very well. But not as well as her father who owned a large city electrical firm.

The two men did not get on. Different personalities; different interests; different callings. Carrie loved both of them but from her mother's side of the family she had inherited a great love of the "arts," a sphere that held little interest for her father, her stepmother Glenda and her stepsister, Melissa, three years her junior.

"Like some coffee, darling?" James Halliday asked, looking at his niece searchingly but with great affection. She had suffered a devastating blow and in many ways it showed. Her characteristic sparkle had banked down but he knew in his heart she had the inner resources to pull through this major setback to her life's plans.

Carrie sank into a plush, leather-upholstered armchair, sighing gently. ''I'd love it. No one drinks coffee at home anymore,'' she added after James put through his request. ''Glenda has convinced Dad it's bad for him. Bad for everyone. She doesn't like my buying it, either. I'll have to move out. It was always going to happen. Now I'm not going to New York, the sooner the better. Dad won't be happy but he's not around much to know just how things are between us.''

''It's the greatest pity you and Melissa aren't close,'' James mourned.

''Isn't it? Glenda's fault, I'm sure. Mel would never have felt the way she does if Glenda hadn't stirred up such feelings of jealousy.''

''I know your stepmother has made life difficult for you.'' James confined himself to a single remark when he wanted to say lots more.

''She never wanted me, Jamie. She didn't want a ready-made child who just happened to be the image of her husband's first wife. I swear to this day she's jealous of my mother.''

James nodded his agreement. He'd seen too many upsetting signs of it. ''She can't help it. It's her nature. We both know, too, she's deeply resented your talent. All the attention you got because of it, prizes and awards. It singled you out.''

''And not Mel. Still, she doesn't have to worry now,'' Carrie said wryly.

''You're still a highly accomplished pianist,'' her uncle reminded her, himself devastated by the crushing results of her accident.

''It doesn't seem like much of a compensation. To think I had to be involved in a car crash the very day I got news I'd been accepted into the Julliard. Fate taking a nasty turn.''

''It was a tragedy, sweetheart, but you can't let it ruin your life,'' James warned. ''You need time to recover, then you have to pick up the pieces. It could have been very much worse than broken ribs and a crushed little finger.''

''That won't stand up to the rigours of a career. I know. I'm trying, Jamie. Really I am, but it's hard. The funny part is, Dad is sad for me but he's relieved, too. He didn't want me going off overseas. He wants me at home. Safely married. He wants grandchildren in time.''

He wants. He wants, James thought. He'd wanted my beautiful sister but never made her happy. Trying to confine her fine spirit as he had never succeeded with his daughter.

''Your father has many good qualities but he isn't musical.''

''You mean he hasn't got a musical bone in his body.'' Carrie gave a broken laugh. ''Dad has always been proud of me but he can't come close to the music I play. *Played.* I haven't touched the piano since the accident.''

''Nearly a year ago.''

''No time at all.''

''I agree.'' James couldn't meet her glistening topaz eyes. ''Not for your heartache and bitter disappointment, to heal.''

''I don't enjoy teaching, Jamie. I suppose I was too much of a performer.''

''And you're so *young,*'' James returned. ''Twenty-two is no age at all.''

''Old enough to move out,'' Carrie retorted. ''I'd have done it before today only I didn't want to hurt Dad. Glenda is *never* going to like me. We can't be friends.''

James snorted in disgust. ''I don't want to be unkind but Melissa is very much like her mother or she's rapidly becoming that way. I think a shift might be best for all. Where would you like to go? You know you can come to

Liz and me. We'd love to have you. Not blessed with children of our own, you've been everything to us.''

''And you've been wonderful to me. Liz has been far more of a mother figure than Glenda could ever have hoped to be, but it's time I struck out on my own, Jamie. You know I'm right.''

''Your father would buy you an apartment, surely? He's a wealthy man.''

''I'm not going to ask him, Jamie. Glenda would bitterly resent that. I bought my own car. I'll rent my own flat.''

Protective James didn't like the sound of that at all. ''What about if I bought you one? I can afford it. Of course I wouldn't like to go against your father. Add to the...'' He almost said, chip on his shoulder.

''List of resentments,'' Carrie supplied. ''Bless you for everything, Jamie, but I'm ready and able to stand on my own two feet. Lord knows I spent long enough as a student. I suppose I should undertake a doctorate. I may not be able to make the grade as a concert artist but music has been my life. I worked so hard. All those years of practice! I guess I'm stuck with a teaching career so I'll need all the qualifications I can get.''

''Agreed. But how can you support yourself if you won't allow help?'' There was worry in Jamie's voice. ''Part-time work won't be enough. Lessons here and there.''

''I still have Grandma's money.'' Carrie referred to her inheritance from her maternal grandmother who had pined away from grief at the loss of Carrie's mother, her only daughter. ''It'll see me through. The thing is, Jamie, I want to get away. I need to find a bolthole. At least for a while. I have to get away from the whole music scene until I can come to terms with what has happened to me.''

There was deep feeling in her uncle's answering tone. ''I can understand that, darling. The funny thing is I have a client, our most valuable client I should add, who's looking for a governess for his little daughter. Not that you're governess material,'' he quickly considered.

''Who said?''

''Sweetheart.'' James gave a fond laugh. ''You're not. Take it from me. You're so gifted. So beautiful. A young woman to show off not hide in the wilds.''

''The wilds?'' Carrie's arched brows shot up. ''Tell me more.'' She fought down a very sharp ache inside.

''I'm sorry I started this,'' James paused as a tap came on his door. A young female office worker entered wheeling a trolley set with what looked like a mini-banquet. James Halliday had a sweet tooth but showed not an extra ounce for it.

''Over there, thanks, Ann.'' He gave the girl his charming smile. ''Looks good.''

''All lovely and fresh, Mr. Halliday,'' Ann smiled, turning her pretty face to Carrie who returned her pleasant greeting.

''How you don't get fat!'' Carrie wondered affectionately, after Ann had departed. ''Just as well you have your sailing.'' She got up from her chair to pour.

''I'm going out on the bay this weekend. Want to come?''

''Yes, please!'' Carrie's golden-brown eyes brightened. She loved boats. Loved the water. She had sailed with her uncle since she was a child right up to the Whitsundays in the glorious Great Barrier Reef.

When they were both seated, coffee in hand, three delicious little pastries to James' left, Carrie picked up where he had left off. ''I take it the governess job is on an Outback property.''

''Property doesn't say it, love.'' James stirred his coffee with vigour. ''More like a private kingdom. The family are big operators. They control over four million hectares spread across ten stations around the state. My client is one of the nation's largest private land barons. Queensland remains home to the country's biggest cattle kings, as you know."

"So we're talking the Channel Country in the far southwest," Carrie concluded. "Couldn't get farther away." Well over a thousand miles.

"No." James shook his thickly thatched head. "The chain does extend to the Cattle Country but the family base is in North Queensland. It's the linchpin in the whole operation. Not their biggest holding but perhaps the best. A marine flood plain that provides pretty well constant lush green feed. Cattle from all over their holdings can be fattened there. It's a Brahmin stud."

"Called?" Carrie savoured her coffee. As usual it was very good.

"Maramba Downs. Maramba."

"I'm sure I've heard of it."

"Very likely," James answered complacently selecting a mouth-watering patty. "Royce is often in the news."

"Royce who? Come on, you're being very cagey."

"Carrie, love, this job wouldn't suit you," James said, wondering why he had even mentioned it.

"The fact is I'm becoming more interested by the minute."

"It's not going to happen. I understand the little girl is…difficult. Other governesses haven't lasted long."

"What does the little terror do?" Carrie asked, having a special soft spot for "little terrors." She had been one herself.

James laughed. "I know what you're thinking. Didn't Glenda complain a lot about you? Royce sees it differently of course. The *governesses* are at fault."

"Aaaaah! Does the dragon have a surname?"

"Royce McQuillan. Splendid fellow. One of the finest

young men I've ever met. Hasn't had an easy life, either. He lost his father and mother a few years back. They were killed in a plane crash holidaying overseas. Then his marriage broke up.''

''Oh, dear!'' Carrie slumped, knowing what heartache meant. ''The mother didn't take the child? That's unusual.''

''Didn't want her, it appears.'' James' kind eyes grew soulful. ''I don't know the full story in that area, Royce doesn't explain much. You'd have to know of *her,* though she'd be some years older than you. Thirty, maybe thirty-one. Very glamorous woman. Almost a beauty but too brittle. Sharon Rowlands, that was. Hugh Rowlands heads the Standford Pastoral Company. Ruth Rowlands and her daughter spend most of their time following the social scene. You see them in all the magazines.''

''Except I've been too busy to read them. The little girl must have been devastated when her parents split up. How old is she?''

''A very precocious six going on seven,'' James said.

''So they were married young?'' Carrie observed, making calculations.

''According to Liz the marriage was arranged while they were both in the cradle.''

''That's how it works in some families. It didn't take them long to grow apart.''

''No.'' James truly, genuinely, felt very sorry for his client. ''Royce has very big responsibilities, big commitments. The talk is Sharon got bored.''

''Bored?'' Carrie was stunned. What sort of life did this Sharon want? ''So you've met her?''

''A few times,'' James said.

''What did you think of her as a person?''

''Too shallow for Royce. Liz thought so, too. She's an excellent judge of character.''

''Yes, she is.'' Carrie had turned very serious. ''The mother must have a heart of stone if she could bear to leave her child.''

James stared into his coffee cup. ''I hate to say it but the word is the little one might interfere with her pleasure. I expect she'll remarry though Liz thinks she'll never get over Royce, let alone find another man like him.''

''Maybe if she still cares about him they could get back together,'' Carrie said reasonably. ''Make a go of it for their child. They can't have any of the financial worries that put a strain on most couples.''

''Money doesn't ensure happiness, my darling,'' James said heavily, thinking of any number of his wealthy clients who had finished up in the divorce courts. ''I thank God for my marriage every day of my life.''

Carrie gave him the old warm smile. ''You're beautiful people, Jamie. You and Liz. Beautiful, tolerant, generous, caring people.'' Determinedly she pushed all thought of her stepmother's mean-spiritedness from her mind. ''I love you. Always will.''

They sat quietly for a few minutes, the atmosphere full of an easy companionship. ''You know I'm like your father in this respect,'' James confided after a while. ''I couldn't bear the thought of your going away. I know you had to for your career. I was terror stricken when I got that phone call….'' He broke off, the news of Carrie's accident embedded in his consciousness.

''I know, James. It could have been much worse.'' Carrie forced a smile.

''Much, much worse, my darling. Losing my sister was a terrible blow. I couldn't face anything horrible happening to you.'' James spoke huskily. ''There's something else in store for you, kitten.'' He used an old pet name. ''Something wonderful. It may not seem like it now.''

''It doesn't.'' Carrie swallowed. ''It's hard for me, Jamie. Very hard.''

''Yes, yes.'' James reached over to grip his niece's left hand. ''Liz and I understand what the loss of your career means to you.''

''Of course. I may not have had a career.'' Carrie tried to look at it another way. ''I mightn't have made the grade. There are many, many fine young pianists out there. One almost has to have a gimmick.''

''Your beauty? Your personality?'' James suggested, then stopped abruptly, realising it was all over.

''But I don't need a gimmick after all.'' For a moment Carrie had a stark image of the crash. Horror then sudden darkness. Then the full realisation when she woke up in hospital. ''I need a job, Jamie,'' she said. ''You can help me. You're handling this matter for your client?''

''I was going to allow Galbally to conduct the interviews,'' James said.

Carrie allowed herself a little gasp of dismay not lost on her uncle.

''Dearest, *I* don't have time,'' James explained. ''Women are so much better at these things.''

''Not Ms. Galbally.'' Carrie raised her eyebrows.

''She takes her responsibilities very seriously,'' James said loyally.

''I'm sure she does. Can't *you* recommend me, Jamie?''

James dropped his head forward. ''Your father wouldn't like it at all. I can just image his response.''

''Glenda would.''

James responded to the irony. ''But it mightn't work out at all, Carrie. I don't want to put you into a situation where you might be unhappy. Cut off and depressed.''

''Unhappier, don't you mean? I can look after a little girl. She must be especially vulnerable. Like me. Maybe I can bring something to her. Two female creatures under pressure.''

James nibbled his nether lip. ''Royce is coming to the office in a half hour. We have business to attend to. The revival in beef prices has boosted sales in the rural property sector. He's thinking in terms of expansion.''

''Does he want to own the whole country?'' Carrie asked with mild sarcasm.

''We need men like Royce McQuillan, dearest.''

''I know,'' she relented. ''Would it be okay if I waited?''

James sat back, focusing totally on his niece. ''You're serious about this?''

''Yes.'' She touched the little finger of her right hand, and rubbed it in a distracted fashion. Strange, it still *looked* okay. ''Of course I won't know how serious until I lay eyes on the great nation builder, but as you like and approve of him he must be okay.''

''Indeed he is, which is not say he's an *easy* man,'' James considered. ''He's only into his thirties but already he has extraordinary presence. Such an aura! It takes most men years of achievement to acquire that.''

''Must be all the money,'' Carrie quipped dryly.

James nodded. ''That helps. The break-up of his marriage changed him in significant ways. Less likely to relax. Let down his guard. He's more formidable.''

''He sounds an uncomfortable person. Is he bitter?''

James pursed his lips. ''Not bitter as in surly or unpleasant. Nothing like that. He has great charm when he cares to use it. But the marriage break-up took away a certain lightness of spirit. The capacity for easy laughs.''

''Made him more wary of women I expect?''

''*Beautiful* women.'' James looked full at her, captivated as ever by the lovely classical features, the bright colouring, most of all the close resemblance to his much-loved sister, Caroline.

That same lovely face now fell. ''You mean he's looking for someone very *plain?*'' The idea was unsettling.

''I think *pleasant* would be his choice.'' James glanced off.

''Then pleasant I'll be,'' said Carrie, all of a sudden sure life on an Outback cattle station would solve her problem.

She was holding the fort for Debra, Halliday, Scholes & Associates' receptionist when he came through the door, confounding her. The blood drummed in her ears. The world tilted again.

''Why, hello there.'' He spoke very smoothly as she looked up. ''This is just *so* unexpected.''

Somehow mercifully the moment passed. She was able to breathe again. ''It is…odd,'' Carrie agreed, aware those brilliant black eyes were filled with amusement and mockery. ''May I help you?'' She was rather proud of the calm detachment of her voice.

''It's your boss I'm after. James Halliday.''

''You have an appointment?'' It couldn't be. It *couldn't* be.

''Of course I have an appointment.'' He gave a brief laugh. ''You must be new. Royce McQuillan.''

She was struck by dread. There goes the job. The bolt-hole. ''Of course, Mr. McQuillan.'' She stared back at him. ''The receptionist will be back in a moment but I'll ring through for you.''

''No matter!'' He dismissed that with a slight impatient gesture of his hand. ''I'll go along. Mr. Halliday is expecting me.''

''Then allow me to take you,'' Carrie offered, coming around the reception desk as Debra approached from the opposite direction, increasing her pace as she recognised the client.

''Good morning, Mr. McQuillan,'' she carolled, packing a lot of feeling into her voice. ''Or is it afternoon?''

''In a few minutes.'' He glanced down at his watch. ''How are you, Debra?''

''I'm well. And you?'' The receptionist came to a halt, staring up into his face, obviously thrilled he had taken the time to say a few words to her.

''Fine.'' There was a brief glimpse of his devastating smile. Very white against the dark tan. ''Busy as usual. This young lady here,'' he turned to Carrie now standing at his shoulder, ''is going to escort me to Mr. Halliday's office.''

''That's nice of you, Carrie,'' Debra said, her colour warm, eyes bright. ''Carrie is…''

''In the office for the day.'' Carrie cut the other girl off smoothly. She didn't want her relationship to James explained quite yet.

Debra smiled touching a hand to her soft bubbly curls. ''Nice to see you, Mr. McQuillan. I won't be here when you get back. I'll be going off for lunch.''

''Joining the madding crowd?'' He gave her a little salute.

''What part do you play in the scheme of things?'' he asked Carrie as they moved off. ''I recognise you from somewhere and I don't mean our previous encounter.''

''I'm not famous,'' she said. It came off her tongue rather acidly.

''Is *that* what's tearing you apart?'' He glanced down at her from his arrogant height.

''You're wrong. Believe me.'' Carrie kept on walking, slightly intimidated by his long stride.

''I don't think so.''

Little flames glowed in the pupils of her eyes and she tilted her head. ''You must spend your time trying to psychoanalyse people?''

"I haven't actually met anyone who acted quite like you," he returned blandly.

"I'm sure—absolutely sure—I don't understand you." She raised her delicate arched brows.

"Then I'll explain. In simple terms, you're *hostile.*"

"You could very easily arouse those feelings in anybody." It slipped off her tongue before she could consider.

"For all I know you could be frightened of me?"

"Nonsense."

"Street terrorism?" the dark voice mocked.

"Have your bit of fun."

"Are you a lady lawyer?" He gave her his all-encompassing sidelong glance. "You don't look old enough, yet I'd say you're a match for most people."

"I'm not a lawyer." She turned to him sweetly. "I don't work for this firm."

"But you're somehow connected to James? I've finally figured it out." He paused so she was forced to pause, too. "I know he doesn't have a daughter. Come to think if it," he laughed suddenly as full comprehension set in. "There's quite a resemblance. You must be the niece. The brilliant young pianist?"

Except now I've been whittled down to size. "You *are* a detective," she said lightly. "Poirot on his best day."

"Why so snappy?" The striking face tautened as he stared down at her. "You have a wonderful future ahead of you, I understand?"

"An unfortunate part of my nature." They had turned into the top hallway, and now James Halliday himself emerged from his suite, anxious to greet such a valuable client personally.

"Royce," he cried with genuine pleasure, moving forward, hand outstretched. "Good to see you."

The two men shook hands.

"I see you've already met my niece?" James' smile widened to include the two of them.

"We haven't gotten around to formal introductions yet," Royce McQuillan drawled.

"Please allow me." Suddenly conscious of a certain tingle in the air, James performed the introductions, while Carrie, ashamed of the way she'd been acting and doing her utmost to avoid being overwhelmed, gave him her hand.

"*Catrina,* may I?" he asked.

"Everyone calls her Carrie." James smiled, extending an arm to usher them through the door.

She didn't have a clue what she was doing. She had never felt remotely like this around anyone else. The shooting sparks of electricity didn't stop even after he'd released her hand. She couldn't look at him. It was the dynamic aura, she consoled herself. Even James felt it and James was the complete man of the world.

A little later by the time they were inside James' office, she found her voice. "It's been a pleasure meeting you, Mr. McQuillan, but I should be on my way."

James' eyes found hers in perplexity. Something drastic must have happened to alter Carrie's plan. "But I thought, kitten..."

Carrie felt McQuillan's amusement. Kitten? How long since Jamie had called her kitten? Now twice in the one day. She turned to face Royce McQuillan square-on. "Goodbye."

She didn't offer the hand again but lifted a thick silky section of her hair from her collar as she spoke, tossing her head slightly to redistribute the mass.

An extraordinary alluring gesture, he thought. Kitten? She certainly had the colouring of a beautiful marmalade but this young woman had sharp claws. He noticed, too, the knuckles of her right hand were clenched white. They were beautiful hands. Long-fingered, strong-looking. A pianist's hands.

"I was rather hoping you'd stay and have lunch with us," he found himself saying. "My business with James won't take long."

"We're going to Oskars, sweetheart. You like it there." James weighed in, trying to encourage her. "They won't have any difficulty changing two places to three."

She wanted to go, unwillingly in thrall of him. "That's very nice of you, but…"

"Please, sit down both of you." James indicated the comfortable seating arrangement. "I was telling Carrie about your need of a governess for Regina," he said, turning his eyes in Carrie's direction.

"*Were* you? You can't have thought *she'd* be interested?" McQuillan returned suavely, waiting for Carrie to take a seat in the armchair opposite him, before sitting down.

It was time for Carrie to speak, James considered, or let the whole thing slide. Knowing her so well, he could see her moods, however, were fluctuating wildly.

"Actually I've been working so hard on my career I'm in need of a complete change."

Royce McQuillan stayed quiet for a moment wondering if she'd suffered some kind of nervous collapse. A burnout.

"I hardly see you as a governess," he said. "What do you know about the job?"

"Nothing!" Her amber eyes sparkled. "But I like children."

"Being able to handle them might matter more," he observed, his eyes touching on her slender body in a summery two-piece outfit of blouse and skirt, white with dark blue polka dots, the short skirt showing off her beautiful legs, the V-neck of the top revealing the slight cleft between her milk-white breasts. She had the flawless skin of certain redheads. Not a mark on it for all she lived in a subtropical climate.

Carrie bore his scrutiny by sitting very quietly. A kind of balancing act. "Who said I couldn't?" she retorted. "I've had quite a bit to do with talented children, coaching, giving lessons, master classes for the little ones."

"Regina is a child who likes getting her own way," he said matter-of-factly as though it needed to be said. "I don't know what James told you," McQuillan glanced in her uncle's direction, "but her mother left her in my sole custody. Regina isn't desolated but understandably she's found that difficult to handle."

As well she might, Carrie thought. Abandoned so early in life. This dizzyingly dynamic man for a father. "I had to live without my mother," she said quietly. "I've had a stepmother for most of my life."

"You don't like her?" he asked bluntly.

"There's no point in talking about it." Carrie shook her head, not wanting to be humiliated by this man any further. He didn't like her. She wasn't being terribly likeable. Under no circumstances would he employ her. She made to rise. "It was just an idea I had. A spur of the moment thing. Besides something about the story moved me. Regina's feelings that can't be dismissed and I need to help someone." To help myself, to survive, she thought but didn't say. "I'm sure Uncle James will find you someone you consider suitable, Mr. McQuillan." She stood up in one swift graceful movement. "I must decline your kind offer to have lunch. I have to see someone this afternoon at the Conservatorium." Easy to make it up.

He, too, stood up, his expression a little darker. "What a pity. I would have liked to get to know you better instead of a few snatched words. James has spoken of you often. I've just recalled where I saw you though I can see it has since disappeared.'' He turned to James. ''Remember that photograph of a little girl you used to have on your desk. It had a lovely antique silver frame.''

''Carrie, of course!'' James' face lit up. ''It's at home. Liz went off with it. She loves that one.''

''I was ten at the time.'' Carrie looked at Royce McQuillan in surprise.

''You haven't changed at all.''

''I have, too.'' I'm falling apart, Carrie thought, stunned how well she hid it. I just have to get away from this man.

''You're wonderfully observant, Royce,'' James said in his charming voice, fully conscious of the charge in the atmosphere.

''It's not a face one forgets.''

''No.'' James smiled at his niece, his heart in his eyes. ''Carrie is the image of her mother, my darling sister, Caroline. Having Carrie, Caro is always near.'' He reached out and slipped an arm around Carrie's waist, drawing her to him.

''Love you,'' she murmured, turning her head into her uncle's shoulder. ''Well, I must be off.'' Her voice picked up briskly. ''Enjoy your lunch.''

''Let's see, I take it you've withdrawn your candidature?'' Again Royce McQuillan cast his spell over her, his brilliant black gaze suggesting she was a highly volatile individual.

''I didn't think you liked me?'' she answered solemnly.

''Did I say so?''

''I believe you did. In certain ways.''

''Really?'' One black eyebrow shot up. ''I'm sorry you thought so. I didn't mean it in that way. If you *are* serious, perhaps we can discuss the matter again as you absolutely must rush off.'' It was obvious he hadn't believed in her excuse.

''When do you fly back home, Royce?'' James Halliday

asked, not quite sure what was going on. But something certainly was.

"Tomorrow."

His gaze held her as though she was pinned to the wall. "I think you want someone very different from me," Carrie said, suddenly anxious to back out of a dangerous situation while she could. This man could change her life. She knew it. And not for the better. She wasn't such a fool or so traumatized it hadn't struck her, though her reactions were multiple, the overriding one was sexual. The slightest contact with his hand had somehow compromised her. This man still had an ex-wife in the background. An ex-wife who wasn't over him yet. The mother of his child.

Carrie tilted her head to kiss her uncle's cheek. "See you, Jamie. Give my love to Liz."

"You are coming sailing with me?" James was mystified by her thoughts.

"Of course I am. Let's hope for a perfect weekend." Her skirt flaring as she changed direction, Carrie dared to glance in Royce McQuillan's direction. "I'm thinking how I'm going to get out of my parking spot. You're still there?"

"I don't know if I should let you do it," he said with a provocative stare.

"Do *what?* It would be nice if you'd let me in on this," James complained.

"I met Mr. McQuillan earlier on," Carrie explained. "We're both parked in the side street."

"I can come with you if you're worried," Royce McQuillan offered suavely. "Perhaps extricate your car."

"This time I might have to allow you." The accident had made her lose so much confidence. "I wouldn't like to do the slightest damage to your car."

"Not mine. A friend's."

"I see." She nibbled her lip. "If it wouldn't be too

much trouble. I have many talents but I'm not the greatest parker in the world."

"So you've said." He took her arm lightly though he might as well have shaken her such was her reaction. "Won't be more than five minutes, James."

"Take your time." James was doing his level best to assess this surprising situation, but was content to let fate take its course.

"Are you really meeting anybody?" Royce McQuillan asked when they were out on the street.

"I wonder you doubt me." If he hadn't released her she would have had to pull away.

"I do." He wondered what it would be like to kiss her mouth. *Hard.* Kiss the curve of her neck, the swell of her breast. Dangerous to have such thoughts about someone so young. Too young. He remembered James had told him all about his niece's twenty-first birthday party. But hang on, that had to be a year or more ago. Time went so swiftly.

"Stay like that," he ordered when they reached the footpath alongside the parked cars. "Just give me your keys."

"You *will* be careful." She couldn't understand why she was trying to provoke him. She closed her eyes as their fingers touched.

He didn't bother to answer. Instead he crammed himself into her tiny car, shot back the driver's seat as far as it would go, then in a matter of moments had the car waiting, ready for her to get into it and drive away.

"How very nice of you," she said, unable to get the cool satirical note out of her voice. She stood well back while he extricated himself from her car.

"A pleasure, Miss Russell. You quite interest me."

"Surely I'm not important enough for that?" She slipped into the driver's seat, aware she was being drawn into a dark whirlpool.

''I suspect not,'' he gave a low laugh, ''nevertheless you might tell me why a beautiful girl like yourself, a gifted performer, would want to hide herself away in the wilds. You have an aura of intense excitement swirling all around you yet you want to get away. You must have some idea what station life would be like? You'd be so isolated much of the time.''

''I know that.'' Her eyes looked straight ahead.

''So what's the reason?'' His voice was like black velvet against her skin. ''You've split with a boyfriend? You've changed your mind about your big career?''

Some things you couldn't help. ''My career is *demolished,* Mr. McQuillan,'' she gritted, her voice harsh so she could keep it steady. ''Thank you for helping me out. Of course if you hadn't parked so close behind me you wouldn't have had to worry.''

The whole attitude of his lean powerful body changed. ''Look,'' he said.

''No, *you* look.'' She lifted a hand in farewell and drove off.

She could still see him in her rear-view mirror. He was standing in the middle of the quiet street looking after her. God! He probably thought she was mad. She didn't have any appointment at the Conservatorium to keep. She couldn't bear to go home. Glenda's manner was so unpleasant these days. She'd thought to get rid of me but my accident changed that. It changed everything.

Tears sprang to Carrie's eyes but she blinked them away furiously. No use crying. What's done was done. Like Jamie said, she had to pick up the pieces and find strategies to propel her through life.

CHAPTER TWO

WHEN he returned to James' office, Royce got straight to the point. ''Your niece just shocked me by telling me her career is demolished. What on earth happened? You've never said anything.''

James found himself apologising. ''Of course I should have. To be honest, Royce, I haven't felt able to talk about it. Carrie has grieved. We've all grieved for almost a year. She was involved in a car crash the very afternoon she had word she'd secured a place at the Julliard Academy in New York. The accident wasn't all that bad. A friend's car and a taxi collided. Carrie broke a couple of ribs, suffered a few abrasions but the worst part was the little finger of her right hand was very badly broken. The orthopaedic man did a marvellous job. For most purposes it's perfectly all right. She's still a highly accomplished pianist but he warned us the finger won't stand up to the rigours of a concert career. It will let her down, perhaps during a performance. I haven't got words for how we feel. Carrie has changed in little telling ways. But she's very brave. A fighter. In many ways she's been fighting all her life.''

''You mean in terms of her relationship to her stepmother?'' Royce asked perceptively.

James trusted this man so he gave an unhappy nod. ''Like Carrie, my sister was so beautiful. Unforgettable really. When she died—a tragic accident, she fell and struck her head—Carrie was only three. Her father nearly went out of his mind. Jeff and I have never been close friends so I wasn't able to help him as I could have had things been different. He started to drink pretty heavily.

He hadn't before and he doesn't now, but out of his despair came a very quick second marriage. Glenda, his present wife, was his secretary. It appears she'd always been in love with him.''

''So she made things happen,'' Royce said quietly.

''Yes.'' James swallowed hard. ''Melissa was born soon after. Carrie was never wanted by her stepmother. Her father adores her but he doesn't understand her any more than he understood my sister. Glenda is always very careful when Jeff's around but the relationship seen through my eyes and my wife's has never been caring. Not affectionate. Certainly not loving. To compound it all Carrie was by far the brighter child in the family. As you'll know from that photograph she was the prettiest little girl imaginable. She shone in the classroom. Right from the beginning she was brilliant at the piano, which I insisted she learn in remembrance of her mother who was a fine pianist, as was my mother. It runs in the family.''

''So the stepmother was not only jealous of her husband's attention to his firstborn she was jealous and resentful of her capabilities,'' Royce remarked.

''I'm afraid so. Carrie was always classed as a gifted child. Glenda saw the two girls in competition, which was sad for Melissa. Melissa had her mother's views and attitudes forced on her. I think the two girls could have been good friends but Glenda didn't want that. She wouldn't *permit* it.''

''And Catrina's father didn't put a stop to this?'' Royce asked almost curtly.

James shook his head. ''Glenda is clever. Outwardly she's as proud of Carrie and her achievements as ever Jeff is. Inwardly I think she struggles with her rage. She was thrilled at the thought of Carrie's securing a place at the Julliard. That would have taken Carrie off her hands. Very very sadly it didn't happen.''

''I'm sorry I didn't *know,*'' Royce said, like he bitterly regretted the fact.

''I think I would have told you at some point but you've had lots of problems of your own, Royce,'' James answered in a conciliatory voice.

''Your niece is very unhappy.''

It couldn't be denied. ''She's struggling to overcome it. She hasn't touched the piano since the accident.''

''So what is she doing with herself?'' Royce McQuillan asked outright. ''Teaching? That would be very hard at this point.''

''*Very.* Her whole training has been geared to performance.''

''I don't think she's governess material,'' Royce said. ''Too many strong emotions working through her. A trauma to battle down. I was looking for a quiet capable young woman who wouldn't be discontented far away from boyfriends and the city life.''

''I agree. I don't think Carrie is governess material, either, but she made it clear to me she wants to get right away from the world of music. For a time.''

''*How* long?'' Royce asked in his direct manner.

'Who would know?'' There was deep concern in James' voice. ''I think Carrie feels all the pain and bitter disappointments like it was yesterday. She's right about one thing. She's great with children. Or she was until her world changed. She had such sparkle. Such vitality. Saddest to me is she's lost a lot of her natural confidence.''

''Her accident has made her fearful?''

''Of certain things, yes,'' James agreed. ''Her father would never hear of her leaving home. She's tried before but a large extent with her studies she's been dependent on him. He wouldn't thank me for interfering in any way. As I say, we don't get on. But Carrie told me today she is determined on moving out.''

Royce didn't give that another moment's consideration. ''It sounds like the obvious solution. Where will she go?'' He narrowed his brilliant eyes.

''Wherever she wants to go. Liz and I will help her. Carrie is the love of our lives. She's given us such joy. She'll have a battle with her father, though. He's a born controller.'' James' largely hidden antipathy came through.

''Except he lost control all those years ago.''

James nodded. ''All that's history. Almost any other young woman would have made a better mother for Carrie than Glenda. A better mother for Melissa in a way although Glenda dotes on her. They present a united front socially but it's really a dysfunctional family.''

''Then it can't be nice for Catrina to be around.''

In that moment Royce McQuillan made the decision to act.

Carrie spent another hour in town drifting through a department store, buying nothing. Nothing appealed. She was simply putting off the moment she had to return home. There was such a soul-destroying drawing up of sides; Glenda and Melissa; she and her father. Instead of taking any advantage from the situation Carrie had found it a real burden knowing her father enjoyed her company better than her sister's. Not only that, he made no bones about showing it. His insensitivity had created many problems. She'd had the unenviable role of being the favourite. It had caused a lot of pain. On all sides.

Now that Carrie was a woman, Glenda hated her. Carrie felt almost positive Glenda felt no guilt because of it. Now that she wasn't going overseas to continue her studies Glenda was coming more and more into the open. When her father wasn't around Glenda didn't hesitate to use a cutting tongue. She did it with an air of triumph, knowing Carrie would never complain to her father. It had always been so. Carrie, even on Glenda's admission, had never used her unique position in her father's life to gain the ascendency or come between husband and wife. But it hadn't won her Glenda's friendship. That was the irony.

Driving into the garage, Carrie reflected the position and delightful appearance of their beautiful old colonial riverside home that proclaimed her father's affluence. The interior decoration was all Glenda. Glenda and the interior designer currently in favour. The spacious high-ceilinged rooms were choked with an overabundance of everything. Too much money gone mad, in Carrie's opinion. She always felt trapped inside.

The splendid Steinway her father had brought for her when she was eleven years old and already showing signs of promise had been banished from the living room to the soundproof studio Glenda had convinced her father ''darling little Carrie'' must have. Her father hadn't taken all that much persuasion for the good reason much as he loved her and was proud of her successes, he couldn't bear to hear her practising. Her father, she had long since accepted, would never make a music lover. She had given up wondering how her mother and father had come together in the first place. ''Sex appeal,'' James maintained. ''Jeff always was this great big handsome virile guy. They had little or nothing in common.''

Glenda and her father had a good deal in common; likes, dislikes, mutual interests. That didn't prevent her father revealing on rare occasions the unique place Caroline, his first wife, had had in his life. To this day Carrie thought he was tormented by it. The sudden violent loss. The end of a golden period in his life. A golden period that had never really started for her. She was deprived and she knew it. No one should have to do without a mother. Her immersion in her studies, her preoccupations with succeeding as a pianist, could have been the result of too little bonding at home. Her music had shut her off from Glenda's own unresolved resentments. She had poured out her own yearnings on a keyboard. Now she had the feeling of being profoundly at a disadvantage. At Glenda's mercy unless she moved out. Ultimately though, it was her father she would have to confront. This was the father who had told her not so long ago if she left home it would break his heart.

She let herself into the house quietly, coming in through the rear door so she could escape to her bedroom. She couldn't let these feelings of isolation get a hold on her. It was a tragedy her stepmother and her own sister offered her no support at this bad time, but she wasn't alone. She had James and Liz, a whole lot of friends. The only thing was most of her friends were fellow musicians. Their careers went on. Hers had badly faltered.

Someone was in her room. She knew it before she opened the door. Melissa was standing in front of the mirrored wall of wardrobes, holding one of Carrie's evening dresses to her body. The dress she had last performed in. It had a shell top, a beautiful full skirt, and was a rich orange, a difficult colour but it suited her.

"Hi, what are you doing?" Carrie tried not to show any irritation. Melissa was always borrowing her things when she had much more of her own. Items she wouldn't have loaned under any circumstances. Melissa wasn't a lender.

"We didn't expect you home," Melissa said, continuing to preen. "I'd like to wear this on Saturday. Can I?"

Carrie had to smile.

"Mel it won't fit you," she pointed out reasonably. "The skirt will be too long, for one thing." Melissa was petite if well covered. "It won't even suit you. We're different sizes, different styles. I love you in red. It brings your colouring to life.'' She said it naturally, helpfully, but it angered Melissa.

''That's it! Go on, remind me. I *need* bringing to life.''

Carrie didn't worsen the situation by saying she did. ''We all benefit from wearing the colours that suit us. Don't get cranky for no reason,'' Carrie implored.

''Oh, and you aren't?'' Melissa turned around to throw the dress on the bed. ''The tragedy queen with the little smashed finger. Who said you were going to be a concert pianist anyway? If you'd ever got there you'd have probably found plenty better than you. You were just a big fish in a little bowl. New York is the centre of the world.''

''Well, I'm not going, Mel. So settle down. I'm not a whinger, either, so don't try pinning that on me.''

''Why, will you tell Dad?'' Melissa looked back belligerently, her voice on the rise, a pretty girl, dark curly hair, hazel eyes, a little overweight, but the expression on her face made Carrie want to give up.

''We can't talk, can we?'' she said quietly, feeling pretty well numb inside. ''We're sisters. That's wasting a valuable relationship.''

''Sisters?'' Melissa shouted, her face energised by jealousy. She followed Carrie up closely, hands on hips, obviously spoiling for a fight. ''Does that mean we're supposed to love one another?''

''It happens in most families.'' Carrie turned, picking up her dress and carrying it to the wardrobe.

''But you're too good for us, Carrie. Too clever for Mum and me. Mum says having you around has ruined our lives.''

Though the sort of stuff Glenda fed her daughter made Carrie feel sick to the stomach, she faced her sister calmly. ''How do you want me to react, Mel? Scream back? I was little more than a baby when my mother died. Three. I didn't want to come between anyone. I'd have adored having my own mother. You might think of that.''

''Oh, for God's sake, the gorgeous, the beautiful, the adorable Caroline.'' Melissa's pretty face was working.

''Who died when she was only a few years older than me,'' Carrie retaliated. ''Thank *you,* Melissa. Doesn't that defuse your rage a little? She had her whole life in front of her.''

''But haven't you ever thought she's more glorious in death,'' Melissa cried almost hysterically. ''That's what Mum says.''

''Then Mum has a lot to answer for.'' Carrie felt her own temper rise.

''You hate her, don't you? You hate me,'' Melissa insisted, dragging at her curls roughly.

''Mel, that's so unfair.'' Carrie put her hand on her stepsister's arm, grateful Melissa didn't shake it off. ''That's some dreadful propaganda Glenda has fed you. It desperately hurt me to hear you say that. Glenda and I might never get on, but I wouldn't like to lose you. We're *blood.*'' She could feel Melissa trembling.

''How dare you!'' a voice shouted from the door. Glenda dressed to the nines was standing there quivering with outrage.

''For what it's worth,'' she fixed her greenish eyes on Carrie, ''I'm your stepmother. I've looked after you and looked after you *well* for all these years, you ungrateful creature. Now you try to turn Melissa against me.''

''Oh, please, Mum, don't start,'' Melissa wailed, her eyes filling with tears.

''Look how you've upset her,'' Glenda accused.

Carrie took a deep breath. ''Why don't you stop right now, Glenda,'' she said. ''I'm having a bad enough time without your starting.''

''Is it pity you want?'' Glenda demanded, her expression distorted.

'Understanding might say it,'' Carrie answered briefly.

''You think yourself so extraordinary,'' Glenda said. ''Anyone would think you were the only one who has ever suffered a setback. Between ourselves I've had a lot to contend with.''

''You've never had talent like Carrie's,'' Melissa burst out unexpectedly. ''I've never heard her big noting herself, either.''

Glenda's impeccably made-up face drained of colour. She looked at her daughter as though she couldn't understand what she was saying. ''Excuse me, Melissa, haven't I heard you endlessly complaining about Carrie's airs and graces?''

Melissa's reaction was even more unexpected. ''Maybe I'm just jealous,'' she said. ''I'd give anything to get covered in glory. To be lovely. Just a tiny bit like Carrie. To see Dad's eyes light up. To feel his pride in me. I'd have given anything to be Dad's perfect little girl. Ah, hell....'' Melissa couldn't bear it any longer. She broke into sobs, trying to flee the room but Glenda stopped her forcibly, grabbing her wrists.

''My darling, don't you ever put yourself down. Your father *adores* you.''

''Like hell he does, Mum. Beside Carrie I'm pathetic. A failure. I couldn't even get a place at uni. Dad was so disappointed in me.''

''Ah, don't, Mel. Please don't.'' Carrie was deeply affected; answering tears sprang to her eyes. ''What's so important about going to university? You'll find something you love doing.''

''Then tell me what it is.'' Melissa was back to shouting. ''I can't do a damn thing. I'm stupid. We all know that.''

"You haven't begun to find yourself," Carrie said. "You have to try things, Mel. You're the best cook in the house."

"I beg your pardon." Glenda, who took particular pride in her culinary skills, looked affronted.

"Why not train to be a chef?" Carrie suggested. "You have a real way with food and food preparation. The way you're always experimenting and making new dishes."

"A chef!" Glenda looked totally taken aback though she couldn't deny Melissa was very good. "What nonsense you talk. Mel is able to turn out an excellent meal—perhaps a touch too exotic. I don't want her spending her time hanging around restaurants."

"She has to train first."

Melissa looked astonished. "Why not?"

"Oh, please!" Glenda shook all over in disgust. "Your father is a rich man, Melissa. Come to that, you don't have to work at all. You can help me."

"How? Chauffeur you around all day?" Melissa looked over at Carrie and actually smiled at her. "Do you think I could become a chef?"

"Of course I do," Carrie said briskly. "I'm greatly surprised you haven't thought of it before."

"Now look here, Carrie," Glenda began a shade helplessly. "Don't go putting foolish ideas into Melissa's head."

"It's quite an attractive idea," said Melissa, now oddly calm.

"My God!" Glenda held her head. "I want you out of here, Carrie," she said harshly. "I don't care how you do it—what you say to your father—I want you *out.* You've disrupted my home long enough."

Even Melissa flinched. "Mum don't!"

"That's all right." Carrie looked at Melissa reassuringly. "In lots of ways it will be better if I go."

"Not when you're being ordered out," Melissa said. "That's dreadful."

"Keep out of this, Melissa," her mother warned sharply, her expression furious. "Do you think because Carrie has suggested a job for you it's going to make things better? You girls have had a very spiky relationship for years. You want your father's attention? You'll get more of it with Carrie gone."

"Well, maybe..." Melissa looked confused.

"So that's settled," Carrie said, trying to absorb the blows. "I'll speak to Dad then I'll set about finding a place of my own."

"I'm sure you'll be a lot happier in it, Carrie," Glenda said in a much gentler tone, though the expression on her face was almost exultant. "You must realise how I've tried, I've..." She broke off, diverted by the sound of the front door chimes. "That must be the florist," she murmured, looking a whole lot brighter. "I've ordered a new arrangement for the entrance hall. Leave your sister now, Melissa, and come downstairs. I'm sure Carrie has lots to think about."

Carrie felt cut to the bone. Hot tears welled but she fought them back. She'd done enough crying in her pillow. It was time to rise above it. A few moments later Melissa rushed back into the room, appearing surprised, but very pleasantly so. "Carrie, there's someone downstairs who wants to see you. The best-looking guy I've ever seen in my life. You've gotta come clean."

"About what, then? Who is it?" Carrie turned away; quickly brushing a few unshed tears off her eyelashes.

"Says his name is Royce McQuillan. Got a great voice. Real cool."

"You're joking?" But Carrie knew that she wasn't.

"Mum offered him something but he didn't want it.

They're in the living room talking. Mum seems to be enjoying it. She loves the tall dark handsome types.''

''I'll be there in a moment,'' Carrie said, walking through to the adjoining bathroom to run a comb through her hair, but mostly to check the sign of tears didn't show.

They did. Or she thought they did, she was so emotional.

''You don't have to touch anything,'' Melissa said, following her into the en suite. ''You're perfect. You've got this incredible skin. Why haven't I? You never have a breakout. It's not fair.''

''We both know you have very good skin, too, Mel. And big hazel eyes. I don't have a curl in sight.''

''Curls aren't special,'' said Melissa.

Glenda and Royce McQuillan were seated in the living room, apparently enjoying a pleasant conversation. ''Oh, there you are, dear.'' Effortlessly Glenda assumed a fond voice. But then she'd had so much practice. ''You have a visitor.''

Royce McQuillan stood up, unbearably handsome and *physical.* Giving her that coolly sexy smile. ''Catrina, it's wonderful to see you. I just happened to be in the area.''

''How nice of you to call in.'' She marvelled her own voice rippled with pleasure.

''I'll be flying home tomorrow,'' he explained, ''I thought we might have dinner tonight if you're free?''

''That would be lovely.'' Such an unexpected saviour!

He had moved right up to her, taking her hand, staring down into her face. ''So I'll see you tonight then?''

''Marvellous. I'm looking forward to it. What time?'' She almost begged him to take her with him.

He shot a cuff, and glanced at his watch. ''If you could be ready at seven? I haven't given you much warning.''

''Seven will be fine,'' she said, with a quick smile. ''I won't be late.''

"I'll pick you up." He turned to look at Glenda who was staring at them both in a kind of open-mouthed fascination. "A pleasure meeting you, Mrs. Russell. You, too, Melissa." He gave her a smile that might haunt her for the rest of her days. "Catrina has spoken of you both. I must apologise for tearing off but I'm cutting it rather fine as it is. I have to see someone before I go back to the hotel."

Glenda rose, looking at Carrie as though she was precious. "It's a great pity you'll miss my husband," she said. "He's working late tonight. You know how it is?"

"My busiest times are the mornings. I'm a cattle man, Mrs. Russell. My home is North Queensland."

"How exciting!" Glenda was studying him in detail, wondering where on earth Carrie had found this prize.

"It's a very beautiful part of the world, north of Capricorn," McQuillan said, towering over the petite, very trim Glenda. "Catrina, would you like to walk me to my car?" he asked with a turn of his head.

She smiled at him and he smiled back.

"Goodbye, then." He gave the mesmerised women, Glenda and Melissa, a charming salute. "I'm sure we'll meet again."

"That's great!" The nineteen-year-old Melissa burst out.

They walked in silence out of the house and along the front path bordered by an avenue of palms and farther back an avalanche of azaleas and flowering shrubs intoxicating in their perfume.

"You've been crying?" he said.

"I have not." She knew she sounded nervy.

"Your stepsister doesn't look in the least like you."

"Not surprising, I'm said to be the image of my mother."

''She must have been very lovely.''

''Yes.'' Carrie answered simply as though it wasn't a compliment to herself.

''I can well see your stepmother might give you a hard time,'' he remarked rather grimly.

She turned her head in surprise. Glenda had been at her social best. ''Didn't she act welcoming enough?''

''Indeed she did. She was very pleasant. I just happened to spot something in her eyes. Are you all right?'' he asked after a minute.

''I'm absolutely fine.'' Carrie decided it was time to get right to the point. ''Why are you here, Mr. McQuillan? Somehow you've given my stepmother and sister the impression we're...friends.''

Quirky little brackets appeared at the side of his mouth. ''Well, it's hard *not* to like you, Catrina. And I have to say it was good to find out you're not nervous of me *personally.*''

''Jamie told you about my accident,'' she said a little fiercely.

''He did.'' He opened the front gate for her, marking the beauty of her hair in the golden sunlight. ''I wish he had told me before. We've become closer than the usual solicitor/client relationship, but he loves you so much he found your pain unbearable. I can understand that.''

''Can you?''

His smile twisted. ''You don't think I've ever loved anyone?''

She stared up at him, the brilliance of the sun flecking her eyes with gold sparks. ''I'm sorry. What you must think of me! Of course you have. You *do.*''

''That's better, Catrina,'' he said crisply. ''If I were a betting man as well as a horse breeder I wouldn't put money on whether you and I will get on.''

"I share your alarm," she said, too agitated to watch her tongue.

"Very wise of you," he drawled, holding her gaze for a minute. "It seems to me, however, having heard your story, I can help you out of a very difficult situation. At least for a time. You on the other hand might well be able to help me with Regina."

Carrie drew in a raw ragged breath. "You mean you're *hiring* me?"

"What does that bloody woman say to you?" he asked, his scrutiny intense.

For a moment she felt drained of all strength. "I'm not her child, *her* daughter. I desperately need to get away."

"So she won't damage you further."

"You can't *know,*" she protested. "Glenda isn't all that bad."

"Isn't she? James filled me in. Besides, I've had a pretty event-packed life. I know a lot more than you, Miss Twenty-Two."

"A great deal more," Carrie said. "I'm sorry I'm being rude. You must bring out that side of me."

"I expect being mad at the world has helped a lot." He studied her with a mixture of mockery and sympathy.

"It's not easy to come to terms with the shattering of one's dreams."

"My feelings exactly," he replied with quiet irony. "You can tell me all about it over dinner." He bent suddenly and, while she felt a rush of pure panic, kissed her cheek.

"What did you do that for?" She tried but couldn't find more than a shadow of her voice.

"What do you think, Catrina? For the benefit of step-mamma. She hasn't moved away from the curtains."

"She'll tell Dad!"

"I don't care who she tells. Do you? Besides a peck on

the cheek doesn't mean I'm about to steal Jeff Russell's little girl.''

''Then *who* exactly are you supposed to be?'' she asked with difficulty.

He gave a brief amused laugh. ''I know it's a dreadful role but at the moment I'm your knight in shining armour. Don't worry, Catrina. We'll decide on a story tonight. Now I simply must go.'' Briskly he moved around to the driver's seat of the parked Jaguar. ''By the way...'' A moment's hesitation before he got behind the wheel. ''Do you have a yellow dress in your wardrobe?''

She was astonished by the turns in the conversation. Astonished at his being there at all. ''You like yellow?''

''I think it would be perfect for you, Catrina,'' he said as though he knew she needed cheering up. ''I want you to dress up. We'll go to Vivaldi's. I'm in the mood for something grand.''

It was the perfect way for a knight to exit, Carrie thought.

When she returned to the house, Glenda and Melissa were very nearly dancing on the marble floor of the entrance hall in their excitement and need to know.

''What have you got to say for yourself?'' Glenda challenged her. ''You *are* a dark horse.'' She laughed with a shadow of bitter envy. ''So secretive. Were you frightened your father was going to forbid you to see him? Is he married? He *must* be married. There isn't a woman alive who'd make the mistake of letting him get away.''

''Come on, Carrie,'' Melissa urged when her stepsister remained silent. ''At least you can tell us now?''

When she was on the verge of being thrown out. ''Why exactly, Melissa?'' Carrie asked. ''It's not your business really. Now more than ever. Wasn't it decided I move out only minutes before…Royce arrived?'' She barely tripped over his Christian name.

''Is it possible you're thinking of moving in with him?'' Glenda abruptly questioned, her eyes narrowing to mere slits.

''Why would that upset you, Glenda?'' Carrie said it as though it were of no consequence.

''You know I have to tell your father.''

Angered but trying to hold on to herself, Carrie made a move toward the stairs. ''Glenda you have no authority over me,'' she said quietly. ''I'm twenty-two years of age. I love my father but it's high time I stood on my own two feet. Royce McQuillan is a friend. He comes from a highly respected family with a fine pioneering name. He *was* married, as it happens. He has one child, a little girl in his custody.''

''You mean he's divorced?'' Glenda gasped, her skin flushing a dark red.

Carrie hesitated, one hand on the banister. ''Unhappily many marriages lead to divorce, Glenda. The happily ever after we'll have to leave to you and Dad.''

''Are you in love with him, Carrie?'' Melissa called, her hazel eyes round with excitement. ''You must be. He's gorgeous.''

''No, I'm not in love with him, Mel.'' Carrie paused on the first landing, wondering what they would say if they knew she and Royce McQuillan had only just met.

''Don't think you can escape your father's questioning,'' Glenda cried in a threatening tone. ''He looked a dangerous man to me. Striking, rich, years older than you. Light-years in experience, all that suave charm. Without doubt you're having an affair. A secret affair it now seems.''

''The one thing you won't be able to interfere in, Glenda,'' Carrie called down lightly.

"Your father will be shocked when he discovers it." Glenda moved to the base of the staircase, looking up.

"Well, maybe he will be, but Dad trusts me to look after myself, to do the right thing."

"And to think the way you've taken us in!" Glenda was the very picture of betrayal. "Pretending your life was ruined and all the time you had a man like Royce McQuillan tucked away. McQuillan....McQuillan...surely I know the name?" Glenda shook her head vigorously as if to clear it. "It will come to me," she muttered.

"Gosh, I think it's wonderful!" Melissa exclaimed, totally ignoring her mother and her sentiments. "You lucky thing, Carrie, you've found your dream man."

At least one who might take me out of my misery.

She had the choice of two dresses, both slip dresses, very much in fashion. One white chiffon with yellow stripes and yellow daisy appliqué. The other, which she finally settled on, golden-yellow chiffon with a rather exquisite floral print; gold high-heeled evening sandals on her feet. Her father's twenty-first birthday present, which had been made to order, went perfectly with it. A large topaz pendant set in 18 kt gold hung from a beautiful gold chain with topaz gold earrings to match.

She was applying a dab of perfume to the insides of her wrists when Melissa came through the bedroom door without knocking, a large book under her arm.

"Mum finally cracked it," she chortled, opening up the coffee-table-sized book at a marked page. "'Kings of the Cattle Country,'" she read. "Your boyfriend's grandad is in it. The book's a bit old but it's all about the cattle empires and today's cattle kings. Here he is, Sir Andrew McQuillan, the master of Maramba Downs. A pretty glamorous figure, don't you think? You can easily see the resemblance. There's a picture of the homestead, too. It looks out on a lagoon. It looks fabulous. *Huge!* And there's a photo of a lot of cattle standing in a kind of billabong with the Great Dividing Range or spurs of it in the background. Tropical North Queensland. Don't you want to look?''

Carrie pretended to be unimpressed. ''I know all about it,'' she said casually. Lord forgive me for the white lie. Nevertheless she couldn't resist moving behind the shorter Melissa to glance over her shoulder, catching an aerial view of the station and its numerous outbuildings and a large herd of Brahmins penned in a holding yard.

''I'm just staggered you never told us, Carrie,'' Melissa said, her voice light with disbelief.

''There's nothing to tell,'' Carrie answered mildly. ''I don't even know Royce particularly well.''

''He *kissed* you,'' Melissa pointed out, making it sound like a passionate embrace.

''On the cheek. A friendly farewell.''

Melissa, looking unconvinced, returned to the book. '''The McQuillan operation encompasses a chain of strategically placed stations to safeguard against drought stretching from the Channel Country in the far southwest right to the Northern Territory border,''' she read. ''Here, I can't hold this, it's too heavy.'' She set the book down hard on the long chest at the foot of Carrie's bed. ''You look beautiful,'' she suddenly said at a rush, a trace of real caring in her eyes. ''I bet *he* thinks so, too.''

''Thanks, Mel.'' Carrie gave her stepsister a poignant little smile, wondering how Glenda could have spread such devastation. ''I want to say I'm sorry you think I robbed you of Dad's attention. I never wanted that.''

There was a long wait for a response. ''On my good days I realise that,'' Mel said with a kind of embarrassment. ''The trouble is, *always was,* you're far more *everything* than I am. It's not easy being outshone. I guess that's why Mum and I are always attacking you. I'm sorry for that, Carrie. If you'd have been ordinary like me we'd have gotten along fine.''

''But aren't you going to be a cordon bleu?'' Carrie asked in a challenging voice, catching up her gold evening purse. ''What's ordinary about that?''

''I hope Dad lets me.''

This could be their last conversation for a while, Carrie thought. ''My advice, Mel,'' she said earnestly, ''is don't let him stop you. You've got to make a life for *yourself.*''

''Well, we'll see.'' Melissa blushed. ''Enjoy yourself, Carrie. Deep down I think I really love you.''

CHAPTER THREE

ROYCE MCQUILLAN arrived on the dot of seven, spiriting her away with such practiced charm Glenda was left with very little to say.

"I don't think I could have liked a dress more if I'd picked it out myself," he complimented Catrina as they walked to the car. "No trace of tears, either," he added, experiencing a powerful urge to see this young woman out of the house. The "atmosphere" could have been cut with a knife.

"You're just too observant," Carrie managed wryly, so overwhelmed by his sudden appearance in her life she was floating.

"Very much so," he said briefly, not adding because it would panic her she had aroused in him a potentially dangerous sexual response. He couldn't dress it up as anything else. Now he had more or less committed himself to taking her under his roof. This beautiful young woman wasn't in the least what he wanted as a governess for Regina. She had problems of her own to cope with, most notably coming to terms with the destruction of a promising career. That presented quite a trauma in itself. He had to be mad. Yet her light fragrance filled the interior of the car with such images of spring blossom and sweet breezes. "Your stepmother seems most insistent I meet your father," he remarked when they were underway, driving down the street with its splendid old colonial homes set in leafy gardens and river frontages.

Carrie glanced out the window, into the star-filled indigo night. "Please don't be angry, or worse, *laugh,* but she's under the impression you and I are having a secret affair. Nothing I could possibly say would affect her thinking. Glenda believes what she wants to believe.''

''That was fairly obvious. So what did you tell her?''

''Only that you were a friend. That you were divorced and you have a little girl aged six.''

''Nothing about coming back with me to Maramba?''

She was shocked by the effect of his words on her. ''I wasn't totally sure you wanted me,'' she confessed.

''I would have hoped for someone quite different.''

She turned her amber head, the long full pageboy swinging to her bare shoulders. ''What have you got against me? My education hasn't been neglected. I was an excellent student. Teaching a six-year-old her lessons couldn't be difficult.''

He glanced at her. ''Catrina, I'm not referring to that aspect of it. I'm not telling you anything you don't already know. You're *over* qualified and you're lovely, not the sort of young woman who can escape into the background.''

''Of course I am,'' Catrina contradicted, a soft flush rising to her face. ''I've had to be very self-effacing at home. My stepmother and I have had a *very* difficult relationship. It's useless to hide the fact her attitude poisoned my relationship with my sister. She set us up as competitors and it wasn't fair to either of us. If you want me to disappear into the furniture I'll do it.''

''Okay.'' He laughed. ''You really *want* this job?''

''At the moment I desperately need it,'' she admitted frankly. ''Before you arrived this afternoon, Glenda and I had a few words. She wants me out.''

''Does she!'' His voice deepened with evident disapproval. ''What does your sister have to say about that?''

''Mel does what she's told. She's only nineteen. She doesn't have a job yet.''

''I understood from James you're very much the apple

of your father's eye.'' He eased into the freeway traffic, a scintillating ribbon of light.

''I suppose you could say that's been a lot of the trouble. I don't make mischief. Dad misses a lot that goes on. He's a very busy man and Glenda is always very careful when he's around.''

''How will he take your coming with me?'' he asked bluntly, turning to look at her as they stopped at the red light.

''Badly, I would think.''

''You're twenty-two. You can't be Daddy's little girl forever. I'll speak to him, naturally.''

''You will?''

''Of course.'' His mouth compressed at her surprised tone. ''I wouldn't want *my* daughter haring off to the wilds with a complete stranger. Moreover a divorced man. It might help for you to know—you're so traumatised you haven't asked—I have a fairly full household so you'll be well chaperoned. There's my grandmother, Louise. My father's mother. She's into her eighties now and a remarkable woman. Then there's my uncle Cam, my father's younger brother, and his second wife, Lindsey. His first wife was killed in a riding accident on the station. A great tragedy. I was only a boy when it happened but I clearly remember how warm and attractive she was. She and my mother were very close. In fact she was my mother's bridesmaid. Cam remarried only two years ago. A whirlwind affair. Lyn swept him off his feet. And of course there's Regina.''

''Your uncle's wife can't help with her lessons?'' Carrie asked.

''Children aren't Lyn's scene,'' he answered briefly.

''Oh! How depressing for Regina.''

''We've had two governesses already.''

"I hope they were suitably plain?" she couldn't resist asking, but absolutely sweetly.

"To tell you the truth I didn't notice. One was better than the other but unfortunately neither could handle the job. Regina didn't make things easy. She can be a little terror."

"I'd like to meet her." Carrie laughed.

"You should do that more often," he commented.

"What?" He had *such* an expressive voice; her musical ear was vastly unsettled by it.

"Laugh."

"Does Regina see her mother?" she asked.

"She hasn't seen her for some considerable time. It's very hard on Regina, but it suits me. My ex-wife is not my favourite person."

"You must have loved her once?" she commented in a low voice.

"I thought I did." There was an underlying note of self-derision.

"I'm sorry."

"Nothing for you to worry about." He turned his handsome head briefly. "My wife's sister, Ina, comes to visit from time to time."

"Regina would enjoy that." Catrina absorbed this new piece of information with a sense of affirmation in family, but she was soon put straight.

"Not noticeable," Royce McQuillan commented dryly, "although Ina is very much like Sharon. I suppose as a family we're every bit as dysfunctional as yours appears to be."

The maître d' showed them to a candle-lit table for two with the best view of the multicoloured dappled river and the city night-time glitter from high-rise towers to spanning bridges. What was total astonishment at what was happening to her if not a cure for the miseries? Carrie thought. She felt stirred and excited; her confidence such, she resisted the temptation to smooth her shoulder-length hair, which in fact looked perfect. Before today she had never even heard of Royce McQuillan, tonight she was dining out with him, attracting a great deal of attention in the process. Without vanity Carrie didn't fully understand the attention from the spacious beautifully appointed dining room was about equally divided. The men, recognising a beautiful young woman when they saw one, were looking at her; the women couldn't force their eyes away from the charismatic Royce McQuillan. Carrie in fact had to swallow every time she looked at him. He was an extraordinarily compelling man. A man who did things with style. Too daunting and too coolly charming all at the same time. Puzzlingly she vaguely resented it even as she blessed his intervention in her life. With Glenda on the attack she had been feeling all but worn out.

"Hungry?" he asked as Carrie began to peruse the lengthy menu.

"I can't honestly say I am." She was absorbing so much excitement from him it was frightening. "The turn of events left me unsettled. I never dreamed this morning I'd be having dinner like this tonight."

"I'm that kind of man," he answered casually. "You ought to try and relax. Have you been here before?"

"No." She shook her head, glancing around the room. It was decorated in luxurious European style in keeping with its name. Beautiful blue moiré silk on the walls, large floral paintings in gilded frames, dazzling chandeliers, impressive china, silver service, crystal, formally dressed guests. "My father and Glenda come here often. It's very impressive."

"So is the food." He scanned his own menu, his striking dark face downbent so she could study him without his noticing. The golden flame from the candle-flower arrangement centre table lent his skin the sheen of polished bronze. Hair and brows, ebony. ''What about seafood? That's light.''

It really didn't matter. She felt so strange she was content to follow his lead. The wine waiter approached and without even looking at the wine list or consulting Carrie—perhaps he knew full well how she was feeling—he ordered a vintage Bollinger.

''I don't believe anyone can have a glass of really good champagne without feeling better,'' he commented lightly. ''Don't worry, Catrina, I'm not going to ply you with alcohol. I'm in pursuit of a governess, remember?''

''I know that,'' she responded a shade tartly.

''So why the look in those amber eyes?''

''Describe it,'' she challenged.

''All right.'' His tone was soothing. ''You look like you're trying to decide whether you should pick up that daffodil skirt and run.''

''Do you blame me?'' she asked in a low voice. ''You're a *stranger.*''

''No I'm not.'' He looked at her amusedly. ''I told you I'm your knight in shining armour.''

''Dragooned into the job.''

''Don't think that.'' His fingers just brushed the tip of hers yet she felt the hot wave of reaction wash over her from head to toe.

''That blush is exquisite, Catrina.'' He watched the apricot colour spread over her flawlessly creamy skin. ''I haven't seen a woman blush for years. Make that a decade,'' he added rather bitterly.

Why wouldn't she blush with so much heat in her blood? ''Perhaps we'd better establish at once exactly who I am,'' she suggested. On the defensive. ''The new governess. An employee.''

"Perhaps a distant cousin?" He held her golden gaze. "If you're uncomfortable with kissin' cousin."

She couldn't speak for a moment thinking this man unanswerable. "I can understand why the other governesses left and I don't believe Regina was all to blame," she finally managed briskly.

He smiled and the faintly saturnine expression was totally banished. Instead sensuality dwelt in the depths of his eyes. "If you think I teased *them* you couldn't be more mistaken. You're as unusual to me as I am to you. Besides with that little air of hauteur, you're exactly right to tease."

She knew she was playing with fire but the flame was too bright. "Perhaps now and again I might even respond?" she quietly replied, aware she was feeling a little dizzy and she hadn't even touched a single drop of wine.

For answer he turned his attention back to the leather-bound menu. "I'd like that, Catrina, but it won't actually happen. I think we both know where that path might lead."

She had never met nor expected to meet a man so dangerous, so mesmerizing in her life. For the first time since her accident she felt acutely alive, all her senses returned to her. Probably by tomorrow she'd return to earth with another sickening crash.

The food was superlative, the sauces that accompanied the seafood dishes so delicious, so creamy, so beautifully flavoured, she found she was hungry. Both had settled for a starter of Moreton Bay oysters in an amber-tinted champagne sauce with caramelised spring oysters followed by the lobster dish Vivaldi's was famous for, the main course. All through Royce McQuillan quietly entertained her with a fund of stories about station life, some of them brilliantly funny, deliberately so because he told her he liked to hear her laugh. It was when they were debating a dessert versus a cheese platter with the cheese platter ahead, that the strange harmony of the evening was shattered. With her back to the entry Carrie wasn't able to observe the late arrival of a very glamorous-looking foursome but she couldn't help remarking the spectacular change to Royce McQuillan's expression. Perceptibly the lean powerful body tautened, the brilliant black eyes became hooded and the muscles along his hard firm jaw line clenched.

She remained perfectly still, asking quietly. ''Is everything all right?'' Obviously it wasn't.

He frowned heavily. ''A shame to have the evening ruined. Don't turn your head, it's possible they'll miss us.''

Whoever they were. Faint hope, she thought, of missing him. Not with his height, breadth of shoulder and striking good looks.

In another few moments a woman's bright brittle voice exclaimed from somewhere just behind Carrie's shoulder. ''But how absolutely charming!'' The remark to Carrie's sensitive ear was charged with venom. Yet she fully expected Royce McQuillan to rise to his feet. Instead he remained seated, staring up at the ultra-slim woman who moved into view, standing over the table. How utterly sophisticated she looked! She wore a very sexy side-slit silver dress, her dark head with its full fringe pulled into a high knot with a long fall at the back. She was looking at Carrie oddly, pale blue eyes like ice chips. ''Why, isn't she like a flower?'' she cooed in a frankly sarcastic tone. ''A bright orange lily. And so *young!* Aren't you going to introduce us, darling?''

''Sorry, Sharon,'' he drawled. ''I'm not going to introduce you at all.'' The perturbation was now very successfully hidden beneath coolly amused detachment.

''A man like you always needs a beautiful woman around,'' the woman Sharon observed, continuing to stand there staring from Royce to Carrie with extraordinary intensity. ''How are *you,* Babs?'' she suddenly addressed

Carrie directly. "I'm Sharon McQuillan by the way. Yes, I *do* exist. Very much so. And you are?"

"No one of any interest, Mrs. McQuillan," Carrie replied, keeping her tone courteous but neutral.

"But I feel—I just *know*—you are." Clearly under the icy sarcasm Sharon McQuillan was disturbed, maybe even furious.

"You should just accept you're past tense, Sharon," Royce advised.

"I won't!" she responded, her expression so tight for a moment she looked almost plain. "You always were a cruel devil, Royce."

"I don't think that would stand up to examination." His answering tone though low definitely grated. "Anyway, don't let it bother you. I'm out of your life. Now why don't you rejoin your friends? They're throwing all sorts of looks in this direction. I see Ina is with you?"

Sharon McQuillan gave an odd almost contemptuous laugh. "Ina is very insecure. My sister has accepted she can't move out of my shadow. I'd appreciate it, too, Royce, if you didn't allow her to visit the station so frequently. Of course she's using poor Regina as an excuse. It's *you* she comes to see."

So that's it, Carrie thought, hearing the ring of truth.

"Still jealous of one another? I don't know how you find the energy." Royce McQuillan sounded sharply amused. "Why don't you leave quietly, Sharon? You've stood there long enough. It's rather sad."

Sharon McQuillan countered by leaning closer, her confident voice floundering slightly. "Don't let him humiliate you as he has humiliated me," she warned Carrie. "He might bewitch you now—he's bewitched us all—but he'll starve you of affection in the end. I know."

Empathy for another woman moved Carrie to respond. Rightly or wrongly, Sharon McQuillan was suffering.

"Mrs. McQuillan, I told you, you're making something out of nothing." Not that it was any of her business.

But Sharon McQuillan continued to stare bitterly into Carrie's great golden eyes. "I'm sorry, that's impossible to believe. I've had a lot of experience in these matters. You're *someone* in my husband's life."

Utterly fed up, Royce McQuillan rose to his impressive height, dominating both women. "Ex-husband, Sharon," he corrected her. "Surely it's not necessary to remind you? We'll say goodnight. Best wishes elude me."

It was then Sharon McQuillan made her move. She put one hand on his shoulder, then raised herself on tiptoes just long enough to land a kiss clearly meant for his mouth on his cheek. "'Night, darling," she breathed in a voice that combined ecstasy and torture. Then she rounded on Carrie, putting an oddly sympathetic expression on her face.

"Goodnight, Miss Who-ever-you-are. May I compliment you on your hair? It's absolutely beautiful. Though I can't distinguish if it's natural or from a bottle."

"You really need to look at the roots for help." Royce's voice had a hard mocking edge. "'Bye, Sharon. I won't forget to give your love to your daughter."

"Do that, darling." Sharon waved over her shoulder, already beginning to thread her way back to her table.

"Lord!" Carrie murmured after a long moment's hesitation. She was used to infighting but was unnerved by the quality of this exchange.

"'I'm sorry about that," Royce apologised. "The timing was terrible. It's the first time I've been out to dinner in months and I have to run into my ex-wife."

"It must have been very painful." She recognised his upset.

"Not in the way *you* mean. The pain is for Regina. Sharon rejected her from day one."

Carrie's own sense of fairness made her read for an excuse. ''Could it have been possible she was suffering from postnatal depression?'' she suggested.

He thought on that very briefly. ''I do have sensitivity, Catrina,'' he answered, his handsome face dark and moody. ''Sharon couldn't bond with her child because she *didn't want her.* She demonstrated that over and over again. Regina has never known a mother's love.''

Carrie shook her head in a kind of denial. ''That is so sad, but she must be very close to you?''

''Intensely so,'' he said in a gentler tone, ''but unfortunately it involves a lot of screaming and yelling. Regina wants to come with me to places I can't possibly take her. She's only a little girl and I have a huge cattle chain to run. I have to be away from home at different times. I can't dance attendance on her and she can't and won't understand. In that way she's a little bit like her mother. In other ways, too. Sharon was always what they used to call 'highly strung.' I thought it was simply being spoiled rotten, but I soon learned.''

''It's upset your evening.''

''And yours.'' His voice was quiet. ''You've gone pale.''

''She still loves you,'' Carrie said.

He looked back into her eyes with brilliant irony. ''Sharon can't bear to let go of anything she thinks is *hers.* Love doesn't come into it. She needs to retain possession.''

Carrie wasn't convinced. ''And her sister, Regina's aunt is with her? I don't want to turn my head but I can feel eyes boring into my back.''

''All four pairs of them,'' he said. ''The men because you're beautiful. Sharon and Ina have been in competition ever since I can remember and I've known them both forever. By and large Sharon always comes out the winner.

Why don't we have coffee somewhere else?'' he suggested.

Carrie felt quite in control. ''Please don't bother about me. I've had a very enjoyable time. I'm quite happy to go home.''

''Surely that's just an expression.'' He raised a black brow.

''Yes it is,'' she was forced to admit. ''I mean, I'm ready to go home.''

He raised a hand to summon a waiter. ''No, we'll have coffee,'' he said. ''No need to rush. You know all the in places better than I do.''

''Well, I know where they serve the best coffee,'' she said. ''Look, I really don't...''

''Forget it,'' he said. It was as they were preparing to leave the restaurant that Sharon's younger sister, Ina, made her own move. She rushed up to them, a little breathless though Royce had acknowledged her presence with a little wave directed to her table.

''Royce!'' she cried, smiling at him brilliantly. ''How marvellous to see you. What brings you to town?''

''Business, of course.'' He accepted her quick peck on the cheek fairly charmingly. ''How are you, Ina?'' Again defying conventional manners he didn't introduce Carrie who took her cue and wandered a little way off.

The two sisters shared a strong resemblance, Carrie thought. Both tall, ultra-slim, dark-haired, light eyes, very sophisticated in their dress. The elder Sharon was the more striking, sexier, sharper, with a slightly febrile look about her. Ina appeared softer, less overwhelmingly self-confident. Her voice was more attractive, too, lacking her sister's less pleasant brittle note. Though she wasn't looking in their direction, Carrie was aware part of Ina's forward rush was to find out exactly who Carrie was. It could even have been at Sharon McQuillan's insistence. From all accounts, she was the dominant sister.

Carrie was pretending to be engrossed in a very beautiful arrangement of spring flowers when Royce returned to take her by the elbow. "I'm terribly, *terribly* sorry about that," he said. "You'll have to forgive my bad manners not introducing you but I don't want you drawn into this." He didn't add, though Carrie guessed, his ex-wife wouldn't rest until she had found out exactly who Carrie was. A private investigator wasn't out of the question. Sharon McQuillan had used one before.

"I didn't know I was so interesting," Carrie responded lightly, though she was becoming unbearably aware of his proximity.

"Extraordinarily enough, interest becomes fixated on anyone on my arm," he told her dryly.

They walked in what seemed a loaded silence along the brightly lit waterfront promenade with its strolling couples, the breeze fresh and clean, tangy with salt, the sky full of stars, the Milky Way a flittering trail of diamond daisies. Luxurious yachts were moored out front, the City Kats, the ferries in operation, the big beautiful paddlewheeler, *The Kookaburra Queen,* the cruise craft docked at the pier. Nearing where the Jag was parked on the street, a short distance from the restaurant, a very expensive sports car going much too fast suddenly shot out of a hotel drive causing Carrie to react with alarm. Her fears and anxieties had not diminished in the many long months since her accident. They had increased.

"Catrina, it's all right." Instantly his arm went around her, gathering her in. Just like that. Her body had come to rest against his, her head pressed into his shoulder. "There's always some fool showing off to his girlfriend," he muttered, staring after the car with its young male and female occupants. "Probably over the limit."

Carrie scarcely heard. Her whole body had dissolved. Or that was the way he made her feel? Liquified. She'd been much too busy with all her studies for a close relationship but she knew enough to realise real passion, *burning* passion, violent desire was unknown to her.

Until now.

How utterly senseless.

One of his arms was cradling her back. She only had to lift her head for her mouth to brush hotly against his brown throat. She knew she was trembling. Her body was emitting all the wrong signals; the most terrible folly of female surrender. She could inhale the wonderful male scent of him, the power and glamour, feel his masked strength. She even thought she murmured something. Or was it a soft moan that escaped her lips? This was a man who could break her heart. Instinct born of a lifetime of pain.

If Carrie was buckling under the weight of desire, Royce McQuillan, too, felt its extraordinary impact. How could feeling like this spring from nowhere? Her body was so soft, so female-fragile in his arms. He wanted to slip his other hand across her breast. He wanted to bring his mouth down on that alluring little beauty spot. He wanted to kiss her open mouth. He didn't want to stop there. He hadn't been celibate since he and Sharon had broken up. But he'd always known how to contain himself.

Until now.

His sudden violent need of her was akin to man's need of pure water. He had a clear image of himself in the desert. A dry canyon of reflected colours, his throat badly parched until he turned and saw a crystal spring. He wanted to gather the silvery droplets on his tongue...

How could one moment go on forever? He forced himself to breath deeply; telling himself it was a man's primitive response to a beautiful woman. But control didn't come easily when adrenaline was like fire in his blood.

She was resting her soft weight against him, her own breathing ragged.

God, what was happening, he thought, stultified at the speed of it? It was like being on a wild ride. Terrifying and at the same time exhilarating. He couldn't seem to contain the ferocity of desire despite the tight rein, as his fingers found her nape beneath the thick silk of her hair, traced the curve from neck to shoulder.

Stop now. He gave himself the stern warning though little frissons of arousal were running up his arm. Desire was hell. It ruined lives. Alive with self-contempt, he took her lovely face in one hand—he could feel the heat of her flush—his voice deeper than usual but fake-casual.

"I'd love to prolong the moment, Catrina," he said, "but there's someone on a bicycle about to ride over us." In fact the bike rider was walking his bike to the traffic lights. But no matter. He had to abide by the rules. This was one girl he couldn't ravish. God, he hardly knew her. Regina's new governess. A young woman with her own problems so the potential for trouble was enormous. He had to focus very hard on that.

CHAPTER FOUR

CARRIE had a task in front of her convincing her father she needed to get away. They were seated at the breakfast table—her father had delayed his leaving time for the office—and the atmosphere was very tense.

"But a governess, Carrie?" Jeff Russell exclaimed, hurt and surprise on his face. "Why on earth would you want to do something like that?" He made the job sound like the most menial of domestic positions. "You've spent all these years training to be a musician now you want to bury yourself in the jungles of North Queensland. I don't understand it. There must be something more to it. This man McQuillan," he asked forcefully, "have you fallen in love with him?"

Carrie stared back at her father without answering. She hadn't. She believed she hadn't. She didn't want to think it had happened. She had decided absolutely not to. Yet last night she could have stayed with him forever. At one point he could have picked her up and carried her right away. A fatal attraction? That's what it was. God, why not? The man was devastating.

"Carrie? Are you going to stay like that, not opening your mouth?" Jeff Russell, a dominating sort of man, demanded.

Carrie paid attention, her body taut and strained. "I'm sorry, Dad. I know you love me. I know you want the best for me, but I don't think you truly understand what my injury has done to me. I might sound spineless but it's upset my whole world. I just want to get away for a time. I don't want to have anything to do with the music scene."

Her father muffled an explosion of disbelief. ''After all the money that's been spent on you. Why the price of the Steinway alone! Good God, what father pays that kind of money?'' Jeff Russell threw up his hands in despair. ''I don't know how you can think I don't care. You're *my daughter.*'' His dark blue eyes flashed. ''I've always done my best for you. I can't let this happen.''

Carrie clasped her two hands together to stop them trembling. Her father was such an overpowering man. ''I'm twenty-two, Dad,'' she pointed out quietly. ''An adult. I have to find my own way in this world.''

''Without money?'' he retorted angrily. ''You've never taken money seriously. I've always had plenty of it.''

Carrie measured the extent of his anger and bewilderment. ''I'll be in your debt, Dad. But you have to give me a much wider latitude. With the position I've been offered I have free board and a generous salary. I have Grandma's money, too, if I ever need backup.''

''You don't understand,'' her father said in a near fierce tone. ''I don't think I could endure your going away, Carrie. You're the light of my life. My firstborn. Your mother's greatest legacy to me.''

Sorrow brushed Carrie's face. ''You have another daughter who loves you, Dad, very very much. You have Glenda.''

Her father turned his handsome, aggressive head away. ''I know and I love them both but my deepest feelings are for *you,* dammit!''

Almost an obsession, Carrie thought. ''That's turned us into a triangle, Dad. Me at the top, Glenda and Mel at the sides.''

Her answer provoked her father to anger. ''I hope your sister has nothing to do with this departure?'' he thundered. ''A blind man could see how jealous she is of you.''

Carrie almost sagged. ''Mel has absolutely nothing to

do with it,'' she told her father resolutely. ''I *must* leave, Dad, my own decision. I must be on my own for a while. Mr. McQuillan,'' she sensed she had better stick to the strictly formal, ''will call into the office today to see you. He'll ring beforehand to check if it's convenient.''

''Will he now!'' Jeff Russell fumed. ''I'll see him. I certainly shall. I'm very curious about this McQuillan. He could hire a dozen governesses. Go to an agency. What does he want with you? Glenda tells me he's a divorced man.''

Carrie studied her father quietly, feeling love and pity for him. ''It happens, Dad. Without it being anyone's fault.''

''And he has a child?''

''Of course. Regina will be my charge,'' she returned levelly.

''It's bloody ridiculous!'' Jeff Russell cried in a great burst of agitation. ''Trust James to involve himself in all this. Always so gentlemanly but he's always been hostile to me,'' he sneered. ''I believe James is capable of setting this whole thing up. Probably McQuillan has fallen in love with you. You're a very beautiful young woman with lots of fine qualities. I can't imagine for the life of me why he wants to employ you as a governess for his child. I suspect he wants you but he's trying to make it seem respectable. I won't have it!'' He jumped up from the table, pushing his chair back so forcibly it scraped along the tiles.

Carrie rose, too, facing her father squarely, something not a lot of people were capable of. ''Dad, your estimate of the situation couldn't be more wrong,'' she said levelly. ''Mr. McQuillan is actually being kind to me. He had another type of person in mind. He told me so. I'm the one who pressed for the job. I need to get away from everything to do with my old routine. I need a totally new environment for my feelings of frustration and grief to go away. I beg you to understand. You say you love me....''Abruptly she cracked, tears filling her eyes.

''Carrie, sweetheart!'' her father exclaimed, staring back at her in worried perplexity. ''You're far more disturbed than I thought. I don't like to see you in this agitated state. It breaks my heart. You need the love and support of your own family, whatever you might think. Perhaps a holiday. Anywhere in the world. Glenda and Melissa can go with you for company. Stay at the best hotels. I should have suggested it long before now.''

''I don't want a trip, Dad.'' She couldn't add, never with Glenda.

''Depression, that's what it is,'' her father said, his face full of concern. ''You don't have to tell me anything about that. I went through hell after your mother died. Hell!'' he repeated as though the grief was still too hefty for him to shoulder. ''Let me speak to McQuillan. I'm good at sizing men up. Glenda has told me all about his background. Pioneering family and all the rest of it. Chain of cattle stations. That doesn't mean he's the sort of person I want my daughter associating with.'' Jeff Russell reached out and patted his daughter's shoulder several times. ''Leave it to me, Carrie. Leave it to your father. A move away might be all right as long as it's not extended.''

Glenda waited until her husband had left, kissing him goodbye in the entrance hall, before she joined Carrie in the morning room where the family had breakfast.

''So how did it go?' she asked, her tone rather brutally avid.

Carrie looked up from where she'd been sitting, looking out at the prolifically flowering garden. Not Glenda's work. They had a wonderful gardener come in three times a week. ''My coffee is cold,'' she said evenly. ''Would you like a cup if I make some?''

''I'd like to know what your father had to say?'' Glenda answered bluntly.

''Well, let me put your mind at rest.'' Carrie had already

started to move. ''Whatever Dad says, and he doesn't want me to go, I'm accepting the job.''

Though Glenda brightened with relief she still managed to sneer, ''What job? You must think I'm an idiot if I can't read the signs. You're after him, aren't you?'' she said crudely.

''If you think that then you *are* an idiot,'' Carrie replied, her expression calm and cool.

''That's right, abandon the too-good-to-be-true-golden-girl act.'' Glenda moved so the two women stood facing each other. ''Don't trip up with this one, Carrie,'' Glenda warned. ''I've done my level best for you but it's all gone on far too long. You've cut Melissa off from her own father. You've done everything you could to divert his love from me.''

For the first time in her life Carrie felt utterly free of her stepmother. ''Oh, come on, Glenda, that's a lie, and you know it.'' Carrie moved a decisive step forward so the petite Glenda had to fall back. ''My father's behaviour is his own. I bent over backward trying to deflect attention from me. And don't kid yourself you did your best for me. You were a rotten caretaker from day one. A woman so mean-spirited you couldn't take a helpless little child into your heart. I could have cared for you but you wouldn't let me. You know my friend Christy Sheppard? She has a stepmother. She adores her. Lucky Christy. Now I'm going to be in the house for a few days more until I can get myself and my things together. I'd advise you—and you'd be wise to observe this to the letter—if you so much as look sideways at me, you or Mel, I'll tell Dad what a rotten bitch you've been to me all these years. And you know what, Glenda? Dad will believe me.''

A truth that Glenda recognised with a bitter twist of her mouth.

* * *

Her father drove her out to the airport, smiling through his upset. Whatever Royce McQuillan had said to him, or how he had handled himself, Jeff Russell had settled down from the time of their meeting. He now accepted a complete change of environment on the McQuillan historic station would be in Carrie's best interests.

Royce McQuillan had told him about his family, his grandmother, his uncle Cameron and his wife and his small daughter Regina, all of whom resided at the homestead. Naturally Jeff Russell was happy about that. In fact it was clear to all of them Royce McQuillan had made a decidedly good impression on the notoriously hard-to-please Jeff Russell. It made it possible for Carrie's father to accompany her to the airport and to hug her supportively when she left, telling her if things didn't work out she knew she had a loving home to come back to.

Astute as he was about many things, and Jeff Russell was a very successful businessman, Carrie reflected, her father had been as good as blind as to what went on in his own home.

The thousand-mile flight took her north of Capricorn and into the tropics; over glorious tall green cane country an eternal presence for hundreds of square miles; the great mango plantations, the banana plantations, pawpaws, passionfruit, all manner of exotic new tropical fruits, alongside the Great Barrier Reef, the eighth wonder of the world stretching away out to sea for twelve hundred and fifty miles. As a Queenslander Carrie had visited many beautiful islands of the Reef, swum in the magnificent lagoons, drifted with face mask and snorkel around the submerged coral gardens and hired scuba gear to further explore the incredible beauty of the undersea realm. She'd almost got to the Daintree Rainforest, which joined the turquoise sea, but Melissa had become sick on that particular trip and they had had to return home. Perhaps she would get the opportunity now.

Carrie stared out the porthole at the thick carpet of clouds, marvelling that she was here at all. She'd advised Royce McQuillan by phone she couldn't return with him but needed a few days to ready herself for the trip. As requested she'd faxed him details of her arrival. Either he would drive in from the station to meet her or if he couldn't make it he would send someone, probably his overseer.

The flight was pleasant and uneventful. They landed to brilliant sunshine, the air even brighter, the countryside more densely green and colourful than the subtropical capital. Crimson, white, mauve and orange bougainvillea spilled over fences and pergolas around the airport, the great poincianas were already coming into flower, the tulip trees and the cascara trees lacing their hanging bean pods with yellow bloom. It was much hotter than it had been at home. She was glad she had worn something crisp and fresh, a white cotton and lace shirt with a matching skirt, sandals on her feet. She hadn't forgotten to bring a wide-brimmed hat with her, either, an absolute must anywhere in Queensland with its perpetual sunshine.

A little flushed with excitement, Carrie composed herself to wait. She didn't expect it would be long. Royce McQuillan was very much the sort of man who followed through. The plane had been packed mostly with tourists who used the large coastal town as a jumping off point for the Reef islands, the luxurious Port Douglas resort on the coast or the rainforest. They were waiting now, assembling their luggage, relaxed and carefree, holidays in front of them.

I'm here as a governess, Carrie thought. If anyone had

told me that even a week ago I'd have thought them mad. Her talents such as they now were, lay in a different direction. But she was determined to do a good job. She felt confident about giving Regina lessons, perhaps helping her a great deal. She had been an excellent student herself. Better yet she hoped to make friends with the child, win her confidence and liking. Why not? She'd always got on well with children. In fact she had really enjoyed helping out with students from the Young Conservatorium. But then, she reminded herself, those children were exceptional. They wouldn't have been there otherwise. Regina McQuillan had been labelled "a little terror" by her own father. Albeit he was smiling at the time. The one thing she couldn't be was a failure. She really needed this time out even if Royce McQuillan never spared another minute for her again.

The very strange thing was that nobody came. Not Royce McQuillan. Not anyone from the station. She'd been waiting well over an hour and a half, staring out the window at the landscape. Once she got up to buy herself a Coke. Another plane had arrived, offloading passengers and cargo. She was beginning to feel depressed. Was it possible everyone had forgotten about her? She realised Royce McQuillan would be a very busy man. Perhaps something had gone wrong at the station? Someone had injured themselves? She'd read it happened fairly frequently on Outback stations.

The same female airport attendant who had approached her once before came up to check again if she was all right. It was midafternoon now. Two long slow hours had gone by.

"I was supposed to be met by someone from Maramba Downs," Carrie now explained. "I have to say I'm getting a bit anxious. Would you happen to know the station at all?''

The young woman's face lit up. ''Everyone knows Maramba up here. It's one of the best cattle stations in the country. The McQuillan family is big in this part of the world. Something like royalty. You know Royce McQuillan?'' the attendant trilled. Obviously she did.

''I'm here to be governess to his little girl,'' Carrie told her.

The other young woman squealed. ''Boy, you'd have fooled me. You don't look like any governess I've ever seen and I've seen a few passing through.''

''Why is that?'' Carrie asked, thinking governesses had to be intelligent young women.

''Heavens, you got off the plane like a movie star going incognito.'' The attendant studied her afresh. ''Say, why don't you ring the station? Check on whether someone's coming. It's getting pretty late and it's one heck of a drive. A good two hours and that's really movin'.''

''I suppose I'd better.'' Immediately Carrie stood, looking 'round her.

''I'll keep an eye on your luggage,'' the young attendant promised. ''The phones are over there.'' She pointed.

''Yes, I know. Thank you.'' Carrie returned the friendly smile. ''Won't be long.''

A woman's voice answered the phone, sounding very, very surprised. ''But, my dear, I'm absolutely certain Mr. McQuillan knows nothing about this,'' the voice informed her. ''Why ever didn't you let us know? How very foolish!''

Carrie launched straight into assuring the voice—it turned out to be the housekeeper—she had sent a fax the day before containing all the relevant details.

The upshot of the rather jarring conversation was the housekeeper advised her to take one of the airport buses into town and check into the Paradise Point hotel. Mr. McQuillan would be informed as soon as he came in. The inference plainly was Mr. McQuillan would be displeased and there was a certain amount of dubiousness about whether Carrie had in fact notified the station at all.

"Now, you've got that straight?" the housekeeper double-checked as though Carrie could very well be dimwitted.

"Yes, thank you. The Paradise Point hotel."

"Just tell them you're going on to Maramba Downs," Carrie was further advised. "You won't have to pay for anything."

Carrie hung up, feeling slightly jaundiced. This definitely wasn't a good start. She was highly relieved, too, the housekeeper wasn't a member of the family. She sounded a real dragon.

She watched the tropic sun go down in fiery splendour from the small balcony off her room. They must have thought she was to be a guest of the station because she'd been booked into a room overlooking the sea that was definitely deluxe. Oh, well, if she had to, she'd pay the difference between it and what a station employee would normally rate.

Whatever had happened to her fax? The journal printout on the home office machine had given the OK result, so it must have been received. Yet the housekeeper, her voice saturated in doubt, had given the decided impression all faxes to the station were dealt with promptly. A mystery!

By six-thirty she was starting to get hungry. She'd had a light breakfast at home, keeping out of Glenda's way, no lunch, nothing on the plane. A Coke at the airport terminal. Should she add dinner to the tab? The answer was yes. Royce McQuillan, if she ever saw him again, could dock her wages.

Carrie was running a brush through her hair when there was a knock on the door. She hadn't asked for room service. Maybe they were going to downgrade her to a lower floor. She was determined to make light of this. She put down the brush, glanced at herself briefly in the mirror, then went to open the door.

Like the first moment she'd laid eyes on him she lost time. Royce McQuillan was standing there looking dazzlingly attractive in a khaki shirt, narrow jeans, dusty riding boots on his feet, his black hair glossy as a bird's wing, wind-ruffled into curls, one of which had descended onto his bronze forehead. This was a seriously sexy man.

His very first words, however, were crisp and to the point. "Couldn't you have let us know?"

"I did let you know." She threw him a look of pure censure.

"How?" He surveyed her loftily from head to toe.

She eyed him back, struck afresh by such blazing vitality allied to nonchalant grace. It was even more evident on his home ground, dressed like a cattle man. All he lacked was the big rakish Akubra.

"By fax," she told him, feeling totally connected again. "I can prove it if I have to. At least I think I can. I might have thrown the result slip out. I wanted to leave Dad's study neat."

"You sent a *fax?*" Unexpectedly he lowered his rangy height into the nearest armchair, long legs out in front of him.

"You don't believe me?" She tilted her chin.

His black eyes sparkled like jets. "How can you talk that way when you're supposed to be the governess?" he drawled.

"What way?" She couldn't quite understand him.

"I'm not used to bits of girls tilting their chin at me," he explained.

''Right. I'll stare at the floor.'' Hadn't she first thought his employees would address him staring at his feet? ''I'm so sorry you didn't get my message. I did send it. Perhaps it's been missed.''

''Nope.'' He ran a hand over his dashing black head. ''I believe every last fax has been checked.''

''Then I don't understand.'' Carrie gestured a little wanly.

''Me, either. Anyway I'm here.''

''You drove in?'' And it was such a trek she'd been told.

''I didn't *fly,*'' he said dryly. ''It's a long drive but too short to take up a plane.''

''How kind of you,'' she murmured sweetly into the pause.

''Isn't it? I'm damned hungry. It was one hell of a day. Have you eaten?''

Carrie shook her head. ''I was just about to commit a mortal sin and put dinner on the tab.''

He laughed as though she amused him. ''I have to wash up.'' He got to his feet, waves of pure energy coming off every movement. ''We'll stay the night and travel back first thing in the morning. Suit you?''

''Whatever suits *you,* Mr. McQuillan.'' It was not said provocatively yet little lights sprang into his eyes.

''It was Royce the other night,'' he retaliated, rolling his own name off his tongue.

''This is different,'' she pointed out. ''You're my boss now.''

''Well, I don't care. As long as it's all right with *me* you can keep on calling me Royce.''

''With a title perhaps? Mr. Royce?''

He shot her a slow, admonishing look. ''Okay, have fun, Catrina. I may yet call you Cat. You have claws.'' At the door he turned. ''I won't keep you waiting long. Give me twenty minutes. I booked a table when I came in. A lot of monied tourists are in town.''

I've only known him a handful of hours and already I'm in too deep, Carrie thought, torn between excitement and dismay.

When they walked into the dining room people nodded and waved from all directions. Obviously he was very well known. In fact it appeared when he was in town he was the hotel's number one diner. Curious eyes flickered over Carrie. Men and women, prompting her to say governesses didn't normally get invited out to dinner.

''You're not invited out,'' he said, one black brow arched. ''You just happen to be here and you're hungry. You're also the one who got me to drive in hell-for-leather after a long hard day. I really should have sent you off to bed without dinner.''

''I'm glad you didn't.'' She blushed.

''What were you thinking all the hours you were waiting?'' He lifted his eyes from the menu to ask.

''Life is never meant to be easy,'' she said sweetly.

He laughed beneath his breath. ''I wonder if I can get you to sample one of this restaurant's best dishes?''

''Not kangaroo. Please not kangaroo,'' she begged.

''You wouldn't know what you were eating if I didn't tell you.''

''But I do trust you to tell me. I guess it has to be crocodile?'' Her amber eyes sparkled.

''How clever of you, Catrina. There's a marvellous tian of smoked crocodile and corn-fed chicken on the menu served with a lettuce leaf mixture, diced apple and avocado in a dressing topped off with tomato coulis. You could have that as an entré.''

''Sorry, I'm going to have the crab and paw paw salad,'' she murmured. ''And seeing I'm in cattle country privileged to be dining with the local cattle king, I should try the beef tenderloin with red wine shallot sauce and sautéed mushrooms.''

''I'm pleased you said that, Catrina,'' Royce cautioned. ''It's all Maramba beef.''

Afterward they went for a short stroll along the seafront, the water glimmering with luminescence, a drench of sweetness from the flowering shrubs, a heavenly sea breeze blowing, setting the fronds of the great palms in motion, seductive pockets of shadow that filtered out the street-lights. It was bliss after the brilliant glare of the day, the starry fastness of the night sky so beautiful it made Carrie ache to see it. She realised with a profound sense of shock from the moment Royce McQuillan had come into her life her internal focusing had shifted. Her preoccupation with him had set up some kind of a pain barrier. She had stopped thinking about her accident or what it had done to her life carrying her from a peak into a deep trough. Instead she was thinking almost exclusively about him. About how women fell madly in love with certain men. What was it about, then? Their overwhelming masculinity? Their physical beauty? Virility? Their toughness, their lean hard bodies as compared to a woman's soft yielding satin flesh?

There was a real buzz about this man. Like electricity in the air. Sex appeal, they called it. He had it in abundance. Yet his marriage hadn't worked out. She had seen his handsome face set in sombre lines when he spoke about it. She had seen the glitter of obsession in his ex-wife's ice-blue eyes. Carrie just knew Sharon McQuillan would come back into the picture. At least there was no bitter struggle for custody of Regina. Peculiar as it was, Sharon McQuillan, according to her ex-husband, had never wanted her own child. It was one of those things that happened occasionally, leaving anguish in its wake.

They walked in harmony, hardly talking, each ostensibly enjoying the night, yet deep down intensely aware of each other. Feelings were gathering like a storm. Each realised this sudden violent attraction that had sprung up between them had to be crushed. Yet to Carrie it seemed as though the world had changed. She felt slightly wild, out of control, yet ready to sheer off like the cat he had called her.

"I suppose we'd better go back," Royce murmured eventually as they came to a small resting point along the promenade, the water lapping peacefully. "Fairly early start in the morning. I won't get you up at dawn but you should set your alarm for six, with breakfast at six-thirty. Ring room service. We'll take off after that. I have a couple of buyers flying in the afternoon. I have to be there."

"Your uncle couldn't handle it?" she asked, wondering how much he delegated.

"Better if I'm there," he said briefly, a touch of his hand turning her.

They were a short distance from the hotel, walking out from beneath a huge poinciana surrounded by a bed of cool ferns, when a lone flying fox on its nocturnal haunt all but dive-bombed them flapping its leathery wings. It shrieked so strangely for a moment, Carrie who was well used to the sight and familiar whirring sound of fruit bats invading their own fruit trees, scarcely knew what manner of bird it was. But it was as aggressive as a nesting magpie.

"There's one bat looking for trouble," Royce rasped, one arm around Carrie who had her head bent to protect her face, the other still holding the long twig he had snatched up as a defensive weapon.

"Maybe it just got lost?" Carrie's voice quavered, almost drowning in sensation having him so overpoweringly close.

"The damn thing was huge!" He sounded both amused and outraged. "You're okay, aren't you?"

When every muscle, every sinew, was twitching under her treacherous skin. "Of course I am!"

Yet she was as poised and alert as a dancer, he thought, ready to spring away across a stage. The breeze had begun to play with her hair, skeining it like a cloud of silk across his cheek. Perfumed, buoyant, so soft and warm. He caught a handful in his fist, relishing the texture. Her slender form was wedged against his hip, alluringly female. Shining skin so beautiful it begged to be touched.

God, this was madness, he thought, trying to abide by common sense. It had taken him too long to get control of life to fall into the labyrinth again. Catrina Russell, the new governess. Poised and controlled one moment, a panicked little girl the next. He was half horrified by the extent of his own desire. It was unimaginable the way it had all happened. Outside forces ruling one's life.

She straightened, trying to joke. "I'm sorry, you must think me a real cream puff."

"Ice cream," he corrected with a self-mocking half laugh. "Vanilla and apricot." He could taste her soft mouth against his. The upper lip was finely cut, the lower enticingly full. Her body was in silhouette as the darkness beneath another poinciana deepened. She was increasing her speed, long lovely legs moving easily over the ground, carrying her away from him. "No need to apologise, Catrina," he called after her dryly, "the damn thing startled me, too."

She paused beneath a streetlight, her hair billowing, doubled by the breeze into a gleaming mane so it resembled a bright satin cloak haloing her face. Her eyes had a glittery look to them and her cheeks were darkened with blood. She had a high mettled look to her, a capacity for passion she must bring to her music. He could imagine what she would be like under his hand....

When he reached her he was so moved by her beauty he pulled her into his arms, wondering if his life was ever going to be normal again. Desire was like an avalanche thundering down a mountain. You couldn't get out of the way. Acutely aware of her *stillness,* her intoxicating fragrance all around him, he all but seized her up, his breathing a little harsh. "Maybe if we get this over, we can settle down," he suggested with acid self-mockery.

Boundless excitement spread rapidly all over her body, flooding her. She felt dizzy with shock and unbearable tension, her open mouth soft and vulnerable, waiting for his as though her body was in sole charge and her mind had gone numb. In her whole life for all her small triumphs on the concert stage there was nothing to measure against this. This excitement was so extreme.

He drew her back into the shadows, shifting her weight onto his heart, taking her mouth in a kiss that went on...and on...and on...the most ravishing invasion, Carrie totally submissive as though forbidden fruit was all the sweeter. He kissed her until her wildly beating heart was ready to explode, then he released her from the spell, his dark vibrant voice bizarrely normal, even conversational.

"We both wanted that, Catrina," he said briskly, "even if it might have been the worst thing I could have done. If it's any consolation, I promise it won't happen again."

She was shaken to the core, but years of conquering nerves stood her in good stead. "Which is a blessing," she managed calmly even if her voice was very soft. "I really don't think I could handle it."

"Me, either," he said smoothly, still trying to analyse his complex feelings. Kissing her was akin to a storm blowing up inside him. It had taken every ounce of his self-control to let her go, when he couldn't get enough of her. Something so dangerous he instinctively had to step back from it. He thought of her vulnerability at this time when she was attempting to build a new life for herself. It would be callous to threaten her further.

Carrie didn't have to rely on an alarm as a safety net. Dawn cracked open to frantic birdsong, sweet, melancholy, warbling, the reckless cackle of the blue-winged kookaburras in the trees beneath her room. It was impossible to go back to sleep, though her night had been disturbed by broken dreams. Her subconscious was so in thrall, Royce McQuillan had figured in them all, his presence so deliriously strong at one time she awoke heart thudding, thinking he was in the bed with her, his hand on her breast. Small wonder she felt too keyed up to eat much breakfast—orange juice, tropical fruit salad, coffee—but she was dressed and waiting when he knocked on her door.

"All set?"

She was almost relieved to see his brilliant gaze was impersonal as it ran over her, checking out her attire for the long trip. She had dressed coolly but sensibly in a navy T-shirt with a designer label worked into the front, white cotton jeans, and navy sneakers. Because of the heat, she had caught her hair back into a gold clasp at the nape. She followed his cue, speaking as though not one moment of passionate intensity had passed between them. "I hope I didn't bring too much luggage?" She indicated the three pieces.

"Does a princess take too much luggage?" He pretended to lift one of her suitcases with difficulty.

"I can take one." She wanted to be helpful.

"That's a relief!" His mouth quirked. He was determined to start the day off lightly. Cut the fuse that ran directly to dynamite. "No, I can manage, Catrina," he told her casually. "We don't need to bother with room service.

You've only got the three pieces. I'll tuck one under my arm.''

She watched him, as he went about doing it, his movements lithe and economical, while he told her to leave the keys on the small circular table and the door open. He'd settled the bill the night before.

''I hope you've got a wide-brimmed hat?'' he paused to ask.

''Of course.'' She reached behind her for the straw hat lying on the bed.

''Plenty of sunscreen?''

''Never leave home without it. Believe it or not, I don't burn.''

''Let's keep it that way,'' he said briefly, his striking face as calm and inscrutable as a mask.

Ten minutes later they were underway, driving out of the large prosperous town and picking up the main highway, Carrie in the passenger seat of the Range Rover, Royce behind the wheel. At this hour the heat of the day was diffused, the morning incandescent. Open savannahs rolled away from the highway to the range, the lush green strip of coastline overlooking a sea ablaze in blues, ultramarines, cerulean, turquoise, cobalt.

''Do you mind if I put the window down?'' she asked a few miles on.

''You don't get car sick do you?'' He glanced at her. ''Or does the air conditioning bother you?''

''Neither. I wanted to smell the bush. I love the way the sun warms the leaves on the gums! It releases the most marvellous aroma.''

''It's the distinctive scent of the Australian bush.'' He lowered his own window only a short way so he wouldn't create a cross draft, letting in the fragrance of the flowing morning. Across the grasslands, Carrie glimpsed kangaroos bounding as silently as spirits into the shade of the trees. Their benign presence gave her such a warm feeling. The Range Rover was moving smoothly at speed, on the two-hour journey that would take them into the heart of Maramba. Once an emu paced the 4WD showing a short but fantastic turn of speed—60 m.p.h., Royce told her.

All along the route Carrie was fascinated by the towering purple and cerise banks of bougainvillea gone wild. It rose like brilliantly coloured ramparts to either side of the highway. A veritable jungle with those dangerous hooked thorns, but magnificently showy. In the gardens at home a whole range of cultivars thrived, the Thai golds, the hot pinks, the scarlets, the bronzes and burnt oranges, showy and relatively easy to handle, but they never attained the incredible height and splendour of their bush cousins. Away to the west rose the ragged peaks of the Great Diving Range, mauvish purple against the cloudless deep blue sky.

"They really do look like larkspur," Carrie observed, harking back to a famous Australian poem listing the beauties of the homeland.

"At this time of day," he agreed. "Later on they turn to grape. The truly spectacular changes occur in the Red Centre. I don't think any other region can rival it, glorious as our tropics are. Those uncompromising ochres. The primeval beauty. You've been to Ulura and the Olgas?"

She shook her head regretfully. "Even to an Australian it's *so* far away! I've been studying most of my life. There has never been time. But I would adore to go."

"Then you might make it," he surprised her by saying casually. "We have stations all over. From the Channel Country in the far southwest up to the Gulf of Carpentaria. Jimboola in the Channel Country would be the best jumping off point. I fly down fairly frequently. You can come with me for the trip. But in the months ahead it's going to get damned hot. You could very well melt away."

"I won't. I know how to keep my cool."

His white smile gleamed. "I've noticed that." He made a brief gesture toward the ever-present ranges that rose like a great barrier between the verdant benevolent coastal strip and the sun-scorched vast inland. "The most dominating geographical feature of our continent," he pointed out, "rambling way down the eastern seaboard, some 500 kilometres. From the tropical tip of our own state of Queensland, through rain forest, semi-desert, snowy alps and beautiful pastoral country to end in the Victorian Grampians two states away."

Carrie saw it, as it must have been. "A very frightening and daunting obstacle to the first settlers in Sydney," Carrie said.

"Twenty-four years to cross the Blue Mountains and open the great western plains to the infant colony. What Blaxland Lawson and Wentworth must have looked out on? In any man's language, the Promised Land. The pastoralists lost no time taking up their grand selections. My own family included. The first McQuillan to arrive in Australia was one James Alastair McQuillan who arrived in the colony with his wife Catriona—which is one reason I like to call you Catrina—and their two young children. That was Christmas 1801. They must have nearly died of the heat after Scotland. James, a younger son, was the only member of the McQuillan family to come to the new colony. He wanted to make his fortune. And he did. From all accounts he was very friendly with Governor Macquarie. Anyway he was granted a big parcel of land outside Sydney at Parramatta. The old homestead is still there, very well looked after, incidentally, by the family who took it over some hundred years later. James' son, Bruce, had a difficult and strained relationship with his father. He migrated to Queensland in the mid-1800's. James himself was killed in a shootout with a band of escaped convicts.

"How terrible!" Carrie was a little shaken by the thought.

He shrugged. "I don't think James McQuillan, though a 'gentleman' and a free settler, would have been classed as a kindly man. Desperate times produce desperate men. I can't help feeling sorry for a whole class of so-called 'convicts.' Poverty and starvation begets all sorts of crimes. Ferocious cruelties play a big part. The brute with the whip, savage guards, harsh overseers on pastoral properties. Some sixty percent of the convicts who were sent out here had never before committed a crime. And such crimes! Petty theft. Stealing a loaf of bread. Apples from over a wall. Poaching a rabbit from some rich landowner. Theft of any kind was always punished by transportation. Those crimes would hardly earn a fine in today's society, but criminal law in Georgian England was brutal.

"Then there was the wave of 'political' and 'agricultural protester' crimes. The 'utterings' in the streets, voices raised against the government. The dissidents quickly found themselves transported. The irony is as an English historian pointed out, the worst criminals remained in England while a whole class of 'victims' men, women and children, suffered being torn from their country, their families and sent to our wild shores. No wonder the ones who survived were tough. Many of the emancipists, the risen convicts, became very powerful and wealthy with immense land holdings."

"Yes, I know. It's an extraordinary story," Carrie agreed. "My own family on both sides hailed from England. Strangely they all migrated at the same time. After World War I. The men had fought in France and managed to survive. They and their wives decided they wanted to get as far away from Europe as they could."

"Then Australia would have done it," he said dryly.

"So the only one hundred per cent Australians are the

Aborigines,'' Carrie said, definitely sympathetic to the aboriginal displacement.

''The historic custodians of our land. Nowhere on the continent do you feel their 'presence,' their Dreamtime culture, more strongly than at the Red Centre. When I take you there, you'll know what I mean.''

''I'm astonished at your continuing kindness.'' She smiled. ''Meanwhile we're in the glorious tropics. It has its own unique characters.''

He made a little sound of agreement. ''Brilliant skies, brilliant sea, brilliant landscapes. The dazzling light more than anything. The heightening of the senses. The most spectacular time is on the verge of the Wet that will come up in a month or so. The Wet brings the bush to flower. It brings cyclones, too. The big heat and humidity when you just want to sit with an ice-cold beer in one hand staring out over the garden. I never seem to get the chance. Do you ride, by the way?'' he asked, suddenly serious.

''I haven't done for a couple of years but I was taught properly. Dad saw to that. All of the children I knew, all my friends, belonged to a pony club.''

''Well, at least that's off my mind!'' He gave a low laugh. ''The Australian love affair with horses. They've played such a role in opening up this country, especially the Outback. At one time I was pretty serious about joining the Australian Olympic team. The team Three Day Event and Show Jumping. I'd won a few trophies. I was good. I'd received a few approaches. That was when my father was alive and expected to go on living to a ripe old age. It didn't happen,'' he said grimly, ''neither did my Olympic dream. I play polo. We all do and we still use horses to work our cattle. When anyone says horses are stupid creatures I see red. A horse's courage and intelligence has saved many a stockman's life. Horses are our mates in the Outback.''

''You won't get any argument from me,'' Carrie reassured him. ''They're magnificent creatures. I cried when our Three Day Event team won their third consecutive gold at the 2000 Olympics. Our horsemen are marvellous when it's tough, dangerous, going. As a complete contrast, I loved the horses performing to music in the dressage section. Responding to all those signals. If that's not high intelligence, what is?''

''I agree.'' He nodded. ''So many who performed brilliantly. I was actually there in Sydney to congratulate Andrew Hoy and other members of the team. It's still in my blood. I stayed for the pool and the equestrian events then I had to head back home.''

''Lucky you!'' Carrie said lightly. ''The TV coverage had to do me. It was wonderful.''

The miles flew and the talk became animated as they relived the Olympic experience.

''So it wasn't *all* half crazy with grief over the loss of your career?'' he asked eventually.

''Whole hours out,'' she admitted, ''with my accident forgotten. Those horrible moments when I knew we were about to crash. I even knew I was going to get hurt in a way that would affect my life.''

''Then it's a bit of serious experimentation, isn't it, being a governess?'' He swung his head. ''I've transported you out of your sheltered environment into the wild bush. Maramba, though, it doesn't suffer anything like the isolation of Jimboola in the Channel Country or another outstation of ours up in the Gulf in crocodile country, is cut right off from all the excitements and activities of city life. You'll be starved of a lot of things you've got used to.''

''I'll cope,'' she said briefly.

''You'll have to,'' he told her bluntly. ''I'm a very busy man. I wouldn't know how to act nursemaid.''

"Nursemaid! Heavens, I'm not going to bother you," Catrina protested.

He didn't try to hide his concern. "Regina is a great little kid. A real survivor, but like I told you, she's a fair terror. She has a really worrying trick of hiding. She can find places no one including me has ever thought of. I *cannot,*" he emphasised, "do this baby-sitting thing. My grandmother suffers badly from arthritis. Some days she's in a great deal of pain. We have a good aboriginal woman called Jada, married to our leading stockman, who looks after my grandmother's needs. She's like a personal maid but much closer, more family. She was born on the station. Neither can help out with Regina. My uncle's wife has no great feeling for children. She doesn't want children herself. Regina's mother is, as I told you, a write-off. Our housekeeper, Mrs. Gainsford, runs the homestead like a five-star general. She's super-efficient if not kind and cuddly. She does her best to control Regina's little excesses of temperament but she can be a touch stern. Needless to say she and Regina don't hit it off."

"She wasn't too sweet to me, either," Carrie said dryly.

"You mean she didn't believe you'd sent word?"

"That's what I mean."

"I expect Regina nicked it just for the hell of it," he suggested wryly.

"She's old enough to check the faxes and take mine in?" Carried asked in surprise.

He groaned. "Regina is six going on six hundred," he said. "An *old* soul. I care about her very much."

Although the tone was deeply sincere to Carrie's ears it sounded a shade odd. "I would think so," she said. "Who better than a father to love his daughter?"

"You would know," he said, still with that undercurrent in his tone. "Anyway, you're the boss. She's a dreadful eater by the way."

"That's it. Give it all to me now," Carrie crowed.

"Pecks at everything like a budgie. Has numerous hates. Throws things all over the place. Is very wilful. Always makes a drama of mealtime. Otherwise she's a great kid."

Carrie was undismayed. This was a child, after all, and a child in need of love and understanding. "I'll just have to work out what she likes." She spoke simply. "One thing I wanted to ask you?" She turned her head to look at him, struck by the bronzed glow of his skin, the inky blackness of his well-shaped brows.

"Fire away!" He gave her a brief brilliant glance.

"Did you tell anyone about my background?" she asked quietly. "The fact I was going to New York to study. My accident?"

"My grandmother only," he told her. "It was told to her in confidence. She will respect it. Whatever you wish to do, Catrina, is up to you. All the rest of the family was told you were handpicked by my trusted solicitor."

"Good. I don't want to talk about my accident," Carrie said. "You do understand?"

"Whatever makes you happy," he responded almost gently. "*For now.* One day you're going to have to talk it out. I know about bitter disappointments, Catrina, I can spare you the time."

CHAPTER FIVE

MARAMBA Downs, taken up by Bruce McQuillan in the 1870s, started its huge run on the coast and ran in a north-westerly direction right up to the thickly wooded slopes of the Great Dividing Range. Driving through it, Carrie thought she had never seen more exotically beautiful country in her life. The sparkling clarity of the air rendered more brilliant the full palette of colours. The mountain ranges formed a backdrop, the turquoise sea to the east, the offshore islands and the Great Barrier Reef beyond, immediately inland superb grasslands; endless lush pastures of blue and green grasses with sleek Brahmin cattle grazing alongside prolific birdlife.

On the many lagoons Carrie was enchanted to see great flocks of swans, pelicans, ducks, the entrancing blue brolgas, the huge jabirus, the biggest bird in Australia, and flights of magpie geese that had ruined the rice industry in the tropical north to the extent not even the manoeuvres of the Australian Air Force could deter their attacks on the crop. In one pond white ibis had staked total claim, probing the bottom of the emerald pool with their long beaks, the surface laced with pink and white waterlilies. The atmosphere was so peaceful, so open, so free, she could literally breathe it in.

As they drove further into the heart of the station a large flight of birds suddenly rose from the waters, numerous in the air, the Royal Spoonbills she could identify and concentrations of ducks with very pretty pale yellow plumes. She was about to ask Royce McQuillan their name when he spoke.

''Outbuildings coming up.'' He lifted an indicating hand from the wheel. ''The hangars and landing strip off to the right. One for the Beech Baron, the other for our two helicopters. We use them for musters and other purposes. The landing strip is all-weather, as it would have to be when we get the rains. There's a building for just about everything. Freezing rooms, machinery, equipment, tack, saddles. We cure and tan our own leather. It's important to have materials on hand for repair. Staff bungalows and bunkhouses on this side.'' He indicated again. ''The building with the blue roof is the gym and entertainment centre when the men can relax. You might think they get enough hard work in the saddle but they like working out. You won't see the homestead until we're almost upon it. The home gardens in some places have turned into a jungle. I'll have to have it cleared. It's almost a rainforest. Near the house it's more open woodland. We don't want snakes in the house but I have to warn you, you're going to see a few. The thing to remember is snakes do their level best to keep out of our way. Of course if you're unlucky to stand on one....'' He shrugged expressively.

''I'll watch where I put my feet,'' Carrie guaranteed.

The outbuildings behind them, Royce drove more slowly, pointing out different features. ''We're in the home gardens now.''

Carrie was silent for a moment, thinking it was more like an enchanted forest than a garden. She stared out the window, transfixed by the extent of it, and the great diversity of vegetation. Palms towered, staghorns and elkhorns of incredible size were affixed to the great shade trees, tropical orchids quivered in the breeze, yellow, palest green, pure white, the rich purple of the Cooktown orchid, the state emblem. There were flowery shrubs of all kinds, hardy bromeliads, agaves and aloes, gorgeously coloured beds of foliage to rival the dense green and cascading everywhere flowering vines in every conceivable colour, the bright violet-blue of the morning glories, the pink, white, scarlet, orange and sunshine yellow of the trumpet flowers.

As she continued to look, the curving drive became straight, now it was lined on either side by sentinel Cuban Royals, their fronds moving above the shadowy canopy of the giant shade trees, the poincianas. It would be paradise when those trees broke out, Carrie thought. There were so many of them they would colour the very air.

Almost before she was aware of it the homestead rose up.

It was *huge!* Even bigger than she had envisioned from the photograph Melissa had shown her. A tropical mansion constructed of dark timbers, to meld perfectly with the environment. The building was two-storied, with great wrap-around verandahs on all sides, at least twelve feet in depth, she gauged, the roofline dipping protectively over it like a great shady hat. It was enormously impressive. Enormously picturesque. Just as in the photographs, a lagoon lay at the homestead's feet ringed by all manner of tall water grasses and aquatic plants, sections of it floating the blue lotus, sacred flower of ancient Egypt, native to both Australia and North Africa. There was even a small boat amid the reeds.

''What a wonderful place to live,'' she exclaimed. ''It's like something out of a Somerset Maugham story.'' She loved the way the landscape flowed toward the house. Massive in anyone's language, there had been minimal impact on the site.

He glanced at her, well pleased by her reaction. ''That was the intention, Catrina. This isn't the original homestead, by the way. That was destroyed in a cyclone many years ago. This one is cyclone-proof. *We hope.* My grandfather built it. He'd travelled widely in South East Asia. You'll see the influences, outside and in.''

"Your own private kingdom," she marvelled.

"It is." There was pride in his voice, but an unmistakeable thread of grief. "But no man has complete control over life. Over nature. This may look like a man's dream but life isn't. Dreams as we both know can be very easily shattered."

They arrived to a situation. Regina had gone missing, Royce was informed the moment he set foot on the verandah.

Mrs. Gainsford, a tall thin woman, thin face, thin body, thin voice, but looking decidedly frazzled, attempted to explain, standing there, hands folded, awaiting some kind of judgement. Never once did she look in Carrie's direction. No, it was the "master" who was the only one of importance.

"I've done everything in my power, Mr. McQuillan, to see that Regina was here when you arrived," she burst out. "In fact I was congratulating myself I had won the battle. It wasn't until a half hour ago I realised Regina was nowhere in the house. Or nowhere I know about. It makes me look so foolish, so ineffective," she concluded hotly, ready to put the blame on a six-year-old.

"Try to forget about it," Royce McQuillan advised sardonically. "I know you do your best, Mrs. Gainsford." He turned to Carrie. "This is our new governess, Catrina Russell. She'll be responsible for Regina in future."

"Splendid!" the housekeeper clipped off, her expression conveying she didn't believe for a moment Carrie would succeed where she couldn't. "I have your room ready, I'll show you to it."

"Thank you." Carrie offered a smile before addressing Royce McQuillan directly. "Where do you suggest I might look for Regg… Regina?" She almost slipped and said Reggie. She had come to think of this little "terror" as Reggie.

"She'll come out when she's good and ready," he said wryly. "Regina needs to make a statement more than most. Of course if she hasn't shown herself by lunchtime we'll have to organise a little search party."

"She never touched a bite of breakfast, either," Mrs. Gainsford broke in, looking like this was yet another grave offence. "I'm *so* sorry, Mr. McQuillan. I simply dread what more shocks Regina has in store for us."

Perhaps it wasn't the right moment but Carrie burst out laughing. A laugh she quickly snuffed at the cold stare in her direction. This was a woman she would have to work with, Carrie thought, though she had the decided feeling she and Mrs. Gainsford would never be onside.

"And where's Mrs. McQuillan?" Royce was asking the housekeeper rather pointedly, giving Carrie quite a chill. For a moment she thought he meant his wife.

"Here, Royce!" a voice called, heavy with overtones. As though she had been watching, waiting in the wings, a striking-looking woman in her mid to late thirties with short, thick, smartly cropped fair hair, tanned skin and very bright blue eyes appeared, offering the master of the house a strangely provocative smile. "I wanted to be here the moment you arrived but I've been looking for Regina. Not that any of us can stop her when she wants to hide. And this, I take it, is the new governess?" The electric-blue gaze moved to Carrie.

Just a wee bit….astonished? Definitely not friendly. Expect no support there, Carrie thought. An element of the furious look Sharon McQuillan had given her.

"My dear, you couldn't have arrived at a better time," this striking woman said, stalking forward on sandals with very high heels. At the last moment she paused beside Royce McQuillan, lifted her head and gave him a kiss on the cheek that lingered far too long. "Welcome home, Royce, I've missed you."

He glanced down into her upturned face. ''What in a matter of hours?''

To Carrie's acute ears the tone was cutting, but Lindsey McQuillan—it had to be—appeared to revel in it.

He made to introduce them and Carrie found herself subjected to an even more intense scrutiny.

''I gather James Halliday recommended you for the job?'' Lindsey McQuillan asked as though she was about to make notes. ''I never did hear your exact qualifications?''

Carrie wasn't flustered although it looked very much like Mrs. Lindsey McQuillan had taken a dislike to her on sight.

''They're adequate, Mrs. McQuillan,'' she said courteously.

''Well, we'll see.'' The other woman stared back as though she didn't want to leave it there. ''Regina's governesses haven't done so well in the past.''

''Maybe you had something to do with that, Lyn,'' Royce McQuillan tossed her way. ''I'm hoping you'll give Catrina your support.''

''Oh, I will. I will. Quite rightly.'' She smiled back at him in that ominous intimate way, when she might have said, Not me! I haven't got the energy. ''Anything you want to know you must come to me.'' She eyed the label on Carrie's expensive T-shirt and didn't appear comfortable with it.

Carrie obliged her with a thank you.

''Where's Gran?'' Royce suddenly asked, sounding to Carrie's ears as though he didn't want to leave her alone with his glamorous ''aunt.''

''Resting,'' Mrs. Gainsford supplied as Lindsey McQuillan held back from an answer. ''It's not one of her good days, but she'll be wanting to meet the young lady later on.''

''Well, Carrie, I'll leave you to get settled.'' Royce gave her a bracing glance. ''I have things to do.''

''Fine. I'll be fine.''

Carrie's assurances were all but drowned by Lindsey McQuillan's cry of dismay. ''But surely you've got time for a cup of coffee, Royce? I want to tell you all about a phone call I had from Ina.''

Immediately his face hardened. ''It'll keep. If Regina doesn't show up in an hour or so, get word to me. I see Arundi working around the grounds. He can take one of the Jeeps. I'll be at the Four Mile. Cam's there, isn't he?'' he asked Lindsey with a twist of his raven head.

''I expect so,'' she answered languidly. ''He's where you told him to be, Royce, darling. *Naturally.*''

Royce McQuillan moved off. They heard his voice outside telling someone to take Carrie's luggage into the house.

''Come this way, Miss Russell,'' the housekeeper said.

''Carrie, please,'' Carrie suggested pleasantly.

Mrs. Gainsford scorned that. ''I prefer to call you Miss Russell, if you don't mind.''

''Makes me seem too much of a personage.'' Carrie smiled.

''You'll have to be something of a personage to keep Regina under control,'' the housekeeper said with a tight mouth. ''No mother! It's showing dreadfully. Mr. McQuillan is a wonderful man. A very important man. He shouldn't have all this worry on his mind.''

''I expect you spare him a lot with your competence.'' Carrie offered an olive branch. ''He told me you ran the homestead splendidly.''

That brought an instant reaction. A dark red flush and a complete softening of the rather harsh face with a smile. ''Did he now?''

"Certainly. He must greatly appreciate having the house run so efficiently."

"A perfect gentleman he is!" Mrs. Gainsford put real feeling into her voice. "A perfect gentleman. It's a wonder to work for someone like that."

Carrie couldn't help but agree.

The room she had been allotted was much more than Carrie had expected. In scale with the rest of the house it was huge. Maybe three times the size of her bedroom at home. Here was the Asian influence Royce McQuillan had spoken about. Thai, she considered thoughtfully. The family had holidayed in Bali several times. A marvellous teak bed occupied centre room, slender four posters holding up the billowing folds of the white mosquito netting, edged top and bottom with heavy white embroidery that matched the white bed linen. There were two carved teak chairs and a small matching table with an eye-catching floral arrangement on top. A comfortable day bed was near the window with an Oriental chest at the foot of the bed. There was a teak cabinet holding a collection of Chinese blue and white porcelain, a deep comfortable armchair upholstered in white Indian cotton, an ottoman with a brilliant throw across it, an Indian-style carved armoire in one corner, and a tall bookcase filled with books in another. She caught a few names: Isabel Allende, Sharon Maas, P.D. James, Kathy Reichs.... On one wall was a brilliant painting executed in oils of outsize golden sunflowers surrounded by colourful foliage set against a cobalt sky.

"Oh, I'm going to love staying here," she said, her topaz eyes full of pleasure.

"I'm not surprised!" Mrs. Gainsford sniffed audibly. "No other governess has been given such a room. But Mr. McQuillan gave orders."

"Aren't I lucky!" Carrie moved across the polished floor decorated with a single exquisite Oriental rug.

''You are indeed,'' Mrs. Gainsford pronounced, back to her reedy tone. ''There are some really valuable things in here. All that embroidery on the bed linen was done by hand, you know.''

''It's lovely. I'll look after it.''

''I change the bedding twice a week. One of my girls will do the cleaning. You don't have any chores to take up your time.''

''Thank you for making it so welcoming for me,'' Carrie said, giving the older woman a happy smile. ''The flower arrangement is quite beautiful.''

Mrs. Gainsford glanced toward the teak table where the rich red of anthurium lilies glowed against three large dark green leaves, a piece of strangler vine to one side, a burst of grevillea to the other. It was a most unusual arrangement, perfect in its ceramic container with what appeared to be aboriginal motifs.

''Jada did that,'' the housekeeper said without enthusiasm. ''She thought you might like it. I prefer a good straightforward bunch of flowers any day, but Mr. McQuillan allows Jada do the flowers for the house. Keeps her busy when she's not attending to Mrs. McQuillan senior.''

''I'm so sorry Mrs. McQuillan isn't well,'' Carrie said carefully.

''A marvellous lady! Never complains. She said something about seeing you when you're settled. I'll let you know. Meanwhile we've got no other option but to wait for Miss Regina to appear. More than anything else she needs discipline that child.''

And a mother's love. If there was anything about Royce McQuillan Carrie might have criticized it was his casual attitude to his little daughter. Couldn't he have said, I love her deeply, rather than I really care about her. Even Uncle James told her frequently how much he loved her. Yet

Royce McQuillan had used the word ''cared.'' There was a good chance Regina wasn't getting enough love from him, Carrie thought.

Mrs. Gainsford went to the door; turning to tell Carrie a light lunch would be served at 1:00 p.m. Meanwhile she was free to settle in and have a rest after her trip. ''I expect you've done quite a bit of travelling in the last couple of days.''

''Some,'' Carrie smiled. ''You never did find my fax?''

''I apologise if I ever doubted you,'' the housekeeper said abruptly. ''You look a responsible young woman. It was Regina for sure. She's always doing silly things. Now I must be off. You should rest now.''

''I'm sure I won't be able to nod off without knowing where Regina is,'' Carrie said.

''No chance of your finding her if she doesn't want to be found,'' Mrs. Gainsford said, frown lines forming between her sparse brows. ''I wouldn't have thought she had the brain power to get up to the things she does. She's a *child,* yet she gives as much trouble as a woman.''

''I hope Regina and I are going to be good friends,'' Carrie said quietly.

''Then, my dear, you're hoping a lot. This is no little sweetheart you'll be dealing with. This is an exceptionally naughty girl.''

Again Carrie felt like laughing out loud. Such a very capable woman to be outplayed by a six-year-old. It reminded her of the way Glenda used to call her ''an uncontrollable child.''

With the housekeeper gone Carrie wandered out onto the verandah, looking down its long length. Golden canes in huge pots glazed a deep bronze were set at intervals at either side of the pairs of French doors. She couldn't wait to see over the house. The entrance hall was enormous, the soaring ceiling the full height of the building with two broad staircases leading off on either side to the upper gallery that ran right around the second floor. Asian influences appeared to be everywhere. She had taken that in at a glance. This was a marvellous tropical house.

She was humming quietly to herself, unpacking the luggage a gently spoken aboriginal man had brought to her door only a few minutes before. He had introduced himself as Arundi. The same Arundi who had to carry word to Royce McQuillan if Regina didn't surface by lunchtime. Carrie just hoped she would. She really wanted to meet Miss Regina McQuillan.

No way did she imagine Regina would be in the armoire.

Carrie's heart leapt in shock as she opened the carved door. She had, in passing, noted it wasn't quite closed, but never did she expect a small girl to confront her, all thin arms and legs, pulling a ferocious face, no doubt meant to be frightening.

Carrie had to wait a full minute before she could talk. "Heavens, Reggie, you scared the life out of me."

"That's great!" the little girl responded triumphantly. "No one *ever* looks for me in the right place."

"You mean, you were here all along?" Carrie wasn't happy about what Mrs. Gainsford had said.

Regina gave her a disgusted look. "I've only been here since Ethel checked. That's her name," she started to giggle, "Ethel Gainsford."

"Are you going to come out?" Carrie asked, putting out a hand. "I want to put my clothes away. You can help me if you like."

Regina sprang out, ignoring Carrie's hand. "Why should I? You're supposed to be doing it."

"That's okay. You might miss the present I bought for you, though. It's in with my dresses."

Regina's plain little features—how could she be plain with such good-looking parents—contorted. ''Why would you bring a present for me?''

''Why, to make an occasion of our meeting,'' Carrie said cheerfully. ''What else? I'm very pleased to meet you, Regina. I've heard so much about you.''

''I bet.''

Royce McQuillan hadn't exaggerated when he said his daughter was going on six hundred.

''What did you call me when you first opened the door?'' Regina now enquired, looking at Carrie's hair so close to flame.

''I'll try to think…''

''It was Reggie. You called me Reggie.''

''I won't if you don't like it.''

''I *do.*'' Regina dressed in a simple T-shirt and shorts suddenly jumped into the armchair. ''You must have known I wished I was a boy.''

Carrie was upset by that. ''What would you want to be a boy for?'' She started to hang up her clothes.

''Royce would have liked it,'' the child said, getting up and absentmindedly handing Carrie another garment. ''Royce wants a son.''

''Okay, he wants a son.'' Carrie turned to stare at her. ''He wants a daughter, *too,* Reggie. You call your father Royce?'' Carrie asked.

''Of course,'' Regina shrugged her thin shoulders. ''He doesn't mind. I think he likes it. I *love* him. He's the best father in the world. You're going to find out sometime, but my mother *hates* me. And that's the truth.''

''No, Reggie. Don't think that. Not for a minute,'' Carrie protested, distressed.

''She's a terrible mother!'' said Regina. ''She never comes to see me. *Ever.* She never thinks of sending me a present. Where is it, anyway?'' The wrath evaporated into curiosity.

''At the bottom of the suitcase. It's wrapped up.''

''I hope it's not a doll,'' Regina said, sounding like she'd burn it. ''I'll swear if it's a doll. I know a good few swearwords. I hear the men.''

''It's not a doll, Reggie,'' Carrie assured her instantly. ''There are lots of words you can use besides swearwords, you know.''

''Oh, sure, and I could use them if I wanted to. I can *read.*''

''I'm sure you can,'' Carrie said in a matter-of-fact voice. ''Do you like the Harry Potter stories?''

Regina was busy making a mess of Carrie's careful packing. ''If I could ever get anyone to buy me one,'' she growled.

''Well, you're in luck.'' Carrie sat down on the bed. ''I brought some with me. We can read them together.''

Regina looked at her in astonishment. ''Why are you being so sweet to me?''

''Let's say friendly.'' Carrie smiled into the big grey eyes. ''I want us to be friends, Reggie. I want that very much.''

For a moment the child looked pleased: small, soft and vulnerable. Then she nodded darkly. ''You're just after Royce. They all are. Lindsey says there's not a woman alive who wouldn't want to grab him.''

''You're kidding. She told you that?''

''No one *tells* me anything.'' Regina dug deeper. ''But I find ways to hear. Lindsey doesn't like me, either. She told Royce I sneaked your fax.''

''Did you?'' Carrie asked simply.

''No, I didn't.'' Regina stared her in the eyes. ''I don't tell lies. *Not one time.*''

''So I believe you.'' Carrie shrugged.

"Those other governesses, they were *wicked!*" Regina told her with some relish.

"That's hard to believe, Reggie," Carrie protested.

"You didn't see the way they acted. Both of them were madly in love with Royce. And there's more." She leaned close to Carrie, her whole body confiding. "Lindsey is in love with him, too." So said, the child began to bounce up and down.

"Reggie, you can't say things like that," Carrie told her.

"I *didn't* say it, Ina did," Regina corrected her, the gymnastics over. "You don't know my aunty Ina. Boy, can she talk! They must think I don't have ears."

Or they didn't care what they said in front of the child. "Here, let me find the present for you," Carrie offered by way of diverting the child's attention. Regina had been rifling through the suitcase, upending everything in the process, now Carrie found the package and handed it to the child.

"What is it?" Regina looked down, somewhat overcome.

"I won't tell you. It's a surprise."

Regina spoke up. "Listen, I'm not going to tell anyone else, but I like you. You're beautiful. I just hope you don't fall in love with Royce."

That brought Carrie up sharply. "Reggie, I'm here to be your friend," she said, ruthlessly suppressing all thought of the child's father.

"So how come you're a governess?" Regina asked. "The other two didn't care about me." While she spoke Regina was making short work of opening the thoughtfully wrapped present, her expression puzzled as she looked down at a gold-lacquered toy trunk. "I can't even guess," she said softly, then opened the lid.

Immediately a clown with a brightly painted face dressed in a polka-dotted nightshirt with a matching bed cap on its head sprang up, waving its arms and turning its head from side to side. It startled the child, making her laugh.

"Isn't that cute!" The big round eyes were filled with radiant pleasure. "The trunk is the bed. Didn't they make a great job of his costume and the bedclothes?" She smoothed them with a finger.

"I'm glad you like it, Reggie." Carrie was really pleased. She'd spent a lot of time choosing the little clown.

"It's cool." Regina looked so soothed Carrie risked asking, "Don't you think we'd better tell Mrs. Gainsford you're found?"

Regina began waving her arms, perfectly mimicking the clown. "Do we have to?"

"Everyone is worried, that's the problem."

Regina waved that possibility away. "I've hidden lots of times before. They don't come looking like they used to."

"As much as you want them to?" Carrie asked, thinking it was Regina's way of getting attention. "You wanted to be found today."

"Yes, I did," Regina confessed, polishing the little clown's red nose. "You wouldn't have found me otherwise. I *wanted* to meet you. Royce said you reminded him of the girl in the painting downstairs. It's supposed to be haunted." She giggled nervously.

"So what does it do?" Carrie asked, "make weird noises or spin upside down in the frame?"

Regina giggled appreciatively. "I don't know *precisely*... But Lindsey told me it was haunted when I went to touch it."

"You do see she was trying to get you *not* to touch it? The painting isn't haunted, Reggie. It's probably very valuable."

"When I told Royce he said, 'you never can tell,' then he laughed."

They were both sitting on the bed playing with the clown when Regina leaned right over speaking in a loud stage whisper. "Don't look now, but Lindsey is behind you."

"She is *not.*" Carrie didn't bother to turn her head.

"She is so."

Carrie was just beginning to wonder if the child was serious when Lindsey McQuillan spoke, her voice as sharp as the crack of a whip.

"This won't do at all!" She threw Carrie, who had sprung up off the bed, a look of such severity it would have shaken most governesses to the core.

Carrie, however, turned to face the older woman full-on. "I'm so sorry, Mrs. McQuillan, Reggie and I were on our way downstairs."

Multiple expressions played across Lindsey McQuillan's hard, good-looking face. "Reggie? Is that supposed to be a nickname? The family won't be comfortable with that. Personally I detest the habit of shortening names."

"Well, *I* don't," Regina said flatly, coming to plant herself beside Carrie. "It's my name and *I* like it. Anyway, Royce calls you Lyn. Isn't that the same?"

"That's enough from you, young lady," Lindsey cautioned, visibly angered by the child's rudeness. "You've had the entire household including your father concerned about your whereabouts while you and your new governess—" she shot Carrie another venomous glance "—are calmly sitting up here playing with a toy."

"It was only a few moments, Mrs. McQuillan," Carrie protested.

"It's totally irresponsible," Lindsey pronounced, looking like she wanted both of them flogged. "If you can't do better than that, my advice to Royce will be to send you packing.''

''You're not the boss around here.'' Regina suddenly started to jump up and down. ''I hate you.''

For answer, Lindsey McQuillan looked directly at Carrie and said in disgust, ''This child is neurotic. Am I right?''

''Gabble...gabble...gabble...'' Still yelling, Regina darted out of the room and along the verandah.

Not caring what the other woman thought, Carrie took off after the child, so fleet of foot she caught her up, grasping her in her arms. ''Gotcha!''

The yelling and screaming broke into guffaws. The little girl began a mock battle with Carrie who made her own mock attempt to subdue her. ''I want the cops right now!'' Regina cried, laughing hard.

''I *am* the cops,'' Carrie said.

''Show me your badge. So where is it?''

''Your father's got it. It's with my references.''

Abruptly, Regina abandoned the game. ''Bloody Lindsey!'' she swore, causing Carrie to take the little girl's thin shoulders and hold them.

''Reggie, you can't use any old swearword that pops into your head. It's not ladylike. Also, you must show your grandaunt the proper respect.''

''I didn't tell her to shut up, did I?'' Regina asked reasonably. ''I didn't like the way she was talking to you. Blaming you for everything.''

''She was worried.'' Carrie tried to make excuses.

Regina groaned. ''No, she wasn't. She's lived here for years. You've just arrived.''

''That's true. So will we go downstairs and try to smooth things over?'' Carrie suggested.

''Not me.'' Regina shook her tangled mop of light brown curls.

"Fine." Carrie patted the child's arm. "I'll go on my own."

"Okay." Regina cheerfully took Carrie by the hand. "Do you think I could ever get to have a hamburger for lunch?"

For a moment Carrie stared at her. "Why ever not? I like hamburgers."

"That's good. I got kicked out of the kitchen the last time I asked for one. Ethel is supposed to be this great cook yet she won't make me a hamburger. With chips. I *love* chips. I hate vegetables, especially broccoli, and I hate cereal for breakfast and I hate eggs."

"Right! I've got the message." Carrie briefly considered Melissa had been a poor eater as a child. "I don't see why you couldn't mix up a drink for yourself for breakfast. Use the blender. I'm sure Mrs. Gainsford has one. A banana smoothie, or you could use pawpaw or cantaloupe. Put some honey on it. Ginger, if you like. We could experiment. Add a scoop of ice cream. You need fattening up."

"And that's not all! Everyone thinks I'm terribly plain." Regina hung her head.

"Who's everyone?" Carrie appeared to challenge.

"All the family, of course. My mother can't bear the sight of me."

"That's really tough." On the evidence, Carrie couldn't argue. "As you're being frank, I might tell you my stepmother couldn't stand the sight of me."

"Really?" Regina looked up at Carrie to make sure she was telling the truth. "She must be a real bitch."

Carrie nodded, so much in agreement she didn't attempt to modify the language. "I'm telling you this in the strictest confidence of course."

"That's okay. I won't tell anyone." Regina reassured

quickly. "How could anyone not like you when you're so beautiful?"

"How can anyone not like you when you're so bright and clever?" Carrie returned.

"You're lying to me," Regina accused solemnly.

Carrie responded quickly. "I'll never lie to you, Reggie. And you'll never lie to me. Will we shake on that?"

Very intensely Regina put out a hand. "Let's," she said.

And that was how Royce McQuillan found them as he reached the upper verandah, Lyn and Mrs. Gainsford in tow. Just like a lynching party, he thought in extreme irritation.

They were solemnly shaking hands.

Brilliant! He studied them both with a shock of pleasure. Only minutes before he'd been informed by an outraged Lindsey in concert with Mrs. Gainsford who raced straight from the kitchen eager to join in, that the new governess was far from an immediate success. Not only had she deliberately withheld vital news Regina had been found, she had given the appearance of actively encouraging the child's bad behaviour.

Now to his great relief it seemed the two culprits were quietly going about the business of making friends.

Thank God! He started counting ten in his mind to bring down his own intense annoyance. He hadn't even left for the Four Mile, taking time off to speak to one of the groundsmen about clearing the overgrown sections of the home gardens when Lyn managed to locate him, which she did with depressing efficiency. She was full of her poor opinion of the new governess. Not that he wasn't used to this lack of enthusiasm. She had given the other girls hell.

Evidently Catrina had hit an especially raw nerve. He'd expected it. Catrina Russell wasn't your everyday Outback governess. Lyn would hate her for that alone. Now he was here to play the heavy. He was sick to death of it. Sick of the constant demands on his time. Sick of Lyn's overbearing pretentious manner with the household staff. Including the dreary but otherwise excellent Mrs. Gainsford.

Now he greeted Regina with an affectionate smile of relief and Carrie with a calming look. "Hi, poppet. So you decided to turn up?"

"I'd had enough," Regina announced joyfully, puffing out her thin little chest. "I was in the armoire. I frightened Carrie. Now I'm sorry." She ran to her father, clutching him around the knees, such a look of adoration on her small freckled face it gave the tender-hearted Carrie a hard time.

Lift her, she willed Royce McQuillan silently. Lift her. Go on, you're a big strong man. She'd be a little feather in your arms. This is *your daughter.* Kiss her. Hug her. Do something. Don't just stand there, tousling her already over-tousled hair. Disappointment and acute censure stabbed her when he failed to do so, although he continued to smile warmly into the plain little face.

There was not a trace of him in the child, Carrie thought. Not in colouring. Not in feature. Not in potential for height. No trace of her glamorous mother, either, for that matter. Reggie hadn't been fortunate enough to inherit her father's brilliant black eyes, or her mother's ice-blue. They were grey. And I'm going to do something about her hair, Carrie vowed. It could be a big plus for Reggie if it was well cut and properly groomed.

Royce McQuillan catching her naked glance read her thoughts with great accuracy. Obviously she thought him a poor father. Undoubtedly he was. But hell, he wasn't the father and he was doing his best. God only knew who Regina's real father was. One of Sharon's one-night stands when she was drunk. He'd tried to control his bitterness toward Sharon's parents over the years. They had kept

Sharon's instability, which at times became manic, one *huge* secret, though he had to concede childbirth had exacerbated the predisposition.

McQuillan found he didn't much like the look of censure in Catrina's golden eyes. Who was she to judge him? He and Gran were the only ones including Regina's maternal grandparents and her aunt Ina, who actually cared about the child. He hadn't even confided in Gran that Regina wasn't his, though he suspected she had her doubts. The blow had gone too deep. He had fallen out of love with Sharon very quickly but he had been prepared to honour his marriage.

Until she told him with vicious triumph Regina wasn't his.

Now this young woman with an angel's bright aura was judging him and finding him badly wanting. It hurt and he had to admit it made him angry. It was a blow to his self-esteem when he was long accustomed to respect.

Royce was returned to the present by Regina pulling strongly on his hand. ''Carrie calls me Reggie. What do you think about that?''

''Reggie's a boy's name,'' he teased.

''You *want* me to be a boy, don't you?'' Regina countered sadly.

''The heck I do!'' Now he lifted her, swinging her around and around so she squealed. ''Don't *ever* feel I'm not happy with you just the way you are, Reggie. Between the three of us—'' he glanced rather coolly in Carrie's direction ''—I think it suits you. A bit of fun. One thing, young lady, you have to put on weight.''

Reggie hugged him, whispering over his handsome face conspiratorially. ''Carrie says I can make my own breakfast. Banana smoothies with ice cream.''

''And that's all?'' he queried, not thinking it enough.

''A glass of milk,'' Carrie intervened at this point. ''Reggie tells me she doesn't like cereal. Or eggs.''

''I can't have a child in my kitchen,'' Mrs. Gainsford protested, looking quite miffed. ''Regina might well have an accident. I don't know what Miss Russell is thinking about.''

''Obviously trying to ingratiate herself,'' Lindsey McQuillan supplied lazily. ''I presume you're talking about using a blender?'' She shot Carrie a challenging glance. ''Regina's too young to be fooling around with appliances. I would have thought you'd know that.''

''Well, for a start, I'd be with her,'' Carrie said, thinking Lindsey McQuillan, striking though she was in appearance, was an awful woman. ''There'll be no problem.''

''I'd rather they don't do this, Mr. McQuillan,'' Mrs. Gainsford said reedily, unable to keep her feelings of territorial invasion bottled up.

But Royce McQuillan turned on her smoothly. ''As far as I'm concerned, Mrs. Gainsford, we'll employ any method that works. Reggie can have a baked chocolate soufflé fresh out of the oven for breakfast if it will make her *eat.*''

''Can I really?'' Reggie was delighted, grinning broadly and showing quite a gap between her two front teeth.

''Well, we won't make it routine,'' he told her. ''Now and again.''

''You're kiddin' me.'' She gave him her sunniest smile.

''Miss Russell is the boss,'' he said suavely.

''No, listen.'' Reggie shook his hand. ''Her name is Carrie. Carrie for Catrina. Isn't that beautiful?''

Royce McQuillan looked at Carrie over the child's head. ''I know this new idea won't give Mrs. Gainsford any problems.''

''I'm sure we'll be able to manage nicely.'' Carrie spoke

confidently, aware of his edgy mood toward her. ''I expect the kitchen is very large.''

Lindsey McQuillan's electric-blue eyes were shooting darts. ''Don't think I don't know what you're trying to do,'' she told Carrie. ''But good luck, anyway. I don't plan to be around when Regina sends things crashing to the floor.''

That set the complacent child off again. ''You're always nasty to me. *Always.*'' Reggie suddenly screeched in a lightning mood swing, ''Bitch. Bitch. Bitch.''

''Lovely!'' Lindsey mocked while Carrie got her hands beneath the child's armpits and hauled her away saying, ''No one has shown me over the house. I'll soon find myself lost if you don't help me, Reggie.''

Wiggling, Reggie quickly broke Carrie's restraining grasp but she was calmer now. ''It's a pretty good house,'' she said, taking Carrie's hand. ''I won't promise I'll tell you all my hiding places, but I'll tell you some.''

''That's okay.'' Carrie looked down at her, greatly relieved the little girl had settled down. ''You won't want to hide with all the good things I've got lined up.''

''Tell you what, why don't we start with downstairs?'' Reggie swung her head. ''Is it okay, Royce, if I show Carrie your study?''

''As long as you promise you won't touch anything,'' he called, at that moment prepared to forgive Miss Catrina Russell anything for her easy ability to handle this child. He'd never seen Regina, now to be known as Reggie, show this much friendliness to anyone outside himself.

With his plans so disrupted he decided to call in on his grandmother again, walking down the long gallery to the west wing. His grandmother was into her eighties now, her once vibrant health a thing of the past. In fact it was starting to grieve him she just might slip from his life altogether, while he was somewhere out on the station or away on a business trip. Almost time to get in a nurse, though his grandmother would fight him on that one. Jada suited her. Softly spoken, sweet-natured, dignified Jada, she *knew*. But soon the role of minder would be too much even for Jada.

As it was he found the two of them together, talking quietly, companionably, their long thirty-year friendship golden. His grandmother fragile as porcelain but fully dressed in what she called her ''uniform,'' stylish loose shirts over comfortable trousers, lay on her daybed near the French doors, Jada close by in an armchair, a cooling breeze blowing in from the garden, filmy curtains swaying gently. Both looked toward him with smiling surprised faces, Jada, plump with delicate almost birdlike arms and legs, rising out of her chair immediately. ''I thought you'd be long gone, Mr. Royce.''

''Hell no!'' he joked. ''Didn't you hear the ruckus?''

''You know we don't hear anything up here, darling.'' His grandmother tilted her head, her hair beautifully arranged by Jada in a thick French pleat. Another common point between the two women, both had copious snow white hair though Jada wore hers standing up in all directions.

''I thought you two used telepathy?''

Jada chuckled. ''Don't need telepathy to guess it was young Regina. She's just gotta be the centre of attention.''

''Right on.'' He saluted her.

''Don't run away too far, Jada,'' Louise McQuillan called as the aboriginal woman moved to the door. There was something so immensely benign in Jada's spirit just having her around helped ease Louise's pain.

''I'll be right outside the minute Mr. Royce comes down,'' Jada promised.

''Thank you, dear.'' Louise McQuillan sighed gratefully. ''So tell me, what happened?'' With Jada gone she turned her attention to her grandson, fixing him with attentive eyes.

Royce took Jada's unoccupied chair, running the events of the morning before her, making a good story in the process.

His grandmother listened in silence until he'd finished, then she sighed deeply. ''I hope Lindsey isn't going to try to make it a trial for this young woman the way she did with the others?''

After what he'd just seen, that amused him. ''I think she'll find Catrina quite a different proposition. Catrina grew up holding her own against a stepmother who was no mother at all to her. As for Lindsey…'' He shrugged, leaning back into the chair. ''I think I'll have to stop her altogether.'' He'd been thinking that for some time, but Louise McQuillan looked anxious.

''In what way? What do you mean, darling?''

''I'd rather she was out of the house,'' he answered bluntly, realising his grandmother wasn't fully aware of Lyn's pathetic attempts to fascinate him.

There was an answering sentiment in his grandmother's eyes but an overriding love and pity for her son. ''But what about Cameron?'' she asked. ''He needs us, Royce.''

Royce didn't answer, looking down at his hands. No use worrying his grandmother with his scarcely mentionable concerns about his uncle's wife.

''I don't know what demon possessed my poor Cameron to marry her!'' Louise McQuillan moaned. ''She only married him for money, for so-called position… Even Cameron must be aware of it.''

''Of course he is.'' Royce grimaced in embarrassment. ''I think it took him roughly as long to wake up to Lyn as it did for me to wake up to Sharon. Nothing like marriage to help things turn nasty,'' he added cynically. ''I've been thinking very hard of letting Cam take over River Rock.'' He named a distant station in the McQuillan chain.

Louise looked past him to the dancing sheer curtains. ''God forgive me for saying this, my darling, but are you sure Cam could handle it? Both of us love him but both of us know Cameron switched off his engine a long time ago.''

''Doesn't mean he can't rev it up again,'' Royce said a little too crisply, but he was being sorely provoked. ''Cam gets through life just doing what I tell him. It's not the way for a man to go.''

''He hasn't got *your* toughness, my darling,'' Louise pointed out, wryly knowing her grandson didn't even realise just how strong he was. ''Cam never even got a chance to step out of his father's shadow. Trish was the woman who would have been the making of him, but losing Trish the way he did…!'' Louise moved her hands in a desperate little gesture of utter helplessness. Twenty years ago, but she remembered the terrible day of her daughter-in-law's riding accident as though it were yesterday.

''I wonder why it is the good ones are taken?'' Royce asked without ever expecting any answers. ''Unfortunately Cam is married to Lindsey now and she's as good as useless to him. In bed, obviously as they've moved to separate rooms, and as a helpmate. She alienates all the staff. I'm the last person to recommend divorce but I think Cam should cut his losses. God knows I had to.''

Louise nodded sadly. ''To think there was a time I was fond of Sharon,'' she wondered aloud. ''But then, those were the days Sharon and her family were very eager to impress us. It was all such a dreadful, dreadful pretence.''

''You mustn't think about it, Gran,'' he told her briskly. ''Don't add to the stress.''

Louise McQuillan turned her head a little fretfully. ''I know I *shouldn't,* but these days I have too much time to think. Too much time to go over our tragedies. But don't worry, my darling.'' She suddenly bucked up. ''I'm not going to die until I see you happily remarried to the right woman. I've struck a bargain with the Almighty.''

''Great!'' He gave her his beautiful heart-melting smile and stood up. ''If anyone has the clout, it's you. You could be my only salvation, Gran.'' He bent to kiss her.

''No!'' She patted the strong hand that was resting on the head of her daybed. ''There will be the woman for you. I can feel her coming closer. The answer to my prayers.''

He had reached her bedroom door before she called after him rather coquettishly. ''Your Catrina sounds a very interesting young woman.''

''*My* Catrina, Gran?'' His brilliant black eyes mocked her.

''Odd the way our first McQuillan bride was Catriona,'' Louise mused. ''That rare amber colouring, as well.''

He gave a little hoot of laughter. ''Don't start seeing omens, Gran. Our new governess was a student up until a year ago. She's very *young* and she has a trauma to overcome.''

''Does she know I was a fine pianist in my day?'' Louise McQuillan asked.

''Haven't said a thing. It didn't seem the subject to get on to.''

''She won't fail to notice the concert grand. Even if Mrs. Gainsford keeps covering it up.''

''Gainsford means well, Gran,'' he told her. ''No one has played the piano for years. The cover keeps the dust out.''

His grandmother smiled and waved him off. ''But pianos are meant to be played, my darling. Your Catrina might very well come to it in her own time.''

CHAPTER SIX

THE lights were on in this huge house. Carrie walked down the left side of the divided staircase that made such a striking approach to the principal rooms dazzled by the astonishing brilliance of Maramba homestead at night. Everything was light and glitter. Recessed spotlights flared over the wonderful collection of objects evoking the South East Asian heritage, the tall eight-panel Coromandel screens inlaid with jade and ivory and semiprecious stones, the rugs and sculptures, the tall Chinese vases, including the big matching fish bowls on carved stands that flanked the staircase at ground level.

Someone in the last hour or so had filled the bowls to overflowing with golden-yellow cymbidiums. She caught her breath at their beauty, pausing to admire them. The bright yellow was in wonderful contrast to the inky blue-and-white pattern of the large porcelain bowls.

She knew from her tour with Reggie, the magnificent living room was to her right. It housed not only the ''haunted'' portrait of a ravishingly pretty young girl in a sunlit garden setting who just happened to have Carrie's own unusual colouring, but a nine-foot concert grand someone had swathed in a gorgeous bolt of brocade. Seeing the piano had given her an actual frisson of shock as though what she sought to escape had followed her to this remote place; wasn't the world big enough or wide enough for there not to be a piano? No ordinary piano, either. Although she hadn't approached it and it appeared to mean nothing out of the ordinary to Reggie, it was obvious someone in the family had played the piano at some time. Because of the size and value of the instrument, she concluded that someone had played it extremely well. Yet Royce McQuillan had never said a word.

Carrie continued on, passing through the library that contained an extensive collection of books to the formal dining room beyond. This was a huge room used for large gatherings, beyond that was the informal dining room used by the family. She understood that was where they would be dining tonight. Voices reached her as she approached the lovely luxuriant plant-filled room with its floor-to-ceiling glass walls that allowed a wonderful view over the lush tropical grounds.

Inside, seated at ease in chairs, was the family who all turned to look at her. Royce McQuillan—stunning enough to set *any* woman's heart racing, she excused her own reaction—who immediately stood up and walked toward her; and a frail little lady with the sweetest face and expression, dressed in elegant silver evening pyjamas. Mrs. Louise McQuillan, it had to be, Carrie guessed. A tall, gently distinguished-looking man rather like a university professor but enough like Royce McQuillan to be his uncle, now also stood and, her face turned in a practiced silky smile, the glamorous Lindsey in a floral print halter dress that showed a bit too much cleavage for a family dinner.

"You timed that nicely," Royce McQuillan told Carrie when he reached her, taking her lightly by the arm. "How lovely you look," he added quite without thinking. She did indeed look lovely. "We were just having a predinner drink. Come meet the rest of the family."

She was content to let him steer her, feeling his dangerous power as his hand closed over her bare arm. She stood first in front of his grandmother who greeted her with unconcealed pleasure and interest, right hand up-stretched.

"I want you to be happy here, my dear." Louise McQuillan smiled. Her smile was beautiful just like her grandson's, and there was a real light in her still fine dark eyes.

"I adore it already, Mrs. McQuillan," Carrie answered with happy emphasis. She had taken to Mrs. McQuillan senior on sight, thinking she must have been very beautiful when she was young. As they spoke Carrie found herself gently stoking rather than shaking the hand offered her for fear of crushing it. The fingers were so fragile, even though the joints were knotted and swollen. Long fingers that once must have been as strong as her own. It was an oddly intimate moment that passed between young and old but neither woman seemed to find it strange.

Royce McQuillan's uncle Cam in turn took Carrie's hand as gently as she had taken his mother's, his manner almost "old worldly" courteous. He was one of those men usually defined as a "perfect gentleman," handsome, erect, his manner graceful, but he had none of the vibrant energy, that aura of power that made his nephew so outstanding. Rather he seemed like a man not really *involved.* Not the quintessential cattleman.

When she reached Lindsey, Carrie was offered a rather flippant "hello there," but Lindsey's electric-blue eyes moved over Carrie's outfit like a monitoring device, totting up each individual item. Carrie had chosen a dress that suited her well, a deceptively simple peach silk shift but with a very clever bias cut. Strappy sandals were on her feet. Sale price Ferrangamo and even then they had been dear enough.

"Don't tell me you managed to get Regina to bed?" Lindsey finally asked, apparently not happy about the final figure.

"No struggle at all." Carrie smiled. "The two of us started on one of the children's stories I brought with me. Eventually Reggie nodded off."

"Reggie only needs the right handling," Louise

McQuillan said gently, picking up on the new nickname and looking at Carrie with open approval. "I've been saying that for quite a while."

"Early days, Gran," Lindsey warned, her strong features sceptical.

It was over dinner Carrie was treated to one of the reasons the less than mellow Mrs. Gainsford had managed to keep her job. She was a great cook. In fact Carrie thought Mrs. Gainsford could teach Melissa a lot. Carrie didn't know how Mrs. Gainsford did it—surely most great cooks had a little bit of the show-off in them?—but dinner was superb. It took Carrie a little while to realise only she and Royce McQuillan were actually doing justice to such a beautifully cooked and presented meal. Louise McQuillan ate very very sparingly, tiny mouthfuls of the great North Queensland eating fish, the barramundi, served with a crab cream sauce on a little white vegetable mash. Lindsey delicately forked over her seared scallops; while Cameron McQuillan seemed to be lost in some monumental problem he couldn't tell them all about. He appeared to come out of his reverie briefly to say he might try a slice of orange and Grand Marnier soufflé cake with coffee. No mascarpone, thank you.

The conversation was general but when Carrie expressed her fascination with the broad landscape and the wonderful sense of "belonging" with both the homestead and the home gardens, Louise McQuillan came to full life. She turned to Carrie with a flush of pleasure. "My first job as a bride was to make a great tropical park out of what were then *wild* surroundings. It was an immense challenge. I was only twenty yet my husband gave me complete control and an army of helpers. One day when I'm feeling stronger I'll show you what I had done all those years ago, Catrina, as you're interested."

"Indeed I am. I'd enjoy that very much, Mrs. McQuillan."

"It was Royce's idea to construct the waterfall at the narrow end of the lagoon," she said, looking down the dark polished table to her grandson.

"A real brainwave." Royce smiled, his glance resting on Carrie, who looked as colourful and shiny as a day lily. "I had boulders brought in from all over the station. God knows how the great landscape gardeners of centuries past managed without modern machinery to perform the Herculean tasks. I used bulldozers, backhoes, excavators, even the station helicopter. While we were at it we contoured the surrounds of the lagoon to make it even more attractive. Roughly five thousand litres of water a minute pass over the waterfall when the valve is fully open. The water supply comes from the dam behind the homestead. I'll show you when I have the time."

"I'd love to see the waterfall in operation," Carrie said, not sure of the exact nature of her feelings toward Royce McQuillan, but they were powerful.

"You will," he promised lazily. "Gran and I decided on a tree fern forest at that end, then with so much water about she hit on the idea of stepped terraces of water iris. There are millions of them, as you'll see. Great beds of day lilies and arum lilies, too. My mother and Gran spent endless hours working out different themes for the grounds."

"Rosemary and I were such friends!" Louise McQuillan shook her head sadly. "The home gardens were our passion. If you want to see truly wonderful fruit and vegetable gardens then you'll have to find your way to the rear of the house near the old stables. That's where Rosemary truly reigned supreme. It was absolutely thrilling picking all the fruits and vegetables she had grown.

The extraordinary thing was neither of us had any great expertise when we started. Just a great love of gardens.''

''I couldn't bear to break my fingernails,'' Lindsey McQuillan volunteered languidly. ''My pleasure is looking at the gardens, not breaking my back. Whilst we're on the subject of gardens, I do hope you told Carrie about the snakes, Royce? That may very well bother her.''

Louise McQuillan opened wide her eyes. ''I've lived here for sixty years, without incident, Lindsey. Snakes do their best to keep out of the way. I can't think Catrina would ever be foolish enough to try to pick one up?''

''I'll leave the snake charming to those who can handle it.'' Catrina laughed. ''Snakes or not, I'm enchanted with everything.''

It wasn't until they adjourned to the seating area for coffee that the general conversation turned to the specific as Lindsey decided to show her talent for investigation.

''A little bird tells me you play the piano, Carrie,'' she announced brightly, glancing closely at Carrie to see how she was taking this disclosure. ''You'll have easy access to one here. That's if Gran will allow you to play her Steinway?''

Carrie felt too shocked to be angry though the speed with which her confidence had been breached filled her with the sick realisation. Royce McQuillan must have told this malicious woman all about her. Either Royce McQuillan or his grandmother. Whoever it was Carrie felt a jolt of betrayal.

It must have showed.

''Oh, I'm sorry. How awful. You had an accident didn't you?'' Lindsey cried as though she only just recalled that piece of information.

That appeared to arouse Royce's disgust. ''And how did you stumble on this?'' he interjected before Lindsey could continue, not bothering to dissipate the hostility in his dark vibrant voice. ''Don't tell us.'' He laughed without humour. ''Sharon, through her willing stooge, Ina?''

''But, Royce, I thought you liked Ina?'' Lindsey eyed him mock quizzically. ''I told you this morning I had a conversation with her. But you didn't want to know about it.''

The knowledge Royce McQuillan hadn't confided in Lindsey did much to restore Carrie's composure. ''What I don't understand is why either Mrs. Sharon McQuillan or her sister would be interested in me?'' she queried.

Lindsey laughed, a flash of white teeth between very red lips. ''That's simple, really. Sharon continues to be interested in any woman who comes into this house. You appear to have gone a little pale, Carrie. I do hope I haven't upset you?''

Carrie was quiet for a moment, considering. ''You've surprised me, that's all. I was hoping to forget my accident for a while.''

Lindsey nodded sympathetically. ''I can understand that, but surely it won't go away?''

''Lindsey, please!'' Louise McQuillan looked distressed. ''I do wish you would change the subject,'' she requested. ''Catrina is handling her own problems in her own way. I might mention here and now, Catrina,'' she turned her small face to Carrie, ''you're more than welcome to go to the piano whenever you feel you can.''

Carrie smiled at the old lady gratefully. ''Thank you, Mrs. McQuillan. It's not easy at the moment, as you can imagine.''

''No, my dear,'' Louise soothed. ''But I know you will find courage.''

At the sympathy and liking in the old lady's voice, Lindsey's jealousy cracked open. ''Surely it isn't that much of a tragedy?'' she asked. ''You can lead a full life.''

She looked at Carrie challengingly. ''It's not as though you've lost a limb.''

Suddenly her stepmother's face came back to her. This was the sort of thing Glenda said. ''I really don't think you'd know much about it, Mrs. McQuillan,'' Carrie answered quietly. ''I've been very involved in my music all my life. I love it. I've trained for it. I could have had a career.''

''Then it's decidedly odd you accepted the post of governess,'' Lindsey retaliated. ''Whoever suggested it?'' Her bright blue glance whipped from Carrie to Royce.

''Don't bother asking,'' Royce said. ''It's none of your business, Lyn.''

''That's perfectly true.'' Cameron McQuillan had taken overlong to curb his wife. ''It might be best, too, if you don't give Ina the slightest encouragement to gossip, Lyn. Sharon is not part of the family anymore.''

''Someone should tell *her.*'' Lindsey flushed at her husband's mild reprimand. ''It wasn't as though I was asking for information about Miss Russell. It was volunteered. Personally I can't see why the secrecy.''

''I wasn't aware Catrina kept any secret from *me,*'' Royce drawled. He looked at Lindsey, his black eyes sardonic. ''Catrina has to deal with the loss of a promising career. If she doesn't want to talk about it, that's her affair. When you're talking to Ina next you might break some news to her. She won't be on the guest list this Christmas.''

''How drastic!'' Lindsey sneered before she could help herself. ''She lives for these visits. Like Sharon, she'll never get you out of her system.''

''As though I care about such things,'' Royce told her with slow cruelty. ''Gran, this can't be very pleasant for you.''

''On the contrary, it's been delightful meeting Catrina.''

Louise McQuillan smiled. ''I'm hoping, Catrina, you won't leave me to my solitude,'' she said charmingly. ''You must come visit me. We can talk.''

''I'd like that, Mrs. McQuillan.'' There was gratitude in Carrie's golden eyes. She felt touched and honoured the old lady had made the effort to come down to dinner to meet her.

''Now—'' Louise McQuillan looked at her grandson once more, her delicate head shaking almost imperceptibly on its fragile neck ''—my bed calls. I think you can help me upstairs, my darling.''

''Sure, Gran.'' Immediately Royce stood up, as did Cameron who went to his mother, bent over her and kissed her cheek.

''Goodnight, Mother.''

''Goodnight, Cameron, dear.'' She patted his large, strong hand.

Carrie excused herself after saying she was going for a walk leaving that extraordinarily ill-matched couple, Lindsey and Cameron McQuillan together to perhaps bicker lovingly. They didn't appear to have a thing in common, but far more worrying to Carrie's mind, was the fact Mrs. Lindsey McQuillan appeared far more attracted to her husband's nephew than she ever was to him. A potential mine field? Almost unreal.

It was with a feeling of relief Carrie found her way out to the huge lobby, from there taking the front stairs to the home gardens. It was a beautiful night, the vast landscape lit by a huge copper moon, the languorous golden moon of the tropics. She took the broad gravel path set with irregular-shaped paving stones that meandered around the house, intending to take a short walk before retiring. She had never in her life ventured into a garden of such immense proportions, a million blossoms scenting the night with their presence. Bright moonlight lit her way burnishing the shining, still waters of the lagoon. She was tempted to walk down to the water, it looked so inviting but decided until she knew more about her surroundings it would be better to stick literally to the garden path.

It perturbed her Royce's wife had gone to such lengths to check out her background. And so quickly. She must have spies everywhere. It hadn't helped Ina's cause, either, getting straight onto Lindsey to relay the findings. Three women all obsessing about the same man. Royce McQuillan very obviously was one of those men women found irresistible. It wasn't just his handsomeness though "handsome" didn't say it, it was his whole aura. She felt like she was unravelling more and more herself. Even her accident didn't seem to matter as much as it had. Carrie pressed her injured finger, the little finger, against her warm cheek. She was far away from everyone she loved, her father, Melissa, Jamie and Liz. Far away from her friends. She could see how it was going to be with Lindsey McQuillan. No ally there. In fact, an enemy. Feeling the way she did about Royce McQuillan, why was Lindsey staying here? Surely it would be better for her and her husband to set up a home of their own. Their marriage had no chance of survival with Lindsey feeding on forbidden fantasies.

Carrie continued to walk, lost in thought. She didn't think she was going to have that much trouble discharging her duties as governess. Reggie, after an initial shaky start, had turned out to be surprisingly amenable. On their tour of the house she had been an engaging little companion with a knowledge of beautiful objects and far-off places far beyond her years.

To ease the meal hour, Carrie had persuaded Mrs. Gainsford to cook morsels of fish in batter for Reggie's tea served with chips and presented in a little basket lined with a strong paper napkin. Carrie who knew a little bit about napkin art then went to the trouble of making a waterlily for Reggie's plate, later showing the child how she went about folding the napkin over and over before she was able to gently pull the corners upward to make the petals. Reggie had been fascinated, eating her meal with every evidence of enjoyment, something that pleased Mrs. Gainsford so much she went to a drawer, pulled out a large starched napkin and proceeded to fashion it into a bishop's hat, which she set beside the waterlily. Reggie had clapped. Mrs. Gainsford had smiled. Simple little measures but they succeeded in making the mealtime quite pleasant.

Some twenty or so minutes later Carrie, refreshed, her lungs filled with the pure night air, turned to retrace her steps, her eyes delighting in the spectacle of the house lit up like an ocean-going liner at night. This was such an experience for her. A tropical adventure. One she had never even imagined a little more than a week ago. She was finding out things she hadn't even known about herself. Things inside her. Wild stirrings in the blood, the ravishing pleasure of just being able to look at a certain man. To study the planes and angles of his face. The set of his shoulders, the elegance and strength of his body. To listen to his voice. Get caught up in his smile. To sink near to drowning in the sparkle of his eyes. Her own extravagant feelings invested Lindsey McQuillan's barely concealed longings with pathos. Here was a woman who had married a much older man for status then fallen in love with his nephew. What a recipe for disaster.

Carrie was nearing the corner of the east wing outside the library when she saw through the open French doors a sight that froze her with dread. Royce McQuillan in a temper—or some flame of passion—was gripping Lindsey McQuillan by the shoulders, his striking face usually so vivid with life, taut with fury. She was staring up into his face, rapt, stupefied, begging? Her head with its short crop of blond hair flung back, in some turbulence of her own. Whatever words were passing between them, Carrie couldn't catch but the body language was abundantly clear. Both were intensely aroused.

The shock was so extreme Carrie felt as winded as if she'd been struck in the chest. She recoiled in misery, left the path and broke into a run clutching at the heart that had leapt up in her breast. This can't *be!* she cried raggedly, talking out loud like a child. They can't be having an affair. No matter what she saw, what she thought she saw, it couldn't be true. For all he incited strong passions, she couldn't see Royce McQuillan betraying his uncle.

Where there was smoke there was fire, the night answered her.

Carrie's headlong flight took her down the grassy slope to the sanctuary of the lagoon. Her insides were contracting, a taste of bitterness was in her mouth. That grass was so thick and plush the heels of her sandals were sinking into its deep pile. She could smell the water, hear the ghost of music in the vibration of the reeds, see the luminous heads of hundreds of white arum lilies. Inevitably her mind grappled with the thought of snakes. What to do next? Wait until her heartbeat had settled and she had regained her composure before making her way back up the slope onto the path. She didn't know if she had it in her to hum some snatch of melody to warn of her approach. Hadn't Lindsey told him the governess had gone for a walk? Or were both so far gone as not to care?

Bemused, Carrie hovered in the dark shadows at the water's edge, relegated to the role of unwitting voyeur. The things one saw through windows! Enough to shatter lives. Darkness was all around her. She couldn't be visible from the house yet moments later she saw Royce McQuillan's tall figure silhouetted against the brilliant lights from the lobby before he strode out onto the verandah like a man in need of a great breath of fresh air.

He stood for a moment, looking out into the night, then he plunged down the stairs.

Carrie's need to avoid him burned so strong she found herself taking off, running through the grass following the upward contour of the lagoon until she could reach the protection of one of the great shade trees. From there, after a minutes respite, she could make her way to the house, perhaps entering through one of the multiple sets of French doors. Entry by stealth, she thought. My first night and I'm sneaking back into the house.

It's all your fault, Royce McQuillan, she thought, her mind locked into an obsessive replay of what she had seen. Lust? Guilt? Anger? Degrees of all three. Carrie realised she was trembling, her breath coming in little keening sounds through her nostrils. If she fell she could ruck an ankle. This was like some hellish dream.

"For God's sake!" A man's voice astonished her. How had he got there? Yet arms like steel bands locked around her, bringing her flight to a shuddering halt. "If I live to be a hundred I'll never understand why women do the things they do," Royce McQuillan rasped.

She tried to laugh but, couldn't possibly succeed. Instead her breath spasmed. "I'm sorry I became disoriented in the dark."

"Couldn't you have stuck to the path?" He could feel the tremble in her body through her silky taut skin, moonlight pearling down on a face sheened with heat. He recognised the sensation every time he touched her. Tried to disconnect it.

"I wanted to look at the water." She was fighting for breath, for control.

"Listen." He continued to keep hold of her, barely preventing himself from shaking her. "I can't tell you more than one time. Don't go straying from the paths at night. Especially don't go walking around near the water. Some areas are swampy, you could have got locked in reeds. I would have thought you'd have more sense. You haven't even got anything substantial on your feet. Little bits of leather!''

''I forgot. I'm sorry.'' She stood like a statue within his arms, willing herself to feel nothing. ''I won't do it again.''

''Hell, girl, it's my responsibility to see you're safe,'' he said with sharp impatience.

''Look, I'm all right.'' Carrie felt her energy returning as though she had drawn off some of his virile strength. ''I don't need you to walk me back.''

He turned her face fully to look at him. ''Something has upset you.''

''I can deal with it.'' Her body went very tense.

''*Tell* me.''

''I'd rather die first.'' Hostility flooded her.

''It must be pretty awful. You were out on the path, weren't you?'' His voice cracked with a kind of contempt.

''I hope I'm not going to have to account for all of my movements?''

''Ahh, the little flash of hostility. Such a dead give-away.''

''I really don't want to talk about it.'' Indeed she didn't, feeling sealed off in a strange world.

''You don't have to hide anything from me,'' he jeered. ''You saw something—you *thought* you saw something—that made you so uncomfortable you tore off into the night?''

''Why don't we just leave this?'' Carrie knew immediately her voice sounded too tense, too judgemental.

''How sanctimonious can you get?'' he swore gently. ''Leave *what?*''

She dropped her head, her hair falling around her face

like a curtain. ''I suppose sometimes only the truth will do.''

''And you're sufficiently sure of your facts to know it? Let me spare you the telling, Carrie. You looked into the house and saw Lindsey and me having a few heated words?''

''Something like that,'' she confessed in a low voice. Even now he hadn't settled down.

''Why should it upset you so badly?'' He stared at her. ''It's hardly any of your business.''

''I don't see it like that. I was very disturbed.''

''You thought you'd actually stumbled on an illicit love scene?'' he scoffed.

''No need to be so cutting.'' She felt a wave of shame.

''No need for you to play the shining paragon of virtue, either. So bright and so innocent. For your edification, Miss Russell, I am not, repeat, *not* having an affair with my uncle's wife, if that's the conclusion you jumped to. Did you really think I was? Did you *really* think that of me?''

She shook her head wretchedly. ''No, I didn't. I certainly didn't want to. But she's in love with you. You must know that.''

''That's what it looked like?'' he asked in a harsh, drawn voice.

''That was the message I've got since I arrived.''

''Congratulations!'' he groaned.

''What did you say to her?'' Carrie found herself asking before she could stop herself.

''Just who the hell do you think you are?'' he asked in amazement, trying to rein in his own feelings. ''You're obviously not happy just being Reggie's governess.''

''I'm no more a governess than the hostess of a game show,'' she said with a spark of anger, not going to stand there and be humiliated. ''I didn't pick the place and I didn't pick the time. I just happened to look into a brightly lit room—''

''Be sure to add, and passed judgement on what you saw.''

Carrie glanced up at the moon as if for guidance… ''So I regret what happened. I regret if I've offended you. I know you'd never betray your uncle.''

''Is there anything you'd like to add to that?'' he demanded, closing his fingers around her wrist.

''Yes, don't be mad at me. Please.''

Abruptly he relented, his thumb almost absently stroking the transparent blue-and-white inside skin. ''Okay, a cease-fire. We'll walk for a while, then we'll go back to the house. But first I'd like to tell you the idea of Lindsey's being in love with me is a joke. An embarrassment. There's a whole body of literature about women who put themselves through torture with their ridiculous longings. To put it crudely, Lyn isn't getting the kind of sex she wants and she seems to want it pretty badly that's my interpretation anyway, but she's not getting it from me. We can all be very certain about that. I've made it so plain I expect she's going to devote the rest of her life to hating me.''

''Lord!'' Carrie ached. ''Love is an illness.''

''*Not* love.''

''It must seem like it. Sexual confusions. Couldn't Lindsey and your uncle live somewhere else? I understand he's very well off.''

''A fact that appears to have all but destroyed him,'' he answered bluntly.

''Your uncle should be enjoying life. He's a charming man.''

''And *kind,* which I remind you, I'm not. Cam's too withdrawn if not actually out of it. In many ways he's his own worst enemy.''

"That's sad." Carrie's voice wavered. His touch was inducing such excitement.

"Okay, it's sad, but I'm losing patience."

"They're such an unlikely couple." She toyed with the idea of pulling her hand away but didn't.

"Hell, he's not the only man to marry the wrong woman." His voice carried self-disgust. "Cam and I between us have made it a family affair."

She tried to absorb some of his anger. "You'll meet the right woman," she promised.

"What, are you going to set up shop as a clairvoyant now?" he scoffed, glancing down at her silky head, her pure profile outlined against the gilded purple of the night.

"No, I'm just trying to be cheerful."

"How sweet of you." The vibrant voice was attractively discordant.

"Don't be bitter. The smartest people can make terrible mistakes."

To her surprise he gave a hoot of genuine laughter. "Catrina, for one so young your insight is tremendous."

"Insightful. That's me. Dammit!"

"Hey, I like it." Before she knew what he was about, he turned her to him, cupping her oval face in his hands. "What are you doing in my life?"

She had no time to answer even if she could because he bent his head to kiss her parted mouth. Gently…so gently, yet her heart beat like a wild thing, nibbling at her cushioned lips as he might at wild strawberries. It was utterly bewitching, emotive enough to make her want to cry. She could have spent her life kissing him. Yet when he finally withdrew his beautiful seductive mouth from hers she could only find a stammer. "You said you wouldn't k-k…kiss me again," she reminded him.

He nodded. "I meant it, too. At the time." His tone was

both erotic and tender as he pushed the hot silk of her hair behind her ears.

''Well, you shouldn't do it. I can't think straight,'' Carrie answered.

''That's your punishment,'' he said crisply. ''Never, never, spy on me again. I'm your employer, after all. Which is a kind of shame.'' He caught her hand and began to swing it, urging her on toward the house.

''Did you have these little problems with my predecessors?'' she couldn't resist asking as he hauled her up onto the path.

''They weren't as shatteringly attractive as you are,'' he mocked. ''I just can't believe it! I didn't know you a fortnight ago.''

''It is odd,'' Carrie agreed as he steadied her. More than odd, astonishing! Suddenly after all the many long months of her crushing disappointment the whole world looked different. She raised her face to him as they walked up onto the drive.

''Look at the stars,'' he said, pausing to rest his hand on her delicate shoulder. ''The Southern Cross. Orion the mighty hunter with his jewelled belt. The others like diamond clusters through the trees. No matter what happens to us they never change. They endure.''

''As we're supposed to do,'' she said quietly, feeling the warmth and the energy spreading out from his hand. She had to find a way out of her own confusions. Her long years of training couldn't be lost.

''Sometimes things get worse before they get better, Catrina,'' he warned as though he had read her mind. ''Put up a fight.''

''I'm going to.''

They lingered for a little while longer, he talking, Carrie listening, perfectly in tune with his mood.

Neither noticed the woman standing in the shadows of the upstairs verandah. Nor did they know how long she had been there.

CHAPTER SEVEN

REGGIE, to everyone's delight, slipped virtually overnight into another skin. She became a pleasant and co-operative child blossoming under Carrie's gentle understanding hand, secure in the knowledge Carrie really liked her, for Carrie's approval and quick affection for this motherless little girl was transparent.

By the end of a month, in the light of what had gone on before, they had established an excellent working routine; three hours of lessons in the morning; two in the afternoon. Again contrary to all Carrie had been told, Reggie proved an apt pupil. The trick Carrie had found from her own teaching experiences with gifted young musicians was to make the subject matter interesting, something she gave much thought to. That done, learning flowed very naturally. Reggie had a large vocabulary for her age—even excluding the swearwords which continued to pop out from time to time—but her disinterest in numeracy took an upward turn when Carrie hit on using an assortment of large, brightly printed cards to help Reggie see problem-solving more as a game.

Meal times, too, were much less of a battleground. Even Mrs. Gainsford had to admit Carrie's methods were working. Reggie learned how to make her own breakfast smoothies—banana remained the favourite—and Mrs. Gainsford capitulated to the extent "kid's meals" were on the menu with Reggie making a big concession by eating certain julienned raw vegetables she could dip in a sauce. All this along with many chocolate-flavoured malted milks resulted in a pleasing weight gain. Reggie had never had such a benevolent guiding hand. And it showed!

So it wouldn't be all work and no play, they often drove out for a picnic lunch followed by a nature ramble always within a specified distance of the homestead. Royce McQuillan had put at Carrie's disposal a nifty little Toyota Rav 4 which gave her considerable mobility. In fact she sometimes thought he would give her just about anything if it would make her stay happy and Reggie a contented child.

Reggie adored their little forays into the bush but not for the life of her could Carrie cajole the little girl into learning to swim. There was a beautiful big swimming pool in the rear garden of the homestead but of far more interest and pleasure to Carrie was a wonderful rock pool fed by a fresh water spring some four miles from the main compound. Almost perfectly moon-shaped, it nestled in the shelter of a series of low jutting rocks massed like an amphitheatre, crystal-clear, rather cold even in extreme heat, surrounded by tall spears of blue native grasses overhung at this time of the year by a feathery tree with dazzling yellow, large-petalled flowers.

On this particular day they had finished their picnic lunch. Reggie dressed in a pink T-shirt and shorts, sat on a large flat rock overlooking the pool, watching Carrie taking her swim.

"You look like a mermaid," Reggie called as Carrie floated on her back, her hair streaming around her.

"It's lovely in here." Carrie would have loved to induce the child to enter the water. But all in her own good time.

"No way!" Reggie shook her head. "There are spirits at the bottom of the pools."

"Spirits?" For a moment Carrie thought she hadn't heard right. She swam over to the child, treading water. "Did you say spirits?"

''They'll get you, too,'' Reggie warned.

Carrie shook her head. ''This is a beautiful place, Reggie. Can't you feel peace and harmony all around you?''

''Yes, I can,'' Reggie answered simply, ''but there are all spooky things, too.''

''Who said?'' Carrie pulled herself out of the pool, water streaming from her slender long-legged body, clad in a streamlined dark blue swimsuit with a splash of green and yellow flowers.

Reggie ran to pick up Carrie's towel, passing it to her and gazing up at Carrie with open admiration. ''You've got a beaut figure.''

Carrie could feel herself smiling. ''Why, thank you, Reggie. I'm getting a lot of exercise these days.''

''Uncle Cam told Royce you're the most beautiful girl he's ever seen. And you know what? He said it in front of Lindsey.''

''Ouch!'' Carrie rubbed herself down briskly, thinking Lindsey wouldn't have liked that.

''Uncle Cam just says what he thinks.'' Reggie smiled. ''He's a nice man, isn't he? But so *quiet.*''

''He's a perfect sweetie,'' Carrie said honestly. She had got to know Cameron McQuillan better. ''I think his quietness is the result of a lot of unresolved sadness, Reggie.''

Reggie, justly proud of her word comprehension was lost. ''I just forgot what that means?''

''Unresolved?'' Carrie asked.

Reggie nodded.

''It means sadness not properly dealt with. When your uncle Cam lost his first wife the grief was so terrible he couldn't ever break it down into little pieces. Something he could manage. It has never gone away. Some people are like that.'' Carrie thought of her own father and the unresolved grief over her mother he had expressed. "Men can feel things very deeply."

Reggie nodded in near adult agreement. "So why did he marry Lyn then?" she asked reasonably.

"He must have thought she'd bring joy back into his life." Carrie towelled her hair. "She's a striking-looking woman."

"That's not her own blond hair," Reggie said. "Haven't you seen the roots?"

"Lots of women colour their hair, Reggie. It looks good."

"She doesn't frighten me anymore," Reggie said, pitching a small pebble across the water.

"I should hope not," Carrie breathed, very protective of the child.

"She *did.* She even told Ina she never thought I was one of them."

"One of what?" Carrie looked at her in dismay.

"I dunno. I think she's mad. Anyway she's the one who told me about the spirits at the bottom of the lagoon at home. Evil little things that will catch you around the ankles and drag you down to the bottom. She knows I can't swim. I would drown."

Carrie made a note to speak to Lindsey. "I could teach you to swim in no time, Reggie, if you'll let me." Carrie put certainty and commitment into her voice. "You could never be frightened with me?"

"Don't be silly! You're neat! I'll think about it, Carrie," Reggie promised. "But not today."

"That's okay." Carrie was satisfied with that much progress. She ran a wide-toothed comb through her wet hair then pulled it back into a ponytail. "I suppose we should think about starting back," she said regretfully.

"Don't you want to dry off?" Reggie was happy where she was.

''I'd like to.'' Carrie weakened.

''I love it here.'' Reggie sighed in contentment as Carrie spread her towel on a rock then lay down in the shade of the overhanging tree, with diamond chunks of sunlight falling on her long legs. After a while Reggie spoke. ''You know we've got crocs on Maramba?''

Carrie's breath literally whistled. ''Wh-a-a-t!'' She pulled up her long legs so swiftly a great armoured reptile might have lunged out of the water beneath her.

''Not here, silly.'' Reggie giggled. ''This is freshwater. So are the billabongs. I'm talking about upcountry. Royce might take us. Up near the estuary where the salties, that's the salt water crocodiles, come in. Not so many as there used to be. You don't think Royce would let us swim anywhere there was a salt water croc?''

''Hang on, I'm feeling a little weak,'' Carrie begged, still startled. ''No, of course not. You gave me a start.''

''I'm so sorry!'' Reggie sweetly apologised. ''I didn't mean to. I was hoping you'd ask Royce to take us up-country. We could go in the helicopter.''

''I don't know I'm all that interested in meeting your rough-skinned pals,'' Carrie said wryly.

''They're fascinating!'' Reggie breathed. ''The first time I saw one out of the water I thought it was a great big log.''

''Some log!'' Carrie shuddered, turning her head at some disturbance behind them.

A lone rider was coming down the trail, calling out to them as he approached. ''Want some company?''

''Nah, you're supposed to be working,'' Reggie called back, laughing. ''I'll tell Royce.''

''Gimme a break, princess.'' The rider dismounted, hitching his horse's reins to a branch. He was young, lanky, whip-cord thin, attractive with straw-coloured curls and bright hazel eyes. His name was Tim Barton. He was the son of a wealthy Melbourne merchant banker, a long-time friend of the McQuillan family, and he was doing a year's work experience on Maramba as a jackeroo. A kind of toughening-up process before he joined the family firm, Carrie gathered. She had met Tim several times on her trips around the station and quite liked him though it was obvious Tim wasn't taking his duties as seriously as he might have done. On his own admission he wanted to extract every bit of colour and fun he could out of his stay. Carrie he had taken to at first glance.

Now he ambled down the grassy slope, swaggering a little in his riding boots, cream Akubra in hand.

"How are you, Carrie?" He stared at her with open admiration, eagerly soaking her in.

"Fine, Tim." She gave him an uncomplicated smile. "Doesn't this come under the category of wasting time?"

He laughed good-naturedly. "Never wasting time talking to a pretty girl. *Girls.*" He bowed in Reggie's direction.

Reggie shook her curly mop. "You're here to see Carrie. Royce said you fancy yourself as a lady's man."

Tim's ears reddened. "You're something, you are, Reggie. Carrie taught you to swim yet?"

"The water's not warm enough," Reggie explained. "Like an apple?"

"No way I'm going to take it off you."

"That's okay." Reggie threw a shiny red apply his way. "What do you want, anyway?"

Tim glanced at Carrie, a wry expression in his eyes. "I swear this kid's a grown woman. Actually I wanted to ask Carrie if she'd like to go riding at the weekend. I know plenty of great trails. I have Saturday afternoon off."

"Sure, we'd love to come," Reggie answered promptly for both of them.

''I don't know that I asked you, princess,'' Tim said mildly. ''Anyway, you're too little to ride.''

''I am not! Don't say that,'' Reggie answered indignantly. ''I haven't been ready for it, but I am now. Carrie is going to teach me.''

''Seems to me Carrie doesn't get enough time to herself,'' Tim exclaimed.

''Carrie is *my* governess,'' Reggie answered him primly. ''Maybe we could go in the Rav?''

''Why not!'' Carrie took pity on Tim. ''Does that suit you?'' She gave him a lazy smile, wishing it was Royce McQuillan who had asked her to go riding.

''You can't get rid of this sweetheart for the day?'' Tim only half joked.

''No, she can't,'' Reggie said, grinning and showing the wide space between her front teeth. ''I'll be—'' she snapped her fingers ''—what's that word…?''

''Chaperone?'' Tim asked sarcastically.

''That's it!'' Reggie crowed. ''Anyway, Carrie has a boyfriend at home.''

''Have you?'' Tim looked at Carrie with a twisted grin. ''Why wouldn't you, you're so beautiful!''

''I bet they're going to get engaged,'' Reggie said. ''Carrie is going to sell the pictures to *Woman's Day.*''

Carrie stood up, laughing, looking around for the colourful matching sarong to tie around her waist. ''Reggie's talking about a friend of the family. I believe she was offered twenty-five thousand dollars for wedding pictures.''

''You think she'll accept?'' Tim flashed the child a glance.

''You bet she will,'' said Reggie airily.

Both Carrie and Tim burst out laughing, which was the way Royce McQuillan found them. What a tableau! he thought. Innocent youth, carefree, snatching fun, yet it irritated him enormously.

Tim, who really needed ticking off, was looking at the very light-clad Carrie with a positively worshipful expression on his face; Carrie, all pale honey limbs and an exceptionally beautiful body apparently quite unselfconscious under that drooling regard; Reggie, sitting happily on a rock munching on a red apple.

Royce sat his bay stallion for a moment easing back on his frown before calling out to the young jackeroo. "Tim, aren't you supposed to be giving Lance a hand?"

Immediately Tim spun around, all respect. "Sorry, boss. I heard the girls splashing so I decided to come down and say hello."

"I'm sure they appreciated that," Royce clipped off. "Say goodbye now and get on with it. There's a whole lot more for you to do before sundown." He had taken it fairly easy on Tim knowing Tim was basically filling in time but the boy's little breaks were becoming too frequent. He would have a private word with him later on in the day.

"See you Saturday, then, Carrie?" Tim murmured swiftly, watching Royce McQuillan dismount.

"Better get going, Tim," Carrie said, reading the older man's body language. "I'll pick you up at two outside the bunkhouse."

"That'll be great!"

"So long, Tim!" Reggie called brightly. "We might take a nice picnic."

Picnic? Royce walked on, pretending not to hear. As Tim reached him he added a few more instructions, then he continued on to the spring, its dark green surface sparkling with tiny bubbles like the bubbles in champagne.

"How's it going?" he asked, watching Carrie stoop

gracefully to pick up a sarong which she tied native-fashion around her slender hips.

''Really, really good,'' Reggie said in a high sweet voice, looking more like a little boy than a girl in her serviceable T-shirt and shorts, but she was filling out, McQuillan thought with satisfaction. There was flesh on those little chicken bones. And she looked contented, eyes bright, a ready smile on her lips.

''How long has Tim been here?'' he asked, avoiding sounding stern.

''Only a few minutes,'' Carrie supplied, trying to fathom why when she never felt the least bit self-conscious in her bathing suit in front of Tim she felt close to stark naked under Royce McQuillan's brilliant gaze. Not that he was looking at her in any sexual way. All in all the look was a mix of arrogance and irritation.

''He asked us out Saturday,'' Reggie supplied with enthusiasm.

''I don't believe it,'' he said.

''You'd better believe it.'' Reggie nodded her head owlishly. ''It's true, isn't it, Carrie? I think he's fallen in love with her,'' she told Royce in an aside.

''Nonsense,'' said Carrie, not at all disconcerted by the child.

''Hold on, he isn't *available* Saturday.'' Royce bent his gaze on the child's face.

''That's awful,'' said Reggie. ''He said he was.''

''I know how disappointed you must be,'' Royce glanced briefly at Carrie who looked more than ever like a day lily. ''Tim just occasionally forgets he's supposed to be here to *work.* He had last weekend in town.''

''Gee, we were going on a picnic,'' Reggie told him dolefully.

''Okay so *I'll* take you,'' Royce said.

Reggie rushed at him, grasping him around the knees. "You promise?"

"Reggie, I'm a man of my word." He ruffled her curls.

Reggie gave a whoop of delight. "And I love you!" she yelled. "Don't you just love him, too?" Reggie turned her head to appeal to Carrie.

"Your father is a wonderful man," Carrie said sweetly, feeling her face flushing.

"Why thank you, Catrina," he drawled with just the faintest hint of mockery.

"I mean, everyone says it," she added.

"Let's all pray for a beautiful day." He let his eyes rest on her until she felt her knees buckle.

"So where are we going?" Reggie asked, clinging to his hand.

"I'll have to give that some heavy thought," he told the child. "If we make it a day trip we could take the helicopter and visit the rainforest. We'd have to leave the helicopter, of course. Set up the next leg of the trip."

"Oh, can't we, Royce?" Reggie sounded thrilled out of her mind at the offer. "I'll be so good. Carrie will love it."

"It sounds marvellous." Carrie, too, found herself responding with enthusiasm. "But what am I going to do about Tim?" She looked directly into Royce's sparkling jet eyes.

"I'll tell him," he said.

When Lindsey heard about the proposed trip to the rainforest she decided she wanted to go. "It will make a nice break in the monotony," she said as they lingered over coffee.

"If you're bored, my dear, you could always take a trip to Brisbane. You have friends there," her husband told her.

‘‘It’s no fun on my own.’’ Lindsey regarded him coolly. ‘‘They’re all happily married. No one wants a woman on her own. If you’re young enough and attractive enough you’re seen as a threat. No, the rainforest will do fine.’’

‘‘I’ll have to check with Reggie,’’ Royce McQuillan said smoothly. ‘‘It’s *her* trip.’’

‘‘You can’t be serious,’’ Lindsey flared.

‘‘Indeed, I am. You and Reggie aren’t exactly on the best of terms.’’

‘‘In fact, my dear,’’ Cameron McQuillan said mildly, ‘‘You’ve given the child a rather bad time.’’

Lindsey blinked. ‘‘That’s a bit much,’’ she protested. ‘‘Regina has been a lot more civil since Carrie arrived. I scarcely ever hear her uttering her swearwords anymore.’’

‘‘She might break out again if I tell her we’re taking extras,’’ Royce said, swallowed his coffee hot and strong. ‘‘Needless to say, Lyn, I’d love you to come along.’’

Reggie, when she did hear Lindsey wanted to come, whipped out her worst word, so cross she scarcely heard Carrie’s remonstration. ‘‘She’ll spoil everything,’’ Reggie fumed. ‘‘She always does. She’ll want to talk to Royce all the time. It’s no good trying to get a word in. Why doesn’t he just tell her she can’t come?’’

Carrie swallowed. ‘‘I expect he’s concerned about hurting your uncle Cam’s feelings. After all, Lindsey is his wife.’’

Reggie sank to the floor and buried her face in her hands. ‘‘I knew it was too good to be true. I wish she’d step on a taipan.’’

Carrie crouched down beside the child. ‘‘Oh, don’t say that, sweetheart,’’ she shuddered. ‘‘You mustn’t say things like that. God is listening.’’

‘‘He knows how nasty I am,’’ Reggie said with a helpless shrug. ''Can't you please ask Royce not to take her? He listens to you.''

''I don't know that he will,'' Carrie groaned, not happy about Lindsey's coming along on the trip, either.

''He's very pleased with the way you take care of me. He told me. Anyway he doesn't even like Lindsey. Want to hear something? He and Gran begged Uncle Cam not to marry her. Uncle Cam should have listened. You should hear what Aunty Ina calls her, and they're supposed to be friends.''

''No, thank you, Reggie. I don't want to know.''

''Well, it's slut,'' Reggie muttered.

''How very unkind. You've been listening to far too much talk for a little girl.'' Carrie frowned.

''That's because they forget I'm there. I don't want her to come, Carrie. Please speak to Royce.''

So Carrie waited that night for Royce McQuillan to go to his study, then she followed him.

''May I have a word?''

''Come in,'' he said briefly. ''Shut the door. I suppose you could even lock it.''

''Isn't that a bit drastic?'' She glanced behind her.

''It's the only way to keep people out.''

''Am I people?'' she asked nervously.

''No, you're okay.'' He gave her just a glimpse of his beautiful smile. ''Fire away.''

Carrie slipped into a chair facing his massive partners desk. Directly behind him was a portrait of his grandfather, Sir Andrew McQuillan, a handsome stern-faced man with thick, silvered hair in stark contrast to the now familiar jet-black eyes. The artist had caught perfectly the aura of power and distinction.

''Reggie has asked me to beg you not to take Lindsey on our trip,'' Carrie began.

''Splendid!'' He looked up from some paper in front of

him. "I don't just insult Lindsey, you know. I insult my uncle."

"I know. It's a difficult situation."

"My God, tell me about it!" he invited. "Problems and troubles. That's what my life's been up to date."

"You might solve a few things if you…"

"Show them the door?"

"I wasn't going to put it quite so bluntly."

He was silent for a while, staring at her. "I like you in white. White for the pure of heart."

"It's cool in the heat. Are you sure we're not going to get a storm?"

"Are you feeling in need of a bit of excitement?" he asked suavely.

"I'm just commenting on the heat of the night. The humidity is very high, as well."

"The tropics, Catrina." He stood up and flicked a switch that drove a five-bladed dark timber and brass fan. "Better?" He looked down at her. Her beautiful skin was matt and flawless. Hair and eyes shone. She looked the picture of youth, beauty and health. In fact she tore his sore heart.

"Thank you. So what do I tell her?"

"Tell her she's the one who spilt the beans," he said dryly, resuming his seat.

"She was excited, that's all. It was my own reaction."

"I'll have a word with Reggie," he told her.

"Don't you ever want her to call you daddy?" Carrie found herself asking wistfully.

"Royce is a good name," he answered crisply. "It's on my birth certificate. You're sure not backward in coming forward, are you?"

"I suppose not. I plunge right in. It's just that it seems a little…" She shrugged. "Reggie loves you so much. I'm certain letting her call you Royce is well intentioned, but daddy has to be one of the most beautiful words in the world.''

''Thank you for sharing that with me, Miss Russell,'' he mocked, ''but you must respect *my* decision to allow Reggie to call me Royce.''

''I'm sorry.'' Carrie bit her lip.

''I trust you are. Whose idea was it for Jada to give Reggie drawing lessons?''

''Mine. You should see them together. They love it. I can't draw very well at all.''

''Surely you have enough talents. Like your music.'' He stared at her with his lancing eyes. ''If you don't go to the piano soon you'll forget how to play.''

''The piano is all covered up.''

''What an excuse. I'll have the cover removed. If you're qualified to give advice, so am I. I'm sympathetic to your great disappointment, Catrina, but, we agreed, I thought, you can't brood on it overmuch. Try to let go of the pain. I'm genuinely very interested in hearing what you can do. Want to try playing something?''

''No,'' she said emphatically, backing off when faced with it.

''Okay,'' he said equably, ''not tonight. You probably want to practise first.''

''I hate you.'' She looked at him and suddenly her great golden eyes blazed.

He sat back casually. ''I can live with it. However, if you dare repeat it, I'll terminate your employment.''

''Would you?'' Her anger evaporated.

''Not really. I value your services too highly. Now, Catrina, I have work to do. Tell Reggie, on condition she can keep her mouth shut, there'll be just the three of us.''

''You're saying you're going to tell Lindsey she can't come?''

''You're questioning I'm not game enough to try it?''

"No way!" Carrie stood up and smiled. "I figure you can handle just about anything."

Carrie was making her way along the quiet gallery when Lindsey emerged from her private sitting room to call her. "Can you spare me a minute of your precious time?"

It wasn't the friendliest greeting in the world but Carrie answered pleasantly. "Certainly, Mrs. McQuillan." She'd taken note of the fact Lindsey McQuillan preferred the formal address.

"Come in," Lindsey indicated with an abrupt movement of her hand Carrie should join her in the sitting room which was furnished with fine pieces taken from all over the house. If nothing else Lindsey enjoyed luxury, Carrie thought. She had never seen Lindsey in the same outfit twice. All of her clothes bore a top designer label. In the heat of this night she was wearing a deeply dipping short sapphire-coloured dress which enhanced her eyes, matching sandals on her feet. She could have worn it to the most chic party but she dressed day in, day out to dazzle. For a married woman, her judgement was seriously under question.

Carrie felt yet another stab of pity for her, wondering how and where Cameron McQuillan had met his wife and married her despite deep family misgivings. Reggie, who had heard far too much for a child, let alone one of her tender years, was a mine of information.

"I saw you follow Royce to his study," Lindsey said in an intense accusing voice, moving into an armchair and crossing her legs. "What was that all about?"

Carrie with the redhead's temper felt her teeth go on edge. "A private matter, Mrs. McQuillan, to do with Reggie."

"Don't you think you overdo running to Royce?" Lindsey's remarkable eyes flashed.

"I don't at all." Carrie managed to speak calmly. "I can't see how you can accuse me of that. What is it you *really* want to talk to me about, Mrs. McQuillan?" No sense in not getting to the point.

"Thank God you're not stupid!" Lindsey said. "I want to warn you not to go falling in love with Royce. I can't help thinking you're well on the way."

Carrie didn't even stop to think what she was saying. "It must be the norm around here," she said wryly. Causing Lindsey to sit high in her armchair.

Her mouth worked for a minute before she could speak. "I beg your pardon?" The expression on her face was of complete shock.

"Look, I don't want to upset you," Carrie said, *meaning* it, "but it's very obvious you're attracted to Royce yourself."

Lindsey sat staring at her. "What a colossal cheek! How dare you!" She was so startled her voice actually shook.

"I'm trying to be a friend to you," Carrie said quietly. "It's a sad situation."

"And none of your business," Lindsey cried sharply. "I remind you we're talking about *you.*"

"Oh, no, not *me.* I'm not your enemy here, Mrs. McQuillan," Carrie said. "And I don't allow women to attack me. You asked for it."

"And I got it in spades." Lindsey blinked.

"I'm sorry. I really am."

"You'll be sorrier if you ever try to come between Sharon and Royce," Lindsey warned, a curious, almost exultant expression on her face.

"You mean the *ex* Mrs. McQuillan?" Carrie pointed out.

"She's still very much in the picture." Lindsey laughed.

"I don't think everyone knows about that," Carrie answered mildly. "Certainly not Royce."

This conversation wasn't going at all as Lindsey intended. "My dear, there's *lots* you don't know," she said very coldly.

"I daresay there is. But I wouldn't care to hear it from someone like your friend Ina. I'd watch out for her if I were you." Carrie threw in a warning of her own.

Lindsey turned an odd colour. "What are you talking about?"

"Just a rumour. Be more careful, she's not to be trusted."

Lindsey took a deep shuddering breath, her anger momentarily abated. "Hang on, who's giving you all this information. Is it Gran? You're spending more and more time with her."

Carrie shook her head decisively. "Mrs. McQuillan doesn't *gossip.* She loves to tell me stories about the old days on the wilderness coast. I love to listen. It's a real insight into what must have been a unique way of life. She's a fascinating woman with many fascinating stories to tell. I enjoy her company and I've grown fond of Jada, too. She's so devoted to Mrs. McQuillan. It's lovely to see."

Lindsey's expression was cynical. "My dear, you don't think I've got the picture? You've done everything in your power to ingratiate yourself since you arrived here. You've even got poor old Cam eating out of your hand."

"Your husband is a very nice man, gentle and charming," Carrie pointed out.

"No he's *not,* he's a bastard," Lindsey burst out, her face working. "He's got *nothing* to offer me! I thought we were going to travel the world. I thought we were going to have a good time. Instead he can't bear to leave his bloody home. If that isn't pathetic, what is? God that man has a lot to answer for."

It was certainly a different point of view. "Surely you

can convince him you want a home of your own?" Carrie challenged, feeling the other woman's inner rage. "You'd feel so much better in different surroundings. Don't you want children?"

"No, I don't." Lindsey sat there, face white. "Children were never on the agenda. I want a *life*."

"Then you'd better move away from Maramba," Carrie suggested. "I'd say right now."

Lindsey was silent, absorbing Carrie's frank advice. "Why am I letting you talk to me this way?" she asked finally.

"I expect you need someone to confide in. I'm sympathetic to your plight."

"Hell, yes." Lindsey stood up and stalked to the French doors. "You're in love with him yourself. Don't bother denying it. We women can read one another like books."

"Mrs. McQuillan, I'm keeping my head down," Carrie said. "I'm here as Reggie's governess. I'm not about to empty my innermost thoughts into your ear. While we're on the subject of Reggie might I ask you not to fill her head with stories about evil spirits at the bottom of the home lagoon. She pretends to be so confident but she's only a little girl. It scares her. I can't begin to teach her to swim."

"Oh, no, I just thought it was a way of keeping her away from the water," Lindsey apologised with huge difficulty. "She's such a mad little devil. In fact she's a lot like her mother. Sharon is very unstable. If you ask me Sharon's a manic depressive. If she's not on some great high, she's in hell. The child's the same."

"I don't accept that," Carrie answered flatly. "Reggie has been neglected, starved of a mother's love."

Lindsey gave her a bitter smile. "So that's the plan? You're going to make yourself indispensable to Reggie so you can get Royce?"

"Looks like our little conversation is over," Carrie said, standing up. "I'm not a manipulative person. I'm not greedy or ruthless. I don't have a plan. I have a few demons to wrestle myself before I can even start making plans of my own. I can only tell you I'm not your enemy. Please don't treat me like one."

The trip to the rainforest—minus Lindsey—was a wonderful new experience for Carrie and Regina. Royce had organised a guide and he led them through part of one of the last great remaining rainforests of the world. Warm, humid, golden-green, the plant life was overwhelming in its profusion and diversity, the great trees with their crowns interlocking formed the forest canopy covered with other plants, mosses, ferns, orchids, elkhorns and staghorns on a massive scale. Ferns stood the size of trees while the wonderful ancient cycads dominated the lower levels. It was a very hot day when they started on the verge of the wet, but on the rainforest floor everything was quiet and calm. Thick woody vines lay all over the rainforest floor, or hung like gigantic ropes from the trees. Epiphytes heavily adorned the tree trunks or even bare rocks while beautiful posies of flowers, a phenomenon called cauliflory dotted the trunks of the forest giants, climbing a hundred feet or more.

At one point they had to come to a complete halt, Reggie hushed and excited, as a giant bird called a cassowary, black-feathered and flightless with brilliant blue and red colours on its head, neck and wattles, stalked out of the forest undergrowth. They all stood perfectly still, the guide in front, Royce standing protectively in front of Carrie and the child, his arms stretched back. The bird moved quietly, booming and rumbling, obviously looking for food. Five feet tall, heavy birds, cassowaries could be dangerous and were known to attack man if the nest was threatened. But there were innumerable wild fruits in the forest. The cassowary moved off, despite its size difficult to see against the great profusion of plants.

Afterward when Reggie grew tired Royce carried her back to the rainforest edge where butterflies in their thousands, a giant kaleidoscope of colour were swarming all over the massed stands of pink and purple lantana; lace wings, cruisers, birdwings, spotted triangles, the magnificent iridescent blue Ulysses with its huge wingspan. Here, too, in the sunlight they were able to appreciate the brilliant plumage of the birds, so difficult to see in the density of the rainforest branches.

It was a perfect day but that perfection wasn't to survive the night.

When they arrived back on Maramba, later afternoon, Royce was greeted by his overseer, who appeared to be waiting just for the purpose of telling him a charter plane had flown in that afternoon with Mrs. Sharon McQuillan as a passenger.

"Mummy?" Reggie asked in wonderment, her eyes round with surprise.

"She's got a bloody nerve!" Royce McQuillan muttered, shaking his head disbelievingly, his voice bitter.

"You're not going to fight, are you, Royce?" Reggie asked after such a happy day, on the verge of tears.

"No of course we're not, poppet." He recollected himself instantly. "Let's go and see what she wants."

"It can only mean trouble," he told Carrie, as Reggie made a beeline to get into the Jeep.

Carrie stood her ground, experiencing a whole jumble of perturbing emotions; panic, anxiety, an unwelcome rush of jealousy she couldn't fight down. Worst of all, she felt threatened. What were the consequences of their own deepening relationship, very serious on her part and, she'd hoped and believed, on his.

"It might be best if you and Reggie keep out of the way until I can see what this is all about."

"You mean out of sight?" She wasn't certain how to do it; wasn't certain she wanted to.

"Sharon didn't come to see Reggie," he said bluntly, "hell, don't you think I want the child to have a loving mother? Tragically that's not on."

Somehow they made it into the house without encountering anybody, Royce McQuillan instructing Carrie to take Reggie upstairs.

She obeyed, shaky inside and absorbing the danger. She wanted to stay near him. It was obvious he was deeply disturbed as she was herself. What hold did this woman have over him? She had seen him directing his men, noted his easy bred-in-the-bone authority. He had no problem being master of a great station, but he still had a problem with his ex-wife.

Was it possible he still cared for her? Carrie agonised, painfully aware of her own lack of worldliness. If he did, how could she possibly cope with it? Sharon McQuillan was a woman who damaged lives, but she was very sexy with a lot of style. Also, and Carrie had seen it with her own eyes, Sharon had not succeeded in breaking free of her ex-husband. Were both of them left with feelings they didn't want? Was it possible Royce McQuillan was out of reach altogether?

Holding Reggie firmly by the hand, praying the child wasn't going to get out of hand, they made the upper gallery where she saw Jada beckoning to her from the far end.

"Your grandmother wants to see us, Reggie," Carrie said, going toward the aboriginal woman.

"Gran doesn't like Mummy." Reggie spoke huskily, as though her throat was red raw.

"Everything will be all right, darling. Don't you worry," Carrie tried to reassure her. "Your mother and father are adults. They can talk in an adult way."

"You haven't heard my mummy when she's *mad!*" Reggie said, clutching Carrie's hand tighter. "She can screech like a cat. Maybe she wants to stay?"

"Would you *want* her to stay?" Carrie asked. Sharon was the child's mother, for all that.

"Gran said Mummy doesn't know how to behave," Reggie said as though that settled it.

"Gran didn't *tell* you that?"

"No, she was talking to Royce."

"You'll have to stop listening in to the adults' conversation, Reggie," Carrie warned. "Think of it as a little sin."

"No it's not," said Reggie. "It's not at all. It's my way of finding out what's going on." And in its way it was very effective.

Jada let them in to Louise McQuillan's bedroom. Carrie was quite familiar with the layout of the west wing having spent companionable time with the old lady. She had brought Reggie with her several times and Reggie had behaved. Carrie hoped that state of affairs was going to hold, especially as the old lady looked frailer than ever, almost diminished.

"Sharon is in the house," she announced, and the words came out like a sad wail.

"I'm sure everything is going to be all right, Mrs. McQuillan." Carrie went to the old lady and gently took her hand. "You're upsetting yourself for nothing."

The old lady gave a hollow laugh. "Difficult not to, my dear." She lay back on the pillows.

"I'll look after you, Gran." Reggie followed Carrie to

the bed, speaking amazingly soothingly for such a young child. ''Maybe Mummy's come to be friends?''

Weak tears sprang into Louise McQuillan's eyes. ''You're a good little girl, Reggie. Would you go with Jada for a minute while I speak to Catrina?''

''Sure, Gran.'' Reggie bent over and kissed the old lady's hand on the coverlet. ''What do we do if she wants me back?''

''Would you want to go, Reggie?'' Louise McQuillan asked very gently.

''I don't know. I don't think so,'' Reggie's voice trailed off. ''Maybe just a holiday. But I don't want to be away for Christmas. I don't want to go anywhere without Carrie.'' She started to sound agitated.

''Come along, child.'' Jada took the little girl's hand, smiling down at her.

''I've got a nice drink for you. Let your gran talk to Carrie now.''

Reggie went off willingly, walking with Jada into the adjoining sitting room.

Louise McQuillan waited until she heard their voices in the next room before she continued. ''You haven't been with us that long, Catrina, but I feel I know you. I trust you. I know you're mindful of Reggie's welfare. I have to tell you I'm worried and I can't hide it. I don't know what Sharon's visit means, coming like it does out of the blue. Or worse, someone could be feeding her information. She picked her day. I'd like to think she felt compelled to see her child but we've all learned the hard way. My great fear is Sharon is going to try to use Reggie in some way.''

''You mean as leverage, bargaining power?'' Carrie asked, not really understanding at all.

''She's not above it,'' Louise McQuillan said. ''I want you to stay close to Reggie. Protect her if you can. Protect her from what she might hear.''

Carrie felt brave enough to risk it. ''Is there something I don't know about, Mrs. McQuillan?'' she asked simply. ''Something that might help me do my job.''

Louise moved her knotted hands. ''Just be warned. Royce has a temper. He won't take too much without exploding. Sharon will do everything in her power to provoke him. She can't *let go* but she can never be allowed into this family again.''

''But what about Reggie?'' Carrie asked in concern. ''Does her mother have *no* love in her heart for her?''

Louise bit her lip. ''The awful truth is Sharon has never wanted Reggie from the moment she was born. She never loved or tended to her. Royce had to get in a nurse. Sharon was treated for postnatal depression though her doctor doubted she had the condition at all. I believe Reggie was an unwanted pregnancy. Poor little Reggie has had to pay the price.''

Carrie looked at her in bewilderment. ''But a woman so madly in love with her husband, bearing his child...'' It was incomprehensible to Carrie.

''Maybe if she had looked like Sharon.'' Louise shredded a tissue. ''Sharon was a striking little girl with her dark hair and those ice-blue eyes. Reggie will come into her own when she's older.''

''Reggie is remarkably intelligent,'' Carrie said loyally.

''It might be better if she were just an ordinary little girl,'' Louise answered bleakly. ''Reggie's a thinking child. She's been very badly hurt. Be there for her, Catrina. That's all I ask.''

CHAPTER EIGHT

MRS. GAINSFORD served them a meal in Carrie's bedroom, her manner more subdued than ever but surprisingly kind. "I've made those noodles you like, Regina," she said gently, "and a chocolate pudding. I hope you enjoy. Chicken salad for you, Carrie, as it's too hot. Nice fresh rolls. A family dinner tonight, I understand." She didn't mention Sharon but they were all intensely aware of "A Situation."

After the housekeeper had gone Carrie wheeled the trolley out onto the verandah, pulling up chairs and encouraging Reggie to eat up her meal. She had lost all appetite herself but for the child's sake she pretended interest in her meal, which really was delicious, the fresh garden salad flavoured with a piquant Thai dressing. Though she expected to hear a knock on the door at any moment requesting Reggie come down to see her mother, none came. Even Reggie gave up expecting it, making no fuss about going off to bed, closing her eyes as though she wanted to escape the whole unhappy business.

After a stifling night, Carrie was aroused in the early hours by the wind. It gusted into her room at near gale force, lifting the sheer curtains so they danced with spectacular abandon, the edge of one catching an ornament and sending it crashing over.

"Damn and blast!" A little dizzy from the heat and humidity, Carrie pitched the pillow that had been tucked under her head out of the way and leapt out of bed, adrenaline pouring into her body. Now she could see the lightning that momentarily blinded her and bleached the world before disappearing into the walls of jungle. Hastily she closed one side of the French doors, catching the curtains back in their loops. Distant rumbles of thunder were swiftly coming closer.

After the trials of the evening why not a fierce storm? she thought a little desperately. A storm might clear the air but it could be dangerous. Not that she hadn't lived through many a bad electrical storm at home but she had never seen lightning like that. If her curtains were thrashing about wildly so would Reggie's. She didn't want the little girl awake and frightened. With the shutters secured inside the bedroom would be relatively calm and she had turned on the ceiling fan for coolness. The good thing was Reggie, childlike, could sleep through just about anything including morning calls to rouse her.

Without bothering to pull on her robe, Carrie took to the verandah rushing down its length to Reggie's room, starting back as hundreds of fruit bats who had been feeding on the mangoes, the bananas and the custard apples, flew screeching over the roof in their race for shelter. It did nothing to soothe her agitation. Her hand lifted to her throat as the crickets, the cicadas and the frogs joined in the general din. It all sounded barbarous, an assault on the senses. Lightning flashed again, then a great crack of thunder so loud she thought it might do permanent damage to her ears. Shudders ran up and down her spine. The force of the wind was whipping her long hair, making it sail around her. Her nightdress felt like it was going to be shredded to ribbons. The rain was coming down now. Huge drops that splattered. Even the rain was hot. She rushed for shelter, pitching headlong into someone emerging from Reggie's room…

For a moment he was as startled as she was, his heart

contracting before expanding, his arms locking around her, capturing her as if she were some wraith of the storm.

"Good God, what have I got here?" he murmured from a husky throat.

Such a question when no one absolutely no one else could have aroused such lavish arousal. She was just barely covered in the finest cotton, dressed up with little bits of ribbon and lace and tiny buttons that pressed into his chest. The nightdress was clinging to her body, scented with the nectar of her and the sharp blood-warm greenness of the rain. She didn't struggle. Indeed her bones seemed to turn to liquid so she was like silk in his arms. As they stood there, lightning blazed in the lacquer-black night, burning his downward view of her into his retina. Her breasts were barely masked by the feather-light fabric. They gleamed opalescent; the tips bruised a dark rose. He wanted to stoop and cup her breasts in his hands. He wanted to suckle the sweet budding nipples.

Catrina, he thought. My God, my heart!

Desire licked through his flesh; a frantic need for gratification. She was no sacrifice to his disturbed dangerous mood. He was in love with her. He had been from the moment he'd laid eyes on her. Everything leading him to that point in his life like a revelation. But there was danger for both of them in its driving force, the thought he couldn't stop. She was whispering to him, looking urgently toward the small figure of Reggie curled up sound asleep in her bed.

"I was going to close the shutters." Her breath came in little exhalations.

"My thought, too." Abruptly he released her, trying to beat back the desperation that was in him. "Why don't you move back onto the verandah while I do it? You'll have to change your nightdress anyway. It's damp."

He, on the other hand, was fully clothed. In fact he

hadn't gone to bed, too deeply disturbed by his ex-wife's visit and its implications for Regina.

Incredibly Sharon hadn't made an immediate request to see her child as almost any other mother in the world would have, saying she preferred to wait until morning to give Regina "a few early Christmas presents." She was, however, "absolutely ecstatic" to see him. A woman so ego-driven she couldn't see it was one of the great turn-offs of his life. Innocent little Reggie's birth had destroyed any tender feelings he might have had for Sharon though it took him eighteen months to find out for sure Reggie wasn't his.

Swiftly he closed the timber shutters leaving the French doors open for the heat. The verandahs were deep. Even in the worst of storms the full force of the rain didn't reach the central core of the house. Reggie was lost in her dreams. He hoped they were good.

His hand stretched out to take hers as he led Catrina back to her room. The spray from the rain, swirling a blue mist as the lightning lashed, enveloping them both, slicking their skin and wetting their clothes, but never cooling the waves of fire in the blood. They had barely reached Carrie's room before the force of his feelings overcame him. His arm cradled her back as he bent her over his arm.

"God, I want you!" he uttered, the soft moan edged with a trace of violence as passion and a self-imposed restraint warred within him. He lowered his head over hers, took her mouth, found it open and waiting, wet and tasting of rain. Her nightgown was plastered to her and he had the most powerful urge to ease it from her body. To hold her naked in his arms. He couldn't even hear the thunder that was cracking overhead so great was his own agitation. Just how much was a man supposed to take? To have this young woman under his roof. A young woman so good at communicating with his family, leading a troubled child with the gentlest of reins. To see her day in and day out. Dine with her at night, see her behind his eyelids as he finally closed his eyes for sleep.

As he withdrew his mouth momentarily to give her breath, something flickered on the periphery of his vision. In an instant he was alerted. Someone was moving along the verandah. A woman. He wasted no time. Now wasn't the moment for some shocking confrontation. With the tall curving fronds of the golden canes screening them he lifted Catrina clear off her feet and carried her back into her room.

"Go to bed!" he clipped off with so much urgency, Carrie found herself obeying. He sounded too remarkably sober for a seduction scene, a feat in itself after the tumultuous passion of his kiss. Even though she was all but soaked to the skin, she lay down on the extreme edge of the bed, watching him make short work of closing the other French door before shooting home the bolt.

It was beyond Carrie's understanding. A bizarre melodrama but despite that she trusted him with all her heart. Moments later with Royce standing well back in the dark recesses, a woman's figure appeared ghostlike outside Carrie's locked doors. It gave Carrie such a fright she uttered a strangled little cry in her throat that mercifully was lost in the turbulence of the night.

Sharon! Carrie had a moment of devastating revulsion.

She turned on her back, half closing her eyes and pretending sleep. The room turned luminous as another bolt of lightning zigzagged down the sky. Sharon stared in. Incredibly the doors rocked back and forth as she attempted to open them, but they held. When Carrie turned to look again, Sharon was gone.

Immediately Carrie dashed up, her body shaking, pulling the sheer curtains out of their loops and across the French doors. This was a first in her life.

"Is it possible your wife thought she was going to find you in my bed?" she demanded of the tall figure who moved out of the shadows to be near her.

"My *ex*-wife," he corrected, then inexplicably began to laugh, holding it in before it became a shout. "You have to hand it to that woman for sheer cheek!"

"No way is she *normal,*" Carrie breathed. "She didn't even want to see her own daughter. Would you like to try explaining all this?"

"Catrina, I haven't got the time," he mocked, "and it would drive me crazy."

"So we wait until she comes to the other door?"

He shook his head. "I hope you had the sense to lock up."

"Actually I did on account of her."

He nodded as if he understood exactly. "The time has passed for any reasonable talk with Sharon. I'm at the point of throwing her out."

"She's brought you a lot of misery, hasn't she?"

"Yes, but it's Reggie who has suffered the most." His voice was bleak.

"So what do we do now?" Carrie asked very quietly.

"I know what I'd like to do," he replied with black humour. "Take that nightgown off you and towel you dry."

She was mute for a moment, racked by little ripples that multiplied. "I'm not a child."

"You're telling me?" His low laugh was a shade harsh. "Failing that, I think I should pour myself a stiff drink."

"Well, I don't have one to offer you." Carrie shrugged helplessly. "Just as well. I might be persuaded to have one myself. But I will get out of this nightgown." She began to pad across the room, brought to a gasping halt as something pierced her foot. "Oh, no!"

''What is it?'' he questioned, in his frustration a little fierce.

''I've cut my foot.''

''How the devil could you do that?'' He sounded concerned but very restless.

''The curtain knocked over an ornament. I'm sorry.''

''That's okay, I'll take it out of your wages.'' Again a low laugh as though humour could reduce the tremendous electric charge between them. ''Here, come into the bathroom.'' He found her bare shoulder, couldn't resist palming it.

''I might get blood on the rug,'' she warned. The rug was superb. Persian.

''Okay, so I carry you.'' He swooped and lifted her, kissing her a little roughly but oh so sweetly on the mouth.

''I'm getting accustomed to this, Royce McQuillan,'' she said in a hushed voice. ''Be warned.''

''Maybe it's me who's thinking you'll never get away from me,'' he answered.

Inside the spacious en suite he closed the door first before turning on the light. He deposited her on the marble bench, before gently taking hold of her foot. ''This is what comes of running about in bare feet.'' He examined the soft area to the side of her instep. ''Damn there's a tiny fragment still in it. You're not chilled, are you?'' He dared a brief glance at her, desire still lashing at him.

''You're joking. I'm steaming.'' She gave a little laugh, reaching out for a hand towel, then patting her face and throat dry. ''You're even wetter than I am.'' Her voice shook a little as her own feelings crested. His hair gleamed blue-black in the bright light, curling into damp waves and curls. His skin had the perfect polish of bronze. The soft shirt he had worn at dinner was dyed a deeper blue by the rain. He had undone a couple of buttons and pulled the wet collar back. She could see his muscular chest, the fine whorls of dark hair that lightly matted it. Not only the cut on her foot was throbbing. Her whole body was. The two of them sealed off in this quiet room.

"That's what comes of making love in the rain," he answered her as he walked away to the wall cabinet where he found cotton wool, antiseptic and some bandaids. "Your feet are as beautiful as your hands," he remarked as he went about tending the wound.

"I've been hearing that since I was two days old." She smiled.

"Aren't *you* lucky?"

"You can't really believe that?" She sought his brilliant eyes, her heart beating madly.

"I do." He answered as though it mattered a great deal to him. "I can see into the future, Catrina, and my vision of you is good."

"Do you believe in destiny?" she asked, her voice very soft.

"I surely do." He opened up. "It was my parents' destiny to die together in a plane crash. It was my destiny to marry Sharon and later divorce her. Gran keeps telling me fate is going to step in again, this time with the right woman. The woman who will put me under her spell from the moment I lay eyes on her."

Look at me. Look at me, Carrie begged silently. She had given him her heart. She couldn't take it back.

"Do you know her name?" she asked, her voice so faint she wondered if she had spoken at all.

"Suzanne." He plucked a name from the top of his head, his smile teasing.

"Really?" She searched his face with her great golden eyes, seeing the sparkle of humour.

"We can't stay here, Catrina, you know that." His senses were swimming with her nearness and the sight of her lovely body, much too lightly veiled. Her soft heavy hair was falling loosely, radiantly all around her shoulders, drying fast in the heat, her long legs naked, the skirt of her nightgown rucked up to her fine-boned knees. She looked sexy beyond belief, yet so young and innocent.

"Have you ever had a lover?" he found himself asking, his voice dropping in pitch.

She closed her eyes thinking if she kept them open he couldn't fail to see she was hopelessly, madly in love with him. "No," she answered truthfully. I thought I'd been made love to but I've since learned I was wrong about that. She opened her eyes again and stared back at him. "You make me sad, Royce McQuillan."

"I don't believe that. I can't." His fingers pressed gently on the pulse in her throat.

"Then why do you twist my heart?"

The admission made his senses soar. "Do I?" He was barely aware he moved, yet his hand reached out to caress her breast, pushing aside the low neck of her nightgown to find her seductive silky flesh. "Carrie, what am I doing?" he groaned. He was like a man split in two. One part of him wanted to let her go back to her virginal bed, the other thought there was no possible way he could let her.

She was luring him on, her hands reaching out to clutch his shoulders as he stroked her breast, her head tipped back, her back arching at the pleasure his hands were giving her.

"You are so beautiful!" He heard his own voice purr into her ear as his mouth began to track across her face, covering it with kisses…her throat…the upper swell of her breasts. He couldn't get enough of her.

She gasped when his mouth found her erect nipple, her body for a moment going rigid with that deep inhalation. He lifted his head, trying to contain himself to the point he was sure of her reactions but she cried out softly,

''Please don't stop!'' Sensation after sensation was flashing down her spine, the pleasure so intense it was almost a pain too great to bear.

''I can't do this,'' he said after fevered minutes, even as he lifted her, crushing her in his arms. ''I can't do it. Stop me.'' It was a cry of anguish torn from his lips. The very air vibrated around them, thrumming with shocked sexual pleasure and his violent arousal. She had to stop him. Before it was too late.

It seemed an eternity before Carrie could respond. Her every desire, her every need, her every want was for him. His hands were gripping her hips as she clung to him, his long fingers splayed toward the apex of her body that was contracting sharply in the throes of intense physical excitement.

''I'm sorry...sorry...'' Her knees were almost buckling under her but she somehow managed to fall back against the door.

''God, what have you got to be sorry about,'' he muttered through white clenched teeth. ''I'm acting like a man possessed.'' He raked his hand through his hair.

''I offered myself to you.'' Carrie took her share of responsibility for the explosive loss of control.

''And I'm going to take you, Catrina,'' he promised harshly, ''but it's going to be the right place and the right time. I couldn't bear it if you came to hate me.''

Her mind reeled at the very thought. Hate him? She loved him. Nothing to be done about it. ''How could you say such a thing? You've changed my whole existence.''

''Complicated it, too.'' His striking face was sombre. ''There are things I haven't told you, Catrina. Information I've denied you. But I've felt like a man caged.''

''Then tell me now.'' Her face radiated an intense urge to help.

''Not *now.*'' His smile twisted. ''I can't be with you

like this. My whole mind and body is focused on making love to you. But I couldn't bear to trap you. It's going to be a bad day ahead. I feel it like a black reality—Sharon is a sick unstable woman. For years now my whole experience of her has been either elation or depression. Whatever happens, I don't want you to leave. Promise me?'' He touched her cheek.

''Nothing easier.'' She stared up into his brilliant eyes. ''I won't.''

''I'll hold you to that.'' He smiled grimly, then reached past her to open the door.

''Is Mummy going to want to see me this morning?'' Reggie asked, wringing Carrie's heart. She was laying out the child's clothes. The best outfit she could find. Good quality but dull. Carrie determined on a trip into town in the near future where she could buy the little girl some of the latest gear for children. Bright colours, bright patterns. There were some marvellous labels for kids. She would have Reggie's hair cut while she was at it. Reggie truly did have great hair but it fell into the fairly unmanageable category being thick and extra crinkly-curly. Both her mother and father had very dark hair, Royce McQuillan's blue-black, Sharon's a deep sable. Reggie's was pretty much nondescript, which was unusual. But she could change that when she was much older with the use of colour. Reggie was clever and funny, often hilarious, and Carrie had grown very fond of her. ''Let's go downstairs and see.'' Carrie had come to her decision. ''The two of us can't hide away up here. What do you say?''

Reggie pulled the blouse over her head and grinned. ''Suits me. I haven't seen Mummy in ages.''

''So we're going to show her what a debonair little girl you can be?''

''What's debonair?'' asked Reggie.

''It means you have very charming manners and you're cheerful.''

''That's me.''

After the storm of the night before, it was a brilliant day outside, the sun slanting through the front door into the lobby. Holding Reggie's hand, Carrie made her way down to the informal dining room where she found Sharon and Lindsey seated together. Both looked up, their faces cold and without welcome.

''Good morning.'' Carrie spoke pleasantly, expecting Reggie to let go of her hand and rush toward her mother.

It didn't happen. Reggie continued to cling to her side and instead of holding out her arms, Sharon McQuillan addressed Carrie.

''So, the new governess, so beautiful and so talented! You never had the guts to admit who you were.''

It was quite a frontal attack but Carrie didn't waver. ''I'm sorry, you confuse me, Mrs. McQuillan. You speak as though I'd committed a crime?''

''Well, haven't you? Running after Royce. Where the hell was he last night?''

''I suggest you ask him,'' Carrie answered calmly. ''I'll go away. I thought you might want to speak to your daughter?''

''No, don't go away,'' Sharon suddenly thundered, not able to hold back her jealousy and anger. ''My child doesn't need a governess. I'm here to take her away.''

''Sharon?'' Lindsey flung the other woman a startled glance.

''You keep out of this, Lyn,'' Sharon warned. ''This is *me,* remember. I'm awake to you. I just use you when I need information.''

Lindsey stood up. ''Really? I don't have to listen to this.''

''Then clear off.''

So much for mother love. So much for making the decision to come downstairs. "I'll bring Reggie back at another time," Carrie volunteered.

"Oooooooh, Reggie! What sort of name is that?" Sharon shouted.

"It's *my* name," Reggie answered with more than a touch of her old belligerence, surveying her mother's thin, glamorous figure, dressed in a pink silk shirt and matching narrow-legged trousers. "Aren't you happy to see me at all?"

"And what exactly is *your* greeting?" Sharon countered fiercely. "You have no manners at all. Come here and kiss me."

"I don't want to." Reggie shuffled her feet, a child trying to protect herself from further abuse.

"Reggie hasn't had her breakfast, Mrs. McQuillan," Carrie said, thinking it very necessary to get the little girl away. "I'll take her to the kitchen."

"And who the bloody hell are you?" Sharon asked coldly.

"She's my governess," Reggie shouted. "I love her and you give me the creeps."

Immediately Sharon was on her feet, rushing toward her daughter as though she intended to smack her, but before she could even make it halfway Royce McQuillan's menacing voice brought her up short.

"Cool it, Sharon, for God's sake!" He strode into the room, a tall daunting figure dressed in his everyday working gear of bush shirt, bandana, silver-buckled belt laced into jeans, the cattleman's elastic-sided riding boots on his feet. "Catrina—" he shot a piercing look at her "—take Reggie to the kitchen if she hadn't had her breakfast."

"I'm going." Lindsey flashed past him. "There's no place for me."

"Not any longer, Lyn," Royce McQuillan clipped off. "My family has received no loyalty from you."

"I never knew she was so mean," Lindsey cried, pointing a finger at Sharon. "She's mean, mean, mean. I've never known anyone so locked in on themselves."

"Let's go, Reggie," Carrie said to the little girl quietly, disturbed that the child was cowering against her. It wasn't her spunky little Reggie.

"Come on, sweetheart."

"How lucky you are to have this wonderful young woman as a governess, Royce," Sharon cried. "Have you had her in your bed yet?"

Carrie fled, keeping her hands over the little girl's ears until they were well out of earshot. Inside the kitchen she had to take a deep breath to steady herself. "It's all right, Reggie."

No response at all from Reggie but she continued to hold tightly to Carrie's hand. "Come on, love, let's make a smoothie," Carrie suggested, her voice as soft as velvet.

"I'm ashamed of my mother," Reggie said, suddenly responding to Carrie's stroking her head. "Isn't she awful?"

Perfectly odious, Carrie thought, but she couldn't possibly say. "She's angry about something, Reggie. Anger makes people out of tune with the world."

"I hope I don't have to go and live with her."

"I'm sure your father won't allow anything you don't want, Reggie." Carrie rubbed the little fingers between her own. Good fingers, very nimble. What had happened to her couldn't stand in the way of her helping others. She could teach Reggie to play. It could make the little girl very happy.

They were standing at the blender when Mrs. Gainsford hurried back into the kitchen. "My goodness!" She turned a panic-stricken face to them, chewing hard on her lip. It was obvious she was about to say more but Carrie signalled her with a shake of her head not to. ''It's a pawpaw smoothie this morning, Mrs. Gainsford,'' she tried to speak normally. ''This one is perfect. It looks like you've just picked it.''

''I did, dear. It survived the storm. It's the bats that are the problem. We have to keep the fruit covered.'' The housekeeper hurried over, smiling at Reggie. ''What about a scoop of ice cream in it this morning?'' Her voice was as gentle as either Carrie or the child had heard it.

''Thank you, Mrs. Gainsford,'' Reggie said.

''Carrie, I left a basket of fresh eggs on the chinese table in the hall.'' Mrs. Gainsford turned her head. ''Would you mind getting them for me, dear?''

''No problem.'' Carrie could see the housekeeper was deeply embarrassed and unwilling to venture outside her own domain. ''I'll be back in a moment, Reggie.''

''I'll look after her,'' Mrs. Gainsford said, going to the refrigerator. ''Coconut or caramel ice cream, Regina?''

Very quietly Carrie made her way outside, hearing Sharon cry out, ''I don't care what you think... You're the big man. So powerful! But this is one time you don't have any power over me because Regina isn't yours. *She's not your child!*''

In the ringing silence that followed Carrie felt too paralysed to move away.

''Watch out for me, Sharon,'' Royce McQuillan said in a voice so deadly Carrie came out of her stupor.

She found herself rushing down the corridor to the dining room trying to hold to her promise to Louise McQuillan to keep the family safe. She could hear Sharon babbling on almost incoherently, as she burst into the room.

''What are you trying to do, Mrs. McQuillan?'' Carrie

cried. ''Reggie might hear you. I tell you you'll break her heart.''

''You have to leave here, Sharon,'' Royce McQuillan said. ''That means today. I sure don't know what your real reason for coming here was.''

That was too much for Sharon. She burst out laughing. ''Why to check out your little girlfriend, darling. Lyn told me she'd fallen in love with you just like the others.''

''Did she tell you I've fallen in love with Catrina?'' he rasped. ''Of course not. Neither of you would want to believe it. But I've finally found out about love. It took a while.''

Sharon blanched. ''You just want her because she's young and beautiful. It will wear off, I promise.''

Whatever Royce intended to say it was forestalled by Mrs. Gainsford's shout.

''Regina!'' she cried.

Only she had seen the little girl race through the front door, moaning to herself at what she had heard.

The housekeeper cried out again in a blind panic, consumed by guilt for having turned her back for a minute, only this time all three adults had converged on the lobby, Royce demanding of the woman what was going on.

Carrie knew. She couldn't explain how she knew. But she knew. ''The lagoon.'' She flung a glance of such anxiety at Royce he took to his heels with Carrie racing after him, fear lending her wings.

They both looked on in total anguish as the child ran headlong down the slope, not stumbling as they desperately hoped, but making swiftly, surely for the glittering emerald waters of the lagoon.

''Reggie!'' Royce McQuillan shouted with the full force of his lungs. ''Stop. Reggie, stop.'' His face contorted with dread.

But the little girl ran on, plunging into the lake and disappearing instantly from view.

''Reggie!'' Carrie screamed in an agony. This couldn't be happening. This was anyone's nightmare.

Royce with his galvanic burst of speed far outstripped her so she was able to watch him dive into the lagoon where he, too, disappeared as the sparkling waters of the lagoon closed over him.

Carrie ran on desperately, propelled without incident across the thick grass, still soggy from the storm. When she reached the water she fell into it, surprised at its depth, then dived. Crystal-clear on top, beneath was terrifyingly murky sediment rising from the bottom now that three bodies were in the water. She shot to the surface to take a breath, preparing to dive again only Royce rose from the middle of the lagoon with the child in his arms.

''Oh, thank God!'' the words were ripped from her throat. Frantically Carrie swam toward them but he urged her back. ''Get out of the water, Carrie,'' he called. ''Get a blanket.''

Somehow Jada was there, spreading a rug on the grass as Royce emerged with the child and immediately began to put his training into practice. Big stations were life and death places. It wasn't the first time he'd been on hand at a near drowning. There was no sign of Sharon. Mrs. Gainsford and Lindsey huddled together a distance away, both of them looking white and shocked, overcome by the drama.

While they all prayed, Royce started CPR, continuing until Reggie began to splutter and retch up lagoon water.

Carrie was on her knees beside the child, tears pouring down her cheeks, whispering over and over, ''Reggie!'' She thought she had endured agony with the loss of her career yet here was a little girl so damaged by adult cruelty she had given up on life. It put everything into perspective.

Racing down the slope came Royce's overseer, with two of the stockman and the young jackeroo, Tim Barton. All of them looked deeply shocked.

''God, Royce!'' the overseer spoke. ''Will we get a doctor?''

''She's all right now. I don't think she needs one.'' Royce turned his head to speak to them. ''She wasn't in the water long but I'll get her up to the house and tucked into bed.'' He rose with the little girl in his arms, his handsome face showing all the signs of a profound anger and distress. ''Carrie, get that rug around you.'' He turned his head, his eyes whipping over her.

Tim moved swiftly, settling the rug Jada passed him around Carrie's shoulders. She was paper-white with shock. Tim felt helpless. What had gone on here this morning? They all knew the ex-wife, Sharon, was on the station. For a beautiful woman, and Tim had met Sharon McQuillan twice in his life, there wasn't one person he knew who liked her, including his own father. More important, where was the mother now? Tim looked around. No sign of her. Why wasn't she holding her child? Why wasn't she crying as Carrie was? Nothing made sense to Tim. He looked on with mingled horror and fascination. This was one dysfunctional family! For all he admired the coolest dude he had ever met in his life. Royce McQuillan.

CHAPTER NINE

IT TOOK weeks for Reggie to recover from her ordeal. Years later with Reggie, happy and confident, performing brilliantly both academically and with her music studies, both Carrie and Royce considered the healing began with the piano lessons. The cover of the Steinway had come off and Carrie began to teach the little girl to play. Carrie wasn't looking for big results. This was therapy; an all-out effort to divert Reggie's mind from her sad thoughts. What Carrie hadn't expected was for Reggie to take to the keyboard like a duck takes to water, so by Christmas of that momentous year Reggie was eagerly looking forward to her lessons which she had twice a day to make progress swift.

Without slowing down to identify notation—that could come later—Carrie played little pieces, letting the child watch her hands. As a crash course it had big results. More satisfying to Carrie was the way Reggie showed every sign of being a "true" musician, wrapping herself in an armchair every time Carrie sat down to play, her small face intent and filled with delight. Their music became a marvellous common ground. Indeed Carrie's playing caused family spirits to soar. Even the workers around the homestead found it difficult not to stop work and listen.

As for Sharon, ashen-faced and badly shaken, she had flown out of Maramba the same afternoon as "Reggie's dip," which was the way the family, including Reggie, referred to it. The whole incident of necessity had to be played down. But before departing Sharon had emptied out all her own bitter resentments telling them all near hysterically, she didn't blame herself in the least for what had happened. She felt no responsibility for what Reggie had overheard. The child was an inveterate eavesdropper, picking up things she was never intended to hear. Redemption for Sharon may have lain in acceptance and remorse. Sharon chose the stony path of denial. Whatever transpired between Royce and his ex-wife, Carrie never did find out. All she did learn was Sharon had given up all claim to her child. There was no place in Sharon's busy life for Reggie. Her birth had been "a terrible accident." As far as Sharon was concerned, Reggie could continue to be brought up as a McQuillan. No one was going to hear the story from her. She had a reputation to guard after all. Royce swore she actually said that. Sharon had no sense of irony.

The greatest hurdle lay in Royce's explaining to Reggie just how life was, and the reasons he had kept so much from her, even allowing for her tender years. Royce was able to do this during a quiet discussion with the disturbed little girl, who had all but disappeared behind a fortress in an effort to protect herself. Nevertheless he managed to convince her she was his little girl "by choice." So he wasn't her birth father? They both had to accept that. But in every other respect she was. She was his daughter. He loved her. He wanted her. He would have had a huge problem with her going away with her mother.

As the weeks went by Reggie, mature beyond her years, came within reaching distance of acceptance. She was Regina McQuillan. Maramba was her home. Royce was her dad. She even began to call him that, tentatively at first then it became second nature. Carrie, it became abundantly clear, was very important in the scheme of things. Reggie looked to her for guidance, support and unstinting affection.

At the dawn of Christmas morning, just as they planned, Royce and Carrie took the horses and rode out to the open savannah that stretched away in all directions. This was private time for themselves. Time they desperately needed as their hunger for each other was profound. The homestead was full of Royce's relatives and more were expected to fly in later on in the morning. The extended McQuillan family always made a big thing of Christmas, coming back to the ancestral home for the celebration. This year Cameron and Lindsey would be missing from the festivities. They were currently in Europe enjoying an extended holiday. The matriach, Louise McQuillan who was feeling so much better these days with many burdens off her mind was greatly looking forward to a week long of family. All everyone wanted was for the rain to hold off. This was the start of the Wet. The wild bush heralded it by putting on a phenomenal floral display.

For some miles Royce and Carrie rode over dense wild green herbage scattered with countless little mauve and violet wildflowers. Parrots flashed by in their legions, their colours more brilliant than precious jewels, landing a distance ahead to feed on the abundant seeds and the sea of grasses whose multitude of greens changed shades with the direction of the dawn wind. The peace of the morning was magical. Across the vast open valley sleek Brahmins stood belly-high in the vivid green grasses, turning their heads slowly at their presence. The big muster involving all hands was over in readiness for the Wet. The cattle had been brought in from all points of the station.

On the return ride they came to a curving lagoon where the air was heavy with the scent of wild passionfruit. Prolific vines moored an old fence that had once been part of a holding yard, the globular fruit gleaming a rich purple in the sunlight.

"I want to show you something." Royce turned his head to speak to Carrie, a kind of urgency in his voice.

"We can dismount over there by the fig." He pointed to a massive tree with soaring flying buttresses.

Ducks and black swans in among the pink waterlilies on the sparkling sheet of water, the lilies held their heads high above the water. Some were delicately flushed with red. It gave Carrie a near mystical experience as pleasure flooded through her. She slipped down into Royce's waiting arms. This could only happen once in a lifetime, she thought. If at all. Every time he looked at her it was like actual physical contact. When he did touch her, her whole body sang. It was as if she had shed an outer layer of skin, revealing another all satiny new, infinitely susceptible to sensation. She had never felt voluptuous in her life. Now she revelled in her own skin. And all because of this man.

He bent his head to kiss her until she was shaking in his arms. "Last night the urge to come to you was so bad I spent most of it pacing the floor," he confessed. "I love you, Catrina. No one else will do," he proclaimed, his brilliant eyes holding hers.

"So there *is* such a thing as perfect love?" she whispered, her arms locking around his neck.

"Don't let anyone tell you any different," he answered, enchanted by her response. "You've changed my life. You *are* my life. What I can't take is not being your lover." He reached into the breast pocket of his shirt, pulling out a small box. He looked down into her face as a man looks at a woman he loves and wants. "This says *marry me.*"

"Does it?" Carrie heard her voice quiver before she started to cry.

"Darling!" He gathered her to him, rocking her gently in his arms. "You mustn't do that. I want to make you *happy.*"

"But you do!" Carrie dashed the emotional tears from her eyes. "I love you with all my heart."

"So open the box," he urged, his deep voice indulgent.

"I can't wait to hear what you think. I had the jeweller send me designs. I specified the stones. This is the result."

Carrie opened the box, releasing a little gasp. "I'm dreaming!"

"No you're not," he said vibrantly, the radiance of her expression taking his breath away.

"It's so beautiful, Royce. So precious." She stared up at him with huge golden eyes.

"It's *exactly* the ring for you." He took her left hand, kissed it, then slid home her engagement ring. It was of exquisite design, featuring a superb central stone, the famous Argyle cognac coloured diamond from Western Australia, flanked by glittering ice white pave set diamonds in a white-gold band. It was a very beautiful, valuable ring. "The cognac diamond, beautiful as it is, is no match for your eyes," he told her, catching their glitter.

"Oh, Royce!" She was consumed by a euphoria that had her hiding her head against his chest. "Thank you. Thank you. I love it. I love *you.*"

He let her sob for a full minute before laughter and a wonderful warmth got the better of him.

"Catrina, sweetheart!" He grasped a handful of her hair, making her look up.

"Don't you know women cry when they're ecstatic?" she asked him. "It's almost the rule."

His low laugh was full of an answering love and a certain exultance. "I can just picture you when our son is born."

"Oh, yes!" Carrie breathed, throwing up her arms to the cloudless blue heavens in one graceful sweep. "How is it possible to love someone so much?" she marvelled.

His response was thrilling and immediate. "I'll show you when we're curled up in bed," he promised tenderly.

Like an omen, a breeze sprang up from nowhere. It shook out the flowering gums that grew near the lagoon, scattering them with golden blossom that settled on their hair and their shoulders. Exactly like confetti.

Strategy for Marriage

MARGARET WAY

CHAPTER ONE

Deakin-McKinnon Wedding
Reception—McKinnon Riverside Mansion
Brisbane, Queensland

"ASHE, darling, who is that girl?" The blonde in the exquisite green dress?" Mercedes, his aunt by marriage and mother of the bride, dug him in the ribs, a worried frown on her brow.

"You mean Ms. Botticelli?" His answer, even to his ears, was sardonic. "I've been wondering the same thing." In fact he'd begun to marvel at just the amount of attention he was giving that particular young woman and was amazed at the unprecedented thrust of sexual desire she aroused in him. He'd grown cynical, really cynical, about a woman's beauty and her ability to hold a man spellbound. Beautiful women in the style of this blonde reminded him of his runaway mother. The mother he'd hated and ached for since she'd abandoned him and his father when he was ten years old.

"No one on our side seems to know her," Mercedes whispered with genuine concern, her fingers fidgeting with her extremely valuable string of 19 mm Australian South Sea pearls, the finest in the world. "That is to say everyone I've asked. Oh for heaven's sake why am I worried?" She gave a false little laugh. "It's not as though she isn't beautiful and well behaved but I mean it's fairly obvious our dear Josh seems to know her even if he's not going anywhere near her. Would you mind awfully, darling, getting some idea of who exactly she is?''

The fact was he'd been about to make his move. For one thing ''our dear Josh'' was the bridegroom. A possible ex-girlfriend didn't help. ''No problem, Mercedes.'' He smiled down at her. ''Leave it to me.'' He was extremely fond of Mercedes, and his quiet little cousin, Callista, who looked as radiant as she could ever look on this day of days. Sad to say he hadn't taken to her new husband, Josh Deakin. In his most suspicious moments, which were frequent, he was a suspicious person, he thought Deakin the male equivalent of the proverbial gold-digger. At one time he'd very nearly said so, worried Deakin was only after Callista's money. The problem was Mercedes was very taken with him and Callista was clearly head over heels in love. She wouldn't have listened. She'd have dug in her heels. Although Callista dearly loved her mother, at twenty-nine she was anxious to escape the nest, get married and set up her own home. This was a fairytale wedding he'd been told. Who believed in fairytales? Certainly not him, though he had to admit Ms. Botticelli looked magical.

Mercedes' rich contralto brought him out of his reverie. ''Everything is going marvellously,'' she said as though at any moment all could change. ''The last thing we need is for something—um-um—'' She stared across the crowded room at the beautiful blonde, seeking the right word.

''Don't fret. I told you I'd handle it,'' he soothed, hoping to God it wasn't already all too late. But if Deakin imagined Mercedes and Callista didn't have someone looking out for them, he'd better think again.

''You're my great support, Ashe,'' Mercedes told him fondly. ''I'm afraid I lean on you for so much.''

''We're family, Mercedes,'' he offered lightly when he

didn't feel lightly about family at all. He was head of a clan even if his immediate family had gone. His mother with her lover. They lived mostly in New York. His father and his uncle Sholto, Mercedes' late husband, had been killed in a light plane crash five years ago. An event that made some people say the family was cursed. Maybe it was. It had had its fair share of tragedies. So in his late twenties he had become head of the family, head of the McKinnon pastoral empire, executor of the Family Trust. He took his responsibilities very seriously.

As Mercedes, in a very becoming silvery outfit, sailed off towards her guests he acknowledged he hadn't told her he'd had his eye on Ms. Botticelli since she'd gatecrashed the reception. His well-honed instincts warned him that was the case but he didn't want to put a blight on such a day by overreacting. He'd take his time. She'd done it in the cheekiest way possible. Two ushers were guarding the open double doors of the McKinnon mansion taking the wedding invitations from the guests and checking them against their lists when he spotted her arrival from the head of the gallery. He couldn't look away. He who was very good at taking a woman's beauty and aura in his stride. She was tall, even taller in high-heeled sandals. She wore a ravishingly pretty dress, a froth of chiffon, printed in a swirl of different greens. The crossover sleeveless bodice showed a tantalising glimpse of the curves of her breasts, the short ruffled skirt sprinkled with glittering little beads showed off her lovely long legs. High up on one shoulder was a huge rose made out of the same material sprinkled with brilliants like the skirt. It was an outfit only a beautiful young woman with a perfect figure and lots of self-confidence could wear without risking the dress overwhelming her.

So there she was. A long-stemmed mystery blonde, her hair drawn back from her face into a high knot, the rest of her mane cascading down her back to past her shoulder blades. The overhead chandelier, plus the last rays of sunshine, washed her in light, so she gave off a spectacular sparkle. Her skin, he could see clearly, was a smooth textured cream, blushed over the high cheekbones. There was a shallow cleft in her chin; her eyes even at this distance were a clear light green set at a faint slant as were her darkened brows. She looked excited, a beautiful young thing who inexplicably had no partner, so why did he get the odd feeling all the animation didn't spell happy. Far from it. More like nerve-ridden. He moved further down the staircase feeling another hot surge of desire. It made him irrationally hostile even as it served to remind him he was human.

Who was she exactly? How did she fit in? He thought he knew all of Callista's friends. God knows she and Mercedes had tried to match him up to quite a few, not even listening when he warned them off. He saw her make a little play of rummaging in her glittery purse for her invitation—but then she saw across the marble floored atrium someone she knew. Her face broke into a lovely infectious smile and she waved, calling a name. Instantly, tactfully, the ushers let the beautiful creature go in. Women like that were unmistakably Somebody. Anyone could see that. As a bit of play-acting it was darn near perfect.

Just as he suspected, she didn't head towards anyone in particular. There was no one waiting for her. She walked right on, flashing iridescent glances around the elegant entrance hall massed with flowers. She hadn't been at the church. No way he would have missed her. But she'd turned up at the reception. Interesting! It wasn't a sit-down affair where guests were allotted seats at a table. That might have proved a mite difficult even for an enterprising young woman. Instead a sumptuous buffet had been arranged. It was to be served from the huge bridal marquees that had been erected in the three-acre garden. The dessert table alone Mercedes had told him was one hundred foot long. Mercedes had spared no expense to make this a great day for her only child.

Now they had a gatecrasher. Albeit a woman whose beauty had made the breath catch in his throat. That alone made him laugh and his laugh was deep with self-mockery. In his action-packed life he had no time for a woman who could keep a man in thrall. He had too much on his mind. Too much to do. This woman was Trouble. Moreover she was somehow connected to Josh Deakin, his cousin's bridegroom of only a few hours. The ex-girlfriend immediately sprang to mind. An ex-girlfriend perhaps bent on some kind of disruption. No way! He had the sure feeling at some point he would have to hustle Ms. Botticelli out of the house. And that was quite a while before Mercedes had put voice to her own niggling concerns.

Christy, sick with nerves but too angry and upset to abort her mission, made it through the front door of the two-story McKinnon mansion. Her nerve was holding. It was a shocking breach of etiquette to gatecrash a wedding. On so many levels she deeply regretted it, but her ex-boyfriend, Josh, the man who had convinced her he loved her, deserved a good fright. She had no intention whatsoever of upsetting the bride, the McKinnon heiress. The bride was probably a young woman as gullible as herself. Josh, after all, was all charm on the surface. The only difference between her and the bride was around 15 million, not to mention what that fortunate young woman would eventually inherit from her mother, Mrs. Mercedes McKinnon, a woman of considerable substance and the widow of the late Sholto McKinnon, well-known pastoralist and philanthropist. While Josh had been courting his heiress, he'd also continued his ardent courtship of her. How many times had he told her he loved her? How many times had he brought up the subject of marriage? She'd seriously been considering entering into an engagement. Six months of having a lovely time together. *Fun* really. In retrospect no depth. It all came to a halt when by sheer chance she saw Josh kissing another woman outside the very law courts that figured so often in his fund of amusing stories. Josh was an up-and-coming lawyer. The young woman turned out to be today's bride, Callista McKinnon, now Mrs. Josh Deakin. Even as Josh had been proclaiming his love for her, he'd been courting the heiress. Fate had played its hand. Mrs. Mercedes McKinnon, a favoured client of the prestigious law firm where Josh worked as an associate, came into the offices one day bringing her petite, pretty daughter, Callista. Josh was especially good with female clients so his boss allowed him in on proceedings. It had to be that very day Josh realized a golden opportunity had opened up for him. With a rich wife the world was his oyster. Josh was very ambitious. Money was important to him. *Real money.* Social position. Obviously he saw an instant rocketing up the ladder. She had never fully understood that side of Josh. Not that she had really known him at all. He was a liar for one. A traitor. A good actor who could excel in any number of parts. The very worst aspect was as he told her about his plans to marry Callista he spoke like a man who had come into a huge lottery win. A win they were *both* going to share. She'd have died before accepting that shocking lack of integrity. Josh Deakin, cad that he was, had earned himself this lesson. But she still couldn't stop her nerves crackling.

Halfway across the gracious entrance hall, a perfect setting for valuable antiques and magnificent arrangements of fresh flowers, she became aware she was under close surveillance. She couldn't fail to know by now her blond good looks attracted attention but the gaze that was concentrated on her didn't send out any currents of admiration. It felt more like she was under an extremely daunting inspection. And found suspect. Her senses were so wired she was drawn to look upwards, searching out the origin of that magnetic beam.

Her green eyes widened in shock. Her gaze honed in a man standing at the curve of the elegant staircase, looking down at her with brilliant near-black eyes.

Ashe McKinnon.

It took her less than an instant to recognise him. He was even more damn-your-eyes handsome and arrogant than his photographs. After Josh had told her of his plan to marry into the McKinnon clan, she had felt upset enough to make it her business to find out what she could about them. And there was plenty. They were a pioneering dynasty. Cattle kings from colonial times who had generated great wealth. She'd seen photographs of the current McKinnon and his ancestral home in Channel Country South West Queensland. It was a magnificent homestead. There were photographs of him at different functions, including a brilliant action shot of him playing polo, arm thrown back for a full free swing. She'd know him anywhere. In fact the sight of him gave her the oddest sick thrill. He didn't look a kind man. Far from it. He looked formidable. Certainly not the sort of man who'd tolerate having a gatecrasher at his cousin's wedding.

Christy moved swiftly. All she wanted was the opportunity, however brief, to give Josh the fright of his life. The most she intended was to give him a little wave. Then she'd go home happy, or as happy as a girl could be when a man had humiliated her. She hadn't written Ashe McKinnon into the scenario at all. A huge mistake. She had the shivery feeling he could catch up with her very soon. Christy made her way into the opulent living room, impressed despite herself at the decor and the magnificent artworks on the walls.

"A friend of the groom?" an attractive voice queried at her ear. She spun on her high heels relieved beyond words to see a tall red-haired young man beaming down at her, his bright blue eyes filled with the sort of admiring look she was used to.

She was safe for a while. She intended to stay until she had her little moment of revenge on Josh, and Ashe McKinnon, the big cattle baron, could go to hell.

Of course she had no difficulty easing herself in. Not with that intoxicating image. From the open glass doorway leading into the plant-filled solarium Ashe watched her, openly marvelling at her audacity. He saw all the bachelors in sight make their moves on her. He couldn't believe his response. It angered him. He wanted to tell Jake Reid, a guy he'd known all his life, to take his big hands off her. Even the muscles in his shoulders tensed. This was so unlike him.

The solarium had been turned into a ballroom. Lots of couples had taken the floor to a plethora of styles that ranged from old-fashioned elegance to near gallops. He waited his moment, subtly keeping an eye on her, then he excused himself from the group around him.

"Pardon me." He tapped his friend, Tim Westbury, on the shoulder. "I really ought to introduce myself to your partner."

"Heck, Ashe, we were having such a good time."

For a moment it looked like Tim was going to hang in there until he saw his expression.

"So I noticed. Goodbye, Tim."

"Catch you later, Christy," Tim called before he was swept away by his current girlfriend who eyed "Christy" balefully.

"Wonderful party." He put his arm around her, a strange pleasure, and inhaled her fragrance, freesias spiked with something citrus.

"Wonderful," she agreed, turning her face away, all poise when her heart was thumping with fright.

"Beautiful wedding ceremony."

"It brought tears to my eyes."

"Truly?"

"I never lie."

"Perhaps you have on this occasion. I had the notion you weren't at the church at all. Ashe McKinnon, by the way. I'm Callista's cousin."

She frowned slightly, her eyes as green as peridots. "You don't look in the least alike." It was hard not to be impressed by him. Aesthetically anyway. How best to describe him? All commanding male. A touch severe. Yet the kind of man women went wild over. Not her. She already knew he was too tough for her, but he did look wonderful in his formal morning suit, traditional grey with a very dashing burgundy silk cravat.

She knew from her partner, Tim, he had given the bride away. Head of the family and all that. He certainly looked the part. His height alone made him stand out. He was well over six feet, but lean, powerful. He made her feel small and at five-eight she was tall for a woman. She could feel the whipcord musculature in his arms and along his back. He was very strong.

Christy continued her abstract inspection. A deep permanent tan, not Josh's beach boy stuff, Ashe's was trademark Outback. He had lustrous black hair with a natural wave. If he let it grow a centimetre longer it would spring into curls. His eyes were really beautiful, brilliant like glittering whirlpools. She couldn't see into them but he seemed to be looking right through her.

He wasn't a sweet man. Or a man who would make a woman feel safe. He looked dangerous enough to be treated with caution. There was so much tension there. A hard impatience that was communicating itself to her. Then again he possessed a stand-apart elegance, very much in keeping with a glamorous member of the landed elite. No question about his pedigree. And he just *knew* about her. So what was he going to do, throw her out? For all he knew she could put up a struggle. Or maybe he had taken her measure. There was only one person she intended to embarrass and that was Josh.

He received her long scrutiny, totally unfazed. "I'm dying to know your name," he prompted, dark voice sardonic.

"You have only to ask me. Christine Parker. My friends call me Christy."

Her answer was gentle and low. Music. Another ace up her sleeve.

"Then I'll call you Miss Parker. Are you a friend of the bridegroom, may I ask?" He slid his hand along her back with the surety she had a beautiful supple body.

"Now why does that sound like you've thrown out a challenge?" she parried.

"Possibly because you're the sort of woman who responds to one."

"I mean no harm, Mr. McKinnon. I want you to understand that."

"I'm pleased to hear it." He gave her a sardonic glance. "I can't have you spoiling my cousin's day."

"I have no intention of doing anything like that," she protested. "There's no spite in my nature."

"But you're looking to upset Deakin?"

''Now you sound like you don't care.'' It was wonderful to be able to challenge him. There was something very dangerous about being close to this man. It gave her quite a jolt. In her altered state she compared it to shock therapy. Something was happening to her. She didn't know what.

''My only concern is this reception goes off beautifully,'' he said in a warning voice that left her flushed. ''I'm devoted to my aunt and cousin.''

''Really?'' All of a sudden Christy needed to lash out, her anger and humiliation festering. ''From the look of you I wouldn't have thought you had a tender bone in your body.''

''Play it cool, Miss Parker,'' he said.

There was considerable heat between them. Christy realised with a sense of astonishment a lot of it was sexual. She wondered how that could possibly be when she still considered herself jilted by Josh. She could feel the imprint of this man's hand right through the chiffon of her dress. It might have been pressed against her naked flesh. Her perceptions so long blunted by acute dismay were now razor-sharp. But then he was a striking, powerful, physical man, she reasoned, quite without the easy-going gentleness with which Josh had surrounded her.

Looking down at her telltale face, his expression tautened. ''Let's go,'' he said abruptly. The tips of her breasts were giving him little shocks as they brushed up against him.

''Where?'' She threw up her head, startled. His face was quite unreadable.

''Out into the garden,'' he suggested curtly. ''All the time we've been dancing Deakin has been staring over here. Even with his bride on his arm.''

''Pay no attention,'' she said. But she hoped Josh was staring. He looked so deeply familiar she thought she couldn't bear the whole situation. Callista looked so nice. She deserved to be happy. Christy's instinct told her it wouldn't be for long. Not with Josh. Josh wasn't good enough. Josh's only real fondness was for money. But Callista on her big day looked radiant in her beautiful ecru satin gown that glimmered with thousands of seed pearls. Her billowy floor-length organza veil was held off her small face by an exquisite diamond-and-pearl diadem that looked like a family heirloom.

After all that she knew, Christy still wished perversely things could have been different. That Josh could have been different from the man he really was.

"How well did you know him?" Ashe McKinnon asked her, his dark face taking on an aspect of contempt.

"I don't think you want to listen."

"Try me," he clipped off.

"It's all in the past. Another dimension." She needed a huge breathing space from this man.

"It'd better be." With one hand he lifted her face and turned his black gaze on her.

"What do you want to do, crush me?" She envied him his masculine strength. The hard detachment.

Instantly he eased his grip. What did he want with her? To pick her up and carry her off? To make love to her until she couldn't even remember who Deakin was?

"Are you suggesting I could be *that* physical?"

"I could feel your anger." Yet something about him was giving her a deep, languorous feeling. It was like being engulfed in the black velvet of night. What was she doing twisting and turning in this stranger's arms? He was so totally different from Josh. With a powerful magnetism that reached through her pain. Moreover he was controlling her, pulling her closer.

"So are you going to tell me exactly why you are here? I'm certain you have no invitation."

"I let it get away from me." She glanced at him briefly, her lashes shadowing her eyes. "It flew into the air and blew away." There was no comfort in this man, only astonishing heat. She kept seeing Josh and his bride out of the corner of her eye. Hurt spasmed through her. "Kiss me," she ordered before she started to cry.

He shook her a little. "Because you want to make him jealous? Look at me." He was going to kiss her before the night was over. He had never wanted to kiss a woman more in his life. This beautiful creature who was electric for another man. A man who had his cousin lovingly tucked into his shoulder. "You little fool," Ashe muttered, lowering his dark head protectively over her. "There's no way, no way, you can get him back."

"I don't want him back. I don't!" She knew it was true but she couldn't get herself together almost overnight.

"Is that a prayer?"

Her mouth was trembling beneath his brooding regard. "Could we go outside?"

"Why not? We're leaving a lot of burning curiosity behind."

It was not to be. Callista called to her cousin from across the room.

"Ashe!" No one had told Callista who the beautiful blond girl in the green dress was. She was extravagantly lovely to Callista's eyes. The dress! She could never wear a dress like that. And Ashe? What was he doing with her? The two of them looked somehow torched. As if no one else in the world mattered.

Beside Callista, Josh gave a wry little exclamation. "What with all this talking I'm getting dry in the throat. I think I'll get myself a drink. Could I get you anything, my darling?''

Callista gave him her sweet smile. ''Oh, Joshua, please stay and meet Ashe's new girlfriend. I must say I'm surprised. But then Ashe is the best of anyone at surprises.''

''I don't know…'' Josh's mouth was indeed dry and his heart was thundering. Christy was always such a lady but he knew what angry women could do.

''Please, darling, for me.'' Callista caught her bridegroom's hand.

''I can't do this,'' Christy confessed to Ashe McKinnon as they crossed the floor.

''You can. I'll see you through.'' He took her hand and held it firmly.

''Who am I?'' This wasn't what she intended at all. ''Who am I supposed to be?''

''You should have thought of that.'' His reply was a little harsh. ''You're my deepest secret.''

''You mean *you* asked me?'' She was drowning in confusion.

''Who else? I'm not going to risk Callista's being badly hurt. Do you think you can smile?'' He eyed her critically.

''Of course I can smile, you arrogant man.'' A storm of outraged pride blew up in her. He had calluses on his palm. McKinnon the cattle baron. High power—high voltage. She had an hysterical desire to run from him.

''Would you just look at Deakin?'' he said suddenly in a hard gritty voice. ''My bet is he was trying to make a break for it but Callista stopped him.''

Even devastated by Josh's betrayal, Christy could scarcely blame him.

''So what's the play?'' she asked through small clenched teeth. It was almost as though she'd known this man in another life, but she had no time to dwell on that.

"We'll play it by ear," he told her, giving her, quite out the blue, the sexiest smile.

It was so amazing it put the adrenalin back into her.

And hey! Josh had the frozen look of a rabbit caught in a hunter's sights. Callista, the triumphant bride, was looking from her to her cousin as if she didn't know what was going on. Up close Christy realised Callista was older than she had supposed. Late rather than early twenties. Probably her trust fund paid out at age thirty. The evidence was Josh couldn't wait.

"You look absolutely lovely and so happy, Callista," Ashe told his cousin in a surprisingly calm voice. "I hope nothing ever changes that." He slid his arm smoothly around Christy's waist, drawing her forward. "I'd like you to meet a friend of mine, Christy Parker. She wasn't on the guest list because I didn't know she'd be back from L.A."

Josh, aware he had escaped some terrible danger, fell into his role of loving bridegroom, the expression on his face growing in confidence. "We know one another, don't we?" he asked Christy, quite unforgivably, giving Christy a smile for which one really needed sunglasses. "You're with Whitelaw Promotions, aren't you?"

It was her moment to bring him down. To give him instant payback. Instead she nodded coolly. "That's right. I think I know you, too."

Josh prepared himself again for an onslaught. It didn't come. "So tell me, how is Zack?" he asked in the nicest friendly fashion. He referred to Christy's boss and the head of the public relations company.

"Fine." She couldn't possibly slip into casual mode. She was far too upset. "It's been a beautiful wedding, Callista." She turned her attention to the bride. "I wish you every happiness." Amazingly she was able to say it.

"Thank you so much…Christy…" Callista finally got

her voice going. ''Wherever did you meet Ashe?'' She looked avid to know.

''Well...''

''It's a long story,'' Ashe McKinnon said, locking Christy of the shining beauty to him, aware of her turmoil. She was as jumpy as a cat.

''A story worth listening to, I'll bet.'' Josh's glance lingered long on Christy.

''Christy's not talking.'' Ashe's vibrant voice was saturated in what sounded very much like sarcasm. ''See you later, you two. I know how much you both want to be together.''

''Dear God!'' Christy murmured almost inaudibly as they moved off. ''I don't normally drink but I feel like one now.''

''You did very well,'' he assured her. ''It was plain to me you wanted to slap him.''

''Whereas *you* didn't?'' Whatever this man said, he fired her. ''I thought you came dangerously near to cutting.''

''I'm surprised you said that,'' he drawled. ''But then you don't know me. If I'd been really cutting Deakin wouldn't be standing. 'Don't I know you'?'' He aped Josh's lighter tones then they hardened. ''Only the fact Callista is my cousin and she's wearing a wedding dress stopped me from asking him to step outside.''

''I can't imagine he could stand up to your flailing fists.'' She shuddered. Josh would be no match for this cattle baron. He didn't have that sort of invincible masculinity. In fact, she considered very belatedly, Josh was *soft.*

''My dear girl, I'd drop him in one.'' He signalled to one of the fleet of uniformed waiters who hurried to his side. ''Thank you,'' he said gracefully, taking two glasses of champagne from the silver tray.

"I should go now," Christy said quite sadly as he passed a flute to her.

"My dear, you should be thrown out," Ashe quipped, not liking this beautiful witch's misery.

"I don't belong here."

"I entirely agree with you, but you're not going anywhere. Not yet. Come." He took her arm. Held her captive. "Let's leave all these good people to their exuberant high spirits. I expect you're hungry?"

"No." She shook her head, fighting for her dignity.

"I promise you you will be. Enough money has been spent on the food and drink at this reception to feed the entire Outback for a year."

As they made their way out to the marquee society photographers got in the way. Flashes went off, capturing the two of them strolling along like a pair of lovers. Ashe McKinnon didn't stop to supply Christy's name. He didn't have to, Christy thought shakily. At least one photographer knew exactly who she was since he'd photographed her at various functions a few times before. Without question a photograph of her with Ashe McKinnon at her side would appear in *Vogue*, or whatever magazine had the rights. No matter what, Christy held her shoulders back and her head high.

The food was indeed so sumptuous many of the guests stood gawking in awe before they finally moved in to sample the endless dishes. Ice sculptures in the form of larger-than-life swans decorated the tables, which were festooned with white flowers and trails of ivy down the centre. Billows of white tulle and satin ribbons decorated the tented ceilings with thousands of fresh white flowers including masses of white orchids flown in from Thailand. Christy had already seen the six-foot-high wedding cake, which dominated the twenty-foot-long Georgian dining room table. Obviously the happy couple were to cut the cake in the house. She hoped to be long gone by then. Why hadn't the cattle baron thrown her out? He was a strange perverse man.

Instead he made her eat something. "Go on," he urged. "Everyone is looking at you. Isn't that too priceless? Of course you're the most beautiful woman here, though I expect you still want to change places with Callista?"

She was aghast at his little cruelties. "What a pig you are. *Cochon!*"

"But of course you speak French," he joked. "Anyway I'll pretend I didn't hear that." He bent his glistening dark head over hers, a study in ebony and gold, as though he was whispering endearments.

"No need to overdo it," she said sharply, struck again by the beauty of his eyes. Why did men have such wonderful eyelashes?

"I'm doing what I want to do. It's even possible I've fallen madly in love with you."

"And pray have you?" She could barely conceal her inner rage.

"No. We're co-conspirators that's all. And I'm damned if I know why. Our paths will probably never cross again."

"Amen to that," she flashed. This wasn't a man you sashayed around. He was a big, powerful tough man. The sort of man she disliked.

"You don't see me as eligible?" he mocked. "They tell me I am."

"Why not with all that money," she returned bleakly. Wasn't that how it went with Josh.

"You have such command of diplomacy. I'm sure you weren't always that cynical."

"I was not." There was a headache behind her eyes.

"You're thinking about Deakin, aren't you?" he abruptly accused, the muscles of his face tautening.

"It's hard not to when I've turned up at his wedding," she managed painfully.

"And when did you decide to do that?" He was determined to know.

"At precisely half past eleven last night," she replied.

"What we call a snap decision? More champagne? There's a choice. Moet or Bollinger?"

"Wouldn't it have been cheaper, even smarter, to buy domestic?" she asked tartly, swallowing a morsel of Russian caviar.

"Mercedes thinks our champagne styles lack French subtlety."

"She should go to more wine tastings. Even the experts have been known to be fooled."

Inevitably other guests surged up to speak to Ashe. He appeared to be known and "adored" by everyone on the bride's side, but needless to say none of the super-rich knew her. She only occasionally moved into their world at charity functions. But he introduced her to all his friends who turned searching but approving eyes on her. It was about time Ashe got married, they said with sly glances at her, never guessing she was wincing inside. As urbanely as Ashe McKinnon was handling all this, she just knew there was a dark side to the cattle baron. He was allowing this charade to go on to prevent a scandal. She was determined to get away from him, at the same time filled with the weird notion she couldn't even if she tried. But her moment came. The best-looking of the bridesmaids, four in all, all dressed alike in shades of blue moire silk, determinedly took hold of his arm.

"Ashe, darling, why are you being so cruel to me...?"

Christy waited for no more. She fled across the lawn,

keeping to the shadows and away from the main reception rooms, heading eastwards. If she got lost he would have to send a search party. She'd have really strange memories of all this. They'd probably stay with her all her life.

Just when she thought she was safe, a man's hand suddenly reached for her, drawing her back into a large dimly lit room that looked like a man's study. She had an impression of walls of books, glass cases bearing sporting trophies, paintings of winning racehorses, a desk and chairs.

"Christy!" Josh was staring down at her, soft floppy hair nearly falling into his eyes.

"Sorry, sorry, sorry, I don't want to speak to you." She gritted her teeth.

"Take it quietly, darling," he begged. "God, I thought the bloody cattle baron had abducted you."

"He'll be coming to look for me pretty soon," Christy warned, wanting nothing more than to have Ashe McKinnon explode into the room.

"You *don't* know him, do you?' Josh asked as if he guessed her pitiful secret.

"Pretty soon we're going to get engaged," Christy said briskly, wanting to see how he took it.

The generous mouth dropped open. "Be serious."

"I am being serious," she managed.

"You're not!" Now he gloated. "You don't know him. He doesn't come to the city that often. He has a cattle empire to run."

"I know!" Christy flaunted the knowledge. "He's very rich."

"You don't care about riches."

"I do now. It's ironic, isn't it? I'd say he has even more millions than your wife and mother-in-law put together."

"You're bitter, aren't you?" Josh accused her, his hazel eyes raking her face and body.

"Get a grip, Josh," she said, green eyes narrowing in contempt. "It's okay you married your Callista. There's a big wide world out there full of gorgeous men. Ashe McKinnon would have to be right up there at the top."

"You weren't on the wedding list," Josh pointed out aggressively. "You're a fake, Christy. You don't know him at all." But on his own wedding day Josh's voice cracked with jealousy.

"How would you know?" Christy was finding his behaviour abominable. "It's been weeks since I laid eyes on you. Now if you don't mind I want to leave."

"When you're McKinnon's date?" He challenged her to stop.

"I mean leave this room. You have me bailed up." She stared at him in disgust, willing him out of the way.

"No one will come in here, Christy," he said as if to reassure her.

"Oh, please. You'd better hope and pray not Ashe McKinnon. You could wind up dead. He's very protective of his cousin."

"I can handle Callista." He smiled tightly. "I had to talk to you, Christy. I have to see you later."

"Later?" Her eyes flashed angrily even while her voice rose in sheer disbelief. "Later you're supposed to be on your honeymoon. Not renewing our relationship."

"How I wish it was you," he admitted in a tone of deepest regret.

"Go to hell." She prised her fingers from his arm. "And I hope you stay there."

"Why are you doing this to me?" he groaned, his eyes curiously glazed. "I love you. You love me. Nothing can change that." He reached, as though this time she would surrender and go into his arms.

Instead the tall, powerful figure of Ashe McKinnon appeared in the open doorway. He fairly lunged into the room, looking as daunting as the devil, just as dangerous, and probably just as unlawful.

"This has to be the most stupid thing you've ever done, Deakin," he rasped, eyes like black diamonds. "Get away from him." He turned on Christy, grinding out the order.

Giving orders was a tendency in dangerous creatures, she thought, instantly obeying.

"Hasn't it crossed your arrogant mind that's what I'm trying to do?" The decided edge in her voice matched his own.

"I told you to stay with me," he reminded her, not taking his eyes off the errant bridegroom who had taken cover of sorts behind an armchair.

"And you really thought I was going to obey? What sort of woman do you think I am?" Christy fired, embarrassed beyond words.

"An idiot to begin with," he informed her shortly. "Come over here to me."

She knew better than to rile him further.

"What are we going to do with you, Deakin?" Ashe felt like slamming Callista's brand-new husband against a wall. "My family is very important to me." And in all honesty he was seething at the sight of Miss Parker near wrapped in Deakin's arms.

"It wasn't what you think." The panic-stricken Josh assumed a look of deep apology. Tangling with the cattle baron would be like tangling with a charging rhino. "It's the same old story. You must know it, Ashe." His mobile features took on a man-to-man expression. "Christy and I had a little fling but when I told her it was over she wouldn't let go. Women are like that."

She had never known this man, Christy thought, gazing at him with a mixture of dismay and pain.

"You really think I'm going to swallow that?" Ashe near choked, he was so angry. He couldn't, absolutely couldn't, relate to this guy. What in the name of God did Callista and this girl, Christy, see in him? He was ninety-five per cent toxic waste.

"It's true." Christy picked that moment to be utterly selfless. Not for Josh. Sometime in the future Josh would get his comeuppance. But for Callista. She had no desire to hurt Callista. Callista was just another woman who thought herself deeply in love with a man she couldn't see clearly. "I came here to tempt him."

"What rot!" Ashe bridled afresh. "About as good as it gets." He studied Christy with contemptuous eyes. "You're trying to save his worthless skin."

"Your cousin Callista doesn't deserve this. She's the innocent party. I owe her something. The question I ask myself now is why did *you,* astute old *you,* let her marry him?"

Ashe's dynamic face mirrored his frustration. "The fact is Callista is nearly thirty years old." He rounded on Christy, his anger abruptly abating when he saw how pale she was. Her eyes were enormous, a dead give-away she was deeply disturbed.

"Get the hell out of here, Deakin," Ashe ordered, his voice cracking like a whip. "Your playing around with other women ends today. If I hear one word…!"

"I'm going to be the best husband ever," Josh proclaimed like a professional con man, looking Ashe in the eyes.

"You'd better be, my man." Ashe nodded, his expression grim.

"I love Callista," Josh poured it on while Ashe McKinnon threw back his dark head and roared.

"I have grave misgivings about that. You're dirt."

The rest of Josh's words dried up. Hastily he crossed to the door, pausing a moment from its relative safety. ''As far as I'm concerned Christy is the culprit here. Ex-girlfriends aren't supposed to gatecrash a man's wedding.''

Ashe swore beneath his breath in a near ecstasy of anger. ''Get out of here.'' The attitude of his body suggesting a panther about to spring into action.

Josh wasn't entirely insane. With one last aggrieved look he took to his heels.

''Not his finest hour,'' pronounced Ashe in disgust.

When the time came—by now time had no meaning for Christy—for the happy couple to leave on the first leg of their honeymoon—an overnight stay in the honeymoon suite of a leading hotel before jetting off for three weeks in Thailand—the guests had assembled on the grand sweep of front lawn of the McKinnon mansion to wave them off.

Callista, as pretty as a picture in her pink going-away outfit, turned to throw her bouquet. A surprisingly high sweep. Christy, battling with the illusion she was trapped in a dream, made no move to catch it. She felt quite naturally it was inappropriate as well as the fact she had gone off weddings. She didn't even make a playful gesture of reaching up as all four bridesmaids were doing, but in earnest. The bouquet simply descending gracefully but in a mesmerizing way, twirling and twirling a lovely posy of perfect pink and white roses threaded with traceries of green.

The bridesmaids were running forward, palms up, fingers steepled, each one determined to catch this wonderful forecast. I'm next! Their faces were bright with excitement and anticipatory pleasure.

Me. Me. Let it be me.

But life is full of disappointments and preordained

events. Callista's bouquet fell with a soft fragrant weight into Christy's nerveless hands.

She saw the muscles along Ashe McKinnon's clean-cut jaw tighten cynically before two of the women guests grasped her in affectionate camaraderie and kissed her on either cheek.

"Lucky girl!" They batted speculative glances at Ashe. God, wasn't he a drop-dead hunk!

And why not? Ashe had scarcely left her side. Mercedes had berated him fondly for trying to fool her. Everyone seemed to think she was the new woman in Ashe McKinnon's life. An irony not lost on either of them.

And so it was that Christy and Ashe McKinnon left the wedding together. Christy heading into very deep waters indeed.

CHAPTER TWO

FROM nowhere a chauffeured limousine appeared. At least there were some pluses to being rich. Christy stepped into the back seat. After a moment Ashe McKinnon joined her.

In the silence that followed, Christy stared out the window, devastated by the whole day.

"Silly me, I've forgotten where you live," he said in an ironic tone.

She surveyed him gravely, her faith in life shattered, yet it was he who had rescued her from a very bad situation.

"Goodness me, and you were thinking of moving in. Number 10 Downing Street." At least that was a world away.

"My dear girl they've changed the locks." His black gaze fell on her lovely face, desire lapping in his blood.

"Then I suggest you try 121 Shelly Beach Road."

He lowered the partition window to give instructions to the chauffeur.

"I feel ashamed of myself," Christy confessed after a few unhappy minutes of studying the stars. "Really ashamed."

"Perhaps you ought to be put in prison," he suggested in a mocking voice.

"It wasn't that serious, was it?" She looked back at him. Why was she with this man?

"You do this for a living, gatecrashing receptions?"

"I couldn't face seeing Josh marry your cousin. How petite she is! Doll-size."

"Up until recently I thought she had a woman-sized

brain. As for you, you have to get on with your life.'' He didn't want her mourning Deakin. Not for one minute.

''I don't want to even think about it for at least forty-eight hours. I had maybe one too many glasses of champagne,'' she apologised.

''That's perfectly understandable. It's also the reason why I hired the limousine. I couldn't drive you myself. Not only do I not keep a car in the city but I'm well over the limit. Three glasses of anything is surely not enough to celebrate a wedding? Even an insufferable one.''

''I should have known better.'' Christy gave a bruised sigh.

''Indeed you should.'' His tone used up a lot of censure.

''You've never made a mistake in your life I suppose?'' Christy pressed back exhaustedly against the plush upholstery.

''I think I hate the way you say that. All my ex-girlfriends speak to me.''

''I bet you gave them a hard time,'' Christy answered. He wouldn't lie to them. If anything he was too much up-front. ''I know some women go in for excitement and danger. It must make them feel more alive. It's my professional judgment that you're a dangerous man.''

''All it might take is a little getting to know me.'' He flung out an arm and drew her close to him. His desire for her was blocking out his usual tight control. And he wanted to comfort her. All of a sudden she seemed very vulnerable.

Christy allowed her head to come to rest against his shoulder. ''You know you're not my keeper.'' But he was *very* masterful.

''I am for this evening.'' He brushed a few glinting golden strands of hair from her cheek. ''To be honest, I'm concerned you might go after them.''

She came upright in despair. ''I've learned my lesson.''

''I sincerely hope so.'' He didn't sound impressed. ''Your ex-boyfriend and my cousin have only this very evening exchanged their marriage vows.''

''And good luck to them,'' Christy exclaimed disjointedly. She felt so overwrought she couldn't even begin to describe her emotions. ''I do know one thing. I wouldn't want to marry a man like you.'' She withdrew the ruffled hem of her short skirt away from his trousered knee.

''I hope you weren't counting on my asking you?'' He didn't bother to control the mockery. Who the hell did she think she was? A goddess?

''Getting married is the last thing I want to do,'' Christy said with the sombre gravity of the betrayed. ''Marriages in most cases don't seem to work out. I know any number of couples who have split up.''

''Not counting you and Josh?'' He smiled grimly.

''When I think of you a word comes to mind,'' Christy said in exasperation. Didn't he know she was badly hurt?

''Please don't say it,'' he joked. ''I detest hearing rough words on a woman's tongue. As it happens, I'm not a great one for marriage either. It's something men have to do to get heirs.''

She felt the shock. ''What a rotten thing to say.''

He was silent for a while. ''Being betrayed isn't just a woman's area. Wives and mothers have been known to abandon the marital home leaving devastation behind them. Women don't have a great deal of difficulty stamping on a man's heart.''

Christy was taken aback by the degree of passion in his voice. ''You're beginning to sound like a misogynist.''

''Sometimes I think I am.'' He revealed a white twisted smile. ''A reflection of my background perhaps. But to get back to you, Christy Parker, you could be a whole lot unhappier as an old maid.''

"Don't use that term," she protested. "I'm a feminist, I don't like it. I'm sick of all the words men have thought up to label women."

"You don't think they deserve a lot of them?" he asked with strong sarcasm.

"Women don't need men," Christy said, sexual antagonism thick between them. "I suppose they might need them for an occasional bout of sex."

To her complete surprise given the tension between them, he burst out laughing. It was a very engaging sound. There were some things about him she managed to find wildly attractive. In desperation, not knowing what else to do in the presence of this complex man, Christy closed her eyes. Men of his type were new to her. He was too physically and verbally powerful. She was having such difficulty adjusting to everything that was happening. In a few short hours she'd gone from jilted woman and gatecrasher, to the new woman in Ashe McKinnon the cattle baron's life.

But then it was only play-acting.

Thank God.

"Wakey, wakey," a man's voice breathed seductively in her ear.

"Wh-a-at?" Christy started to say dazedly. "I surely didn't doze off?" She felt such confusion, disorientation, staring up into his fathomless dark eyes.

"You must have. You didn't notice when I kissed you."

"You didn't kiss me." She was absolutely certain she would have registered it. On the Richter scale. She understood already, miserable as she was, Ashe McKinnon was that sort of man.

"No, I didn't," he drawled. "I imagined I kissed you."

"Oh..." She was reduced to silence.

Seemingly like magic they were outside her apartment

block, the surrounding well-kept gardens giving off the scent of gardenia and frangipani. Above her head the Southern Cross was a dazzling presence. It appeared to be right over the spot where she was standing. A billion stars gleamed. It was a heavenly night, velvety and fragrant. It made her feel very very sad. She even yawned. Ashe McKinnon and the chauffeur, however, had their two heads bent together.

What were they planning? Whatever Ashe said the chauffeur threw back his head and laughed. Men! They bonded in minutes. A moment more and the chauffeur got back behind the wheel, saluted briefly before he pulled away from the kerb, then did a U-turn back in the direction of the city.

''Well which is it?'' Ashe joined her, so tall he towered over her. ''The penthouse?'' He tilted his dark head back, staring up at the twenty floors of the high-rise building.

''Don't be stupid. I can't afford the penthouse,'' she said feeling a rush of something like panic, ''neither do I recall asking you in.''

''But my dear Miss Parker, it's totally expected under these circumstances. You need someone to look after you.''

''Not you, Mr. McKinnon. I'm in no doubt of that. Most decidedly not you.''

''That's okay.'' He answered casually as if he wanted no part of that agenda either. ''As it turns out I have plenty of women fighting over me.''

''Men who ooze money generally do.''

''Ouch, that was nasty.'' He made a mock attempt to defend himself. ''Come on, Miss Parker. For all you may have deserved it, you've had a bad day.'' He made a grab for her hand and momentarily defeated she let him take it again, curiously responding to the feel of those calluses against her smooth skin.

''Well if you're coming in for a while, come,'' she said, her voice carrying strain. '' I want to get this damned dress off.'' It reminded her too bitterly of the wedding. Of wasted time. Failure.

He glanced down at her golden head for a moment then looked away. She'd created a sensation tonight. Ms. Bottecelli the gatecrasher. ''Don't you think you're being rather forward?'' he mocked.

She scarcely heard. ''I can't stand it.'' There was nothing left to her but to mourn. Parting with ex-boyfriends was never easy even if they were hollow men. ''I'll never give my heart again. I'll lock it away someplace inside me. I'll never give my trust.''

''Oh stop feeling so sorry for yourself,'' he advised, not without pity. ''You're young. You're beautiful. So you let yourself get involved with a villain, there are good guys out there. Next time,'' he added bluntly, ''you might be a better judge. Callista spent more quality time choosing her wedding gown than her groom.''

Whereas Josh the freeloader had instantly chosen a young woman with money to burn.

They never spoke in the lift. He looked marvellous, she thought somewhere between detachment and admiration. A prince among men. Josh couldn't hold a candle to him for looks or presence. Anything for that matter. If she was going to be fair. Not that Ashe McKinnon was the sort of man she should have fallen in love with. Men like that threw out such a challenge. One she preferred not to take on. Besides he was out of her league and he didn't believe in marriage either. A man like that would expect his bride to sign a watertight pre-nuptial contract.

Thinking about it, it only made common sense.

Christy reached out and dislodged the pink confetti on

his shoulders thinking he'd probably look as wonderful in his working gear—akubra, bush shirt and jeans, riding boots on his feet—as a morning suit. Groovy. Really groovy. That's what her friend, Montana, would say. On the scale of one to ten Ashe McKinnon had to rate an eleven. She dwelt quietly on his physical attributes so as not to think about Josh. Josh would be labelled "unfit" beside this man.

"So what's the verdict?" His eyes glinted.

"Sorry?" They stepped out of the lift together, Christy indicating with a little flourish of her arm her apartment was the one to the far right.

"I'm surprised you haven't noticed my gold tooth."

"You have a gold tooth?" She stood stock-still and stared at him in horrified amazement.

"No I haven't, but if I had I'm sure you would have noticed it. Do you usually eyeball men so closely?"

"I know you look spectacular, but I was looking through you."

"Here, give me that." She was fumbling, something she never did, but her fingers were nerveless, so he took the key off her, turning the dead lock and standing back while she preceded him into her one-bedroom but decidedly up-market apartment. She would spend the rest of her life paying it off but it was an excellent investment.

Inside almost total darkness. He put out a hand and found the panel of light switches.

"How did you do that?" She pushed back her hair.

"What?" He gazed down at her with a puzzled expression.

"Find the lights so easily? I've never thought they were terribly well placed."

"I have X-ray vision. I've spent my life learning how to see in the dark."

"Ah the pleasures of being a cattle baron," she sighed. "Won't you sit down? I have to get out of this dress. Won't be a moment. Then we'll have coffee."

"Take your time," he said very dryly.

"What's so funny?" Christy turned back to ask.

"Oh life in the fast lane. Do you mind if I take off my cravat?"

"Go ahead." She met those eyes and had the extraordinary sensation something was cutting off her breath. "I'm not coming back in a negligee if that's what you're thinking. I intend to burn this dress."

"When I thought you should wear it forever," he said suavely. "I like your abode. Did you do the decorating yourself?"

"Right down to painting the walls. By myself. Now I think about it, Josh always had an excuse to avoid anything like physical hard work."

"You call painting a few walls hard work?" he called after her, his tone caustic.

Josh. Josh. Josh Deakin was *out* of her life.

"By the time I was finished I was burned out."

Left alone Ashe wandered casually around the open-plan living-dining room. His study at home was bigger in area so he took small steps unless he powered into the sliding-glass doors that led out onto a small balcony. He went to the doors, opened them and stepped out to take a look at the view. Or city people called it a view. God, he could never live in the city, he thought for perhaps the millionth time. He could never be contained. But this was nice for what it was. A successful working girl's pad.

He wondered, with a surge of anger that could get him into trouble, whether Deakin had lived with her. Slept with her. Had his morning cup of coffee with her. He hoped not, picturing it but not wanting to.

The decor was entirely feminine yet a man would feel comfortable here. She had great taste, sensibility. Even unhappy she'd filled the place with flowers. He liked that. He liked the books she read. Lots of books. She would love the extensive library he had inherited with many important first editions and historical documents. His was one of the great pioneering families. He liked the prints on the walls. An oil painting of her. Very good. He understood the artist had been in love with her. It showed. He liked how everything was very clean, very neat. Orderly. She'd make a fine wife, he thought with a kind of dark amusement when in reality he was appalled she wanted Callista's brand-new husband. Yet when was the last time he'd found a woman so damned intriguing? Never was the answer. It left him feeling vaguely shell-shocked.

Finally he got his silk cravat undone and placed it on a side table. There was a glass bowl filled with beautifully perfumed yellow roses on it and a silver-framed photograph of her and he presumed her parents. She bore a strong resemblance to the woman, so youthful-looking she might have been an older sister but he knew she wasn't. The man was good-looking, too, rugged, with a look of character. For some reason he thought them landed people. Maybe they owned a farm of some sort. Living on the land was character building in his experience.

Ashe sank down into an armchair with apple green upholstery; spring colours dominated the room, awaiting the drama of her return. He was starting to wonder what the hell he thought he was doing? He wasn't the man to be swept away by a woman's very obvious charms. Correction: he hadn't been up to date. There was her beauty and the rest, the way she talked, the way she moved, but he realised he was getting too big a charge out of being with her.

He wanted her. The thought stunned him. He'd only just met her, under the worst possible circumstances, yet he wanted this woman. He supposed it was the way he lived his life. He was always making instant decisions. Big decisions. But he was never, couldn't afford to be, reckless. This was madness. So ill-advised. How could he possibly want a woman who was tearing herself to pieces over another man? A man moreover he already despised. Worse, married to his cousin. He knew better than anyone what happened to a man who let himself fall very deeply in love. It was like handing over one's soul. His mother had cheated on his father long before she finally left him. He couldn't get her treachery out of his head. More than twenty years later. His father was the finest man he had ever known. He had never grown another emotional layer of skin to enable him to remarry. His mother right up to the day he died had been enshrined in his father's memory. If it had been him…if it had been him…

"Oh dear, what's the matter?" Coming back into the room Christy gave him an alarmed glance. He looked positively daunting, the expression on his face dark and brooding.

"Nothing." He emptied his mind of all violence. "Do come further in and let me see you. Didn't change your mind? No negligee?" He spoke flippantly, trying to kill desire.

"You're a complete stranger." Just as coolly she answered his banter. She'd put on the first thing that came to hand, a pink-embroidered shirt over white cotton jeans. "Would you like coffee?"

"Coffee, the instant cure. Not the instant kind, I hope? You wouldn't by chance have any single malt whisky?"

Her face froze as memories floated up. "I let Josh have

all his liquor back. I'm not much of a drinker. There is however a bottle of Tia Maria. It goes exactly with coffee.''

''Tia Maria it is,'' he answered rather shortly, outraged anew by her feelings for Deakin. ''It's not exactly what I planned but it will do. Strong, black coffee, no sugar. Do you need a hand?''

''There's not the space for you. How tall are you anyway?''

''If I remember correctly just over six-three. Are they your parents over there?'' He inclined his head towards the photograph.

''Yes.'' She came back into the living room, her beautiful face breaking into a smile. ''I miss them terribly.''

''Where are they?''

''I grew up on a sheep and lavender farm in Victoria. My parents are still there. They'll never leave. They adore country life and one another.''

''You're an only child?'' He stared at her with brooding eyes.

''Sad to say yes. My mother had a lot of trouble having me. My father couldn't have borne to lose her. That put paid to a bigger family. But I was never spoilt. I was never of the over-protective one-child syndrome. In fact I ran wild.''

''So you're a country girl?''

''Does that put me up a notch?'' She heard the approval in his voice.

''Indeed yes. When I marry—''

''To great applause,'' she cut in dryly.

''My wife will have to understand what living in the Outback means.'' His vibrant voice cracked right down the line.

''You look extremely sober when you say that,'' she commented.

''It's a top requirement.'' He didn't bare his soul to her. He didn't say his mother had been a beautiful social butterfly. A city girl, born and bred. In fact the last woman his father should have married. The last woman to mother a child. It was a miracle she had stayed so long. She had missed—expected to miss—his tenth birthday. There had been no celebration. His charming extravagant mother had run away. She was an adulteress, goddamn it. Love wouldn't stand between him and a successful marriage.

She brought him a hot steaming cup of excellent coffee along with a small crystal glass containing a dollop of liqueur.

''What are you having?''

''Aspirin.'' She couldn't disguise how she felt.

''Go back and get some coffee. Put a lot of milk in it,'' he ordered.

''You're the boss.'' She walked back into the kitchen and popped a small jug of milk into the microwave. ''I bet you're the boss even when you're asleep?''

''Of course I'm the boss. That's my job. So what next, Miss Parker?'' he asked, quietly surveying her.

''As in?'' Wearily she rubbed the faint cleft in her chin, taking a seat opposite him.

''Plans for the future. You realise you're going to have to cut Josh Deakin out of your life? End of story.''

''Obviously you haven't read my character correctly.'' She didn't know how it had happened but she desperately wanted him to approve of her.

''Not every ex-girlfriend turns up uninvited at a wedding.''

''Go on, rub it in.''

''I have to. I'm excessively biased in favour of my cousin.''

''She's a lucky girl.'' Christy gave a mournful sigh.

There was a little droop to her lovely mouth. It made him want to kiss it hard. A little punishment without hurting her. ''Anyway if you're a good girl and say your prayers, Mr. Right will come along.''

''Mr. Right?'' Her beautiful green eyes were distant. ''What makes men Mr. Right all of a sudden? I don't even want to talk about Mr. Right and marriage. I'm in denial.''

''I recognise that. I can even understand how you feel being burned. The fact is I'm wary of marriage myself.'' He said this with considerable self-mockery.

''Pray tell why is that? You don't look like you'd be wary of anything.''

''I've seen a lot of men lose their good judgment over a woman,'' he remarked cynically.

''Well you couldn't possibly say that only applies to men. Right now I'm feeling love is a four-letter word. And it definitely doesn't last. Well it did—it does—for my parents. But they're different.''

''You're thinking you don't stand a chance?'' He gave a quiet, ironic laugh. ''What about arranged marriages?'' he asked. ''Plenty of precedent for those. This head over heels bit doesn't always come off.''

''You can't be saying you'd seriously consider marrying a woman who doesn't love you?'' He took her breath away.

''And one I don't love either. I've no time for mad primitive urges, all that sweep a woman up and carry her off sort of stuff. One can learn to love, certainly. And, of course there must be trust and respect, mutual commitment and the same goals.''

''Anything else?'' She kept her eyes on him.

''Ideally she'll be good-looking, warm, compassionate, love kids, smart and able to take on a full partnership in the McKinnon operation. At least have input. I don't want any trophy wife.''

''And one who would never be unfaithful?''

The brilliant black eyes turned glacial. ''Why did you say that?'' His handsome face tautened.

She took a little rapid breath. ''I see it hit a nerve? You're certainly looking at me as though I'm not to be trusted.''

''Women as beautiful as you mightn't make the safest wife,'' he retorted.

''Really?'' Colour flared into her face. ''You're a real woman hater, aren't you?''

''I'm just very much against divorce.'' He sounded deadly serious.

Christy half rose, anything but at ease with him. ''More coffee?''

''No this is fine. You're not going to cry, are you? You've been very emotional all night.''

''No I am not going to cry,'' she told him a little fiercely. ''Dammit I don't understand men. You could have any woman you liked. That bridesmaid you were talking to? Did you happen to notice she's madly in love with you? And there were at least a dozen others sick with disappointment you had me hanging off your arm. Is it possible beneath that formidable exterior you're scared of women? Do you look like a panther when you're really a puppy?''

He surveyed her coolly. ''I can't believe you said that. It's just that I want a lot, Christy. For one so recently jilted, you have a great deal to say.''

The phone rang out, saving Christy an answer. They both jumped, so intense was the atmosphere between them. Christy went to answer it. Who could be ringing her this time of night? Her mind sprang, instantly, anxiously, to her parents. Accidents happened on farms. Nerves tightening she spoke into the mouthpiece. ''Christy here.''

Silence at the other end then a man's voice so low she

would have had to ask him to speak up only the voice was too familiar. ''Christy, Christy, don't hang up.''

Her heart contracted. Shock. Sick anger. Utter disbelief.

''Please...hear me out.''

''You're kidding. You've got to be kidding!'' The words burst from her before she could swallow them back. What sort of life form was he?

''Who is it?'' Ashe McKinnon was on his feet. ''Deakin?'' His voice was hard.

She hung up immediately. ''Don't be ludicrous. Wrong number. They were after a woman named Paderewski or Popadiamantris or someone.''

He clicked his tongue disgustedly. ''I can think of a few other things you might be but a good liar isn't one of them. We all know who Paderewski was and Papadiamantris to the best of my knowledge was a Greek writer. That was *Deakin.* Where in hell is he speaking from, the hotel? I'll go round.''

That thoroughly panicked her. ''I tell you, it was a wrong number.''

The phone rang again but Ashe saved her the trouble of answering it. ''McKinnon,'' he thundered. Straight from the Oval Office.

The very last thing Josh would have been counting on, Christy thought, secretly thrilled. Ashe McKinnon in her apartment. If McKinnon hadn't looked like he wanted to lynch someone she might have been able to laugh.

He hung up, obviously having frightened the caller off. ''If Deakin were here right now he'd have to be hospitalised. It was him, wasn't it?'' He drilled her with his brilliant stare.

''Don't jump to conclusions,'' Christy found herself imploring. Usually the people she dealt with were easy to handle. Not the cattle baron. No way. ''It was the wrong number. I get lots of them.''

He stared at her without a flicker of belief. ''As an attempt at protecting your ex-boyfriend that was pitiful.''

So it was, but the whole situation was highly explosive. And she was the cause of it. She should never have gate-crashed the wedding, no matter how badly Josh had treated her. ''All right, then, I'm protecting Callista.'' She refused point-blank to be intimidated. ''From you as much as him. Do you want to get back into town and punch him out? For all your talk of cool, common sense, you're a passionate man.'' She put out a hand and tentatively touched him. Much as a brave or alternatively stupid person would attempt to soothe a big cat. ''Please relax. Settle down.'' But settling down didn't appear to be on the agenda.

''They're supposed to be on their goddamn honeymoon and he's ringing you?'' he retorted in amazement. ''It's enough to make anyone reel.''

''It's been done before.'' She borrowed some of his own cynicism. ''Men ringing their mistresses and old girlfriends from the honeymoon suite. A crime of the heart. But it happens. The thing is you haven't got the right impression of me.''

''So educate me,'' he challenged, looking down that fine, straight nose at her.

''I can scarcely expect you to listen, you're so judgmental, but I don't, repeat, don't, fool around with married men. As far as I'm concerned, they're off-limits.''

''Fine words,'' he bit off edgily, his expression so infuriating, before she knew it, Christy's hand was in midair, carrying all the weight of her unhappiness behind it. He caught it, arresting her fiery reaction. ''Now there's a first,'' he said in very dangerous tones, as she stood there swaying. ''No one has ever taken a swing at me before, much less a woman. I want to believe you, Christy Parker, but I have to say I'm absolutely rattled.''

''Can't you appreciate it's the way I feel myself.'' She concentrated hard on rubbing her wrist. He hadn't hurt her applying just enough force to stop the blow but he had rendered her trembling. God knows what was at the heart of it. ''This has been a dreadful day. A knock-out sort of day. I really should go to bed. Right now. This minute.''

His brilliant eyes suddenly sparkled with black humour. ''Maybe I should stick around in case you decide to call Deakin back?''

Pure melancholy was taking hold of her. ''I can't believe how cruel you are,'' she murmured. ''Not that I care. After tonight I'll never see you again.''

He was aware how violently he wanted to change that. ''You don't believe that any more than I do.''

It was said in such a disturbing voice, with the irony she was becoming used to and something less identifiable. Whatever it was it sent shock waves through her. Feelings very hard to deal with on this day of days.

''I'll speak to you tomorrow.'' He sounded perfectly calm, even calculating.

''About what?'' she asked bewilderedly, trying to find some clue in the unreadable depths of his eyes.

''Oh we'll go someplace,'' he tossed off carelessly. ''I don't have to be back home until the end of the week.'' Not true but what the hell! He marvelled at how completely his focus had changed. ''You need something to shake you out of your misery. You didn't love Deakin. No one could love anyone without a soul.''

Soulless most of all. ''I thought I loved him,'' Christy said, horrified when she felt tears well into her eyes. She couldn't cry in front of this man. She saw him as... Oh, God, what did she see him as? ''You talk about a soul.''

She blinked back the tears furiously. ''I can't even trust my own heart.''

Again that white twisted smile. ''You're not the first,'' he said with the faintest hint of grief. ''Sometimes I think falling in love is a necessary evil. I know it's the reason I'm here. But we both might do better if we used our heads.''

Christy stared away across the room. ''I'm not that wise, I'm afraid. I'm not that cold-blooded either.''

Desire was the most powerful allure of all. It had been drawing him inexorably to her all night. ''No, your skin is like warm milk.'' He lifted her head, one hand beneath her chin, staring into her beautiful eyes, seeing himself reflected, instantly aroused by it. ''In case you're going to lie awake all night thinking how awful life is and how much you still love Deakin, why don't I give you something else to dwell on?''

With his other arm he folded her strongly to him, then he kissed her mouth. Almost gently at first, tasting her lips, savouring them, then more fully, deeply opening her lips like petals to find the sweet nectar.

It was the faultless execution of a kiss by a master. A kiss that would keep her awake for hours. Her heart fluttered wildly, a pretty songbird crammed into a cage. There were flickering lights behind her eyes indicating a high degree of arousal. She knew on one level he was punishing her, but he was effortlessly engineering a response.

She felt it, all along her body. Her face, her throat, her breasts, her thighs. Electric tingles raced lightning-quick, along her limbs, stirring up a heat that moved to the pit of her stomach and the glowing crux of her body. It was a kiss the likes of which she had never known.

When he finally withdrew his mouth she could hear the rasp of his breath. She feared he could hear her own involuntary little moans. She was trembling with an effort to absorb all these new sensations. What had he been attempting here? Whatever it was he had proved his point. Or was proving a point all that it was? She couldn't find words to ask. He had stolen all her breath.

He took her hands, stood with her while they both quietened. "I think that had results." There was a decided edge of self-mockery in his voice. "I don't imagine it's restored your faith in life, but at least it shook you up a little."

Like an earth tremor. She stared up at him with brooding eyes. "I never asked for that."

He gave her that ironic white smile she was fast coming to look for. "Who knows, it might have been destined."

She looked away. "At least I have to thank you for stopping me from making an utter fool of myself." A solitary tear slid down her cheekbone.

Ashe gathered it with his finger and put it into his mouth. "There, gone," he said a little harshly. "No more tears for Deakin."

"I have to swear to it?" she asked quietly.

This time the smile seemed to cost him an effort. "You do. Repeat after me. I, Christy Parker—"

She let him have what he wanted. He had wanted her mouth. "I Christy Parker—"

"Will never allow Joshua Deak—"

"Will never allow Joshua Deakin—"

"Into my heart again." He blurred the anger. "Moreover I will never do anything to threaten or destroy his marriage."

She winced. The tip of her tongue moistened her tingling lips.

"Say it." His expression was still very serious and strangely dark.

She obeyed, quite under his spell. "I will never do anything to threaten or destroy his marriage. There, does that satisfy you? Because I can't take a minute more.'' Not at this level of intensity. The male scent of him was all over her; warm, clean, intoxicating.

''Vows you'll disobey at your peril.'' The dark shadows gradually left his face. ''That's over, I'll let you go to bed, Christy. You're out on your feet.'' He turned to find his cravat, picking it up and shoving it in his pocket.

''How are you getting back?'' she roused herself to ask. ''Let me call a cab.''

''Don't bother.'' He looked down at the hand she had placed spontaneously on his arm. ''I can walk.''

''It's too far,'' she shook her head. ''Miles.'' She knew he was staying with Mrs. Mercedes McKinnon.

''You don't seem to remember I'm from the Outback,'' he scoffed. ''Your idea of miles is a hop, step and a jump. Besides I have a few blunt corners in my head to knock off. A walk will do me good.'' He turned at the door. Tall, elegant, vital, scornful. A man like that could rock a woman to her very core.

''I'll ring you around ten tomorrow. We'll go out for the day. Take a drive, the ocean, the mountains, have lunch somewhere. Okay?''

Who could argue with the man? Compliance was a natural response.

CHAPTER THREE

IN THE morning, it took Christy some time before she could actually look herself directly in the eyes. This time yesterday she didn't even know Ashe McKinnon. This time yesterday she'd considered herself a woman in a sorry plight, betrayed by the man she thought loved her, ready to cause him some fright by gatecrashing his wedding. What was she now? Apparently about as fickle as they come. The very thought seared her with shame and embarrassment. At the same time as she thought she was agonizing over Josh's betrayal another man was making an enormous impression on her. Was that normal? Or would any woman succumb to such a dynamic man?

She was still feverishly working on that when the phone rang.

''So how did the wedding go?'' her friend Montana greeted her with bated breath. ''Did you give him a damned good fright? On the other hand, did you get thrown out? I see nothing in the papers except a lot of gush over the bride and her filthy-rich folks.''

''You really want to know?'' Christy asked. She had confided in Montana about an hour before she had left for the wedding, Montana, being Montana, had egged her on.

''Why do you think I'm ringing? I'm dying to know.'' A crunching sound. ''That was an apple,'' Montana explained.

Christy told her friend in detail, even down to the table decorations. She didn't excuse Josh for his unforgivable behaviour. She told Montana all about the reception. How Ashe McKinnon had saved her from…

''Aaah!'' Montana interrupted theatrically, obviously visualising the whole scenario. ''Ashe McKinnon! I've always wanted to meet a man called Ashe McKinnon and a cattle baron! Lucky, lucky you. If I didn't love you I'd hate you for being so beautiful and never putting on weight. That's a sore point with me.''

''Do you want to hear?' Christy asked patiently. Montana had a delicious curvy figure but she couldn't live without her bathroom scales. And her apple diets.

''Throw it at me,'' Montana invited.

''Then I'm not so lucky. He was doing it all for his cousin. He's extremely fond of her.''

''Oh don't give me that!'' Montana retaliated. ''You're the sort of woman to drive men mad. Personally I think it's just an over-rated thing, long blond hair.''

''You may well be right. Josh wasn't going to commit to it. Or me,'' Christy pointed out, with a sick twist of the heart. ''He quickly stepped away from me for a girl with more money.''

''Okay so Josh Deakin is a scumbag,'' Montana reasoned. ''I had to pretend I didn't mind him.''

''You did a remarkably good job.'' Christy was only half joking.

''But, darling, you thought you were in love with him,'' Montana cried as though that explained everything. Perhaps it did. ''What was the point of saying anything? I had to leave well alone. We all did. Thank God you've had a lucky break. You can start again. Stitch up an affair with this McKinnon guy.''

''Sorry, too dangerous.'' Though Montana couldn't see her, Christy shook her head vigorously.

''I bet he's real groovy?''

''You should see him,'' Christy said very dryly.

''And he's a true-blue, red-blooded bloke?'' Montana joked.

''I think anything else is pretty rare in the Outback.''

''I want to see him,'' Montana crowed. ''Do you think I might be tempted?''

''Absolutely. I'd be tempted myself if I hadn't had such a bad experience.''

''And just how many do you think I've had dished out to me?'' Montana asked. ''Five? Six?'' Montana gave her gutsy, infectious laugh. ''It's really sad you had to find out the hard way about Josh, honey, but something wonderful is in store for you. Remember what they used to say about you at Uni? You'd end up Someone.''

''Spoken by the woman who voted for me.''

''So what's the cattleman like in bed?'' Montana screeched with laughter.

''I'm quite sure he's absolutely fabulous,'' Christy replied.

''Oh God, you must have fallen in love with him?''

''It's hard to fall in love with someone when you're still trying to recover from a broken heart,'' Christy offered very soberly. Although Josh had failed dismally to measure up, it didn't lessen the wounded pride.

''Don't let it warp you, kiddo,'' Montana advised gently. ''So, are you going to see the cattle baron again?''

''We're going out for the day actually,'' Christy confided, thinking the way she was acting was really odd. Maybe it was natural after emotional shock. ''I'm waiting on his call.''

''How about that!'' Montana let out another excited shriek. ''So, didn't I tell you, you can always take the next cab on the rank. I'll get off in case he rings. Give me a buzz tonight, eh, kiddo?''

"Will do." Christy blew a kiss down the phone.

When Ashe McKinnon's call came she had to rush out of the shower to answer it, wrapping herself in a towelling robe trying to compose herself.

"How are you today?" he asked, solicitous but with a bite.

She had a vivid mental image of him. "I'm fine." She was doubly aware, too, of his very attractive voice. Voices were very important to her. His exactly fitted his image. Fascinating, deep, dark, vibrant, kind of edgy.

"So have you decided where you'd like to go?"

"Does this come under the category of keeping an eye on me?" Christy challenged.

"It might well do, Christy, but also I like having your company. Would you consider the beach? I don't see much of the blue Pacific where I come from. More like endless miles of desert and towering blood-red sand hills."

"Uluru is one of my favourite places on earth," the much-travelled Christy told him with a rush of enthusiasm. She had nominated the most famous monolith of the Red Centre. "But the beach is great. Josh and I used to—" She broke off too late, disgusted with herself for the slip.

"Do you really think I want to hear?" Antagonism threaded his voice.

"I was talking without thinking. I need time to get rid of the old baggage. Time to lose the cruel cuts and bruises."

"Josh, my dear Christy, has met and married someone else," he pointed out. "As I've said before, you'd better slash all thoughts of him from your mind. The fact is you made vows remember?"

"Vows you're obviously going to hold me to," she said with a little latent hostility.

"I expect you to hold to them yourself. We can talk everything through later in the day if you like. My cousin, Nicole, has a beach house at Noosa—she and her husband, Brendan. You may remember them from last night. I did introduce you."

Christy considered all the people she had met. Usually she remembered everybody. "I don't think so! I wasn't at my sharpest last night."

"Well they remember you." His tone was as dry as hers, more sarcastic. "Nicole is under the impression you've stolen my heart."

"Instead of causing you concern!" she retorted. "I do remember now. Nicole and Brendan, of course. Brendan is an architect? We only spoke for a moment but I liked them. It struck me Nicole has very sad eyes."

There was silence for a moment, then his quiet voice. "That's very perceptive, Christy. Nic lost her baby earlier in the year. She was ill herself for a time. Complications for mother and child. The little girl survived a day or two. They were devastated."

Sympathy welled up in her. "Oh, they would be. I'm so very sorry. It puts my heartbreak into perspective."

"Except your heart isn't broken." The gentle, almost tender tone toughened. "Your pride has been dashed, that's all. You'll realise that more and more as the weeks go on. Anyway," he continued bracingly, "Nic asked us up for lunch if we care to go. If you're shy or you prefer not to we can go our own way."

"I'm not a shy person," she assured him.

He thought of the way she had returned his kiss. The touch and taste of her mouth. "I know that, Christy. Being shy would seem implausible for such a beautiful woman—"

"Let alone a valued member of a top P.R. firm."

"Ah, yes. Whitelaw Promotions, isn't it?" he asked suavely.

"You have a good memory."

"It came to me in a flash. And then there were the photographers although we tried to dodge them. One called out to you, 'Christy, look this way!'"

"We turn up at the same functions," she explained lightly. "So, it's lunch with Nichole and Brendan?"

"I think you'll enjoy it. Nic is a brave girl. They have two other children. Great little kids, Kate's six. I'm her godfather. Kit—Christopher—is four."

"We have something in common already, a name." A smile sounded in Christy's voice.

"A beautiful name." He said it in such a way it gave her a little shiver. "You'll still want to bring your bikini. I have every intention of hitting the surf."

The Boyds' contemporary beach house, a house of dynamic forms, commanded a rocky hilltop overlooking the glorious ocean.

"What a magnificent site," Christy remarked, staring up at it from the road. They had been driving for well over an hour and now they were due to arrive.

"As you can see, the house takes full advantage of the view," Ashe acknowledged with a smile. "Brendan designed it. They always wanted a house at the beach. Especially when the kids came along. The Pad they call it."

"Some pad!" She reflected for a moment who could afford it. And it was the second house.

He laughed. "Actually though the front facade is quite striking I prefer the house as seen from the beach. It's like a giant sculpture. An extension of the cliff face."

"It's certainly very large." And it spelled money. No one could build a house like that without a family fortune.

''I suppose it is,'' he agreed casually, used to a huge historic homestead from childhood. ''The west wing is for family or guests when they come visiting. Nic's father is a career diplomat. He has a posting overseas. The U.S. of A. They love it. Nic doesn't see much of her parents these days. Her mother is the McKinnon. My late father's sister, Caroline. He had three. One visits me every so often, Zoe. She's a real character, an academic never married, but with plenty of interests. The other was killed in a fall from her horse when she was only sixteen. The fall didn't kill her. The horse took fright and kicked her in the head.''

''How terrible.'' So not such a fortunate life. Christy stared away, knowing how tragic for the family that must have been.

He nodded, his handsome face taking on its somewhat severe expression. ''My grandparents never got over it. At least they didn't live to face the loss of their two sons. My father and Callista's. They were killed in a light plane crash, mechanical failure. It simply fell out of the air.''

The tender-hearted Christy felt like reaching for his hand but didn't dare. ''So life has been cruel?''

''Very much so, in some ways. At one time I thought it was going to be a way of life.'' Grief flickered like a shadow.

''And your mother? Does she live on the station?'' Christy turned her head to look at him. Perfectly straight nose, chiselled mouth, strong chin and jawline. He was a profoundly handsome man.

''My mother left when I was ten years old,'' he said, to her surprise. She hadn't read about that. ''Almost to the day.''

It was said without expression. Yet Christy looked down at her hands. Some intonation in his voice warned her not to ask the reason.

''She was desperate to start a new life,'' he explained after a fraught pause. She was going to hear it sooner or later anyway. ''My mother was bored to distraction with the isolation. Staring out at the horizon. She's a city girl born and bred, she needs lots of lights and entertainment.''

Bitterness and indifference were equally balanced. ''Your parents divorced?'' Christy asked quietly.

''Of course, Christy.'' He threw her a brilliant satirical glance. ''My mother remarried. With a speed that startled us all. Later we found out she was pregnant.''

''Oh!'' Well that explained the flight and the haste. ''So you have a half brother or sister.''

''Apparently,'' he said.

God knows what was behind that shut expression. ''You don't know them?'' Christy, a much-loved only child, couldn't believe it.

''Once or twice I thought I'd like to know them,'' he admitted. ''It's a brother by the way. Duane Moss Huntington III.''

So his mother hadn't run off with an ordinary man.

''But you saw your mother after?'' she asked, agonizing for all of them. His mother would have applied for joint custody. It occurred to her he must have been a most beautiful ten-year-old, curly dark hair and those wonderful eyes. No mother could turn her back on such a child. Any child of her flesh.

''For a while,'' he shrugged, the mask firmly in place. ''My visits weren't successful. I detested her husband, and sad to say, I despised her. I was very difficult. At war with everyone. My main desire was to get away from them and back to my father.''

''It's only natural it very much affected you.''

The shapely mouth compressed. ''For quite a while I must have been out of control. I don't really remember. But eventually it was something I had to accept. And I did. It was my father who couldn't accept his beautiful wife had left him. He loved her. He'd been so proud of her. She had everything a woman could want, but she threw it back in his face."

"Where does she live now?" Christy asked quietly, an answering ache starting up in her.

"California and New York mainly, though they spend time in Europe. Her husband is an exceptionally rich man. Even richer than my dad, though she swore it was love. Love, my God!"

"We can't protect ourselves against it," she offered sadly, her mind crammed all of a sudden with images of her faithless Josh. "Love takes hold of us regardless of wisdom, or even will. Sometimes it never lets go."

"It never let go for my father though I was wild enough in those days not to have made a good stepson. I wanted my own mother back as she was, not a stranger. But what she did was unforgivable in my book. So terribly, terribly cruel." How well he remembered the loneliness his father had endured, the heartbreak. Men didn't ease their feelings with tears.

"You think she should have stayed?"

That roused him. "Yes I do. I know duty is an old-fashioned word but she should have tried to live up to her vows."

"So vows are very important to you?"

"Enormously important." He shot her a sardonic glance. "Please, Christy, spare me the psychoanalysis. People shouldn't get married if they're not prepared to bring everything they've got to that commitment."

"Yet it still goes wrong," she lamented. "That is to say people change. Grow in different directions. Men are the worst offenders in my book. A lot of them go for a stream of women. They have to prove endlessly they're virile. I had absolutely no idea Josh was seeing your cousin until the evening I happened to pass by the law courts and saw them together, kissing.''

''What did you do, throw a rock?'' He glanced at her swiftly, black eyes sardonic.

''Would it have helped? No, I went on my way. I confronted him the next day.''

''And what did he say?''

He actually slowed the Mercedes, his aunt's, who liked the notion of a namesake car, to ponder her answer, but he was the very last person outside Callista Christy thought she could tell. ''He explained he didn't love me anymore.'' She saw no option but to tell the saving white lie.

''Why do I find it hard to accept that?'' he groaned.

''That's the way it was. I expect he rang last night to apologise for not acknowledging me at the reception.''

''You know that's exactly what he said.'' The mockery was very much on the grim side.

''Meaning?'' She stared across at him.

''You don't really think I was going to let that phone call go. I don't like people who play dirty. People who try to put things over my family. Deakin needed to be warned off.''

''You surely didn't go to the hotel?'' Christy felt the quake in her body.

''Listen I would have got into bed with them if it would have helped,'' he exploded. ''I made a call from the lobby. Your Josh hurried down.''

''He isn't my Josh.'' Christy made the heated response.

''He surely isn't,'' he retorted just as smartly, ''but that doesn't make me feel a helluva lot better.''

''So what did you say to him?'' Christy shuddered, conjuring up the scene.

"Among other things, Miss Parker, I told him he wouldn't want to make an enemy out of me."

"Okay, I don't want to make an enemy out of you," she said. "I'm for a quiet life."

"I suggest you'll only have a quiet life when you're very very old. All Deakin could think of was protecting himself. At your expense, anyone's expense, and that goes for Callista. I don't give this marriage six months."

No part of Christy was pleased, something she would later come to appreciate was telling. Now she said, "Did anyone ever tell you you're a very cynical man? Callista might just love him enough to turn him around. She seems like a very loving person, sweet and gentle…"

"Close up Callista can also be tough," he said in an ironic voice. "She's not a McKinnon for nothing."

"What do any of us know about anyone." Christy shrugged, sounding upset.

He reached over to touch her hand. "Please don't, Christy. I want you to be happy."

The charm—all the more powerful because it wasn't turned on—made her heart flip over in her breast. "You can be nice when you want to," she said as though delivering a difficult verdict.

"There are lots of things about you I like," he answered. "That little cleft in your chin, that long beautiful hair and the clear light green of your eyes. I like their slant. The rest of you isn't bad either."

"So what don't you like? Maybe you'd better not answer, I don't want to jeopardize the day."

"I don't like the way you chose a guy like Josh Deakin to fall in love with. I would have thought you had better taste. Not only taste. I thought you were a woman more in control."

"So I've burnt my fingers," Christy said in a slightly

combative tone. "Next time I start a relationship with a man, a whole lot of planning is going to go into it."

"What about a man you don't love? And who doesn't love you. Then no one will get hurt." He glanced at her, a devastating quirk to his mouth.

"Sorry, I'd have to be attracted to him."

"Naturally," he nodded, "otherwise you'd need your head examined. Why don't you sit down one day and itemise your requirements?"

If she did the list wouldn't contain words that fit him. Like difficult, dangerous, gut-wrenchingly exciting, complex, a man who kept a tight rein on his volatile emotions.

"Shame on you, Christy," he drawled, as if reading her mind. He turned his head and gave her a smile.

Ashe McKinnon. Smiles like that even a jilted woman could get hooked on.

The children were the first to greet them, flying out the front door, running so fast Christy was concerned there would be a fall and very possibly tears. It would be no surprise.

"Uncle Ashe, Uncle Ashe!" they cried in unison, their faces reflecting so much happiness it gave Christy yet another insight into this complex man. For one thing it showed he loved kids and they dearly loved him. The little girl, the elder, had no trouble negotiating the driveway lined by Royal Cuban palms with a triangular section of lush green lawn, but the small boy, just as Christy feared, took a tumble, mercifully on the soft turf.

Ashe, who had gathered Kate's flying figure into his arms, looked away in time to see Christy rush to Kit who lay face down, spread-eagled, apparently kissing the grass.

"Poppet, that was quite a tumble." Christy bent over the

child who turned an adorable little face to her, inky-black curls in contrast to sapphire-luminous blue eyes.

"Oh I don't mind flying but I've got all this grass down my throat." The little boy sat up and gave a choke while Christy patted him on the back.

"What about a glass of water?" she suggested, already half rising.

"No that's okay," Kit vigorously spat grass clippings out of his mouth. "I'm all right." In fact he looked all buoyed up by their arrival. "Are you Christine?"

"Christy to my friends." She gave him her hand, not really expecting him to shake it, perhaps take it, but he pumped away happily.

"You've got a name like mine. Congratulations."

"I'm sure it means we're going to be friends."

"Oh yes, you're the prettiest lady I've ever seen, 'cept Mummy. You can call me Kit. Mummy calls me that."

"It's a great nickname!" Christy stood up, bringing the little boy with her. Kit's beaming smile faded.

"Oh look what I've done! I've made a mark on your skirt. It must have been when I was spitting."

Christy looked down, while the sapphire eyes focused anxiously on her. "That's fine. It will rub off. In fact it's almost disappeared." She shook a tiny mound of damp green grass clipping off her jade cotton skirt, which she wore with a matching halter top.

"Oh good," said Kit, grinning broadly, taking possession of her hand. "I told Daddy not to cut the grass but he said he wanted it to be nice. He put the sprinkler on, too. That's why the grass is wet. I slipped."

"Anyone could have slipped," Christy assured the little boy, making him glow.

"Yes!" he agreed happily. "Though Katey never falls

over. You've come with Uncle Ashe. Do you love him?'' he shot her a surprisingly searching look.

What to say? Up until yesterday I fancied myself in love with the man who married one of your cousins? ''You know what a secret is, don't you, Kit?'' Christy said finally, speaking in a low confidential voice.

''What big people won't tell you about?''

''Until it's time,'' Christy nodded. ''But I will tell you I like him very much.'' She didn't mean that at all. Ashe McKinnon wasn't the sort of man one simply liked.

''That's good,'' Kit said approvingly. ''Uncle Ashe is ours. Mummy said he takes care of us all. I wish we were at home, I could show you my goldfish.'' He held her hand so naturally he might have been holding her hand for all of his short life. ''Come and meet Kate. That's her flapping her hands. I don't like it when she beats me to Uncle Ashe. She always gets ahead because she's so big.''

''Being a boy means you'll be taller than her pretty soon,'' Christy pointed out.

''I'll never be as tall as Uncle Ashe,'' Kit lamented, thrusting out his chest. ''He's loads taller than Daddy. Of all our relations I love him the best.''

And there had to be lots of reasons, Christy thought, walking with Kit toward the other two.

''So how's my little pal?'' Ashe called, suddenly tumble-turning a squealing Kate to the ground. Kit ran to him and got hoisted onto Ashe's shoulder.

''Why haven't you brought Christy before?'' He cupped Ashe's face and bent his dark head to talk into his uncle's ear. ''Christy wouldn't tell me if she loved you or not. It's a secret.''

''That's all right, Kit. She hasn't told me either. Come on, Katey, we haven't forgotten you. Get yourself around here.'' He reached back and caught her. ''Christy this is my little god-daughter—''

''Favourite god-daughter,'' Katey corrected sweetly, very much like her brother in features, build and colouring.

''Favourite god-daughter—I was about to say that—Katherine McKinnon Boyd.''

''That was Mummy's name,'' Katey told Christy, coming to take her hand. ''It makes me special.''

''I can see that. My name is Christine Prudence Parker.''

''What?'' Ashe turned to stare at her.

''Why not?'' She returned his glance. ''If you really liked me you wouldn't mind.''

''Only you're fooling, aren't you?'' Katey smiled up at her. ''It's not really Prudence?''

''Actually it is.'' Christy grimaced a little. ''I had a great-aunt Prudence. She was going to leave me her magnificent four-poster bed, with all the trimmings, one day, but she never did.''

''Who got it?' Katey looked at her aghast.

''I bet there are about forty cats on it right now,'' Christy said. ''Aunt Pru was a great cat fancier. She left her home and all her money to her companion on the understanding she would look after her cats.''

Ashe guffawed and the children bent double.

''What's going on?'' a woman's voice called, hearing all the laughter.

''Oh, Mummy. Come and meet Christy,'' Katey begged. ''She's lovely!''

''Hi, Christy.'' Nicole, dark-haired, blue-eyed, was all smiles. ''Hi, Ashe. I'm so glad you came. Brendan is in the house burning something on the stove. Honestly it's enough to make you cry, but he fancies himself as a chef.''

''If the worse comes to the worst, we can always go to

a restaurant.'' Ashe laughed, bending to kiss his cousin's cheek.

''Only joking,'' Nicole said. ''How lovely you look, Christy. Bren and I weren't sure we dreamed you last night.''

''You're being very kind to me.'' Christy met the smiling gaze, wishing she didn't have to deceive this friendly young woman about the exact nature of her relationship with Ashe. ''I can see where the children get their beautiful sapphire eyes.''

''The eyes are mine,'' Nicole said fondly. ''The rest of them is all Bren. Please, come inside.'' She curled her arm through Christy's. ''I thought Ashe told me everything but he didn't tell me about you.''

''It's a secret, that's why.'' Kit's voice rose. ''Christy is not ready to say.''

''Ho-ho-ho-ho,'' was Nicole's response. ''We'll get it out of her.''

In fact they never did, increasing the high level of interest. But then Ashe was very very deep.

It turned out to be a surprisingly lovely day full of peace, harmony, sunshine and surf, with delightful well-mannered children impossible not to like. A great lunch was prepared by Brendan, with everyone serving themselves from a table in the kitchen and carrying their plates out onto the patio with its glorious views of the beach, the ocean and the hinterland. There was a magnificent red emperor, caught only that morning, baked whole with a saffron sauce, John Dory in beer batter, which the children loved, served with lashings of delicious homemade chips, grilled chicken with an Oriental flavour in case Christy was one of those rare Australians who didn't like seafood—of course she did—accompanied by a garden fresh salad with a difference—

Parmesan-crisped fingers of focaccia, again a favourite of the children.

''It's marvellous to see them enjoying salad,'' Christy remarked to Nicole, watching the two little people eating it enthusiastically. ''I have friends with small children who agonize over not being able to get the kids to eat vegetables let alone salad.''

''We started them very early,'' Brendan, a very attractive thirty-two-old, explained. ''This was the food we all ate and miracle of miracles they accepted it.''

''What a blessing!'' Christy smiled. ''They're beautiful children. A great credit to you both.''

''We lost one.'' Nicole's light charming voice suddenly broke, betraying the sad fact the loss was eating away at her.

Christy grasped her hand and held tight. ''I know. Ashe told me. I'm so sorry. Truly so sorry. I can only guess at your heartbreak.''

Nicole tried very hard to regain control. ''But hey, I wasn't going to mention that, was I?'' She glanced at her husband who smiled at her with love and understanding.

''You're allowed to mention it, Nic,'' Ashe told her quietly. ''We all love you here.''

''That includes me,'' Christy added affectionately. It could easily become true. Nicole drew her as a person.

Later they all went down to the beach where Ashe and Christy had their work cut out trying to get out of the shallows where the children, being children, wanted their full attention. Finally, Brendan came to their rescue, extending both hands.

''Hey, you two, Ashe and Christy have been really good to you and now it's their turn to have a swim. Let's make a space station and give them a surprise.''

The children trotted off with their father while Ashe shot

Christy a challenging look. ''So do I need to give you a head start? I don't know if the costume can take it.''

''Of course it can take it! Versace lycra. Like it?'' Soothed by the lovely day, Christy laughingly struck a model's pose. She'd been hanging out at the beach since she'd been a child. She kept herself in very good shape. Why shouldn't she be at ease in a brief Tigerlily bikini even with those brilliant dark eyes on her?

''The word is love. I love it,'' he mocked.

''Thank you.''

For the next half hour they revelled in the blue crystal water. Christy, a strong swimmer, moved out with him to the front line of the body surfers shooting the big foaming waves right in to the shore. The two of them stayed close together, a seemingly spontaneous thing. It was marvellous. Christy would have liked to spend the rest of the afternoon with the two of them swimming together. Out to the horizon, she thought blissfully. She was used to long swims. She had always stayed in much longer than Josh—in fact Josh didn't swim as well as she did. She couldn't say that of Ashe McKinnon, causing her to wonder how and where he got in his swimming in his desert home. Back on the warm white sand, she asked.

''Good grief, we have lagoons.'' He looked at her in amazement, picking up her towel and handing it to her. ''Chains of beautiful, coolabah-lined billabongs crisscross the station. In the bad times many are reduced to a mere trickle but others are deep permanent waterholes and bracingly cold. I'd rather swim there than anywhere else outside the ocean. We have a swimming pool, too, for the convenience of our guests.''

''The unadventurous ones?'' She lightly towelled herself off. The sun would do the rest.

''It's true some people are overawed by the wilderness

and the sheer size of the place. Two million acres. We have a thriving live cattle export market with Malaysia and Egypt going at the moment with 100 million riding on it. A lot of people connected to the industry come and go. We also breed the Australian workhorse, a descendant of the Waler. They're splendid animals with good temperaments, so they're very much in demand for workhorses—the best—and polo ponies. All in all, we do a lot of entertaining in connection with the operation.''

''So you really need a wife, a hostess?'' She turned an enquiring face to him, unnerved by something in his expression.

''Would you care to discuss it with me?''

''What would be the point?'' she answered flippantly, but she shook inside. ''I told you. I'm off marriage as a topic of discussion. For a long time.''

''What a challenge!'' The self-assurance in his black eyes brushed that claim aside. ''Do you know how good you look?'' He reached out and touched the back of her neck. Her warm, thick, golden hair, honey-coloured when wet, was arranged in a long, thick plait so her nape was bare, creamy to his touch.

For Christy, the cobalt-blue sky tilted.

His hand on her skin, the strong pads of his fingers.

She experienced a blind rush of sexuality.

He knew how to touch a woman. Years of practice? Just a stroke, yet her insides clenched. Such an erotic sensation. He was so much taller than she. So much darker of skin. The skin of her salt-glossed body was palest gold against his dark tan. It appeared to be all over. No paler line of skin anywhere. He had a splendid physique. So arrogantly male. All of a sudden Christy had an overpowering impulse to just fall to the sand and lie there in front of him. Could it be she was emotionally unstable? Worse, was she transparent?

Even as her thoughts confused and disturbed her, he pulled her to him and kissed her mouth. Kissed her. *Kissed her.* Kisses didn't get any better. Or so memorable.

"Do you mind?" he murmured as he finally lifted his dark head.

"You could explain what that was all about." While she was almost blind to her surroundings, he glanced casually over her head.

"Nic and the kids are coming back from their walk. They'll expect to see me kissing you. They think you're my girl."

"We could correct that in a minute," she said sharply. "We could tell them the truth."

"The one thing we can't do." He began to slowly unplait her hair, and shook it loose. "Not now. Let's keep this day as happy as we can."

She nodded after a minute and stared at the three figures in the distance. "Nicole is trying so hard to be brave but she's hurting badly inside."

He shrugged a powerful shoulder. "She's not as well as I thought." His expression deepened into concern.

"Maybe there's such a thing as trying too hard to carry on," Christy said quietly. "Forgive me if I'm being presumptuous but I think Nic needs more time to grieve. Brendan, too. I can see how much they love each other. He's doing everything he can to help."

"He's a good man." Ashe gave his hard-muscled body a token rubover with his towel. "Nic couldn't have married anyone better. What they both need is a complete break. I'll speak to them. The kids would adore to come outback."

That was a big surprise. "Could you manage them? I

had the idea you were an extremely busy and committed man.''

''That's where *you* come in,'' he said.

''Me?'' She experienced a sharp fierce moment of shock and glanced up at him quickly; stunned to see he was serious.

''You probably don't remember but you let slip in the car you were owed a month off?''

She floundered. ''I certainly didn't intend spending it with you in your desert stronghold. I'm far from ready for such an experience.''

''It would certainly keep you away from your ex-lover,'' he said, the note of humour off key.

''I thought they were supposed to be on their honeymoon?'' Christy shot back.

''Three weeks isn't long. I don't trust that guy.''

''As it turns out, neither do I,'' she said, still retaining the pain of hurt and humiliation. ''My pride has been badly dented. Remember I was jilted.''

''Jilted?'' He was roused to throw up his high-mettled head. ''When he's so damn desperate to get you for his mistress?''

Only the truth. ''I'm glad the children aren't with us,'' she told him severely.

''You will forgive me, I hope?'' His sardonic gaze rested on her upturned face, the cream skin deepened a little by the golden rays of the sun. ''By the way, how come you didn't arrive at an engagement? Or did you and you've given back the ring?''

''Oh God, let's have a nice afternoon?'' she groaned, trying to hold back a cloud of windblown hair.

''*I'm* having a great time.'' He informed her. ''You're quite athletic, aren't you?''

''I won lots of prizes at school,'' she answered. It was true.

''With a tendency to boast.''

Christy had to laugh. ''I'm not out to impress you. I'm just telling it the way it was. Dressage was an interest for a while.''

''Really?'' One black brow shot up. ''Now that does have a certain cachet, Christy.''

''Farm girl,'' she responded. Horses were a way of life.

''Size of the farm?''

''Oh, close to a thousand acres. A speck compared to your little spread.''

''I see gold and green.'' He smiled. ''Rolling hills. Fields of wheat. Woolly sheep.''

''Beautiful lucent mists in the morning. Sounds like you've been there.''

''I've been just about everywhere in the pastoral world,'' he told her, joining her on the sand. ''Perhaps. Perhaps…'' He looked off pensively towards the sparkling ocean. The surface was spread with glittering diamonds. Seagulls swooped in search of food; foaming white water washed the sand.

''What?'' she prompted. Of course she was meant to be intrigued. She knew that but still she was caught hook, line and sinker.

''I've just had a profound thought. Is it possible you'd consider helping me if I offer to take the kids? I promise I'll do everything to make your stay on Augusta exciting and enjoyable.''

Under the cover of her wide-brimmed straw hat, Christy's face flushed. Augusta Downs, his station. ''You can't be serious?''

''I'm accustomed to speaking seriously,'' he informed

her, giving her what she was coming to think of as his ''lordly'' look.

''Then why have you sprung this on me now?'' she demanded, turning sideways to stare at him.

''Surely because I only just thought of it. Okay—'' he shrugged ''—I had considered getting *you* to the station but that was before I came to fully appreciate how down Nic really is.''

Christy's expression matched her feverish green eyes. ''Don't you think this is just a teeny-weeny bit impetuous?'' she suggested. ''First and foremost, Nic being a most loving and conscientious mother mightn't consent to such a thing. After all they barely know me. *You* don't know me either for that matter, although you seem to be arranging my life.''

His eyes moved along her beautiful pale gold legs. Like a ballet dancer's, slender but strong. ''I'm in my element arranging things,'' he said dryly.

''You're a terrible person.''

His dark eyes gentled. ''You're not joking! Don't you want to do a good deed?''

She sighed deeply. ''I don't understand you, Ashe McKinnon. Yesterday you were angered by the very sight of me.''

''Did I really give you that impression?'' This creature of grace and beauty? Elegant lines and beguiling curves.

''Yes, you did,'' she said, cramming the flower-decorated straw hat further down on her head.

His mouth twisted ironically. ''I didn't want to see you make a fool of yourself either. No matter yesterday, you're in favour today.''

''So there's a good side to this?'' she challenged him sarcastically.

''Shh, they're coming,'' he warned as though the distant

figures could hear every word. "We're love birds remember? You've got a minute to give me your answer."

"Oh my God, it's *no.*" She waved to the approaching figures. They waved back. "I can't, Ashe."

He liked the way she said his name. It lingered in the air between them, curiously like an endearment. "It could mean a great deal. Nic is taking life too hard."

She met his gaze briefly. This man was a hypnotist. Not only that, he was succeeding in banishing Josh from her mind. "For all you know I might be terrible with children."

"No, you're good with them," he contradicted her. "You'll have plenty of help. I have a housekeeper. She has staff. I'm not panting for wild sex if that's what you're worrying about."

"Far from it," she said tartly, keeping her gaze firmly on her bare toes. Wild sex! The very thought made a blinding white light snap on inside her.

"Time's up, Christy," he said, aware of the delicate natural fragrance she gave off like a flower. He wanted her. He wanted her so badly it astonished him. And he wasn't a man to waste time.

"It's blackmail, you know." She surrendered. God knows why.

His dark eyes gleamed. "You're thinking of someone else. Not me."

The children ran to them excitedly, sunny smiles, cheeks rosy with warmth and exercise.

"Hello, beautiful!" Ashe pulled Katey down onto the sand beside him. "Enjoy your walk?"

Christy just had time to stare briefly at the cloudless blue heavens before Kit landed in her lap, dark curls clustering around his angelic little face.

What have I done? she thought.

What have I done?

CHAPTER FOUR

Two weeks later, Christy, a child on each hand, stood in front of Augusta Downs homestead, staring up at the wonderfully pleasing facade wondering how the early pioneers had ever succeeded in their undertaking of reproducing "Home" in the overwhelming vastness and isolation of the Australian Outback, with its heat and blazing colours and the crippling seasons of drought. Augusta, a homestead with its bore-watered home gardens and myriad outbuildings seen from the ground, created the fleeting illusion of an English country estate, emphasizing the importance of the English, Irish and Scottish families in the pioneering annals of the nation. Seen from the air, Augusta, showplace of the McKinnon operation, presented an awesome sight; a settlement like a small township set down in a vast riverine desert with blood-red soil, rolling red dunes, gatherings of great gums along the lagoons and billabongs, dead desert oaks bleached bone-white by a scorching sun on the ancient level plains, no other human habitation to the shimmering, mirage bedevilled horizon.

In such a place as starkly different to the British Isles as it could possibly be, the transported McKinnon family had lived and died. Here, too, they had developed their great selection without pause since it was taken up in the mid 1800s and named Augusta Downs after the bride of the first immigrant adventurer, James Andrew McKinnon.

At barely twenty-one, with the financial assistance of his well-to-do family in Scotland, he'd been able to purchase a great holding, he and others; a very special breed of men, the forerunners of the great cattle kings. James' driving ambition was to breed great herds of beef cattle, in the process founding his own dynasty in this new Promised Land. His extraordinary life one of unremitting hardships, self-denial and indomitable vision paid off handsomely, if not for him then for his descendants.

Eventually James had persuaded two of his brothers, Duncan and William to join him. At first the brothers worked Augusta, then as James began to extend the family holdings to the north and east Duncan and William took over the running of the new McKinnon outposts. Today the total holdings through the giant State of Queensland and the Northern Territory itself twice the size of Texas but with about one per cent of the Texan population, covered an area greater than the size of the McKinnon's native Scotland. In the vast Outback where the pioneering deeds of extraordinary daring do were commonplace, the kings of the cattle country had forged their own special mystique. Fascinating and romantic to the city dwellers, the life was not without its ruinous conditions and the constant dangers of isolation. Cattlemen had to be tough. Cattlemen let nothing stand in their way. Small wonder Ashe McKinnon had swept her off her feet with his sheer audaciousness, Christy thought.

She knew already Augusta remained the family flagship, the jewel in the crown to this day. The homestead, she realised as she studied it, had been added to greatly over the years, obviously to accommodate the growing family. What looked like the original gabled two-storied building, now the central section, without the usual colonial verandahs, had sprouted huge symmetrical wings probably by the turn of the century with the balconies, verandahs, slender pillars and decorative cast-iron balustrades that made it so very picturesque.

"Can we go inside, please, Christy?" Kit piped up, jerking Christy out of her reverie. "I want a drink."

"Of course, darling." She bent to him remorsefully. He had been so very good right throughout the long flight to Longreach where a charter flight stood by to wing them into Augusta Downs. Ashe had intended to fly them himself but something unforeseen had cropped up. Something to do with drilling difficulties associated with sinking a huge bore.

"I'm so sorry, Kit," Christy apologised. "I was busy admiring the homestead."

"It's lovely isn't it?" Katey beamed with pleasure. Despite all the travel she was still full of beans. "This is the McKinnon ancestral home. Uncle Ashe said it belongs to us all. It doesn't really," she confided to Christy, rolling her eyes drolly. "Uncle Ashe is the real owner, but we're his family."

"He certainly loves you," Christy said as though it was something she had just discovered. At least something she hadn't glimpsed at the wedding.

Inside the grandly furnished homestead—Christy didn't know where to look first—Mrs. Davidson, the housekeeper who only answered to Lonnie—later on Christy learned Lonnie had been christened Leonora by her opera-buff mother, a name that clearly didn't suit—bustled around in an all-out effort to make them welcome and comfortable. Their luggage had already been placed in their rooms by the attractive young station hand, Garry, who had been allotted the job of driving them up from the landing strip to the house, close on fifteen minutes away. Their bedrooms in the west wing all adjoined except for Christy's sitting room, which acted as a buffer. It was a lovely mellow feminine place of satin and rosy chintz sofas, with books, a very interesting series of watercolour paintings on the walls, a cylinder front desk with beautiful brass fittings, paired with an antique chair and a broad view of the extraordinary landscape.

"Now young Kit," Lonnie spoke to the little boy who was openly yawning. "You can either have a bedroom to yourself or share with Katey. As you can see, Miss—" Lonnie turned to address Christy now.

"Oh please, *Christy*—" Christy insisted.

Lonnie showed her pleasure, her mouth curling up in a smile. "As you can see, Christy, Mr. Ashe had a second bed brought in just in case."

"In case of what?" Kit demanded.

Christy tousled his hair. "In case you're lonely. The room can certainly take two beds and then some." The bedrooms were huge by today's standards. "And those beautiful embroidered linens?" she queried, thinking them perhaps too delicate and expensive for the children.

"Must use them, Christy," Lonnie assured her. "There are crates and crates of things in this house—wedding presents from way back that have never been opened."

"Good grief!" Christy bent to hug Kit who nuzzled her neck, obviously missing his mother.

"You have to see it to believe it," Lonnie clucked. "They really want opening up, but Mr. Ashe won't give the okay to do it. A lot of it was his parents' stuff."

And he isn't ready for it, Christy thought, releasing Kit who ran off with his sister to make a tour of their rooms.

"I want to share," Kit told Christy when they returned. "Last time I was here I was little."

"Nearly a year ago, pet." Lonnie lay an affectionate hand over his shoulder. "Don't you remember the whole McKinnon clan turned up for Christmas?"

"It was wonderful!" Katey plonked herself down on the long bench upholstered with beautiful needlepoint tapestry at the foot of Christy's huge canopy bed. The bed, which was easily bigger than king size, could accommodate a family. "Uncle Ashe puts up a great big Christmas tree in the front hall," Katey told her. "It's huge and it has wonderful ornaments all over it. Some of them are very old and very precious, a big star at the top, and tons of presents for everyone under the tree. Mummy was expecting our little baby then, but it died."

Christy went to the child and sat down beside her. "Part of us never dies, Katey. The important part, the soul. While we're enjoying this lovely holiday with Uncle Ashe your little sister, I know she was named Elizabeth after your grandmother, is having a glorious time in Heaven. There's no sickness or unhappiness there. God doesn't allow it."

"I still wish she was here," Katey insisted, looking sad.

Christy held her. "Of course you do, so you can really love her, but she's watching you."

"That's what Mummy says," Katey confided. "Then she cries."

"It's the saddest experience in the world, Katey, for a mother to part with her child. Try to think of it as a separation but not forever. You and Kit are a great comfort and joy to Mummy and Daddy. They adore you."

"But we're going to leave them one day when we get married," Kit pointed out, sounding older than his years.

"Don't be silly. No one will marry you. You're way too little," Katey scoffed.

"I mean when I grow up," Kit retorted.

"When you grow up, Kit, you're going to be very, very handsome," Christy said, drawing him to her and examining his face. "You're tired. I think you should have forty winks after we decide on the beds. Come on, let's have a look at the room.

"So which is it to be?" Christy said when they reached

Katey's bedroom. "Seeing this is Katey's room she really should have first pick."

"Okay then..." Katey eyed the beds then the room. "I want this one." She went to the bed nearest the verandah, which looked like it could have been slept in by Queen Victoria. "I love the yellow bedspread. Is the other one right for you, Kit?"

"Boys don't have pink." Kit pulled a dubious grimace.

"We can change the coverlet easily," Lonnie assured him in her easy, comfortable way, her warm brown eyes magnified by her specs. "I have a very nice blue one in mind."

"Anyway I'm the nearest to Christy's room," Kit said, making it sound for all the world he'd be nearest to heaven.

"When he has bad dreams, he cries," Katey told her, mildly scornful.

Immediately Kit looked down, his long eyelashes languishing on his satiny cheeks.

"He won't cry when I tuck him in," Christy promised. "We're going to have such a good time during the day both of you are going to fall asleep as soon as your heads hit the pillow. And *stay* asleep."

"Will you listen for me, Christy? Don't shut the door," Kit asked, anxiety in his sapphire eyes.

"I'll never be asleep so deeply I won't hear you, darling," Christy said and vowed there and then to keep an eye and ear open. "I won't shut the door either."

It had taken some convincing for Nicole to agree to this time apart from her children. On the one hand it was obvious even to Nicole she was desperately in need of time out with her husband, but being such a devoted mother she had been seriously concerned by the idea of leaving the two young ones. She had never done so before. Only the fact Nicole held Ashe in the highest esteem and had taken such an instant liking to Christy had the matter been settled at all. This put great responsibility on Christy but it also brought into play her organizational skills and the deep maternal feelings she now knew were in her.

Christy put an arm around each child; touched and grateful, both of them melted into her. "This is going to be a lovely holiday. It's my first time and the two of you are going to show me everything."

And so it was the three-week holiday on Augusta began. A time that was destined to totally change lives.

While the children went with Lonnie for homemade lemonade, Christy saw Garry off. "Maybe you and I could go riding one day?" Garry suggested, hooking one high-heeled riding boot around a verandah chair. "What'd ya say?"

"At this stage, Garry—" she smiled, not wanting to be unfriendly even if he was being forward "—I'd say no."

"I won't give up." He smiled cheekily back into her eyes. "You just might change your mind."

"That might well be," she answered, somewhere between polite and blithe.

"'Course you're a guest of the Boss." The thought seemed to dissolve a lot of Garry's initial enthusiasm. "I might have to ask his permission."

"Really?" Christy's face reflected her surprise.

"Hell, yes." Garry nodded emphatically. "Don't give me that big-eyed look. The Boss can get really stroppy if anyone steps out of line. Every guy on the station knows they have to be very careful with the ladies."

She nearly laughed. "You mean you can't give in to impulses like inviting the house guests out riding?"

"Something like that." He grinned, showing excellent teeth. "I might get sacked."

''So apparently you've taken a risk?''

''Why not?'' he asked firmly. ''I've never seen such a beautiful girl in my life.''

''Imagine!'' Christy narrowed her eyes against the brilliant glare. ''Unless I'm mistaken, here's the Boss now.''

''Is, too.'' Garry straightened instantly. ''I'd better get cracking.'' He loped off the verandah. ''See ya, Christy.''

Despite his bravado Garry lost no time in drawing away, putting one arm out the window to acknowledge Ashe.

He didn't get a return wave, Christy noticed. She remained where she was while Ashe brought the open Jeep to a halt at the base of the steps.

''Hi!'' His smile lifted the handsome severity of his expression to a flash of radiance. ''I've had to leave them to it,'' he explained. ''I was more concerned about how you and the kids survived all the travel?''

''It was well worth it for all of us,'' Christy said with pleasure, unable to control the involuntary rippling thrills the sight of him gave her. He held his six-foot-three frame with such arrogant male grace, like the hero of some adventure in the Outback commercial. She drank in the pearl-grey akubra he now swept off, his hair tousled into crisp curls, red bandanna, blue denim work shirt, fancy buckled silver belt, fitted jeans, high-heeled riding boots that made him tower even taller.

''You should recognise me when you see me again.'' He moved towards her with a mocking smile and gave a little tug on a lock of her long blond hair.

''It's because you look so good.'' She tilted her head right back to look up at him. ''I like the gear.''

''We all wear pretty much the same thing around here,'' he replied smoothly.

''Some obviously better than others.'' Lanky, lean Garry,

attractive as he was with sun-streaked hair and nut-brown eyes, didn't look anything like Ashe McKinnon.

"What was Garry doing here?" Ashe now asked, a little coolly, untying his red bandanna and stripping it off.

"He brought us up from the airstrip." Christy looked at him, trying to read his thoughts. "I thought you would know."

"His job was to bring you and the luggage. Take the luggage into the house. Not strike up a conversation, for God's sake."

Her eyes lit with a touch of defiance. "So much for democracy."

"Oh I'm very democratic," he said. "Only nothing happens on Augusta I don't want."

"I just hope I remember," Christy retorted dryly.

"If he's gone and asked you to go riding with him, that's never going to happen," Ashe warned.

"Well not this weekend," Christy tossed off mock-sweetly. "Have you come home for lunch?" She hoped he was going to say yes.

"Hmm," he said, eyeing her steadily. Neat little violet top, very feminine and sexy, skinny-legged, bright blue jeans. Her golden-blond hair hung richly around her face and flowed over her shoulders, the green eyes and creamy complexion were as fresh as spring.

"I can't say I blame Garry for momentarily going crazy." Irritation gave way to a wry understanding. "I had to come myself to check if you were as beautiful as I last saw you or you'd wilted away in the heat."

"What heat?" Christy ran her hand up under her nape. It was damp but she didn't tell him. "Shall we go inside?" she asked. He was making her feel too much a woman. "The children will be thrilled you're here."

''And what about you?'' He lay a light staying hand on her shoulder.

''I'm still trying to figure out how I agreed to come out here,'' she confessed, ''to a complete and utter stranger. I'm not normally a reckless person.''

''Come on,'' he jeered. ''Anyway you did it for Nic and Brendan.''

''For their sakes, yes.'' Her pose was casual. Inside she felt electric. ''You have the most wonderful private kingdom. I can't wait to explore it.''

''I'm glad you like it,'' he returned, still lazily studying her.

''Just so long as I don't have to drop a curtsey at your approach.''

''No one around here does that,'' he assured her, ''but if you ever feel inclined…!''

Lonnie lost no time putting the lunch on the table, a deep-dish chicken pie with little herb-and-sausage flavoured dumplings which tempted the children, served with a salad, and for afterwards, caramel ice-cream topped with ginger syrup, which the children pronounced so ''yummy'' Christy had to have some.

Happy, content and drowsy, both agreed without a murmur to an afternoon siesta while Ashe showed Christy over the house. She'd known at first glance it was furnished in a variety of styles, English, French, Oriental, all the rooms down to the guest bedrooms were filled with art and antiques the family had collected over the generations. To Christy's fascinated eyes it was a veritable Aladdin's cave.

She found very entertaining, Ashe's running commentary. It was full of interest, very informative, sometimes revealing and delivered with panache. This was a man who had lived all his life in what was without question a grand house without he or the house being in any way grandiose. No matter the sheer size, and they didn't cover the entire house, Augusta homestead was none the less very much a home where the one family had lived, loved and died, each generation leaving their mark and all kinds of collections.

"My grandfather left this particular collection to me." They were in Ashe's study with beautiful cedar wood panelling and hung with a collection of equestrian paintings and a glass display case filled with sculptures of horses right through the ages.

"Those are Tang." Ashe pointed to a shelf where several proud and sturdy pottery horses in coloured glazes rested.

"I particularly love the one with the rider," Christy said.

"Here, have a closer look," Ashe offered, going to pick up the beautiful little model.

"Oh no, I'd feel frightful if anything went wrong."

He clicked his tongue. "It's not going to go wrong. You love horses."

"I do." Christy took the pottery figure carefully into her hands, admiring the vigour of the sculpture. "It appears to be a different horse from the one beside it," she remarked. "The other has a broader neck. It's taller and more muscular as well. A different breed?"

"Well observed, Miss Parker," he congratulated her. "Although they're both Tang Dynasty and well over thirteen or fourteen hundred years old, the second horse belongs to a breed imported from the West. The little man standing beside the horse is—"

"His groom of course," Christy said in delight. "The glazes on both are beautiful. I feel honoured you've shown me." Christy extended her glazed pottery figure to Ashe who returned it to the cabinet.

"We used to have a pottery horse with a marvellous head from the Han Dynasty. Goodness knows what happened to it. I hate to say it but some guest in the house must have taken a fancy to it.''

''Obviously you mean it was stolen?''

''Of course. I loved it when I was a boy. You could see the nostrils actually trembling. A Bachtrian pony descended from the Perso-Arab horses brought into China to serve to cavalry.''

''So horses are a McKinnon passion?''

''Very much so. The bronzes are very fine. That particular one is by Degas. Many of the equestrienne paintings are nineteenth-century French. My great-grandmother, Celeste, had a passion for the Oriental school of artists as you can see by the large painting over the mantel. You probably know the Orientals flourished in Europe toward the end of the last century. Grandmere Celeste, she was French by the way, a McKinnon family connection, found the paintings very thrilling and romantic.''

''I'm not surprised. That one is marvellous,'' Christy said. It was a scene where a magnificent pure white Arabian horse was being offered for sale in a North African bazaar with all its attendant tumultuous colours and exotica. ''You must be very proud of your home and your heritage.''

He met her gaze. ''Well it's the story of frontier Australia, isn't it? The history and development of a great pastoral industry as well as a rich social history. If you're interested we have a great deal of archival material in the family library. We'll go there now. There are personal accounts of both my family's lives and the intertwining lives of our neighbours even though they might have been hundreds of miles away. My aunt Zoe—she holds a Doctorate of Philosophy—has published three books in connection with our cultural heritage. She's working on another now. You'll like her. Zoe is a very clever and interesting woman.

She also manages to combine her considerable academic knowledge with a great sense of fun.''

Incredulously she heard his words. ''I'm going to meet her?''

''Sure,'' he told her crisply. ''Sometime.''

''You sound very certain.'' She was shaken to her toes by the intensity of his expression.

''Don't panic. I'm not going to hold you prisoner.'' His brilliant gaze, the distillation of a passionate nature, ran over her.

''That's good because I know you could if you wanted to.''

''Come on, Christy,'' he said with surprising gentleness. ''You know you're keen to be my friend.''

She half turned, redirecting her gaze. ''You're far too uncomfortable for that.''

''Uncomfortable,'' he scoffed. ''Now I know where I stand.''

''You know what I mean.'' She turned back with the challenge, ''You darn near held me to ransom.''

''How so?'' His black eyes, so deep, so beautiful, were impossible to read.

''I still don't believe you trust me.'' Why would he?

''I haven't trusted women for many many years.'' His vibrant voice, though mocking, was a touch bitter. ''To illustrate a point. Not so very long ago, a matter of weeks, you were on the edge of upstaging my cousin's wedding.''

''I wasn't.'' She held to the fine edge of control.

''You were where you *weren't* supposed to be,'' he pointed out.

''I did nothing illegal.''

''Not socially acceptable, Christy,'' he said in a low, ironic tone. ''At that same reception my cousin's brand-new husband was using his strength to pull you into his arms. I recall the moment as vividly as though it happened this very morning.''

''Then I hope you noted I was fending him off?'' Christy was shocked by a sudden urge to hit him. Hell, he had no hesitation about hurting her.

''Oddly I didn't,'' he clipped off. ''I was too busy paying close attention to Deakin.''

She was aware of the ambivalence in their feelings for each other, a strong attraction, a threat of hostility. ''I'm sorry about all of it. I must have been temporarily out of my mind.''

''You'd have to be to want to ruin a wedding.''

''What I wanted was to give Josh a good fright. I thought he *loved* me.'' She despised the residual emotion in her own voice. ''I still can't believe the way he acted.''

''So your feelings for him haven't evaporated?'' He sounded distant and very direct at the same time.

''Why don't you try to understand'' She stared up at him, in a conflicting maze of emotion. ''What if someone had done the same thing to *you?* Answer *that,* Ashe McKinnon.'' Little flames lit Christy's eyes. ''I bet you've got a ferocious temper.''

''Which I mostly keep well under control. Right now I'm having trouble.'' He grasped her shoulders, his fingers exploring the delicate bones. What was passing between them was a difficult, dangerous current. He gave in to his desire, bringing his mouth down on hers, aching for it like some powerful drug, remembering the last time.

For Christy a whole range of emotions were fiercely transmitted. She felt the faint rasp of his skin as his mouth crushed her pulsing lips. His tongue engaged in a mad mating dance with hers, as his hands steadied her. It lasted only seconds yet it left her trembling, with no rules to follow. She had never encountered such sexual power. He was the best and the worst of men and he wasn't always kind.

"Why do you do this to us both?" Her powerful arousal made her angry. This was a man who fed on women's faithlessness.

"A summer storm," he said in a faultlessly cool way, easing one calloused finger over the tender pads of her lips. Like a baby's skin. Newly bared. "I'm a man. I have my wants."

"The truth is, you're mocking me. And you like it."

"Now there's an interesting spin." He observed her closely. "If I'm mocking you, Christy, I'm mocking myself."

"You can't keep on doing it," she said jaggedly. "I'm here to look after the children."

"You're also having a holiday. Believe it or not. I want you to enjoy yourself. You're here to spend time with the children, certainly. You're also here to spend some time with *me.*"

She hardened her voice, her eyes darkening. "Ah, the authoritarian cattle baron. Could you possibly tell me in what special capacity?"

Just to confound her, he changed tack, exerting that unpredictable fantastic charm. "Not as my sleeping partner, unless it excites you."

The experience would electrify her. "I'm still grieving my own stupidity," she told him sharply.

"Then it shouldn't take long. I can't believe a man like Josh Deakin left any indelible mark on you. You've never really loved *anyone.*"

"What about my mother and father?"

"Any *man,* I mean. I know you love your mother and father. But you're a big girl now. I'm talking men. Passion. A lot of people believe romantic love is myth. Nothing more than illusion. It exists only for a short time before it fizzles out. I forget the name of the guy who wrote a book about that.''

Christy made a little dismissive sound. ''I don't buy the argument. The bloom of romance has never faded for my parents.''

''Then they're very lucky. I'm equally certain they work at keeping their love alive?''

Christy surrended to her musings. ''Yes they do. They nurture one another. However, I think *you,* like your guru, have probably gone sour on life.''

''So why the hell am I staring into your beautiful green eyes?''

''You just like playing with fire,'' she told him acidly, riding high on the emotion generated by his kiss.

He shook his head. ''A man could get trapped that way. I'm going through a period when I'm considering a good working strategy for marriage.''

His eyes were full on hers. ''Don't look at me.'' She gave a little shiver. ''I still believe in love.''

''A lot of people who fall in love and get married finish up desperate to escape. Sooner or later reality intrudes. Falling in love isn't loving, Christy. That's a misconception, as you've found out to your cost. There must be the right way of going about it to make love happen. The same interests, the same values, the same goals.''

''I could never get married without being in love,'' Christy maintained, when her ''love'' for Josh was little more than a sham.

''Love as in lust? Perhaps a little more elegant than that.''

''A heck of a lot more elegant as you put it.'' He was disturbing her terribly.

''Plans. Flowers. Church. Reception. A solemn and important occasion. Women revel in it like their wedding day is going to last the rest of their lives. A man just gets through it.''

''You're having me on?'' Temper rare in her sparked.

''That, as well,'' he suddenly relented. ''Anyway why get so defensive? That kiss we just shared was quite feverish, I thought. Almost romantic passion. Certainly sexual attraction. The tricks our hormones play to hoodwink us.''

''You terrify me, Ashe McKinnon,'' she said, inhaling deeply.

''I mean to, Christy.'' His tone was an unnerving balance between tender and sarcastic. ''No, I'm fooling. My work is my life. I might be the top gun but I have a family to answer to. Lots of McKinnon money has been put into my hands.''

''So there's really only one thing remaining?'' Delicately she raised her brows. ''You'll have to take a wife.''

''Wife. Mother.'' His handsome mouth pursed. ''Someone very, very real. Young, reasonably good-looking—plain simply won't do—intelligent, warm, trustworthy, responsible—''

''You seem to have everything in order. Anything else?''

''I haven't finished yet.'' He looked into her face, black eyes tauntingly bright. ''Strong. A person in her own right. A woman who could easily become a director, sit on the board of McKinnon Enterprises. It would be an enormous plus if she were also great in bed.''

''Isn't it a mercy I might fail you there,'' Christy snapped.

He met that with a low, unsettling laugh. ''I daresay we could always find out. But all in good time? I wouldn't want you to feel any anxiety about leaving your bedroom door unlocked.'' He lowered his right hand to the curve of her jaw and cupped it with his long fingers. "Let's continue on our tour of exploration, shall we?"

"The house?" Christy tried to block off all emotion.

"Of course the house," he smoothly replied.

The library was very handsome indeed with a series of magnificent bookcases set in arcaded recesses all around the room. The leather bindings of the books glowed richly; ruby, emerald, olive, dark yellow, burgundy and browns, with titles and accents in gleaming gold. There were an extraordinary number of volumes of all sizes, some with elaborate bindings like vellum, velvet and silk. Deep armchairs were set all around the room with small easily moveable tables nearby. A Regency library table holding a large pewter vase filled with pink and cream roses was placed in the centre of the room, directly beneath a massive multi-armed bronze dore chandelier. A beautiful Persian rug, predominantly ruby, covered most of the gleaming timber floor, muffling their footsteps as they walked in.

Christy who loved books was immediately spellbound. This was a place of quiet and contemplation with the dignity and beauty of another era. Quite obviously the McKinnons had been men and women of education and exceptional intelligence. Every part of the house, not just the magnificent library, spoke of the broad scope of their interests.

Ashe studied her rapt face as she proceeded to circle the room staring up at the bookcases and their contents.

"Surely this must be one of the finest private libraries in the country," she asked without turning her blond head. "Few people could own such a large and comprehensive library let alone house all these books."

"As a matter of fact it is. With forms of entertainments so limited, small wonder the people of the Outback are great readers. And collectors. My great-grandfather had a taste for discovery and exploration. Natural history, that kind of thing. The bookcase where you're in front of now holds some rare works."

"Marvellous," she breathed. "I majored in journalism for my Arts Degree. I spent two years with *Impact* magazine. I love books."

"I can see that." He smiled. "You're welcome to browse anytime."

"Could I take a volume up to my room?" She turned to ask, her face vivid with interest.

"Certainly. I know you would care for it."

"And who is this gentleman here?" She gazed at a handsome uniformed officer of perhaps the early nineteenth century.

"An ancestor," Ashe said. "He was killed in the battle of Waterloo."

"How unfortunate. He was so young."

"There were other McKinnons killed young," he replied a little bleakly. "One in a massacre. I won't go into the details. Four from two world wars. There are more portraits in the next room. The family still calls it the smoking room where the gentlemen used to retire, but smoking is taboo these days. It's more like a trophy room, artefacts, et cetera, brought back by various members of the family from overseas trips."

He allowed her to precede him into the room. "Some of the stuff is quite bizarre. A great-uncle was obsessed with all things Egyptian. Another with all things Oriental, yet another adored India. Just a moment I'll turn on the light. Lonnie has drawn the curtains."

Above the richly carved black marble fireplace was a portrait of a very handsome man of middle years who could only be Ashe McKinnon's father, the resemblance was so strong. What distinguished father from son was the colour of the eyes. Ashe McKinnon's eyes were so darkly brilliant they were almost black. His father's eyes, which appeared to follow one around the room, were notably blue. So where had those dark eyes come from? Ashe's mother? The mother he never talked about?

"What a wonderfully handsome and distinguished man," Christy said, noting sadly for all his handsomeness the man in the painting did not have his son's tremendous... Christy could only think of one word...*dash.* Or even that high-mettled look that made Ashe McKinnon appear so blazingly alive.

"What a sad day it must have been when your father and your uncle were killed," she said, voice faltering.

"The worst day of my life."

"Worse than when your mother left?" she asked gently.

"I was a child when my mother left," he reminded her, his face assuming its closed expression. "I felt as a child. I was a grown man when I had to contend with my father's death and my uncle's. They weren't only brothers, they were very, very close. Family and business partners. That's why I watch over Mercedes and Callista."

"Would you be very angry if I asked where you got your dark eyes?" Brilliant jet and very deep.

"You want to know everything," he responded with a slight edge. "My mother was amazingly beautiful, as you are. And she had ravishing colouring. Blond hair and dark eyes. A combination one doesn't see very often. She had Italian blood in her. My eyes are said to be like hers but darker. Satisfied?"

"It's a normal question, Ashe. Your response isn't. You don't have to have me decapitated."

"I'm light-years away from wanting to do that," he said, his voice unbearably ironic.

"Was there ever a portrait of your mother?" she felt compelled to ask.

He shrugged a powerful shoulder. "I wouldn't know where to find it."

"Okay, so it exists?"

"I hope you're not proposing to go in search of it."

"You need to talk about it, Ashe," she said, studying his face.

"Don't be absurd. My mother went out of my life over twenty years ago. As simple as that."

"What was her name?"

"You're extremely inquisitive."

"And you're on the brink of open hostility." She spoke calmly. "I can see it in your eyes. I just wanted to know a little about your life, that's all. Yours is an astonishing one so different from my own. You belong here in this incredible world with a mansion for a homestead and the wild desert heartland on your doorstep. It's so exotic and romantic. It really is!"

"You're coming in from the outside, Christy," he pointed out. "It's unrelenting hard work."

"But you love it, don't you?"

"It's my life," he answered simply.

It was what made him so powerful and strong. "There are so many photographs on the wall of the sitting room you've given me," she said. "I'm longing to have a good look at them. To see the way you grew up. I thought there might be one of you with your parents?"

His laugh was brief. "Sorry, Christy, you'll look in vain. If you're sweetly imagining I might want to move back into my mother's life again, you couldn't be more wrong."

"That's sad."

"It was, but that was many long years ago."

"So she just went away?" She thought of how it would feel for father and son.

"Well she did leave a few clues," he replied. "Christy, do you mind if we get off this? No one has mentioned my mother for a very long time. I'd like to keep it that way."

"I'm sorry," she apologised. "I'm not just being curious. I'm really interested." She gazed around her. "You know this would be a great setting for a book."

"So long as you don't make me one of your central characters."

"I've always wanted to write," she confided.

"Why don't you then?"

"I've been too busy making a living," she said simply. "I wasn't born with a silver spoon in my mouth. I need my pay cheque to get by."

"But you do have the will to succeed?"

"I do." Her answer was emphatic.

"And you're not looking for a wealthy candidate to marry?"

"You mean like Josh." She spoke a little angrily.

"Josh," he answered curtly, "is in for one very big surprise if he thinks Callista is going to be open-handed with her money. She has a very good business head on her shoulders, which she was probably at pains to hide from Deakin in the first flush of their romance. Besides, *I* manage most of Mercedes and Callista's assets, which include grazing properties in the McKinnon chain."

"I just can't imagine all that money." She shrugged. "I read once an Australian heiress said it's just as stressful to have too much money as no money."

He laughed, his dark eyes trained on her. "It doesn't work for playboys. Or playgirls for that matter. As for me, I'm too busy."

"Maybe you're pleasure deprived," she suggested.

"Maybe that's what wrong with you. Maybe that's why you're thinking on lines of marriage strategies. That's it! It just hit me. You haven't got time to fit love into your life."

"But the love of a good woman could save me?" He made her stop her circling to face him.

"Hopefully. You're way too cynical. And I don't like the way you look down that straight nose at me. I know we got off on the wrong foot."

"Hell, yes," he admitted, "but it wasn't all bad. How do you know I didn't want you from the first moment I laid eyes on you? How do you know, for that matter, you aren't the woman who started me on thinking marriage contracts?"

She had to steady herself. "I would never be so desperate as to enter into a loveless marriage contract. It would be like going to prison. You're too complex a man, Ashe. Too brooding."

"But I make your hands shake."

She found herself holding them up. "You spook me."

"Now that's some piece of information." He captured those hands. Staring down at her ringless fingers. "A very pretty hand," he remarked. "So much for a woman's talk. You should wear a flawless, Colombian emerald, flanked by diamonds. You could draw your hair back and wear the earrings to match. A chignon. Isn't that what you call it? A difficult style for a woman without beautiful features."

"What are you talking about, Ashe?" Christy stammered. Something about him triggered shock and alarm.

"I'm not sure," he bit off. "Do you want me to read your palm?"

Excitement jetted like a fountain. Excitement difficult to endure and very hard to construe. Ashe McKinnon had great passion in him. She knew that. But maybe not the capacity to love. An affliction based on grief from the past.

''I'm an open book,'' she told him, too intensely. The current that was running between them had her quaking.

''No, you're not,'' he contradicted. ''You're too fascinating.''

''Give me back my hand.'' This man was a devil.

He stared at her and saw she was perturbed. ''Of course. Sometimes you're so cool, other times vulnerable. I expect it's because you're recovering from a broken romance and all. Just a little warning, Christy. Don't try to understand me. I don't understand myself.''

CHAPTER FIVE

MORNING broke over the Timeless Land; the great shimmering desert that was the oldest part of the earth's crust.

Birdsong rang out to welcome the sun, its power and brilliance resonating away to the horizons; trillions of birds uncaging their hearts. The illuminated sky, the silvery-grey of a pearl, was spread with colours that intensified by the minute; pink, mauve, rose, violet, yellow, streaks of fiery red. All awaiting the sun to turn everything to such a density of blue just looking up made one feel very close to Heaven.

Christy's dreams had been going around in circles. Ashe was in every one and she no longer wondered why. Most mornings she woke to the sounds of a quiet suburban jungle, now she was roused by an avalanche of musical sound; sweet, piercing, warbling, sobbing, the mad gurgling cackle of the kookaburras, one of her most nostalgic childhood memories; a glorious cacophony of sound, so different from what she was used to, for a moment she wasn't sure where she was, or even if she was in the middle of a fantasy. She had never slept in a huge canopied bed. Never possessed such exquisite bed linens. And the sound outside…

Christy threw back the light coverlet and padded out onto the verandah. Fragrance was all around her, its softness, freshness, gorgeous boronia, overwhelmingly close. An abundance of scents. She couldn't possibly track them. She stared out over the great gums that extended their long arms over massed lilies that grew at their feet. She felt flooded with pleasure.

This was the desert. The wild heart. Yet strangely trees and vegetation flourished. It wasn't a desert at all but a place of wonder. She drew in deep lungfuls of the marvellous air like it was some miraculous medication that could offer eternal life. Christy the nature lover, one hand to her breast, her eyes closed, was experiencing a feeling close to ecstasy. Her blood pulsed through her veins. Her soul rose up on wings. Lifted to the skies…

The sun at the horizon was swiftly rising in an incandescent golden arc. Christy could feel its brilliance and heat through her shut eyelids. She thought of the ancients, the aboriginal tribes who understood and worshipped nature. These were the people most likely to die if they were ever locked up. This beautiful morning she felt a great connection…a great understanding…a white woman's Dreaming.

''That's it, hold it. I really need a camera.''

A man's vibrant voice thoroughly roused her. Christy opened her eyes, blinking rapidly. There was too much within her heart to feel any trace of embarrassment.

''Is it some kind of dawn worship?'' Ashe asked.

She leaned right over the balustrade. ''Ashe?'' Of course it was Ashe. No one else had his alluring voice with all the taunting, teasing, downright sarcastic inflections.

''You mean you were expecting someone else?'' His dark head dropped back the better to see her. ''Rapunzel, Rapunzel, let down your hair. That's quite a cascade!''

''You surely don't intend climbing up?'' A wild clamour peaked in her. Why wouldn't he? He was that daring.

''Like to see me?'' he scoffed.

She laughed, uncertain he was serious. ''You're joking of course?''

''No. I seem to be becoming less and less inhibited around you.''

To increase her extraordinary sense of exhilaration, he

strode from his position on the grass directly below her to a spot further up where a vigorously glossy leaved creeper thickly covered the stonewall.

Did he really intend to climb it? Going on what she had learned about him, the answer was yes. Christy flew back into her bedroom and pulled on her pale pink satin robe. She quickly belted it then rushed back onto the verandah already stirred up, unnerved and curiously delighted.

"I think I deserve something for that." He looked so blazingly handsome and vital; swinging one long leg over the balustrade it would have tested any woman's virtue. "Now that's a very classy robe, Christy." He came towards her in his dashing cattleman's gear, brilliant eyes moving over her.

"I'm glad you like it." She told herself to stay calm. A very tall order with this disturbing man. Why hadn't some enterprising woman bedazzled him into marrying her?

"It's gorgeous and so are you," he drawled. "I'm sufficiently susceptible to a woman's beauty to find a nightie very appealing. It's not every woman, either, who can look ethereal first thing in the morning." His gaze slid with lazy admiration over the long blond flow of her hair, the green of her eyes, the sheen of her robe, the swell of her breasts.

Sparks of electricity tingled over her. "I never expected company, but life is full of surprises."

"Isn't it ever! This could well be the thrilling highlight of my day seeing you in a pearl pink satin nightgown out on the verandah, worshipping the rising sun."

"It was the birds. They woke me." Even as she spoke a flock of sulphur-crested cockatoos exploded from the red gums like a great burst of flowers.

"The Outback is famous for its birds and its early morning symphonies," Ashe said. "I accept your exultation. They've been known to affect me the same way. Aside from that, I expect you wanted to catch me before I left for the day?''

She suddenly saw that was so. But she denied it. ''Nothing so planned. I swear I never thought of you for a minute.''

''Then you force me to make a play for your attention.'' He stared down on her, giving every indication of being absorbed. ''Good morning, Christine.'' He gave her name full resonance. ''I hope you slept well?''

''Like a child. Don't do it, Ashe,'' she begged.

''But I want to kiss you. A kiss. Nothing more. I'm not about to tumble you into bed.''

''I *know* that.'' She blushed, her heart skipping several beats as he put his hand beneath her chin.

''You're beautiful. Your hair shines like a halo.''

He amazed her. Utterly amazed her. He shouldn't be seducing her this effortlessly. But it so excited her. Waves of sensation rose then spilled back through her body. Her sensitive nipples puckered with arousal. His mouth covered hers with the most exquisite voluptuousness. It was like he was peeling her clothes off, laying her skin bare to the cool morning air. It wasn't only dangerous. It was crazy. Possibly the start of a life-changing direction.

He must have thought so, too. ''Can't overdo it,'' he murmured, slowly withdrawing his mouth from hers. ''Taste testing. You taste like wild peaches.''

It was an agony of delight, his pushing the boundaries. ''You're having a great time, aren't you? Don't you think I know,'' Christy accused him.

''My marriage strategy, what else?'' He half smiled at her, fingering a long strand of her hair. ''You're an angel and I'm still marvelling. Your mother should have called you Angelica.''

''I'm glad she didn't. I love Christy.''

"In short you love love?"

"And you're afraid of it, Ashe McKinnon," she told him quietly. "Afraid of your own heart."

His expression turned purely sarcastic. "Sweet Christy, that's a line from a soap opera. I can't stand it. I was going to limit myself to one kiss but I think as a punishment I'll go for two."

Her green eyes fixed him with false warning. "I might scream."

"No you won't. I think you like a little suffering." This time he gathered her very closely into his arms, not anticipating a struggle and not getting one. He felt the crush of soft breasts against his hard chest. One of his strong arms was across her back; the other grasped a satin hip. The pressure of his kiss arched her neck. It hauled up raw emotions so deep within her it was as though they had existed in some secret cavern.

"I don't think you hate it so much," he mocked, when finally he raised his crow-black head. "But you *can* apologise."

"For what?" It was difficult to find breath. The rasp of his darkly tanned polished skin chaffed her lips, not painfully, but erotically. Her whole body was literally quaking with excitement and confusion and the enormity of what was happening. Goodness knows what hungers, desires, this man could call up. Then she would really find out what it was like to have a broken heart.

"I think your credibility as a love-lorn jilted woman has been somewhat shattered," he offered a shade brutally.

"You surely don't think I thought you were being *kind* bringing me here?"

"You're the one who went into bat for romantic love, Christy," he reminded her. "So much for your ex-lover."

"I didn't say romantic love doesn't have its downside," she countered.

"Do you want him back?" He turned her fully to face him.

Her heart contracted. For weeks now she had searched her heart, releasing memories she found were no longer painful. She hadn't known the *real* Josh at all.

"You don't even seem to miss him?"

She shook her head. "No."

It had come to her what she had felt for Josh was an illusion.

"You made a terrible mistake thinking you were in love with him," Ashe continued as if driven.

"Yes I did." She was calm with near despair. "Satisfied, you cruel man?"

"For now." His hands circled her skin. "But you're only on probation. We won't know for sure until you see him again. Most of the extended family usually come to me for Christmas."

She gave a tiny moan. "I'm not *family*. I won't be here."

"You will," he said as though that was already settled. "Now I must go. I would have been gone ages ago except you did your level best to detain and distract me. See if you can work out a routine. One of Lonnie's girls will help you with the kids. Probably Meeta. She's good with children and she's very clever and artistic, as you'll find out. I want you to have time to yourself. You'll probably want to ride in the early morning, or late afternoon. Best to avoid the worst heat of the day. I've picked out a suitable mount I'm sure you'll like."

"Oh, thank you." She was so thrilled she reached out and curled her fingers around his arm.

"Enough of your little wiles!" he mocked, but his firm mouth softened momentarily.

"If you weren't being so damned nice I think I'd hate you," Christy said. "You wouldn't possibly have a well-schooled pony I could teach the children to ride? The earlier the better I always think. Both of them told me they've never been on a horse."

His dark eyes narrowed thoughtfully. "We didn't ask Nic but I'm sure she wouldn't mind. You're an accomplished rider. So *you say?*"

"Check me out for heaven's sake. I'm a good teacher, too."

"And you're not crippled with false modesty. Give me today to straighten out a few problems. I've put a Jeep at your disposal. You and the kids can go for picnics, whatever. I'll leave it up to you."

"Yes, Mr. McKinnon, sir." She touched her forehead with exquisite satire yet he gave her a lovely smile, a smile to die for.

"By the way, we're hosting a quartet of classical musicians at the weekend. For the last couple of years they've been coming Outback to bring the bush classical music."

"But how marvellous!" Christy was delighted.

"Think you could organise it?"

She was a little shaken, but excited. "What? Organizing events is my forte. Who gets invited?"

"Everyone on the station," he said. "As Augusta hosts it this year, quite a few from neighbouring stations will fly in. I've got a list. You can bet your life everyone will want to come."

"So where is the concert to be held?" Her voice showed her strong interest.

"In the Great Hall. That's where we usually hold our entertainments."

"Why not outdoors?" she suggested, visualizing the event in her mind. "Under the stars. The night sky is fantastic out here. No pollution to veil the brilliance of the stars.''

''I hadn't thought of outside.'' He sounded a touch dubious.

''Let me think of it,'' Christy said. ''I'll wander around the place—''

''Keep to the home compound.''

It stopped just short of an order. ''Right! I'll toss around a few ideas. Come up with something for you tonight. How does that sound?''

''It sounds very helpful,'' he told her with genuine relief. ''I can't keep on cramming sixteen, seventeen hours into the one working day.''

''So delegate, you poor man. Throw some of your workload at me. If I can't cut it you can always throw me out.''

''That's not going to happen, Christy.'' Another powerful smile. She was starting to count them. ''In all my years I can only remember one guest being turned off the property.''

''So what did they do?'' She turned up her face to ask. ''Just so I'll know.''

His mouth compressed. ''A few objects from the house turned up in their luggage.''

''Goodness! Do you mean to say you check?''

''Not in the ordinary course of events. The thefts would never have been discovered only the contents put too much of a strain on a piece of luggage. It burst open. Dare I add it was a woman journalist?''

She lifted her dimpled chin. ''I didn't know your guests ran to journalists? Anyway your precious objects are safe with me.''

''Of course I know that.'' He made a mock bow. ''Now I'll take a short cut through your bedroom if you don't mind.''

"I think I can cope with that." She was trying to keep her tone light but it came out sort of wavery, a dead give-away. "You can't take any more wall climbing?"

"Once was enough!" He twisted to look at her, blazingly alive, darkly handsome.

"It *was* pretty high."

He just smiled. "So I'll see you tonight." He crossed quietly to the door although the children's bedroom was a comfortable distance off. "I won't be able to get back to the house until sundown. We're sinking another bore, a steel-lined hole through black shale, mud rock and red and yellow clay, and we're still replacing drains with pipes. It costs tens of thousands of dollars but water is a miraculous resource out here."

"Isn't the Great Artesian Basin right under us?" she asked.

"It is. Under most of Queensland. It might be the world's largest underground source of fresh water, nearly nine billion megalitres, but too much of it is being wasted. There are hundreds of bores in our own State, the one with the most to gain and the most to lose, gushing precious water uncontrollably. The whole issue has to be seriously addressed. As vast as it is, the Basin is a finite resource."

"You're determined to stop the waste?" She glanced up, having moved with him to the door, and saw the committed look on his face.

"Absolutely. All open bore drains have to be capped. At the very least controlled by headworks."

"So why isn't everyone doing it?" She hadn't realised there was such a problem.

"Money, or lack of. It all comes down to cost. Many landowners back off because of the big drain on financial resources. Others concentrate on rehabilitation. All new bores have to be fully capped. Governments have to show the way. They have to fully support management plans and release the funds. As far as I'm concerned, it's dead simple. Our huge pastoral industry depends on the Basin. Without it Augusta and all the rest of the cattle and sheep stations in this State wouldn't be worth a cracker. The Basin has to be preserved for future generations."

"So it's a very big issue?" She decided there and then to check it all out.

He didn't have to think twice. "A solution *has* to be found. *Now.* Lecture over for the day," he assured her.

"No, I'm very interested. I'm going to find out a lot more."

"I didn't think you were just a pretty face." Before she could move—indeed all the time he was speaking she'd been rooted to the spot with attention—he dropped a brief near-affectionate kiss on her nose.

Even that she couldn't pass off lightly. After he had gone, Christy walked back to her bed and fell across it face down. What she felt for Ashe McKinnon was far too difficult to put into words. All she knew was the moment he came into her life she had changed immensely. She didn't function in the same way. It was even possible, and she had to face the truth, she had fallen crazily in love with him. She couldn't rule it out. Crazily in love with a man who talked strategies for marriage. Who wanted to banish romantic love for solid, feet-on-the-ground values? Tentatively she brought a hand up and touched the cushioned pads of her mouth. She thought she knew what a kiss was. She didn't. This was madness with the potential to cause heartbreak. But at least it was *her* secret.

The tiring effects of the children's long travels eventually caught up with them. They slept in until well after nine, only stirring when Christy came upstairs to check on them.

''Hey, you guys! Are you going to lie around in bed all day?'' she asked playfully, standing at the bottom of Kit's bed and tickling his toes.

''What time is it, Christy?'' Katey sat up, rubbing her nose.

''Well, not *that* late,'' Christy teased, glancing at her watch. ''Nine-twenty, but you had a big day yesterday. Sleep well, poppet?'' She turned to Kit, the nervous one.

''I can't believe it's morning.'' He pushed up from the bed then ran straight to Christy and hugged her around the middle. ''I just closed my eyes.''

''You've been asleep for hours and hours, silly,'' Katey groaned.

''So up you get!'' Christy encouraged in a cheerful voice. ''Lonnie is waiting to get your breakfast—anything you like outside of cake—then the three of us are going to tour the home compound.''

''What's the home compound?'' Kit asked excitedly, peering at Christy closely.

''The homestead and the stable complex and a few of the other buildings like the Great Hall,'' Katey, who was certainly going to lose a tooth, lisped.

Christy nodded. ''I need the two of you to show me around. Musicians will be visiting the station this weekend with what's called a string quartet.''

''Oh great!'' Katey, who knew about orchestras, clapped her hands. ''Is it nighttime? Will we be able to stay up?''

''I don't see why not. We're on holidays after all.''

''What's a string qu-a-a?'' Kit's voice fell silent, the new word defeating him.

''It's a group of four people, poppet, who play stringed instruments. Have you ever seen a violin?''

''I think I have.'' Kit eyed her doubtfully.

Katey gave an explosive little giggle. ''Yes, you have.

Great-aunt Zoe plays the violin. You know she holds it up like this.'' Katey went through elaborate sawing motions.

''Oh!'' Kit laughed, just barely remembering.

''I'll show you a picture, Kit.'' Christy stroked his cheek. ''The string section is the very heart of an orchestra. An orchestra is lots of people playing together using different instruments. Other people go along to hear them, to enjoy the music they make.''

''We have a very good orchestra at our school,'' Katey told her with considerable pride. ''At your school, too, Kit. Daddy's old school when you're ready to go.''

''I'm never going to school.'' Kit's adorable face was troubled by a frown. ''I'm staying home with Mummy.''

Christy smoothed his glossy curls. ''Don't worry about that now, Kit. We're going to have fun today. It might be good if we learn something about the instruments that go into an orchestra. We could find pictures of them. Trumpets, trombones, tubby the tuba, the drums that go bang and the cymbals that go clang. Then there's the violin and its big sister the viola, the bigger cello and the huge double bass. I'm sure there's a book in the library we could find. Uncle Ashe would be so pleased if you knew something about the instruments the musicians will play Saturday night.''

''Is there going to be a big barbecue?'' Kit asked in a hopeful voice.

It's one way to feed a lot of people informally, Christy mused. ''Everyone on the station is invited. People from neighbouring stations, too. Today we're going to decide where we're all going to eat, then where we're all going to sit to listen to the music.''

''Aren't we going to the Great Hall?'' Katey questioned. ''It's really *big*. Bigger than our great hall at school.''

''I thought a concert under the stars would be lovely,

Katey.'' Christy turned to the children for approval. ''What do you think?''

Both children were silent for a moment then they looked up at her, sapphire eyes identically set shining.

''And I can cook the sausages.'' Kit grinned.

''You can't. You're too little,'' Katey scolded. ''But I can pass some to you to eat.'' Sweetly she took her little brother's hand. ''Come on. Let's get dressed.''

''Let's.'' Kit began to jump up and down with excitement. ''We really like you, Christy,'' he cried.

''Ditto, little pal.'' She put out a hand and they all slapped a high five.

It took only a few days for Christy and the children to settle into a routine that still allowed Christy time to herself. As Ashe had told her at the beginning, Lonnie had staff to help her keep such a very big house in order, aboriginal girls who had been born on the station, went away for schooling after age eight, the cut-off point for the small station school, then chose to return to their families and their desert home, the land of their ancestors and totemic spirits. This was the place where they were happiest. The homeland. One of the girls, Metta, was particularly good with the children, gentle but firm, and it was to her Christy turned most often for help. What was perfect about Metta, Christy considered, was she had remarkable artistic skill, which Christy was soon to discover was inherent in Metta's ancient race.

Metta knew exactly how to keep the children entertained; teaching them how to model good likenesses of desert animals with the Play-Doh Christy had had the foresight to bring with her, teaching them quick methods to get started with the drawing and painting, stimulating them with ideas and stories from the Dreamtime. The results were surprisingly pleasing. Both children, perhaps because they *were* little children, showed an artistic bent, painting on the small square boards Metta provided; part of a hoard Metta's little brothers and sisters kept for their paintings. An area in Christy's sitting room was fast getting covered with examples of the childrens' painting skills, which they intended to take home to show their parents.

Christy was well aware aboriginal art was finding an increasingly wide market both at home and overseas, particularly the U.S.A. with many of the major artists' work being bought up by city galleries, and allotted a hefty price. It was the dealers who got far and away the largest cut, sometimes as high as fifty per cent. There scarcely seemed to be an aboriginal community, particularly in the central desert areas and the Northern Territory, that didn't have at least two highly gifted artists among them all committed to passing on their "stories" and technical skills to their children.

Christy who had always been attracted to aboriginal paintings felt enormously pleased when Metta suggested she might like to visit one of the camps of the desert nomads who frequently stayed on Augusta for varying periods in between walkabouts. The relationship between the McKinnons and the indigenous people had developed over a century or more into a happy arrangement, almost a "family" arrangement where the aboriginal people led a healthy, protected life with employment for all. Aborigines made fine stockmen, fencers, mechanics. Their wives and daughters worked on various jobs around the station, saddle makers, boot makers, basket weavers, whip makers, or on domestic duties up at the homestead. The aboriginal children attended the small station school along with the children of the white and part-white employees. Ashe McKinnon, as young as he was, was regarded as a father figure, a good man, a kind man, the provider.

Riding lessons, much to the children's excited delight, were started on. The basics at least, getting each child to feel comfortable and happy aloft. Neither child had even so much as sat on a horse, so Christy was surprised at the ease and fearlessness they displayed when first lifted into the saddle. Indeed four-year-old Kit sat even more securely than his older sister with a natural balance.

Ashe had provided, from a splendid stable that quite fired Christy's imagination, a beautiful little white pony, Milk Opal. As expected, Opal was sweet-tempered and well-schooled, so the first "lessons" proved a very enjoyable experience with Christy walking around a gravelled enclosure adjacent to the large and fascinating stables complex which employed a lot of historic materials in the construction, holding a leading rein. It was a fortunate start for both children, because not only was Christy an accomplished horsewoman, she had the ability to gain the childrens' attention and impart the basics in such a way they couldn't wait for the next riding lesson.

For her own enjoyment Ashe had provided her with a beautiful mount, Desert Dancer, a supple, balanced animal eager and responsive to her every command. So it evolved Christy started the day with her own early morning ride managing to be back at the homestead just as the children were getting under way. With all the activity and fresh air the children had no problems getting off to sleep, generally going right through until around half past seven when Christy returned.

Christy had already told Ashe what she planned for the concert. He listened, gave her carte blanche to do as she pleased, along with two of the station's carpenters to build a rotunda on the homestead grounds. One of those delightful little timber gazebos that fit perfectly into the desert environment. It was here Christy was hoping the musicians would play. Lighting could be arranged. To be easily accessible to everyone, the concert would be viewed and heard in the round.

The children predictably thought it was marvellous, checking on proceedings each day. ''I'm going to adore it,'' Katey cried, lying on the grass and looking up through the silver-green leaves of a gum to the blue chinks of sky. ''Will we be able to play in it after?''

''Of course. We could bring our lunch out here.'' Really there were so many things to do, so many areas of the great station to see Christy thought it would take a lifetime to acquaint herself with Augusta.

She and Lonnie conferred for enjoyable hours on the food they would serve. Nothing elaborate but a little bit different from the usual barbecue, though food became almost irrestible when cooked over flames in the outdoors. Fifty people including eight young children had to be fed and she'd decided a barbecue was the perfect way to do it. Permanent brick barbecues, massive to Christy's eyes, had long since been constructed in sheltered areas a little way from the rear of the house and the pool area, but with easy access to the kitchen.

In the end it was planned on the classic peppered Augusta beef steaks in beer and garlic; barbecued lamb with a lavender balsamic marinade; sweet-and-sour kebabs, both lamb and chicken, and the obligatory char-grilled beef burgers for the children, all served with cool, crisp garden salads, the perfect foil to barbecued food, plus a sweet-and-sour onion salad and a spiced aubergine salad which, Lonnie told Christy, Mr. Ashe and the men particularly liked. Potato wedges tossed in fragrant garlicky olive oil with fresh chopped rosemary were decided on to add the extra dimension. For a while they considered flying in fresh barramundi, the great eating fish of the tropics, from North

Queensland or the Territory, but decided they really had enough. Dessert would be barbecued fruits served with whipped cream, ice cream, a chocolate fondue or all three. The people who would help with the cooking, men and women, were all judged excellent both at operating the barbecues and cooking the food.

"You don't need to do anything, darlin', you know," Lonnie told Christy in her kindly fashion, "not on the night. You'll want to enjoy yourself."

"I'll be enjoying myself helping," Christy insisted.

"Well we'll have to make an early start," Lonnie grinned. "Even a barbecue takes a lot of work. But you're a great organizer. Mr. Ashe agrees."

By four-thirty late Saturday afternoon, the musicians and guests from neighbouring stations had arrived and been installed either in guest bedrooms at the homestead or, in the case of single men, in one of the stockmen's dormitories where they would get at most a few hours' sleep. Entertainments in the isolated Outback aren't all that frequent, consequently the most was made of any that came along.

Everyone appeared in high good humour, though Christy was sometimes uncomfortably aware there was considerable speculation as to her presence on Augusta and her exact position in Ashe McKinnon's life. This was a man as eligible as they came. They remembered the girlfriends he had over the years. Two stood out.

One was Gemma Millner-Hill who had come along with her parents and two of her unmarried brothers to enjoy the entertainment. Christy had no difficulty in recognising Gemma. She was the best-looking of Callista's bridesmaids. The one who had grabbed Ashe's arm at the reception, demanding to know why he had been so cruel to her.

Gemma, for her part, was so shocked when she first laid

eyes on Christy, she couldn't hide it, her fine, faintly sharp features drawing together so tightly it gave her a pinched look. This was the girl who had captivated so many at Callista's wedding. The mystery woman no one knew a thing about except Ashe, the hardest man in the world to pin down, who had stayed glued to her side all night. Anger, concern, jealousy and bitterness welled in Gemma's heart.

All these emotions were registered by Christy as Gemma grimly regarded her. One didn't have to be a mind reader to realise Gemma had an enormous attachment to Ashe, an attachment that was shared by her parents and two tall, lean, attractive brothers who nevertheless couldn't tear their eyes away from Christy even as they were greeting Ashe with great enthusiasm and pumping his hand.

"So, who's the beautiful lady?" Dalton, the elder, demanded to know, staring with an expectant, eager face at Christy.

Ashe turned to where Christy was standing, putting out an arm. "Christy, you don't know the Millner-Hill family, do you?"

Christy smiled and stepped forward dutifully, refusing to be upset by the veiled hostility that emanated from the Millner-Hill women, even as they kept their feelings at bay with big social smiles.

"I do remember Gemma from Callista's wedding but I don't think we actually met," Christy said pleasantly.

"I don't think anyone missed *you.*" Gemma's smile just missed out on being a sneer. "Aside from your blond hair and your beauty we all wondered who you were. I mean we all thought we knew Ashe's friends."

"Apparently not *all* of them," Ashe intervened smoothly, beginning the introductions through which Gemma was sufficiently off balance as to glower. Not so the men of the family, who responded with considerable warmth. Mrs. Millner-Hill could barely keep the dismay out of her eyes as she queried, ''You're staying here, dear?'' She stared very hard at Christy with her piercingly blue eyes.

''Looking after the children really,'' Christy supplied casually when she felt under threat. ''Ashe's cousin, Nicole, and her husband are having a holiday.''

''Of course we *know* Nicole and Brendan,'' Gemma informed her just a bit too shortly. ''Nic and I have shared a special friendship for many years now. So you're something of a nursemaid? You get paid for it?''

Again Ashe bestirred his tall elegant body, saying suavely, ''Christine is my *guest,* Gemma. I'm the one who put pressure on her to come out here. Nic definitely needed a break so Christy offered to mind the children. They're taking a nap so they can be awake for the concert, or at least part of it. They don't want to miss out. You'll see them later,'' he promised.

''That would be lovely!'' Mrs. Millner-Hill gushed at the same time, making it sound like she was heaving a great sigh. Ashe and Gemma may have broken up a year back but Mrs. Millner-Hill had never given up hope they would be reunited. Ashe, marvellous as he was, was such a difficult man. He set up his own games; playing by his own rules. A very difficult man to catch. Now this blond girl who looked as intelligent as she was beautiful was staying in the homestead. Unchaperoned. It was intensely upsetting. Mrs. Millner-Hill could only guess at how poor darling Gemma was feeling.

In fact Gemma's emotional turbulence was threatening to get out of hand. Jealousy bubbled inside her like a witch's cauldron. As far as she was concerned, her relationship with Ashe had only been interrupted. Something would bring them together again. She'd lived on hope. If it took her all night she'd find out where Christy Parker came from and exactly who she was. One thing was certain, she wasn't on home turf.

The food was served early as a concession to the children in the audience. Christy and her helpers had set out tables and chairs in the rear garden, the tables covered with chequered patio cloths with bright napkins. A whole range of colourful plates had been chosen, as well, with a little candle-lit lantern centre table. White fairy lights decorated nearby trees, lights streamed from the house and round the pool, the turquoise surface floating masses of wild hibiscus and candles. It looked very pretty even if someone would have a job clearing the pool the next day.

Around seven o'clock they all came together at the front of the homestead for the concert, settling themselves on the lawn on chairs from the piled stack, or on rugs and blankets, the children sprawling out full-length with their chins propped up beneath their hands.

Christy glanced around at the happy expectant faces, disconcerted to catch sight of Ashe and Gemma standing beneath a sparkling lit gum in intense conversation. Or it certainly looked that way.

For a moment Christy was overcome by a sense of not belonging. All these people knew one another. Their families had been neighbours for generations. It was only to be expected their loyalties would be with one of their own. Although Ashe had never spoken about Gemma, it was obvious at one time they'd had a shared personal relationship. Something was driving Gemma to behave with the jealousy that was so badly apparent. The momentum had led her to cornering Ashe. Christy glanced away quickly as though she were a voyeur, pushing a cushion beneath dear little Kit to make him more comfortable.

It was time to start.

The music was beautiful. Dvorak, Tchaikovsky, Borodin. It was wonderfully melodious, at times so meltingly lovely it brought tears to Christy's eyes. Each member of the quartet was a fine musician in their own right yet they presented a most satisfying impression of "oneness," of "wholeness," that was deeply touching and deeply spiritual. There was no intermission to break the spell. Indeed everyone in the rapt audience wanted the spell to continue. Afterwards such was the collective experience there was complete silence for a few moments broken by the call of a night bird, before every man, woman and child broke into long, loud applause.

They were favoured with two encores from the group then one of the violinists broke into excerpts from Gershwin's *Porgy and Bess,* starting with "Summertime," which everyone knew and greeted with delight.

Christy had shared her rug with the children; now it was time for them to go to bed.

"Can't we stay, Christy?" Katey begged.

"Impossible, darling, you're drowsy as it is. Your eyes are half closing and just look at Kit! It was wonderful though, wasn't it?"

"I'm going to ask Daddy if I can learn the violin as soon as I get home," Katey vowed. "I knew some of those pretty songs."

"Let me guess." Christy smiled down at the child. "I think it would be Borodin, the Russian composer. The melodies were turned into songs for a movie called *Kismet.*"

Katey, by this time, was freely yawning. "Here's Uncle Ashe," she cried. Christy turned around. She had no idea where he had sat.

"Time for bed, you two?" He joined them, going down on his haunches. "Enjoy it?" He tickled Kit.

"It was good," Kit said, still hearing the music in his head. While Katey threw her arms around Ashe's neck and kissed him.

"What about if I carry you, Kit?" Ashe suggested, seeing the little boy was all but asleep.

"On your back," Kit begged.

Ashe stayed until the children were tucked up in bed, their eyelids dropping the minute their heads touched the pillows.

He followed Christy out into the hallway. "That went very well. The programme was just right. Beautiful melodies, some of them quite familiar, everyone could enjoy."

"*I* loved it," Christy said, a little in conflict—pain and delight.

"I think everyone else did, too." He took hold of her by the shoulders and brought her back against the wall.

"So what next?" She looked up at him cautiously. What did she really know about this man, only that he was the most glamorous, exciting creature, from another vastly different world?

"Well first of all I'd like to thank you for getting it all together," he murmured, staring down at her. The wall sconce gleamed on her hair and the purity of her skin.

"I had help," she said shakily, as his magnetism took over.

"Nevertheless you brought it off with panache. The settings, the food. A woman can make things so much more elegant."

"Well thank you." Colour warmed her eyes and her cheeks. "But you could have asked Gemma." She hadn't intended to say that, it just burst from her.

"I asked *you*." He lifted a thick strand of her hair, as he had often done before, curled it around his wrist then let it drop.

''Were you ever in love with her?''

''I told you before, Christy,'' he said softly. ''I find it hard to describe love.''

''Put it another way. Did you sleep with her?''

He took her face between his hands. ''What business is it of yours? Surely my masculinity will suffer if I say I've never slept with a woman.''

''I take it the answer is yes.'' She went a little limp.

''Why should it worry you?'' he asked gently, reading her expression.

''Because I'm not stupid.''

''You mean you think I may be working my way up to you?''

She was startled, defensive. ''You *have* made a beginning.''

''But then, Christy, I thought you were enjoying it?''

''Up to a point.'' She hardly knew what she was saying the excitement was so extreme.

''Then let's get married.'' He suggested it as calmly as he might have said, Let's camp out under the stars.

''What?'' Her voice was so brittle it cracked.

''I said let's get married,'' he repeated patiently. ''You want commitment. I'm fighting the never-ending urge to take you to my bed. If you like we can announce our engagement.''

She backed right against the wall. ''So later on we can have a test run?'' Her green eyes were scathing, her body quivering with nerves.

''That's not what I asked you. I'm tired of waiting for cupid's arrow to hit me, aren't you?''

She watched his face, his mouth, those brilliant mocking eyes.

''How do you know cupid's arrow *hasn't* hit me?'' she retaliated, feeling slightly unbalanced.

"Deakin doesn't count." His voice had sting. "You're not in love with *me,* are you?"

"You don't think I'm fool enough to say yes?" Too late she regained some control. She tried to push past him but he stopped her.

"There's a good side to this, Christy." He brought up one arm, resting it against the wall beside her. "I think we're suited. You're beautiful and clever. You feel safe and happy in my world. Don't worry, I've been observing you. You're gentle and kind, I see you with the children, with the staff. Lonnie already adores you. Metta is all Miss Christy says this, Miss Christy says that.... You have a delicate, sensitive hand."

"I hope so," she said seriously. "I believe in being myself. Anyway, both Lonnie and Metta have plenty to teach me. As for you? I think this is part of your plan to keep your ex-girlfriends away. Like Gemma for instance."

His mouth twitched. "I could have sworn Gemma had forgotten all about me."

"But tonight she told you differently?"

"Why do you say that?" he challenged, eyes narrowing.

"Because I happened to catch the two of you talking before the concert started."

He gave a brief laugh. "Christy, Christy, is there no privacy? Gemma is a great one for questions. I think we could stop all the talk in its tracks."

"So there is talk?" She knew it. She could feel it. Why not? Gossip was what most people did.

Ashe shrugged. "You know how people are. Everyone has been waiting for me to get married from the day I turned eighteen. God knows why. I have to tell you, I have a horror of pushy mothers."

"Especially when they look like Mrs. Millner-Hill?"

He shrugged good-humouredly. "Little do you know the tricks Gwen has got up to in her time and she's taught Gemma everything she knows."

"At least you didn't jilt her?" Christy said, her expression turning melancholy.

"Please don't hark back to your little fling with Josh Deakin or I might really lose it." A flame in his dark eyes flickered. She looked luminescent, blooming like some extraordinarily beautiful flower.

The air was suddenly very still, heavy with a tension that ran just beneath their outpouring of words.

"Go on, lose it." Uncharacteristically she provoked him, defying the steely core in him. "There's no one to see you."

It was the match to the fuse. He pulled her forcefully into his arms, allowing her little room to manoeuvre, certainly no escape. His kiss was wild and swift. Passion burst like a damn. It was useless and dishonest to pretend she didn't want this, her body reacting with strange abandon as the tumult rolled over her.

He released her after a spinning eternity, looking for a moment like he wanted to slam his hand into the wall. "You're driving me crazy. You sure as hell know how."

Her long silky hair swept over her shoulder.

"The world is full of sexy women," she taunted, desperate to pierce his emotional armour.

"Not like you. Not a chance."

"So how could we live happily ever after?" she questioned wildly. "I could be just like your mother. I have her hair."

His striking dark face was suddenly very still. "You've seen her portrait?"

"No I haven't." Her hostility collapsed like a pack of cards. "What are you doing, Ashe? What are *we* doing?"

"God knows." The admission was torn from him. "All I know is I want you to stay."

"You can't mean forever?" She knew now how empty her life would be without this complicated man in it.

His tension increased. With Christy he was experiencing something he had never experienced before. Tragedy had touched him deeply, for all his self-reliance, and it had left deep scars. He knew better than anybody "love" laid a man open to a kind of dying when that love was withdrawn. There was a price to be paid for everything. What he felt for this woman, right from the moment he'd set eyes on her, had made him vulnerable. In its way it had opened him up to suffering. He'd survived from childhood by developing an impregnable shell. Yet this beautiful creature was opening up a thousand cracks every day. He wanted her. God knows how he wanted her! He really *liked* her, everything about her. He felt nourished, as were the children, by her company. Was that love? Some very strong thread held them. She was as aware of it as he was. Yet he was rushing her headlong off her feet at a time when she too was vulnerable. He couldn't stop...couldn't... The knowledge he was a driven man mocked him. He could see the little diamond pricks of emotion in her eyes, large and glistening.

"You must be missing what I'm saying, Christy," he offered more quietly, not letting his ravaging emotions out. He took her fingertips and brought them to his mouth. "I want you. Not for some tempestuous affair. I know it's been all too urgent. The timing! But I don't have a lot of time. You know that. I want you with a gold wedding band on your finger. If I were honest I'd admit I want to lock you up so you can't escape me."

She saw stars. Then her vision cleared. "You're manoeuvring me, Ashe." She knew full well a rational argument, even a play for her own integrity, wouldn't stand up against the feelings he aroused in her. ''I don't even know if I want to escape you but I'm frightened of getting in so deep I can't find the shore. I'm only seeing the tip of the iceberg with you. I don't think you realise what a force you are.''

Challenge spilled from his brilliant eyes. ''You're not afraid to cope with it. I'm not wicked. I'm not ruthless. Dogged maybe. Why don't we try easy stages? A trial engagement.'' Smoothly he slipped back to humour, a cover-up for his deeper feelings. ''It would have to be a big wedding, I'm afraid. It will be expected. And you will make an exquisite bride. Don't you think we could live together, Christy?''

His sexual radiance, which she was seeing more and more of, vanquished her. She dropped her gaze before he could spot the tears that sprang into her eyes. How could she deal with him?

''Christy?'' Like the most perfect lover he drew her into his arms with boundless tenderness, lowering his dark head to brush his cheek against the silk of her hair. ''Don't cry. Please don't cry. Your tears bother me terribly.''

Such an infinity of emotion!

Christy tried to get her thoughts together so she could deal with what was happening to her but this man made her perfectly good brain mush. ''What you're trying to do, Ashe, is marry me off,'' she said in a subdued voice. ''You're putting a lot of effort into it. The only odd part is you're trying to marry me off to *you.* You don't love me. Love to you is the forbidden word.''

He was immersed in her intoxicating fragrance yet he held her back from him, and gave her *that* smile.

''I haven't heard you saying you love me,'' he countered, staring down at her.

It was her moment to tell him she had fallen head over heels in love with him, but she had her own needs. Self-protection. She would have to guard her heart. Retain her own identity.

"Christy. It's not like you to be tongue-tied."

In among the swirling emotions she was conscious of her frightened heart. "I'm scared you don't trust me, Ashe. You plucked me out of my life. You brought me here. Maybe at one level you're trying to keep me out of the way."

"Out of the reach of Deakin?" He sounded stern.

"Half a continent away," she continued, determined to have this out. "I don't love him, Ashe. I never did. I can see that very clearly now."

"I just hope you keep seeing it," he said bluntly.

At the fierceness in his black eyes rebellion swept up from the depths of her being. "What did I just say about trust?" she accused him, pulling away. The normal charm of her expression turned tempestuous. "No man and woman can have a good relationship without that."

"What we have is enough!" He knew he could ruin everything but was too caught up in the strength and urgency of ferocious emotion. He thought he could see her heart beating. Her breasts—he longed to caress them—rose and fell, stirring the white silk top that she wore. It was beautiful, stylish, sewn with pink flowers like the paper daisies that covered Augusta after rain. He could smell her delicate fragrance in his nostrils. She was herself. Who was he? A man who needed shock treatment to reveal his heart.

"There's something wrong with your thinking, Ashe," she told him sadly, unknowingly confirming his own thoughts. Christy was acutely aware of the conflict going on in him. It was going on in her. It was impossible for either of them to be calm. Why didn't she tell him what she wanted from him was *everything!* Not the unfathomable unknown.

Seeing her unrest, Ashe curbed his own upheaval, trying to shift some weight of grief off his heart. ''Sexual attraction is a powerful thing, Christy. But what we have doesn't stop at that. If you marry me you can have it all. My horse, my kingdom…'' His vibrant voice, so recently harsh, turned to mock-begging. ''What I need is what every man needs. A good woman. I'd cross the desert on foot to reach her. But she's right here. You'll do just fine.''

How could she possibly answer that? His voice held such endless promise, thrilling excitement. When he bent his head to kiss her, Christy surrendered completely to the torrent of desire that engulfed her.

An unstoppable force had entered her life. Now the force was sweeping her away.

CHAPTER SIX

GEMMA, on the pretext of wanting to see more of ''darling Nic's children,'' begged for an extra day or so.

''If that's okay with you, Ashe,'' she cajoled, her warm friendly smile covering a shocking resentment. In fact resentment was too tame a word. Gemma was furious at Christy's presence in the house. Nevertheless she added, ''Besides, I'll be company for Christy.''

Christy almost winced. That was good. As good as it gets. Gemma's stay-over had more to do with being with Ashe than it had to do with her or the children. When Ashe gave his assent—what else could the man do short of scowling darkly and saying no—Gemma's mood lifted to something approaching buoyant.

The truth was, Gemma had made a career out of waiting for Ashe to ask her to marry him. After all, he hadn't asked anyone else. There were at least a dozen with ambitions, but no one quite as desperate as Gemma to get him for a husband. There was nothing wrong with her, certainly. It might have been straining it a bit to say she was beautiful, but she was good-looking, competent, intelligent, healthy. She was station born and bred; her family was highly respected within the pastoral industry. She knew Ashe had a deep-seated wariness of city women. Of course it all had to do with the trauma of his mother running off. According to Gemma's own mother, Eve McKinnon might have been very beautiful with fascinating thrown in, but she was absolutely hopeless as a station wife. No good at all. Not a *real* station wife.

Many were the stories Gwen Millner-Hill told about "the bolter," which was how she always referred to Ashe's runaway mother. Sometimes Gemma thought deep down her mother actually had hated the beautiful Eve. But then she had so admired Ashe's father. Everyone's sympathies had been with McKinnon and the young Ashe. Which made it all the more astonishing Ashe had a city girl with a mane of liquid gold in his house.

It didn't make sense—any of it—but then Ashe had always been unknowable, constantly confusing her just when she thought she knew him. After a hurried discussion—both saw it as an emergency—Gemma had sent her mother home to run a check on Christine Parker. They should have done it before now but neither of them had had the least idea Ashe had invited the young woman to the station.

Nicole hadn't even called her, Gemma thought, feeling outrage and betrayal. At least Nic could have done that. She desperately needed the warning. She would have gladly kept an eye on the children if it were only for a short time. Children could be very demanding, even tiresome, but the housekeeper was there on call. It would have been wonderful to live in the same house as Ashe, Gemma thought, her anger and disappointment building up to grief. It would have given her so many opportunities to get closer to him. It would have been like old times when they were friends. Real friends, laughing and talking together.

How had this Christy Parker found her way into his life? Gemma, with the help of her mother, was determined to find out. They had a few clues. None of their friends had seen her at the actual wedding ceremony. No way they could have missed her. She was too eye-catching. It made Gemma want to scream. For that matter didn't Ashe have a down on blondes? How then did this particular blonde manage to get into the reception? She had to be a guest from the bridegroom's side. Josh Deakin, legal eagle. At least they had a fix on him....

Although it was still early morning, silvery-blue heat waves danced across the vast open plains. It was an unending landscape, extending to the horizon with the golden spinifex decorating the wind-sculpted sands and the rippling slopes. As the wind shifted so did the fascinating sand patterns that the aborigines depicted so often in their paintings. The dormant seeds of the flowering annuals and ephemerals that came to blazing life after the rains lay quietly beneath the fiery earth as a child lies quietly beneath a blanket. Christy had heard many times of the great glory of the desert heart when it burst into blossom, now she wondered if she would ever see it.

The Wet Season in the tropical north was almost due, bringing monsoonal rainfall to the great desert region via the interlocking river system but very rarely to the Red Centre. Could she be so lucky? There were many photographs on her sitting room wall of McKinnon family members and friends standing amid the floral splendour of Augusta after rain. From sandhill desert to the greatest garden on earth.

Christy sat the beautiful chestnut, Desert Dancer, looking out over the shimmering landscape. This was a favourite vantage point atop one of the low eroded escarpments that dotted the station; the sandstone layered in pink, white, red and yellow. The cattle looked small from this distance. A section of the great herd was grazing the desert floor, finding nourishment and moisture in the pink parakeelya, a flowering succulent peculiar to the sandhills. Stock could live for months on the parakeelya without the need for water. So even in the desert nature provided. Indeed the Great Artesian Basin lay beneath the Simpson Desert. There were springs and waterholes around the desert borders, but no permanent water in the desert proper. Christy had been told the aborigines looked on the desert proper as a place inhabited by evil spirits. So far she could only see its phenomenal primeval beauty.

She marvelled at the splendour of the waterlilies that crowded every waterhole on the station; pink, blue, white, each billabong turning on a display of the one colour. She hadn't so far seen a mix. But then Augusta was so vast she didn't think she could take it all in even if she had a lifetime to do it. She had, however, experienced a marvellous "connection" that had to do with her love of nature in all its moods. Or perhaps the desert only sang its songs to certain people. She could well appreciate how many people would be daunted by this wild environment. The station was so remote; women in particular could be frightened of its loneliness, emptiness, and its "other world" antiquity. Perhaps that was what had happened to Ashe's mother? She may well have tried but been overcome by a lifestyle so extreme, so polarized from the one she'd been used to. There was no use asking Ashe. He didn't want to talk.

Christy looked about the desert heartland amazed by the fiery clash of colours as the sun rose higher. The tops of the desert oaks looked to be on fire. Ashe had warned her to keep a sharp eye out for wild camels, dingoes on the prowl and the herds of wild donkeys that roamed the station, but so far she had only witnessed the thrilling sight of herds of kangaroos, both the desert euros and the more nomadic Red bounding their way across the heavy red sand or the sandstone bluffs of the hill country. Ashe had promised to take her to the caves, which held fine examples of aboriginal drawings. She was looking forward to that but she realised Ashe had little spare time especially in the lead up to the annual big muster.

Descending the rocky slope with its flying pebbles glittering like glass in the sun, Christy kept her eye out for the brightly patterned bearded and netted dragons, the lizards that were widely distributed all over the area. Although they looked extraordinary, even fearsome, they were harmless. Dancer was well behaved but she didn't want her mount startled. This was the home, too, of the biggest lizard of them all, the goanna. She wasn't so keen on being confronted by one of them. Many more than six feet long, they could, and often did, present a problem. In addition to the desert's beauty there were always the hazards, but mercifully most desert animals kept out of man's way.

Christy loved these early morning rides. The desert showed a softer mood with long shadows falling over the dunes, delineating each ripple, revealing the tracks of the mulga scrub spiders, the marsupials, the reptiles and all the other night hunters. She could explore this place forever, but the children were always on her mind.

Safely on the plain, Christy let Dancer have her head. The chestnut thoroughbred was a wonderful ride, highly intelligent and hardy, with no reduction in speed and mobility over the sand. Christy was getting to know more about the station's breeding programme of the Australian stock horse with its strong infusion of thoroughbred blood. Desert Dancer was not a workhorse but a thoroughbred kept for the single great pleasure of riding.

Nearing the home complex Christy eased Dancer up. Lonnie had told her she could always take her time, but Lonnie had quite enough to do, especially after the weekend, which had proved such a great success. Usually, Christy looked forward to getting back to the homestead, to sitting down to breakfast with the children, but not today. Gemma was still in residence even after two full days of her self-invited stay.

Gemma, to Christy's surprise after confiding her desire to get to know the children better, showed no real interest in them. A state of affairs that wasn't missed by the perceptive children. She had also proved arrogant and unsympathetic in her dealing with Metta, going so far as to challenge Christy's decision to allow the children so much time in Metta's company. On a sad note, Christy concluded Gemma was one of those people who didn't believe in encouraging any sort of friendship with the indigenous people, though she would have been highly affronted had anyone labelled her a "racist." One way and another Gemma had thrown quite a few discordant notes into what had been a harmonious holiday.

Children were excellent judges of adult behaviour. Gemma hadn't fooled them. Christy thought of last night's pre-bed conversation with wry humour… "Do you think she'll go tomorrow?" Katey had asked, blue eyes anxious.

"I really couldn't say, poppet." Christy shrank away from saying anything unkind about Gemma much as she deserved it.

"Why does she keep saying, 'if you want my opinion'?" Katey mimicked Gemma's lofty tones comically.

"Oh well, it's an expression…"

"She doesn't like you, Christy," Katey, six going on sixty, told her owlishly. "She never ever says anything nice to you but she definitely likes Uncle Ashe. I 'spose she wants to marry him."

"Gosh I hope she doesn't," Kit suddenly sat up to yell. "I don't like her."

"Neither do I." Katey nodded her head emphatically. "We had such fun when she wasn't around. I'm going to say a prayer her father comes in his plane to pick her up."

Amen to that, had been Christy's silent contribution as she turned off the light.

There was definitely a downside to having Gemma around.

Less than half a mile away, riding back to the homestead, Ashe was thinking much the same thing. He had really stretched himself trying to find time to take Christy and the children on a tour of the station but he didn't fancy taking Gemma along. In fact the very thought was making him so irritable he was close to grinding his teeth. It sure was a difficult thing to put a woman like Gemma off. Harder yet when she had a mother like Gwen.

The worst thing he had ever done was partner Gemma a few times at various Outback functions. Once a post-polo ball. What the hell! He had known her all his life. He had kissed her. God knows she had expected it. He had never slept with her. He hadn't been fool enough to complicate their lives, yet a few kisses had somehow given Gemma and her mother the idea suitability and availability was a big factor in arranging a marriage. Something like his own fool argument. Even Gemma's father and brothers had cottoned onto the idea.

He didn't know why he was being so polite, except Gemma was a guest and he liked to keep a rein on a tongue that tended to be sardonic to the point of cutting. But Gemma's jealousy of Christy was becoming very tedious. Surely, Gemma was supposed to be getting to know the children better when so far as he could see she hadn't bothered with them at all. Also because he knew her so well he was convinced Gemma had something up her sleeve. Some little bombshell she was awaiting just the right moment to explode.

Ashe sent his horse plunging down a steep sandy slope, taking a short cut so he could meet up with Christy after her morning ride. Gemma had hardly let Christy get a word in at the dinner table last night. In fact she was acting pretty much like she was the future mistress of Augusta station and Christy a tolerated guest. Christy was really being very nice about the whole thing but he doubted very much if he could put up with much more.

From a distance off Christy could see Ashe coming at a strong pace towards her, red dust rising like smoke from his horse's hooves. Immediately her heart started its mad fluttering and, unknown to her, her whole face became illuminated with pleasure and excitement. It was very difficult to get a handle on all her soaring emotions when she was so overwhelmed by everything, the station, its environment, the spiritual effects of the ancient desert, and above all, her feelings for Ashe McKinnon. They were so powerful they had invaded every aspect of her life.

After Josh's treachery, which she now saw as a godsend, she had expected to go through a serious emotional slump. Instead in meeting Ashe she felt something momentous had occurred. She had fallen madly in love with him. Rebound? *Irrational love?* That's what Ashe would call it. ''Hormones.'' Except she admired and respected him. Everyone on the station did. There had never been any doubt Ashe could carry on from his father; carry on the proud tradition of the McKinnon cattle kings. And this man had asked her to marry him! Why hadn't she said yes there and then? Marriage to Ashe would be a tremendous experience.

Surely she could face the task of getting him to love her, to look on her as the most important woman in his life. She recognised the fact the sad destruction of his parents' marriage, brought about by his mother's adultery—one had to face it—and her subsequent pregnancy had resulted in Ashe's acute cynicism about marriage and women. Given it was a terrible story, including as it did his own abandonment at such a young age, why couldn't she change all that? The very thought made her dizzy. Whether it was with exhilaration or trepidation she wasn't quite sure.

He was beautiful to look at, riding a handsome white stallion with classic ease and grace. She knew that bred in the saddle he could tackle anything. Station life itself was dangerous. Musters alone were savagely demanding on horse and rider, the wild environment full of challenges. Stockmen had to develop unique handling skills and the stamina for travelling great distances. She knew from her own experiences one had to be fatalistic if one "rode" seriously. Ashe's splendid horsemanship showed.

"You really are a wonderful rider," she told him when he reined in alongside her, vivid, compelling, another colourful bandanna, this one yellow, tied loosely around his darkly tanned throat. "A pleasure to watch."

"Why thank you, ma'am." He swept his cream akubra off in response, giving her *that* smile, albeit mocking. "I was hoping to meet up with you. In fact I made it my business."

"Are you coming back to the house?" She was acutely aware of his brilliant dark eyes moving over her, noting the way she wore her hair in a thick rope down her back.

"I had intended to, but sadly Gemma is getting on my nerves."

"You did invite her," she couldn't resist pointing out.

His answer was a groan. "I hate to say it but Gem invited herself. I'm just wondering when she intends to go?"

"Then you'd better ask before she decides to move in."

You're the one I want to move in, he thought with such certainty the jolt radiated out from his heart. "What do you suggest I say? Your jealousy of Christy is making me angry?"

''Is it?'' Christy challenged, staring into his eyes. ''Doesn't she mean *anything* to you?''

''She's a friend, what else?'' He shrugged impatiently. ''I've known her all her life.''

''Then why is she working so hard to convince me you shared a deep meaningful relationship?''

''Maybe to make trouble. Anyway it was never as deep and committed as your relationship with Deakin,'' he retorted very crisply.

''Give me a break!'' Christy sighed. ''I told you, Josh is ancient history.''

''Frankly I'm relieved to hear that.'' Ashe lifted his head to look up at a hovering falcon in search of prey. ''Because I've had word Josh and Callista want an invitation to Augusta. They've had to come home earlier than anticipated. Poor old Josh caught a tummy bug.'' Ashe didn't try hard to sound sincere. ''Apparently he did too much swooping on the wrong things to eat.''

''How unfortunate.'' Christy was more sincere in her comment. ''You've heard from them?''

''You mean *you* wish you had?'' he enquired acidly. ''I've heard from Mercedes.''

''And they want to come here?'' Christy levelled him with a dubious green stare.

''They want to meet up with Nic and Brendan when they pick up their children.''

''Good grief!'' Christy was stunned. A little distance away the falcon dropped like a stone to pick up a small rodent.

''Would you believe it?'' Ashe said with an exaggerated drawl. ''I hardly ever see them. Except at Christmas. Now *everyone* wants to come.''

''Then I'd better be making plans to go home.''

''Surely you want to see Josh again?'' His handsome

face wore its most infuriating expression. “Just to check on your feelings?”

“What I really want to do is smack that look off your face,” Christy retorted with such spirit Dancer did a lively two-step.

“You want to go easy on the violence,” he scoffed. “I just could retaliate.”

“You'd never strike a woman.” Christy looked and sounded aghast.

“Who said anything about striking? I was thinking something more lascivious. Anyway, as you know, I'm a man who likes to make his plans in advance. Forewarned is forearmed.”

“Meaning?” Christy had to pull a little on the reins. Dancer was getting restive.

“Why don't we find some shade?” Ashe suggested, cramming his akubra further down over his eyes. “I know you're looking after your beautiful skin but you really don't need too much sun. Let's make for the lagoon.”

Why not? The lagoon was beautiful. “Why don't we have some fun while we're at it? Let's race.”

Very provocatively he glanced down at his glinting watch. “I'll give you a three-minute start.”

“Do you want to race or not?” Such a rhythm was building up in her blood, the sensitive chestnut was responding.

“You're on,” Ashe purred, leaning across the neck of his white stallion.

Christy took off like a rocket, never once looking back. She knew Ashe on that beautiful horse could overtake her and Dancer but she was going to give it her best shot. She could make the obvious diagonal cut across the open plain or…spreading out in front of them was a stretch of boulders which she had ridden around on at least two occasions…she could go over the top. She'd soared over fences and ditches many times before in her life. Jumping the boulder in the middle, the highest, would give her a distinct advantage.

What Christy hadn't calculated on as Desert Dancer stretched out in preparation to storm the barricade was that a rock wallaby, in the way of wallabies, chose that very moment to announce its presence, standing up on its hind legs and looking stupid. In a real test of horsemanship Christy held on, as rider and noble animal became airborne, landing cleanly on the other side but so explosively Christy, despite her best efforts, was thrown out of the saddle, the thick fleshy leaves on a spread of parakeelya and button grass absorbing much of the shock.

"My God!" Ashe's reaction initially frantic quickly turned to a curious anger when he found her lying flat out on the carpet of crushed succulents, spitting out bits of grass. "What the hell was that all about?" he demanded, a mixture of high relief and perverse anger tearing at him.

She couldn't answer for a moment, waiting for her lungs to fill.

"Christy?" He dropped to his knees beside her. "You're okay, aren't you?"

She grasped his anger and tried to make light of things. "I would have been if that damned wallaby hadn't messed with us. How is Dancer?" She turned her head in concern.

"He's not hurt," Ashe assured her a little harshly. "He's as worried as I am that you didn't break a limb."

"I'm fine." She fixed her eyes at the blue sky not the burning urgency of his expression. "I'm a bit winded that's all. All this stuff—" she clutched the pink flowers "—broke my fall."

"You're going to hurt someplace," he warned her.

"Without a doubt."

"I hated watching that, you know," he burst out explo-
ively as though it were a catastrophe.

"I can see that, Ashe." She lay quietly.

"You're supposed to take care of yourself." He frowned.

"Look, I'm not hurt." She could laugh still. "I took a
it of a fall."

"Try to sit up." He slid a hand beneath her back, his
xpression taut.

"Listen. I've fallen off plenty of horses over the years,"
he protested with a spark of defiance. "I bet you have,
oo."

"I don't want to see you do tricks." His voice cracked
vith authority. "You're not a stunt rider." He stared down
t her moodily, realising uncharacteristically he was un-
erved. So it was his time to rediscover what caring meant.
'or a moment there, as she and the chestnut were airborne,
e had known blind fear. Experience told him she was
bout to take a fall. It took very little to break one's neck.
'amily tragedy had brought that starkly home to him. The
efences he had painstakingly built up over the long years
vere about to be destroyed. Was this what he wanted? Lov-
ng a woman or living in limbo?

Christy, staring at his passionate, dynamic face was
noved to say gently, "You're making too much of it, Ashe.
'm fine. It was Dancer I was most worried about."

"You owe it to me to take all possible care."

"I know. I'm sorry. It would have been perfectly all right
nly Dancer was spooked."

"Horses spook easily. You know that." He ran a check-
ng hand along the length of her body, still frowning.

Christy knew she had to get to her feet; to prove to him
othing was broken, that she could move freely.

"There." Once up she gave him a smile, feeling she was
rowning in love of him. "Ashe?"

He took her into his arms, trying to impose a hard contro
on his fraying nerves. ''Promise me you won't attempt t
do any jumping without wearing a hard hat, not tha
damned akubra,'' he ordered. ''Make sure you know th
terrain.''

''Absolutely.'' She brought her face up, impervious t
everything around her. Except him.

Something had shifted in their largely invisible relation
ship. In front of the children and the staff Ashe treated he
as ''family,'' a younger cousin perhaps. Now he was com
ing out into the open. Maybe in throwing her, the filly ha
done her an enormous favour.

''I've got something for you,'' Ashe said, taking he
hand and leading her toward the tree-lined lagoon.

''How very thoughtful of you. What is it?' She couldn'
keep the excitement out of her voice, or her fingers fror
trembling in his.

He was regaining control now his voice resuming its ha
bitual self-assurance. ''I hope you like it but it shouldn'
be a big surprise.''

''Now you've got me very interested.'' Her head wa
aching a little so she dragged it out of its plait, shaking he
hair free. ''Isn't this a beautiful spot? Paradise before th
fall. The waterlilies are exquisite. I never knew they existe
in such great numbers or how sweetly they spike the air
I'm planning to come back even if I have to put up m
tent.'' It was nothing more than a nervous outpouring bu
as she met his gaze the rest of her words caught in he
throat. She wasn't at all sure what was about to happe
except it was *significant;* life-changing.

Ashe took her left hand, first raising it to his mouth. Hi
concentration on her was intense. Her hand still captured
he slid a glorious engagement ring down on her finger

cushioning the sudden spasm that passed through her body with his own.

"I offer you this ring, Christy, knowing that if you consent to wear it you will make me a proud man."

She felt her emotions were being pushed to extremity. She felt as though her heart would break. Tears pricked her eyes but she couldn't get out a word.

"It looks like I'll have to kiss you," Ashe murmured, brilliance in his expression. He bent his dark head, taking her mouth like he could draw her heart through her lips; kissing her until she was not only speechless but breathless. "Understand that I want you." He made no attempt to conceal his passionate emotion. "I need you. I need to have you for always."

Christy stared down tumultuously at their entwined hands; his so strong and lean, deeply tanned, hers, in comparison, milk-white. "This is something I could never have foreseen, Ashe," she told him, low-voiced. "We've known each other such a short time. It's like a great leap off a cliff."

"I'd leap off a cliff for you without a second thought." His beautiful black eyes were soft with a smile. "You can take as much time to think about it as you like. Maybe by tonight."

"Sorcerer!" She stared up at him, her green eyes huge.

"You haven't told me you like it." He lifted her hand, watching the flash of the exquisite precious stones.

"I've never seen a ring so startlingly lovely in my life."

"Like you. With *your* eyes it had to be an emerald." In fact a flawless Colombian square-cut emerald flanked by brilliant cut diamonds.

Christy honestly thought her legs would give way. Emotions, his and hers, stormed around them. He never said he loved her, even at that moment something was preventing him from forming the words, but everything else he did saturated her in a feeling she was loved. Loved as she had never been loved before. It was tantalising but deep and constant. She began to cry.

"Darling, Christy, please don't!" The words were ripped from him, the tender weight behind the endearment offering unlimited possibilities. "This is our new life." He bent down to softly kiss her open mouth, his tongue taking up her tears. "Don't be fearful. I won't ever let you down. This is a sacred promise. You have so much to give me. Everything I have is yours." It was way beyond the boundaries of any marriage contract, Christy thought ecstatically.

In fact Ashe's words, spoken in such a way, consumed her. Her heart was beating in rhapsodic time with the chirruping of the birds that flashed in and out of that enchanted place. "You trust me with your life?" To fail him was to be lost.

For an instant his striking face turned faintly bleak. "I trust the soul in you, Christy." He couldn't yet tell her of the loneliness and longings he had capped like a bottomless well.

His face swam before her eyes. She was flushed with high emotion. She could wait for him to tell her he loved her. A man with all that passion locked up in him had already paid too high a price for loving. "I'm going to do the very best I possibly can. I'm not dreaming this, am I?" Christy smiled through the dazzle of tears.

"No!" He drew her towards him like she was infinitely precious.

"Were you that sure of me you already had the ring?"

His laugh was deep in his throat. "I knew it would suit you from the moment I laid eyes on you. There are earrings to match. There was a necklace but somehow my mother got away with that. I might just try to get it back." A faint harshness crept into his tone. ''Every piece belonged to my grandmother, my father's mother. My mother chose a ruby for her engagement ring. She didn't leave it behind. But she never wore your ring though she did wear the earrings with the necklace on grand occasions. If you prefer another ring or another stone you have only to say so. I want to tell you I loved my grandmother very much.''

Tentatively Christy brought up her hand and touched his dark handsome face. ''I love this ring, Ashe. It's so beautiful it takes my breath away.''

More than anything in the world she wanted his love. A vision of Ashe's mother as she imagined her sprang vividly into Christy's mind. Why did she have such doubts Ashe's mother had been utterly callous? Maybe leaving her small son had wrenched her heart out. No one seemed likely to ever know unless by some miracle Ashe was able to speak to his mother. Eve McKinnon's shocking and dramatic flight from Augusta had infected her son's soul. Now all Christy wanted was to make up for the lost years.

After such an experience Christy felt delirious for the rest of the day. Not even Gemma's abrasive presence could sap her of her joy though she couldn't find it in her heart to cause Gemma shock and upset by wearing her engagement ring. She and Ashe had decided they would announce their engagement officially when the family came home.

''The start of our marriage contract,'' Ashe had laughed without irony.

Christy knew Nicole and Brendan would be delighted. Possibly Callista would be greatly relieved although Christy was sure Josh had never admitted to his involvement with her. Josh would be... What would Josh be? Christy found herself quite uncaring. Josh had been a figment of her imagination. Ashe was a real man. He carried the aura of authority and achievement. He commanded respect at the same time treating every man, woman and child on the station the way they wanted to be treated, with kindness and fair-mindedness. They could come to him and tell them of their difficulties and he would listen. Christy had witnessed that many times. Small wonder for such a vast station things ran smoothly.

Gemma waited until after dinner to launch her missile, her sense of triumph barely veiled. Perhaps she wasn't aware Ashe already knew what she was about to tell him? She was leaving tomorrow—her father was flying in to collect her—but before she left she was going to create a few ripples for one Christy Parker who sat at the dinner table in an outrageously pretty dress, her face bedecked with soft smiles.

Christy looked radiant, Gemma thought; jealousy sending icy cold shivers down her back. What new thing had happened to make Christy look so lit from within? She was an impostor, a fraud. She was on Augusta under false pretences. Surely Nic didn't know about her past? Unthinkable she would have kept it to herself or allow this impostor to look after her children. "What I've been trying to figure out," Gemma began as soon as she could, filled all day with a violent urge to get her seething emotions off her chest, "is how you put it over on us all, Christy?"

"What are you getting at, Gemma?" Ashe asked coolly.

Gemma took a long swallow of her delicious wine.

"I really didn't want to upset you with this, Ashe, but did you know Christy here who looks like a model for a medieval angel has been leading a double life?"

Ashe leaned back in his high-backed carver chair, brilliant eyes hooded. "Out with it. I wondered how long it would take you."

For a moment Gemma went quiet. ''Wh-a-a-t?'' No one but no one could look as formidable as Ashe when he so chose.

He leaned forward, snapped his fingers. ''You don't have to be a genius to work it out. You and your mother have devoted some time and effort to checking Christy out. That's it, isn't it?''

''Only because we care for you, Ashe,'' Gemma said, putting out a hand to him, great earnestness in her eyes. ''It looks very much to us as if Christy has planned all this.'' Her voice sounded shocked and saddened.

''What is *this?*'' Christy spoke for the first time, studying the other young woman who faced her across the gleaming mahogany table.

Gemma's whole body language changed. She leaned forward like she wanted to surge across the table, eyes flashing her primitive emotions. ''I'm absolutely certain Nic and Brendan know nothing about your past. Let alone Ashe.''

''You're suggesting Christy has a criminal record?'' Ashe asked in a voice though deceptively soft might have given anyone else pause.

''Not a criminal record, no,'' Gemma continued, unable to leave well alone. ''But she's been enormously deceitful. I don't really like saying this—''

''Then why are you?'' Ashe asked very smoothly, brows like black wings above his brilliant eyes.

Gemma dragged her eyes away from Christy to stare at him. ''I know how much you value the truth, Ashe. Christy Parker has come here under false pretences. I know you'll find this hard to believe. I did, so did Mother, but Christy was seriously involved with—'' Gemma looked down, bit her lip ''—with Callista's husband,'' she finished in hushed tones.

''Is that it?'' Ashe drawled, almost casually.

''My God, isn't it enough?'' Gemma stared at him as though he had suddenly gone mad. ''No one knew her at the wedding. We've asked all around. Finally we got some information from one of Josh's colleagues. He said Josh's former girlfriend was very beautiful. He'd only seen her once. A blonde Josh had been keeping all to himself. No one really got to meet her but he said he thought it was serious. Very serious.''

Ashe's mouth twisted wryly. ''That was before he met and fell crazily in love with Callista and her millions.''

''I mean it's so weird!'' Gemma felt like her bombshell had failed to detonate. ''What was she doing at the wedding? What is she doing here? Who is she? She's not one of us.''

For an instant Christy, catching Ashe's darkening expression, thought he was about to verbally lash out. ''Gemma,'' she intervened quickly, her voice surprisingly kind, ''Ashe knows all this.''

''He can't.'' Gemma tried to swallow the hard lump in her throat. Couldn't.

''He does. What I don't see is that it's any of your business. What did you hope to achieve by saying all this? Josh isn't a bigamist. It's over between us. He married the woman he loves.''

''No, it's not as simple as that,'' Gemma protested, visibly quivering. ''There's a trick in it somewhere. I bet Nic doesn't know about your involvement with Josh.''

''I wonder you haven't gone ahead and faxed her,'' Ashe said.

''I don't know where they are,'' Gemma admitted artlessly, as though she felt thwarted she couldn't contact them with her news.

''Listen to me, Gemma,'' Ashe turned fully on her speaking firmly. ''If you really want to remain a friend, and

I don't want to lose your family's friendship, perhaps you could start by not interfering in *my* family's affairs.''

Gemma blinked hard—''But it's so unlike you, Ashe. So extraordinary. This girl has totally bedazzled you. Why I bet she's no different from your mother.''

Gemma certainly knew how to bring all good feeling to a halt.

Ashe fixed her with brilliant angry eyes. ''Okay, here you are. Your protestations of trying to help won't work. We both know why you're doing this.''

''But you *don't!*'' Gemma all but shouted, strangely pale. ''I love you, Ashe. I'd make you a really fine wife. What you don't need is someone like *her!*'' She threw a vengeful hand across the table, almost upsetting her tall-stemmed wineglass. ''How could a woman like that devote herself to station life? She knows nothing about it. All she can do is ride.''

''I was born and reared on a farm, you know,'' Christy pointed out mildly, when she was feeling the bliss of the day was quite spoiled.

''Why don't you walk away from this, Gemma?'' Ashe sounded a warning. ''You don't love me. You've made an art form out of wanting what you can't have.''

At that Gemma jumped up, in her fury making her substantial, carved mahogany chair rock. ''She's not good enough for you, Ashe. She'll be just like your mother and *disappear!*''

Ashe inhaled on a rasp. He stood up, too, a formidable figure, brow furrowed. ''No more, Gemma. I mean it.''

Gemma could see the hopelessness of it all in his face. Ashe had never loved her but he wanted this girl. ''Wait until Callista hears of her treachery,'' she cried. ''We all grew up together. We care about one another. That can't be lost. *She's* the alien in our midst. She'll bring you nothing but sorrow."

And then she was gone. Racing from the dining room, her slim body hunched awkwardly as though fending off blows.

"Oh my God!" Christy breathed, resting her head on her hand. "I feel so sorry for her."

But Ashe's eyes were hard and cold. "Don't bother. That was just a performance. She's out to cause as much trouble as she can."

"So what are we going to do?"

"I thought we'd done it." He suddenly snapped and banged the table. "As far as I'm concerned we're engaged as from today. I know you hated to cause Gemma any embarrassment—you're too tender-hearted—but you could have worn your ring tonight."

"I'm not so cruel. I didn't want that. We agreed. She does love you, Ashe."

"Like you loved Deakin?" he shot off, then shook his head as if to clear it. "No, no. I didn't mean that."

"I think you did," Christy told him quietly. "I'm as upset you are, Ashe, but no one is going to make me feel guilty. That includes you. I thought I was in love with Josh. I see now that was no more than window-dressing. Josh showed himself in his true colours by going after Callista. He always wanted money. Now he's got it. I'm hoping Callista is woman enough to make him toe the line."

CHAPTER SEVEN

JOSH had picked up considerably since his indisposition. In fact he had never looked better. Boyishly good-looking, tanned from a tropical sun, eyes sparkling, shining sun-bleached floppy hair, stylishly dressed in casual designer gear, well mannered as always, and attentive to his bride who to Christy's concerned eye looked washed out and drained of energy. Not the radiant young woman of her wedding day at all. Though obviously it hadn't been a honeymoon idyll with Josh taking ill.

"You're so good to have us, Ashe," Callista was saying in her soft tones, looking up at her cousin and smiling with gratitude. "I didn't think I could take going back to the city so soon. And Christy!" Callista just couldn't believe it. The exquisite blonde from her wedding day waiting for them at the homestead. She might have been warned!

"How are you, Callista. Lovely to see you again," Christy responded in her friendly fashion. "Josh!" She nodded her head in his direction, not feeling in the least awkward or embarrassed. Ashe's ring hung between her breasts. In a few months' time she would marry him. Tonight after the announcement their relationship would be perfectly open. It would be such a relief. She had hated the deceptions however necessary.

"It was so nice of you to offer to look after Nic's children." Callista was still radiating powerful surprise. "She must think a lot of you?" Instinct warned Callista to be very wary of Christy. There was a story there she hadn't heard. It was obvious, too, Christy had endeared herself to the entire household. Ashe, Lonnie, the children, and the rest of the staff all appeared to look to her as though she were, heaven forbid, Mrs. Ashe McKinnon. Of course any woman could take her cousin Ashe away, Callista had been prepared for that, but she'd been hoping for someone sensible and moderately attractive who would be happy to share Ashe with his family. Someone like Gemma. This young woman was too beautiful, too sexy, too under-awed by everything. Worse, she would take up all of Ashe's attention.

Studying his wife's expression, which near revealed her somewhat bleak ruminations, Josh said solicitously, ''Darling, why don't you go up to the room and rest awhile?'' He was ready to steer her by the elbow. ''I think Callista caught the bug, as well,'' he explained to the others, bending to kiss Callista's temple tenderly. ''She hasn't been terribly well either.'' His excellent spirits were no more than a blind. He had been just as shocked as his wife to see Christy installed at the homestead, which was so big and so grand it pointed up all the things he had missed in his own life. Callista and her splendid arrogant cousin, who Josh knew, had no time for him.

Josh made to move, unsettled at the way McKinnon was looking at Callista, his expression concerned. ''Are you sure you don't need to see a doctor, Callista?''

''Of course not.'' Callista struggled to sound brighter. ''It's all the travelling. Josh has taken the most marvellous care of me. I've never felt so pampered. But I will go and lie down if you don't mind. I want to feel rested before Mummy and Nic and Brendan arrive. Augusta is the best place in the world to feel safe.''

Safe? That was disturbing. The word took Christy by surprise. She'd been hoping Callista would feel perfectly safe with her husband who appeared to be making every effort to cosset her. Maybe it would turn out well after all.

Callista and Josh, arms entwined, retreated to the comfort and privacy of the spacious bedroom that had been prepared for them while Christy continued with her plan to take the children for a drive. Metta was to come along, the most delightful of guides. Metta knew all about the desert's wild fruits and flowers and their medicinal uses, the best lagoons and water channels. She could name all the birds, big and small. She knew the nests for the parrots, the cockatoos and owls and the secretive pelicans. Perhaps the most captivating aspect of her company, Metta had a great fund of stories from the Dreamtime, myths that identified her own tribal past. Ancestral creators had made the world shaping every natural feature of the earth. Metta had a magical story for everything; wind, rain, sun, fire, the blazing rocks that were such a desert feature, the birds and the desert animals. Christy found herself as fascinated as the children by these stories. Their journeys around Augusta had established themselves as happy and educational times.

Ashe walked to the Jeep with them, taking Christy aside for a moment while Metta and the children made themselves comfortable in the vehicle.

"Callista didn't look too well, did she?" he asked, his eyes beneath the wide brim of the akubra sharply keen and a touch worried.

"Some people aren't good travellers," Christy soothed. "She'll probably feel better after a rest. She was very surprised to see me."

Ashe laughed. "Her husband wasn't crazy about it either. Doesn't he look amazingly healthy after so recent a bout of sickness?"

"That he does," Christy agreed wryly. "Maybe it wasn't as bad as they said. The sickness could have carried over to Callista.'' She turned up her face to him. ''We have to tell them the truth, Ashe. The sooner the better. I want to come out into the open.''

''Do you think I don't? What is the truth anyway? You had a brief romance with Deakin. It was all over by the time Callista came into the picture. Naturally we couldn't go into all that at the wedding. It was hardly the time. I hate white lies as much as you but they can act as a social lubricant.''

''Of course. But it *will* come out eventually.'' Christy gave a troubled sigh.

Ashe studied her, gratified Deakin's arrival hadn't disturbed her equilibrium. Finally it was over. ''As far as explanations go, leave it to me. I intend to announce our engagement right after dinner. You want that, don't you?''

''We've made a serious commitment to each other, Ashe.''

''We did and nothing is going to disrupt it.''

''No.'' She looked up at him very seriously. Her identification with Ashe was very new but not fragile. It was strong. She didn't doubt him. Her body trusted him. So did her mind. But there were other people with opinions to weigh in. ''I don't know how everyone else is going to take the news.''

''Frankly, I don't care.'' He tipped her chin, pressing a thumbprint into the shallow cleft, then dropped a kiss on her mouth that set her heart drumming. The first time ever he had done such a thing with the children and Metta looking on in apparent delight. ''Anyway, you're a woman with a lot of grit.'' There was challenge in his black eyes.

''You think it's going to be tested?''

''Well a few things have to be reconciled. Callista won't be full of joy about her husband's knowing you and not saying.''

''She could scarcely catch up with it all at the wedding,'' Christy offered wryly. ''For that matter, no one really got around to explaining why I was there.''

''*I* invited you,'' Ashe said, with magnificent carelessness. ''I didn't have much choice other than to invent a reason to avoid unnecessary hurt. They can accept it, not try to sort it out. I invited you to the wedding. We met when I was in Brisbane for a cattleman's conference some time back. You were doing P.R. work at the hotel. We fell in love at first sight. Such is my nature I couldn't get you out of my mind. I had to have you.''

''Do you?'' Little pulses began to beat inside her, like fiery little prongs.

''You think I like living with you and not having you?'' he said. ''When the house is dark and you're all curled up in bed… I could have walked down the verandah anytime.''

''But you played it safe?'' Her voice was very soft and husky. Didn't he know she yearned for him?

He laughed briefly. ''It would have been the very time Kit would have woken up with a nightmare.''

''So the children have been my little chaperones?'' She couldn't have withstood him otherwise.

''Plus the fact I gave you my word you'd be perfectly safe. Now of course we're engaged,'' he added, his eyes sparkling with dangerous thoughts. ''And the kids are going home. Who couldn't fall in love with you, Christy?''

Whenever he looked at her like that the world was reduced to just him. Christy flushed, a surge of bright blood colouring her skin. ''And with you,'' she whispered, the seed of hope inside her beginning to flourish.

The children were bouncing up and down in the Jeep, unable to contain their excitement and gasping through their laughter.

"We saw you kissing Christy," they cried in unison, flinging themselves forward and waving their hands.

"So you noticed?" Ashe tweaked one of Katey's shiny curls.

"It was great!" Katey grinned broadly. "We're going to tell Mummy and Daddy."

"Whoaa, there!" Ashe gripped their small hands, leaning into the Jeep. "Now listen, guys, it's a secret until tomorrow," he said slowly. "Can I have your promise?" He looked very seriously into their wide eyes.

"*Our* secret?" Kit asked, sounding like that was very important.

"Our secret. You bet!" Ashe confirmed, keeping a hand on each of them.

"Then we'll keep it locked up," Katey promised solemnly, turning to her little brother. "Won't we, Kit?"

Kit was concentrating hard on this. "It's luv-ly you two kissing," he said finally. "It means you're going to love one another forever and ever."

Christy felt her heart swell with such emotion she wanted to cry. Instead she reached in and stroked Kit's warm satin cheek.

It was Ashe who answered for both of them, using a tone of voice so tender, so intense, Christy realised with deep emotion she had never heard him use that exact tone of voice before. "Until the end of the world," he said.

The children were ecstatic when they first caught sight of their parents, waving through the porthole. The Cessna charter flight taxied down the runway and came to a halt a turning distance from the main hangar. Callista, still looking pinched, had remained at the house with Josh in attendance but Christy accompanied Ashe and the children down to the landing strip in good time to see the Cessna bearing

Callista's mother, Mercedes, and the children's parents fly in.

There were lots of hugs and kisses, a few tears from Nicole who had missed her beloved children even as she and Brendan were enjoying a holiday that had turned out to be so piercingly sweet, so full of love and warmth, it had been as Brendan said almost daily, ''a second honeymoon.'' All the old fire was back in their relationship and Nicole had begun to look at life in a new way. Nothing could minimize the loss of her child but she had a wonderful husband and two adorable children to share her life. She realised she was blessed. Mercedes was having trouble locating her luggage. She had brought rather a lot of it for a short stay. Ashe had her driven up to the house by one of the staff. Mercedes was very anxious to see her daughter for any number of reasons. The rest of them tumbled into the Jeep.

''We can't thank you enough, Christy, for looking after the children so beautifully,'' Nicole said, smiling comfortably. This was on the way back to the homestead, Nicole and Brendan having listened to the children's excited chatter and all the wonderful things they had done.

''It was a pleasure.'' Christy returned the smile. ''I loved their company.''

''We're real friends.'' Kit, on his mother's knee, looked at Christy owlishly, letting her know he wasn't about to say anything about their secret.

''That's true,'' Christy laughed.

''And we've got presents,'' Nicole told them in a happy voice.

''My goodness have we got presents!'' Brendan gave a theatrical sigh. ''I know because I had to buy another suitcase to bring them home.''

‘‘And Callista and Josh are up at the house?’’ Nicol
asked of Christy. ‘‘It really is a shame Josh became ill.’’

‘‘He’s over it now,’’ Ashe said smoothly, just barel
turning his head. ‘‘Callista is the one I’m concerned about
She doesn’t look at all well.’’

‘‘It must have been catching.’’ Nicole’s carefree expression became serious. ‘‘Anyway we’re all here now to chee
her up.’’

‘‘Does anyone need cheering up when they’re barel
home from their honeymoon?’’ Ashe asked dryly. ‘‘I hav
to say you two look terrific.’’

‘‘It was a marvellous, relaxed time.’’ Nicole blushed de-
lightfully. ‘‘I desperately needed it. I’m so grateful to you
both for making it happen. Now I’m home with my beautiful children.’’ Nicole hugged Kit to her.

‘‘I can’t wait to see what you’ve got us, Mummy,’
Katey said. ‘‘You and Daddy must see all our beautifu
paintings.’’

‘‘Paintings, oh my!’’ Nicole ruffled her daughter’s hair

‘‘I think you’ll be very pleasantly surprised,’’ Christ
promised. ‘‘Both the children have shown real promise.’’

Brendan turned back to stare at them. ‘‘I was pretty goo
at one time.’’

‘‘You’re still pretty good,’’ Nicole said, nodding he
head proudly, then nodding it again. ‘‘The children hav
inherited their talent from you. Did you know, children
Daddy once had a showing at a gallery?’’

‘‘Why did he stop?’’ Katey asked.

‘‘Because I was responsible for my family,’’ Brenda
explained. ‘‘I’m an architect, sweetheart. That’s my pro-
fession. It satisfied my artistic soul.’’

Hours later Christy was taking care with her dressing whe
a knock came at her door. She went to it hoping it wa

Ashe, instead Mercedes, looking very regal, stood outside the door, her generous figure clothed in her favourite dark blue silk, her trademark South Sea pearls around her neck.

"May I come in, my dear?" She sounded crisply decisive as though she intended to come in regardless of what Christy had to say.

"Why certainly, Mrs. McKinnon." Christy stood back, thinking the time had come to fully explain her presence at Callista's wedding reception. "Won't you sit down?" She indicated the deepest, most comfortable chair.

"I prefer to stand, my dear, if you don't mind," Mercedes said, addressing the chair. "I won't beat about the bush. It's not my way, but I had a most upsetting phone call from Gemma Millner-Hill."

Christy felt the heat in her face. "She seems unable to mind her own business."

"But it's my business, my dear." Mercedes changed her mind and lowered her statuesque figure into the armchair. Her face composed itself into censure and shock. "Indeed it appears that you and Josh, my daughter's husband, knew one another *very well.* I find it absolutely extraordinary it was never mentioned. Would you mind enlightening me?"

Christy shrugged, taking a chair opposite. "I deeply regret the deception, Mrs. McKinnon, but it was scarcely the best time to mention the fact at the wedding, especially as Josh hadn't mentioned it beforehand. The fact is Josh and I had a brief relationship that came to nothing. We weren't suited. It was over before Callista came on the scene."

Mercedes levelled her with a highly dubious stare. "My dear, I'm not happy with that explanation."

"What explanation would make you happy, Mrs. McKinnon?" Christy asked. "I mean no impertinence. The last thing I want to do is upset you or Callista."

''That's true, is it?'' Mercedes couldn't keep the anxiety out of her voice.

''I'm being absolutely honest when I say that.''

''Why did Ashe invite you here?'' Mercedes asked, wanting more clarification. ''I thought Ashe told me everything.''

''Maybe you could ask him,'' Christy suggested pleasantly.

''One doesn't…'' Mercedes hesitated.

''Put Ashe on the carpet?'' Christy cut her short.

''I don't press him about his affairs,'' Mercedes returned very briskly.

''I'm absolutely certain he's going to tell you.'' Christy tried to reassure her. ''What is it that makes you fearful? Can't you tell me?''

The aggrieved look on Mercedes' face disappeared. ''Callista desperately needs this marriage,'' she said. ''She's deeply in love with Josh. Gemma gave me to understand you were planning some sort of upset?''

''Surely not for Callista. I promise you, Mrs. McKinnon, I've moved on in my life. Josh Deakin has no place in it,'' Christy said with great earnestness, looking directly into Mercedes' eyes.

''But surely, dear, he was close to you for a time?''

''He was, but people break up every day. I imagine Josh in not telling Callista only wished not to upset her.''

''Perhaps Josh still cares for you?'' The cloud redescended on Mercedes' fine forehead. ''You're a beautiful girl. You have a very charming manner. Can either of you put your feelings so easily behind you?''

''Speaking for myself, most definitely. I don't regret knowing Josh. But I assure you I have no romantic interest in him now. It's all over, if it ever existed. Gemma was clearly out to make trouble. She didn't like my being here. She didn't like the fact Ashe and I have become close.''

''Close?'' Mercedes cried, as though something awful had happened. ''But my dear, there's hardly been time.''

''Time enough.'' Christy smiled gently. ''I'm sorry you had to find out from Gemma that Josh and I were once friends, Mrs. McKinnon. It's apparent she put the worst possible slant on things.''

''But you *were* going to speak about it, my dear,'' Mercedes challenged, regarding Christy with some worry.

Christy nodded. ''I wanted to desperately but the time was never right. Neither of us can pretend it isn't a delicate matter.''

''That's so.'' Mercedes shook her head ruefully. ''I suppose this is one of these times when one shouldn't delve too deeply?''

Indeed it was, Christy thought wryly. She couldn't endure too much of not being forthright.

''Now why do I believe you?'' Mercedes sighed. ''I don't know you at all and I've known Gemma all her life.''

''Do you think it might be because Gemma is going through a difficult time. She had this big affair with Ashe but it's all taken place in her own mind. One wouldn't have to be a detective to find her aim was to discredit me.''

Mercedes made a jerky movement of the hand. ''But Ashe hasn't given us a hint about any romance with you. You *are* telling me there's something between you?''

''I'd like you to hear it from Ashe, Mrs. McKinnon,'' Christy said. ''He's family. He has a great deal of love for you and Callista.''

On that they were in agreement—Mercedes allowed herself a smile. ''He's been absolutely marvellous to us. A rock, in good times and bad. Ah well, my dear—'' she made a sudden move to get up ''—I do hope I haven't upset you in any way but I thought I simply had to get things straight. I never thought for one moment Gemma was capable of being so vindictive but then jealousy does do strange things to people.''

Both women walked to the door, Christy deciding she could risk a question of her own. ''Mrs. McKinnon, do you mind if I ask you a question? It's not idle curiosity. It's important to me.''

Mercedes nodded her stately head. ''Go ahead, my dear.''

''Your sister-in-law, Eve, Ashe's mother, you must have known her well?''

Mercedes was so surprised by the question for a minute she didn't say anything. ''I did,'' she admitted, a little cautiously. ''Such an enchanting creature but not suited to station life at all. They should never have married but they were both terribly in love.''

''Her leaving had a profound effect on Ashe.''

''Of course it did!'' Mercedes agreed immediately. ''Ashe idolized his father. Looked up to him, respected him. Charles was such a fine man, but Ashe loved his mother in a different way. She was like sunshine. She always kept Ashe happy and laughing. She was a very warm, affectionate person, very demonstrative. Charles wasn't like that. He'd been reared to believe a man should act in a certain way with discipline and authority. He didn't clown around, if you know what I mean. Eve was full of fun. Charles was enormously proud of Ashe. He was very much the son and heir, but they didn't have the marvellous easy relationship that existed between mother and son.''

Christy felt she had learned something entirely unexpected. ''So how did she come to leave him and at such a tender age?''

''She was pregnant, my dear,'' Mercedes informed her

bluntly. "If you didn't know it before you know it now. A mad moment when Charles was away. Of course Duane fell in love with her on sight. I shouldn't excuse him but in some ways he was as much a victim of circumstance as Eve. For one thing, when he visited Augusta—a business trip—he never expected to meet anyone like Eve. In the end he took her away but Charles was never going to hand over his son. Eve was the guilty party and Charles was a very powerful and influential man. There was no question she would get custody of Ashe. She thought she would be able to see him often but Ashe himself made that impossible. Anger used to spill from him in those days and it grew and grew. He blamed his mother entirely for the break-up of the marriage."

"It's a tragic story," Christy said faintly.

"For Charles and Ashe it was very, very hard. Eve keeps hoping some day Ashe will forgive her. He has a half brother you know."

"Yes, Ashe told me." Christy looked into Mercedes' fine eyes.

"Then he trusts you, my dear. That counts for a lot. Ashe doesn't speak about his mother to anyone. I've seen Eve many times over the years when I'm overseas. She's still beautiful. Duane has made her happy. She leads a full life in her own sophisticated milieu, but the memory of her firstborn still haunts her.

"The irony is, Duane Junior is not unlike Ashe in appearance. Both have their mother's eyes, various expressions, the physical grace. But Duane is a softer, easier, boyish version. He doesn't have Ashe's inbuilt air of command or the sometimes daunting aura Ashe can slip into so easily. Duane wants to meet his half brother so much I shouldn't be surprised if one of these days he simply turns up on Augusta. His father doesn't want him to follow up the connection but it's a different story with Eve. Ah well, lots of changes go on in life.'' Mercedes sighed. ''Now I really must go. By the way—'' she half turned, for the first time pleasure in her expression ''—that's an extremely pretty dress. I love the ultra-feminine look but I could never wear it even as a girl. Too tall, too big-boned.''

''You're a very striking woman, Mrs. McKinnon,'' Christy said. It was perfectly true.

''Mercedes, dear.'' Mercedes was inclined to think now what Christy needed was acceptance.

''That's very sweet of you.'' Christy smiled.

''If you ask me,'' Mercedes said prophetically, ''Ashe has a surprise to spring on us all tonight.''

All through the dinner party cum family reunion Josh Deakin held on to his equilibrium for dear life. He couldn't blow it now. He had a wife who to his surprise he didn't mind at all. In fact he had more or less made the commitment to make a go of his marriage but how his heart, or his body, he wasn't sure which, cried out for Christy. He had to brace himself constantly for the sight of her sitting across the gleaming expanse of the long formal dining table.

It was all so spectacular! The table was laid with a sumptuous gold-and-cream cloth, beautiful gold-and-white china, solid silver flatware, flanked by crystal wineglasses that must have cost a mint. Two very tall vases held a profusion of yellow- and apricot-coloured roses. Solid silver candlesticks with cupids cavorting around the base marched down the table. It was terribly impressive, all linked to who the McKinnons were and what they were.

McKinnon presided at the head of the table, insufferably handsome with a striking profile. Josh coveted his jacket. Italian of course, a very fine black-and-white check. He was very much master of a great historic station leading the conversation that sparkled and eddied around him. He hadn't thought the cattle baron could be so witty, so relaxed and charming. McKinnon at the helm of his adoring family. That very much included Callista. She doted on "darling Ashe." A serious and sour note. He would always have McKinnon looking over his shoulder and he'd better get used to it.

While Josh thought himself unobserved, Ashe's dark eyes missed nothing. He could see Callista's husband with a startling clarity; read his mind. Deakin couldn't hide his sense of envy and jealousy. He'd even caught Deakin staring at his jacket. No doubt wondering about the label and how much it had cost as if one piece of information wouldn't reveal the other. Most of all—as host he had to remind himself this would pass—he had counted the number of times Deakin's eyes, subtle and sly, had been drawn irresistibly to Christy. As if any man's eyes wouldn't be, he was dazzled himself, but with Deakin it was different. He and Christy had a past history. He was certain on Christy's part it was just that, but Deakin appeared to be one of those men who didn't like to let go.

On this special night Christy was wearing one of her wonderfully pretty dresses, a kaleidoscope of sea greens and violets, the V neckline plunged down her creamy skin to the rose-tinged cleft. She had beautiful breasts, the skin like the silken petals of a flower. He wanted no other man's eyes on them. Certainly not Deakin's. Nic and Brendan were being nice to him, but he knew, like himself, it was more for Callista's sake than any genuine feeling of friendliness. That was reserved for Christy.

It gave him great pleasure to know Christy got on famously with his family. Even Mercedes appeared to have taken a shine to her, but not Callista, Ashe noticed, and sympathised. Callista was feeling threatened. Perhaps she had already begun to notice how often her new husband's eyes strayed in Christy's direction. It would have that disquietening effect on her. Callista deserved her happiness. His only great regret was she had fallen in love with the wrong man. Reinforcing his own theory love made a person helpless. Love—he knew that also led to betrayal.

He wanted to snatch Christy up and sweep her away. Above all make love to her in the sparkling moonlight. The sensation of it ran up and down his body like a flame, but he was resigned to getting through dinner without actually giving Deakin a punch on the nose.

Sometime later Ashe judged it time to call his guests' attention. He tapped his wineglass and they all fell quiet, leaning forward so they could look at him directly. "With all my family around me, and I welcome Josh to our number—" he was forced to incline his head toward Josh "—I have some news that I know you've long been waiting for. I've finally chosen my beautiful bride. I know I've rushed her terribly, indeed I haven't given her a moment to change her mind, but I knew the moment I laid eyes on her I'd never let her go. Of course I'm speaking about Christine." He turned to Christy, picking up her hand and carrying it to his lips. "Christy has made me very proud and happy by consenting to marry me. This dinner party with us all together marks the official start of our engagement."

While the others looked on in rapt surprise, he withdrew the magnificent ring he had retrieved from Christy from his inner breast pocked and slipped it on her slender finger, her nails lacquered a soft pearly pink.

My God, the family emeralds! Mercedes thought, knowing the full story behind how they were acquired and Eve's defection with the necklace.

Everyone seemed to jump up at once, exclaiming their delight and congratulations. All except Callista who sat cheeks flushed, eyes glittery, trying desperately to get a handle on it all.

And Josh. He sat stunned, the most dreadful sense of loss mixed with anger and envy bearing down on him like an express train. How could this have happened? Christy loved him. He had expected her to keep a place in her heart for him forever. Yet here was McKinnon looking exultant as though his every plan, his every strategy, had been fulfilled. Christy was so absolutely heartbreakingly beautiful it sliced through him like a knife. Her face was illuminated by emotional radiance. She was hugged and kissed, drawn into the family. Of a sudden, a sick fury pulsed out of Josh like blood from a cut artery. He couldn't absorb the shock. It was a wound, so raw, so open, it momentarily overcame him. His hand gripped his wineglass tighter, tighter—he couldn't let go—it fragmented into three large pieces, a shard piercing the skin, causing blood to flow.

"I don't believe it!" he gestured a little crazily, the words bubbling up from his tight throat.

The focus of attention shifted entirely to him. No one could escape his words or his expression.

"Josh, please," Christy appealed in quivering fright, unaware of the hard tension in Ashe. "Look what you've done to your hand!" She said it to deflect Ashe more than anything, but it turned out badly.

Now neither of them could escape their involvement. Neither had a chance to recover. The familiarity with which Christy had spoken Josh's name, the expression on her face, the concern and dismay misinterpreted seemed to speak volumes.

"You know him, don't you?" Callista cried out with a spurt of rage. She made no attempt to go to her husband;

to help him staunch the flow of blood. ''You know *my husband?*''

Here it comes, Christy thought.

Ashe looked at his cousin, a warning in his eyes. ''Don't be so tragic about it, Callista. It's not some terrible thing though you should have been told.''

''By whom?''

''*You* never told me.'' Callista turned her wrath on Christy, a sorry sight as her normal good manners disintegrated.

''I'm not sure *I* had to, Callista,'' Christy appealed, as upset in her way as was Callista. ''We dated for a while but it was all over when he fell in love with you.''

Callista's hurt and anger was terrible to see. ''He *loved* you,'' she said, looking utterly convinced. ''You're just the sort of woman to drive men crazy.''

Mercedes tried desperately to quiet her daughter by putting her arms around her. ''Darling girl, I'm afraid you're over-reacting.''

But Callista shook her mother off with some violence, her breathing coming like a hiss. ''All along I've been worried about you. Little things continually nagging at me. Little things I was trying to forget.''

''Perhaps you didn't hear what I've just said, Callista?'' Ashe's voice was abnormally quiet. ''Christy and I have just announced our engagement. I really can't have you making things difficult for her. Neither do I want to spoil our night.''

Angry as she was Callista had little choice but to back off. ''I'm sorry, Ashe. So sorry, but I can't seem to get things right.'' She closed her eyes as though she was about to step off a cliff. Then of a sudden she jumped, lightning-quick. ''I can't help feeling in marrying this girl—'' with one finger she pointed to Christy ''—you *can't* have known her long enough—you might be doing something you'll regret.'' She completely ignored the fact she only had a short courtship herself, hating Christy simply because she once had a relationship with her husband which in turn gave her a stark and narrow perspective.

Ashe sat back in his chair, frowning. This was supposed to be a night of celebration, ruined by Callista and her no-good husband. Nevertheless he tried hard to temper his words because he knew Callista was at some crisis point. ''Callista, I know you're not well,'' he said with a forgiving air. ''But please stop now. This isn't a matter for you to interfere in. In marrying Christy, I'm doing exactly what I want.''

Shocked and humiliated, her bravado exhausted, Callista abandoned herself to floods of tears. She pushed back her chair, overwhelmed by the enormity of what she had just said. ''Sorry, Ashe. Sorry. I'm profoundly sorry.'' She dashed from the room, not pausing for a moment to look back at her husband of fragile character.

''Lord save us!'' Mercedes intoned, never having sat through such an experience. Ashe had been goodness itself to her and Callista. Now this!

''Callista really isn't herself,'' she apologised. ''I'd best go to her.'' Mercedes followed much less dramatically in the path of her daughter, suddenly struck by the thought Callista could be pregnant. Everything seemed to fuse together. The sickness, the queasiness, the tears and emotional outburst.

''Are you going to go to your wife?'' Ashe demanded of Josh, his patience at an end. Josh was busy pressing Brendan's clean white handkerchief to his cut hand.

That was quite a performance of Callista's, he thought. He didn't know she had it in her, but reacted nervously as they all stared at him. ''She mightn't want me.''

"Right now, I'm not surprised. What the hell were you trying to do?" Ashe's nostrils almost exhaled smoke.

Nicole and Brendan sat uncomfortable and dismayed as Josh tried to pull himself together, knowing above all he had to vindicate himself or he might be standing out on the highway, bags packed. "Your announcement was such a shock to me. That's all."

"The understatement of the year." Ashe's lean handsome face looked contemptuous. "Tell me, what are you planning on next? Are you going to stay with Callista, do you think?"

Josh flinched at the sarcasm. Upstairs Mercedes and Callista would be clamouring for his blood. He longed for the simplicity of his honeymoon when Callista adored him—how things were becoming complex. "I must make Callista believe Christy means absolutely nothing to me," he said finally, creating such disgust in Christy she burst out.

"You miserable..."

"Moron?" Ashe offered as Christy didn't permit herself the next word. It was the real Josh unmasked.

"So, are you going to go to your wife?" Ashe repeated, springing up from his chair, angry and imposing in every way. Disgust pressed down on him as he looked at Josh's good-looking but weak face. "What you should have said was *you* mean nothing to Christy. Or can't you admit that even to yourself? Whatever you do, don't make the mistake of interfering in my affairs. Nobody offers insult to Christy. She's my financée and in a short time she'll be my wife. If you want peace and quiet in your life, remember that."

Josh could have smashed his head against the table so intense was his frustration. McKinnon's wife! What a dream run. So Christy had emerged the victor after all. Christy, the mistress of all this! It was incredible and he had brought it all about. Nevertheless he had to appeal to her. She was the only one who wasn't looking at him with open censure and disgust. ''I guess I've made a fool of myself,'' he said, trying to resurrect his charming self-deprecating smile.

''Here, here!'' Brendan seconded briefly.

''I guess you have, Josh,'' Christy told him gently, ''but it's nothing new. The only thing that can save you is, Callista really does love you. I suggest you go and make your peace with her. I can't feel angry with you. I have to take a lot of the blame myself, but without you I would never have met Ashe.''

A statement that increased Josh's grief. He rose to his feet feeling very much the outsider.

''Do you want someone to take a look at that hand?'' Ashe asked abruptly, just barely remembering Josh was his guest.

''It doesn't need stitching.'' Brendan settled the question by shaking his head. ''The bleeding made it look worse than it really is. If you come with me, Josh, I'll get some antiseptic and some bandages from the first-aid room.''

''I say, that's very kind of you.'' Josh smiled gratefully. He really needed to get away from McKinnon. The man thoroughly unnerved him.

''Better Callista than me,'' Nicole observed after Josh and Brendan had gone. ''He's so charming on the surface.''

''The surface precisely,'' Ashe said.

''I regret I couldn't tell you the exact position with Josh and me,'' Christy said, looking apologetically into Nicole's eyes. ''The timing was desperately wrong.''

''Yes, I can see that,'' Nicole acknowledged, beginning to understand the very tricky situation. ''So you did know him well?''

Christy nodded her gleaming gold head, not looking at

Ashe's darkly brooding figure. She could feel his anger and condemnation. It pierced her like a knife. "He let me down badly. I gatecrashed the wedding reception with the intention of giving him a good fright. Nothing more. Ashe saved me. Hard as it is to believe now, Josh's decision to marry Callista hit me for six. But it was all an illusion."

"It happens," Nicole nodded.

"Well," Christy grimaced, "I thought it was real at the time."

"Deakin could be delicately referred to as an opportunist," Ashe observed harshly. "I sensed that from the beginning, but I knew Callista would run over us all with a steamroller to marry him. She loves him, if that's relevant to happiness?" he added too bitterly, his upset at events and his mother's betrayal stored in his bones.

"I certainly think it is," Christy said bravely, unable to keep the deep hurt out of her voice.

"So do I." Sympathetically, Nicole reached over to cover Christy's hand. "Don't let their outbursts upset your night. It's clear to me Ashe needs you, Christy." To forget his childhood, Nicole thought but never dared to speak aloud. "I couldn't be happier for you both. Ashe has waited a long time to find his true love. Now he has her in you, Christy. I know we're going to be the greatest friends."

Though they all tried hard after that, Josh and Callista between them had wrecked the evening. It wasn't until a good hour later that Ashe and Christy were finally alone. Both of them knew in their bones they were due for a row. Their first. It had been a while coming. Ashe, a passionate man for all his hard-won control, couldn't modify the terrible tension in his gut. He hoped and prayed he wouldn't say anything he would regret, but dammit all this was supposed to be the celebration of his and Christy's engagement, yet a forgettable character like Deakin had had the power to wreck it.

Now Christy stood within his study so beautiful, so feminine, she was transcendant. Her green eyes sparking with little gold currents, revealed her knowledge of the intensity in him. God, the very last thing he ever wanted was for her to be afraid of him. Yet he could see her trembling and anxious when all he wanted to do was take her in his arms. Instead he walked past her and locked the cedar door, so thick and heavy it would muffle all sound.

''Hell, what an evening,'' he groaned. ''Come and take a chair.''

''I thought I was to be put on the mat?'' Christy answered, feeling herself under tremendous strain.

''Don't be ridiculous,'' he answered far too shortly, but his control was collapsing. Not so his desire for her, which was amounting to obsession.

''*Is* it ridiculous?'' she challenged, remaining where she was on the Persian rug. The light from the bronze chandelier like a thousand candles illuminated her beautiful hair. ''This morning I felt wanted, needed, above all *understood.*''

''So what's changed?'' He didn't know, couldn't know, how he appeared to her, his eyes as black as night, his expression broodingly forbidding as he fought the very dazzle of her.

''Josh and your cousin between them have shattered all that,'' Christy said, her voice ragged with disappointment and tight nerves. ''They've shattered your trust in me. Don't deny it. I can see it in your face. You're a hard man, Ashe. Without love in your life you could become ruthless.''

He grimaced with high impatience. ''I don't see that at all. What I did see was your concern and dismay at your ex-lover's cutting his hand.'' He watched her guilty flush, saw her lace her fingers.

Christy could feel herself lose all composure. ''Now *you're* being ridiculous. I didn't give a damn about Josh cutting his hand. It was you I was worried about. You and your temper.''

That rocked him. No one had ever accused him of having a bad temper. ''Have you ever *seen* it?'' he demanded, outraged she should look at it that way.

''I know it is in you,'' she retaliated, at the same time wondering where all this was going. ''I'm seeing it now. Where does your sweet cousin Callista get off abusing me? I've done nothing wrong. The only mistake I made was falling for Josh's superficial charm. And he does have it whether you like it or not.''

That sent a brilliant flash of jealousy through him. ''Listen to yourself,'' he invited, his tone deeply ironic. ''Josh has charm. Charm! My God, you should despise the man. *I* do. With good reason. He married Callista for her money. What he fully intended was to retain you for a lover.''

Christy stamped her foot in rage and frustration. ''How dare you!'' Her rage was also directed at herself. Of course she despised Josh. ''And I'm supposed to be your fiancée,'' she cried scathingly. In her over-emotional state, she began to pull at her glorious ring. It came easily. She threw it at him, knowing with his superb reflexes he would catch it. ''I'm not interested in your blasted marriage contract,'' she told him fiercely. ''I want a man who trusts me enough *not* to have one. You don't. Your supposed trust in me is paper-thin.''

He couldn't stop himself retaliating. ''Your actions tonight didn't help any. We all saw your concern, which you now say was for *me*. Callista didn't see it that way either.''

''That's right, take Callista's part.'' Her voice resounded

with hurt. ''Your precious family. God, I'd always be an outsider. Your wounds have never healed, Ashe. Do you know that?''

''Maybe badly wounded hearts never heal,'' he responded grimly. ''In your place I would have told Deakin off.''

Her voice choked. ''That's unfair, but then you are unfair. It was hardly the time. Or the place. Do you think I didn't want to? You invited them here, not me. I would never have had them. Let them work out their own lives. And just fancy Callista talking about *our* short relationship. She couldn't wait to rush Josh to the altar. If you're jealous—though God knows you don't know enough about caring, certainly not for *me*—there's no need to be. I can't bear to say this one more time. Josh means absolutely nothing to me.''

''Then why don't you tell *him* that?'' An answering anger ripped through him. A terror of losing her. He could feel pain everywhere, to the tips of his fingers. He wanted happiness. He wanted her. He couldn't let it all crumble. He wouldn't. She was going nowhere. It crossed his mind he was going mad. Mad with love for her.

Like a man driven, he went to her and pulled her into his arms. Her beautiful blond hair streamed over his arm, her face averted. Yet he kissed her, not sparing his hard passion.

He might have held a statue. Her arms hung at her sides, never seeking to embrace him. Summoning his strength, he let her go.

She was very pale where she had been flushed before. Her iridescent eyes were filled with tears.

Shocked at his own brutality he fell back against the massive desk. ''I'm sorry, Christy,'' he apologised from the bottom of his heart. ''I didn't mean—''

''You *did* mean,'' she cut him off. ''You've wanted to hurt me and you have.''

Every word was like a nail in him. ''No, please, no.'' He made a grab for her hands, but she pulled them away. ''Christy, please listen…''

''Unlock the door, Ashe,'' she said, her voice cold. ''We've both said things I know we'll regret.''

''Don't let them stay with you,'' he begged. His pulses were pounding, his nerves jangled. He didn't want to let her go but to force her was unthinkable. Whenever he had kissed her before her response had been exquisite. He couldn't bear for her to fear him. But it seemed she did.

Outside the moon was magic. Inside the light had gone out.

Ashe moved to the door and turned the heavy key. As she moved close he put his arm around her waist. ''Do you really hate me so much?''

''No,'' she told him, with bent head, ''I love you, Ashe. God knows why.''

The homestead was very quiet. So quiet Christy could hear the far-off howling of a dingo. Such a weird primeval sound. It made the hairs on the back of her neck stand up. The wild dingos she had seen, especially in the hill country, were magnificent animals, not all of them gold, some nearly pure white, highly intelligent but killers by nature. Their instinct was to hunt. She knew they were a menace to the herd. They were even a menace to humans. Savage attacks were not unknown. The dingo continued his mournful song while Christy padded fretfully round her bedroom, unable to settle. She'd thought Callista's outburst had upset her but it was as nothing to her row with Ashe. And this was supposed to be her engagement night! It had started out so brilliantly only to be shot down in flames.

"I think I can trust you with a little secret, Christy," Mercedes had confided. "It might take some of the upset away and help you understand. Callista thinks she's pregnant."

Christy privately thought if it turned out Callista wasn't pregnant it might be better if she quit while she was ahead. It was evident to Christy a man like Josh—he wasn't a real man at all—would make Callista suffer. Still, Callista wanted him. If anyone said a bad word about Josh she would have exploded like a firecracker. It was their life. They had to work it out.

As for her and Ashe? He almost defeated her. She knew Callista's outburst had upset him, but then, it had upset her.

Sleep was a long way off. She was much too overwrought. Her end of the house was lonely with the children down with their parents. She had never stayed in a house before that boasted twelve bedrooms, all of double size. Would she ever be mistress of all this? After tonight it seemed doubtful. Callista and Josh would be tucked up in bed by now. Perhaps reconciled? No one knew better than Josh how to spin a good cover story. He'd had so much practice.

Mercedes had gone off a little tipsy. A double celebration. It was only to be expected Mercedes would adore a grandchild whether Josh was the father or not. At least Josh didn't have jug ears or any noticeable physical imperfections. The McKinnon blood would help the child. What interested Christy was when had Callista fallen pregnant if indeed she were? Sweet little Callista might have had a few strategies of her own. Maybe forward planning ran in the family?

Eventually churning with regret and forces too strong for her to handle Christy went in search of her impossible fiancé. She had been startled at her own hostility, her mind turning over every hurtful remark to the extent it made her head throb. Ashe could be such a formidable man. She had never known anyone whose arrogant features could so marvellously depict contempt.

Her slippered footsteps were inaudible through the house. She knew he hadn't yet retired. No matter his predawn start, Ashe never went to bed early, thriving on a handful of hours sleep. She could see the brilliant chink of light was still beneath his study door. The rest of the very large homestead was in soft gloom. The sound of her own breathing was startling, so was the swish of her satin robe.

Keep moving or retreat. Especially after that confrontation. She loved him so much but the man was so complicated. She crept a little further towards the light. She stood motionless, listening to her own heartbeat. The grandfather clock further down broke into a series of chimes that nearly made her jump out of her skin. In fact she gave a stifled cry.

Midnight. The witching hour.

Suddenly she began to wonder what she was doing, robbed of confidence in her position in Ashe's life. On this night of nights she had wanted to be feted, caressed, adored. She wanted him to take her to his bed. Passionately desired it, but as the woman he loved, not some damned possession. Christy turned, making up her mind to flee, let tempers cool down, only Ashe emerged from the study, moving so fantastically fast he caught her up before she had gone a few yards.

''So you've come back to me?'' His warm breath was scented with fine spirit. Whisky, brandy, she didn't know. Maybe he'd been drinking away his anger.

She spun in his arms, the agitation of the night fuel to the fire. ''You've got me in a trap.''

''No one gets out of my traps either,'' he said, ''not

alive!'' He laughed beneath his breath then, like a pirate, swept her up into his arms. ''It's been too long. I've tried to be your shining knight but God, I want you too much.''

The electric charge through her blood was fantastic. She struggled though he was much too strong. ''Put me down, Ashe.'' She trembled over her words. ''It's you and your history. You're heartless.'' Glorious. Unforgettable.

''If you think that you're as screwed up as I am,'' he drawled. ''Why don't you just lie quiet?''

''Ashe...please...'' she begged, all helplessness, disorder, long hair trailing, the sash of her satin robe undone.

''You're not leaving me tonight. Not when you came back of your own free will. In fact you're not leaving me at all. Think of that. You and me together. Every night of our lives.''

All manner of emotion charged through her, raising her to an unprecedented pitch. Excitement, passion, residual sadness. This man could break her heart.

''Hush.'' He dipped his dark head to her. ''It would be too, too risky to disturb the household. I just might tell them all to leave.'' He threw her a brilliant smile, taking the rear staircase at an impetuous rush, holding her as though she weighed no more than Katey. At the top, not even out of breath, he went soundlessly down the hallway that led to his private master suite.

A massive wave somewhere between panic and excitement broke over Christy. Inside his massive bedroom with its baronial four-poster Ashe threw her onto the heavy brocade quilt, dark gold in colour. The springs were so good Christy bounced. He put out a hand to trace the curved outline of her mouth. ''That mouth of yours,'' he exclaimed, low-voiced.

Christy's pulses were soaring. Dangerous hormones

flooded her blood. Whatever it was he had real power over her—no question.

"Move over," he said.

"Is this an attempt to seduce me?" She was flushed and defiant, the defiance gossamer-thin.

"No attempt." He bent over her with powerful languorous grace. "If you didn't *want* it, it would be an entirely different matter."

"You're so sure."

"Of you, yes."

Silently she made room for him, lost in her own desperate need. It was overwhelming to be in his bed, his nearness, his male fragrance and strength an invincible force. How she loved the beauty of the eyes that sought hers. He was marvellous. Brilliant. Difficult. She loved him so much all memory of life before him seemed to dissolve.

Christy closed her eyes the moment his hand contoured her breast gently but commandingly, pushing the soft satin aside so he could see her; caress the smooth creamy skin. His thumb circling and circling the tightly furled nipple, his ministrations leaving her trembling in his arms.

"You're so beautiful," he murmured. "I'm so sorry for before. Forgive me."

"I'm sorry, too." How easy it was to say it.

"Of course I trust you. It was jealousy speaking. I've been out of my mind wanting to do this since the night you walked into the reception. So audacious, so sexy."

Her back arched in rapture as he pressed his mouth over hers, kissed and kissed her again, with such sensuality she felt her very bones dissolve. His tongue moved against hers, slid around her teeth. Her robe had fallen away, now his hands moved over her body, tracing, exploring, learning it, now it was his. The stimulation was so enormous he had to cradle her. Christy moaned aloud as he found the valley between her slender legs, his fingers emitting a deep hunger but such tenderness it was almost a reverence.

"You're like silk," he muttered. "I want you so badly the need is almost splitting me open. Yet I want this to last forever." He bent his dark head, his lips brushing warmly, ardently against her throat.

She knew she whispered something, his name, an endearment, but never the forbidden words I love you, though she was leaving herself wide open to the most intimate of caresses. Eventually he levered his lean powerful body over her. He still wore his clothes, his shirt unbuttoned to the waist, but she was barely draped in her nightdress, her breasts and thighs exposed to his touch and his sight. The conjunction of their bodies made her heart contract. Two flames melted into one. She could feel the driving force of his sex. He radiated an exquisite fire, a passion that was sublime. When her heart was almost bursting, and she was unable to contain the need that palpated within her like great wings, he rose from the bed, stripping his splendid darkly tanned body of its clothes.

"My Christine. My angel."

To Christy's immense joy it sounded like a meltdown of all remaining doubt. His vibrant voice was deep, half crooning to her. His brilliant dark eyes were no longer veiled enigmas; they revealed the deep emotions that were in him. Emotions as vast and encompassing as his desert fortress. He was breathing deeply as he covered her, yet Christy heard very distinctly what he said.

"You know, don't you, my darling, this is no more than *love.*"

EPILOGUE

Four months later.
The McKinnon-Parker wedding ceremony and reception—
Augusta Downs Station
South West Queensland

SOME ten minutes before the bride was due to make her appearance in the beautiful old ballroom that had been turned into a flower-decked temple, a tall slender woman walked quietly down the centre aisle and slipped into the front pew. To many of the guests she was not only extremely glamorous but also vaguely familiar. Others knew *exactly* who she was. The former Eve Elizabeth McKinnon. In her mid-fifties Eve was still stunning, her willowy figure dressed in the height of fashion, her beautiful blond hair twisted into an updated chignon. A small turquoise feather and rose creation adorned her head, the chic headpiece colour matched to her elegant two-piece suit and the satin shoes on her feet.

She appeared not to care or even notice that everyone in the ballroom was staring. Eve smiled down the line of seated guests in the front pew. All McKinnons—all extremely sensitive to her presence. Her former sister-in-law, Mercedes, who had never fully blamed her, sat beside her for comfort and support. She desperately needed it. She owed a lot to Mercedes who looked splendid in a light blue outfit with a big blue hat banded with curled silver ribbon.

Further down sat Mercedes' daughter, Callista. Clearly Callista was pregnant but wearing a cleverly cut yellow silk dress with an eye-catching orchid-trimmed cream hat. Her attractive well-dressed husband was beside her. Among the others Eve noted was a very good-looking young woman with startling blue eyes who was regarding her with a hint of gentle encouragement. Could it be Nicole? Eve's mind turned back twenty years and more. Of course, little Nicole. Her husband was one of Ashe's attendants.

Eve focused her gaze with intensity, willing herself to take command of her emotions, which was not easy. Her vulnerability was immense. Her firstborn stood before the satin-draped altar table. At first meeting with him less than twenty-four hours before she had been out of control with emotion, all her hidden grief rising to the surface like a giant gusher, reflecting the great sadness that lay beneath her poised facade. Always she had carried her memories. Carried the guilt for the great wrong she had done her husband, the damage to her son. But her son had survived, to become a magnificent figure in his formal wedding clothes.

Ashe was flanked by his attendants, his best man, a lifelong friend and his two grooms. The youngest of them was Eve's other son, Duane. Duane had been thrilled out of his mind his elder half brother had not only wanted to meet him but suggested he might like to act as his wedding attendant. Why not? In meeting Ashe, Duane was finding his own family. Eve had told herself countless times she couldn't afford to become over-wrought but the scene in front of her threatened to overwhelm her. She knew this room. Many a gala function had been held there. Eve had to fumble in her bag for a lace-edged handkerchief.

Ashe and Duane. Her sons. They had both inherited her dark eyes and other physical features she could rejoice in. She pushed back into the ribbon-decked pew, straightening her shoulders. Her husband hadn't wanted her to make this long journey. He saw nothing to be gained from trying to relive her past. Only she felt this was her golden chance to repair some of the terrible damage she had done. The loss of contact with her firstborn was the central tragedy of her life. Eve acknowledged it almost every day though she had a husband and son who loved her.

"Why deliver yourself up to them?" her husband had demanded, deeply concerned she could be received badly. But he wouldn't go with her. He, too, felt the guilts and burdens of the past.

Mercedes, acutely aware of the crackling static of Eve's emotions, put out a sympathetic hand. Eve had won herself a place at Ashe's wedding but Mercedes knew just how much courage it had taken for Eve to get herself here. Many of the McKinnon clan were still hostile to Eve though social etiquette demanded they try to keep it well hidden. Of course none of this would have happened without Christy. Christy was the architect of it all; the one who had worked the miracle of getting mother and son together. It hadn't happened easily, Ashe had been very difficult to sway, but Christy had never given up. And of course Ashe loved her. That's what settled it. Christy had told Ashe many times the past had to be reconciled before they could look to their future. Christy had become a powerful influence in Ashe's life. Mercedes was happy about that, certain Christy over time would become part of the McKinnon family legend.

At the rear of the ballroom while the wedding guests waited in eager anticipation, Christy took her proud father's right arm. The wonderful entrance music, an emotional force, pealed out to uplift her to the skies. She smiled at her proud father as the bridal procession began its slow stately walk up the ruby-carpeted aisle. Her bridesmaids in extraordinarily beautiful and imaginative gowns, head-dresses on their upswept hair, walked in pairs. There were four: Montana, Suzanne, Philippa and Elise. Slender and glowing as irises in purple, rose-pink, royal-blue and emerald-green silk taffeta. Behind them heralding the bride were her two little friends, Christopher and Katey, page boy and flower girl; Katey dressed in white and cream silk with little appliqués of gold, Kit absolutely adorable in a cream suit with a cream-and-gold brocade waistcoat and white cravat. Their perfection increased Christy's emotional reaction.

She was the central figure. The bride.

Every head turned as she moved into the room. Little ripples of pleasure broke out spontaneously all around the large room. Her friend, Kelly, an honoured guest, had designed all the gowns and the children's outfits. Christy didn't know it then but her truly glorious wedding gown was destined to put the young designer friend on the fashion map. Of magnolia duchesse satin, organza and exquisite gold lace, the bodice was a stunning duchesse satin strapless corset over a fairy-tale billowing skirt with floating panels of gold lace that matched the short flaring veil. The strapless gown showed to advantage the magnificent emerald-diamond necklace she wore around her throat. The same emeralds and diamonds winked at her ears. But what was infinitely more beautiful than her gown and precious gems was the radiance within her. It streamed out of her like rays of sun. Everything about her spoke of her great love and joy. It was this exultation that moved the assembled wedding guests profoundly and reminded them all marriages, in all faiths, had been destined to be a sacrament.

At the altar Ashe stood before the bishop who had baptised him and who was now smiling on him most benignly. Ashe wasn't just waiting for his bride, he was holding his heart in his two hands. His heart was hers. Although he had been told many times he looked superbly in control on this day of days, his throat was thick with emotion. For so long he had become accustomed to suppressing emotion but his beloved Christy had changed all that. She had altered his life in every conceivable fashion and taught him a whole new way of being. Now his heart soared in anticipation of his first sight of her in her bridal finery. He had dreamed of it but today was reality.

She was there! This was a single moment in time he knew he would carry with him all his life. It was all he could do not to seize her in his arms there and then and kiss every inch of her loveliness. He could see his desire reflected in her beautiful sparkling eyes.

What is love? he had once asked, his mind clouded over with doubts. He knew the answer to that now. Ashe turned to his bride, openly adoring her. She took his breath. His so-called strategies had been no more than a last-ditch pathetic attempt to keep his heart tightly closed. It had cracked when his mother had left him. Now his mother and his half brother had re-entered his life. Again, thanks to his serene, compassionate Christy, she had caused it all to happen.

Christy. All the beauty in the world!

''My handsome prince,'' she whispered joyfully to him.

My queen. He would have died for her.

He knew it might take him a little while to fully express his great love for her; for him to really take his mother back into his life, not all of the old barriers had dissolved, but he knew with great certainty Christy would carry his children and the last word on earth he would whisper would be her beloved name.